I0819018

LEAVE YOUR MESS AT HOME

LEAVE YOUR MESS AT HOME

✦ ✦ ✦ ✦

TOLANI AKINOLA

PAMELA DORMAN BOOKS
VIKING

VIKING
An imprint of Penguin Random House LLC
1745 Broadway, New York, NY 10019
penguinrandomhouse.com

A Pamela Dorman Book/Viking

The PGD colophon is a registered trademark of Penguin Random House LLC.

VIKING and VIKING ship colophon are registered trademarks of Penguin Random House LLC.

Designed by Christina Nguyen

LIBRARY OF CONGRESS CATALOGING-IN-PUBLICATION DATA

Names: Akinola, Tolani author
http://id.loc.gov/authorities/names/n2025026522
http://id.loc.gov/rwo/agents/n2025026522
Title: Leave your mess at home: a novel / Tolani Akinola.
Description: New York: Pamela Dorman Books / Viking, 2026.
Identifiers: LCCN 2025017438 (print) | LCCN 2025017439 (ebook) |
ISBN 9780593834190 hardcover | ISBN 9780593834206 ebook
Subjects: LCSH: Nigerian Americans—Fiction |
Adult children—Family relationships—Fiction | LCGFT: Fiction
http://id.loc.gov/authorities/genreForms/gf2014026339 | Novels
http://id.loc.gov/authorities/genreForms/gf2015026020 | Domestic fiction
http://id.loc.gov/authorities/genreForms/gf2014026295
Classification: LCC PS3601.K555 L43 2026 (print) |
LCC PS3601.K555 (ebook) | DDC 813/.6—dc23/eng/20250618
LC record available at https://lccn.loc.gov/2025017438
LC ebook record available at https://lccn.loc.gov/2025017439

Printed in the United States of America
3rd Printing

The authorized representative in the EU for product safety and compliance is Penguin Random House Ireland, Morrison Chambers, 32 Nassau Street, Dublin D02 YH68, Ireland, https://eu-contact.penguin.ie.

For Shefe, who is so much light.

LEAVE
YOUR MESS
AT HOME

ONE

Saturday, October 20

This evening requires an elegance of Anjola that only her sister can bestow upon her. Playing dress-up with Sola has always been a vehicle to a more beautiful, more confident self. When they were both little, Sola would construct wedding gowns from bedsheets, pin Anjola's hair into a failure of a chignon, guide her down the stairs as though she were a dainty English lady, and spin her around for their mother's irritation and their father's bemusement. If Sola hadn't texted the day before to tell her she was in town, Anjola would be going to Neil's party tonight in the same T-shirt dress and black Converse she usually wears for grocery runs.

Sola is casual in that way. When her text came through the evening before, it was the first time Anjola had heard from her since May, when she was supposed to come to Anjola's medical school graduation and never showed. That evening, as Anjola sat with her parents, older brother, and younger sister around a table at New Haven's finest restaurant (it was bougier than most of them were used to, but her mother had decided that Anjola's graduation from Yale had established their family as firmly upper middle class), the text from Sola had come in:

I'm sorry I couldn't make it. So proud of you.

Anjola had shrugged when she read the message, having become accustomed to rarely hearing from Sola, though their mother had found words all day. But it hadn't been a big deal; Anjola knew that Sola would show up for her in her own time. And what a reward for her light approach, Anjola thinks: Her sister has materialized at the most opportune moment.

She waits for Sola in an industrial, loft-style apartment in Logan Square, which she understands to belong to Sola's old friend from high school, Marquise. The space is bright and airy, and when she takes in the overhead windows, she sees tiny particles dancing where the sunlight streams in.

"Your home is so lovely," she says, looking up at the black light fixtures that descend from the beams like steel teardrops.

"Girl, this is not my house," Marquise says, motioning for her to sit at the kitchen island. "It belongs to one of my gentleman friends. He's an industrial designer and he's never here." He pours her a glass of sparkling water, which she hates but does not refuse, because being somewhere so sophisticated makes her want to play the part.

This is the first time she'll have seen her sister in person in ten years. There have been plenty of video chats, plenty of unkept promises, plans to make a visit happen that always fell through. Until Anjola learned to stop asking, learned not to give in to the embarrassment of hoping. Besides, in the intervening years, Sola has still been a confidant. And so Anjola forgives her sister for that time in college when she almost boarded a flight to LA just before Sola called to say she had a sudden engagement in New York and couldn't host her any longer. And Anjola forgives her sister for the time she used the last dregs of her student stipend in her senior year to reserve spots at a meditation retreat in Nevada, only for Sola to drop out at the last second, leaving Anjola to meditate on the end of a situationship all alone. And, of course, she forgives Sola for missing her med school graduation. In place of resentment, Anjola only feels the low thrum of a nervous excitement as she waits.

"Hello, darling." Sola's voice is as dramatic in effect as her entrance. The bathroom door opens suddenly and there she stands, over six feet tall in heels, wearing a denim jumpsuit in the warm yellow light.

The sisters embrace.

"Ẹ̀gbọ́n mi," Anjola says in the little Yoruba she knows. "You look sweet. It's almost like you're aging down." Sola only seems to grow more lovely with time. She is almost an exact replica of their mother, with her honey-hued skin and wide-set eyes, but more stretched out and long in the body.

"And I don't understand how you're a whole doctor and you still don't look a day over twenty-two." Sola takes Anjola's hands and stands apart from her, examining her appearance. "And you dress like it too." She gestures at Anjola's outfit: a blue tee, baggy blue jeans, running shoes. Marquise tsks softly in the background.

"Sometimes I wonder how we grew up in the same house," Sola says.

How did they? When Anjola was in her last year of high school, in the days and weeks after Sola left, she would lie in Sola's bed and inhale from her pillow until her scent faded. She knew that Sola was alive because she'd sent a single text to Anjola telling her not to worry, but in their house Sola eventually became a kind of ghost. First her scent faded, then her absence became less of a spoken thing and more a felt thing, then their mother seemed to act as though Sola had never been there at all.

But she is here. In the flesh.

"How long are you going to be around?" Anjola asks as she watches Sola sidle up to Marquise with her arms crossed. Together they shake their heads at Anjola's clothing in mock judgment.

"Just for a few days," Sola says.

"That's too bad." Anjola pouts, and before she can ask Sola whether she's planning to visit their parents, Sola redirects the conversation to the matter at hand.

"What time is this party again?" she asks. "Whose party is it?"

"It starts at eight." Anjola glances down at the floor, playing with her earlobe. "It's Neil's."

Sola lifts an eyebrow.

"I told him I'd try to get there a little bit before it starts to help him set up."

"No the hell you won't." Sola motions for her to sit back down on the stool. "You're going to arrive fashionably late and stop acting like nobody trained you."

Their mother always made a point to arrive late enough to feel as though she'd been missed but early enough to still be seen—and made sure she looked good while doing so. Sola releases Anjola's hair from the messy bun she'd thrown it into, freeing tiny black locs to cascade down her shoulders and back.

"Look at her hair," Sola says to Marquise. "Beautiful. She's definitely due for a retie though, probably because she's being cheap."

"Wow, so you're really going to talk about me like I'm not here."

"Girl, I could care less about your locs," says Marquise. "I'm still waiting to find out who Neil is."

"He's one of my closest friends. We went to high school and undergrad together."

"So you're really going to sit there and still pretend that you don't want this kid?" Sola asks.

"I used the word 'friend' for a reason."

"Oh, I'm sure," Sola says.

"What's the party for?" Marquise asks, shifting his glasses slightly down the bridge of his nose so he can peer at Anjola over the upper rim.

"It's a surprise birthday party for his girlfriend." Anjola looks up at her sister. "How was I supposed to tell you? You're never here. I don't even like texting that much."

"And all that is why you're single, boo," Sola says, making her way over to an adjoining room.

"Um, can you not?" Anjola calls after her. "I just came for help so I can look the part and be a supportive friend. I don't need a whole lecture about why I'm single. I swear you and Mom are the same."

"What exactly is 'the part' again? And don't compare me to that woman."

Marquise holds out his hand. "Let me see what your friend looks like."

Anjola pulls up Neil's Instagram before passing her phone to Marquise.

"No ma'am." Marquise clicks through the photos with widened eyes. "I could not be friends with this man. Wow. You never let him hit, not once?"

"Again, the operative word here is 'friend,' so no." Anjola tries to reach for her phone, but Marquise turns around and walks to the other side of the counter, his face glued to the screen.

"His girlfriend is so pretty. Is she Black?"

"Apparently."

"I can kind of see it," says Marquise. "Like maybe a quarter."

Sola returns with a few clothing items on her arm and peers over Marquise's shoulder.

"Oh." Her voice is laden with real disappointment. "Okay, sure, she's pretty, but she has nothing on my sister."

"Um, yes she does," Marquise says, finally handing back Anjola's phone. "This is not a slacks-and-button-downs woman, honey. But Sola and I are going to get you together."

"What are you two even going on about? I'm not competing with her for anything."

Sola and Marquise exchange looks.

"At this point I can't argue with you about your feelings," Sola says resignedly. "Hopefully your appearance will do the job for you."

Anjola tries to be patient as they pull at her hair and force her to try on a series of revealing outfits and beat foundation and eye makeup onto her face. By the time they finish and Sola and Marquise can agree on the outcome, it's nearly eight o'clock.

"This is the nicest I've looked in years, actually." Anjola studies her reflection in a large mirror. They've drawn her locs into a half-up, half-down style with a swoop bang, laid her edges, made her face look almost doll-like, and rubbed her deep brown skin with oil until it shone like bronze. She wears a silky, long-sleeved olive top, a flowy, patterned ocher skirt with a slit in the front, and high heels that she insists on swapping out for brown leather boots so she can walk.

"And the coup de grâce," says Marquise, handing her a pair of large gold hoops. "Even if he doesn't leave his girlfriend for you on the spot, he's got to have at least two cute friends for you to mess with."

Sola claps happily beside her. "Yessss. Go get your man, sis."

"I promise you both that isn't the point," Anjola says, gathering up her purse and phone. "But I so appreciate your help."

At the door, Sola pulls her into a tight hug. "We've all gotta be honest about what we want from life," she says.

When Anjola takes her seat on the Blue Line train, Sola's words are replaying in her mind. Knowing what she wants out of life is a hard thing. If she had to describe what she's done so far to, say, a blank-faced God on Judgment Day, she thinks she would say it's mostly been a mixture of what she's been told to do and what seems right. *Want* is something else entirely.

She thinks back to that graduation dinner, that first time she felt the weight of her parents' disapproval.

"The pursuit of elite status and the vocation of providing care are fundamentally at odds," Anjola had said to her mother, trying to explain why she was moving back home to Chicago, why she had ranked its most notorious public hospital at the top of her list for her residency training. The explanation didn't land.

"But, Anjola, you're so brilliant. You told me your test scores were good. Why Cook County of all places?" her mother asked. "What happened?" Her voice was soft and grave, as though she were inquiring about the reason behind a sad misfortune.

"I want to be where I can do the most good," Anjola said.

At the admission that Anjola had done this to herself, that this was not the result of her enemies conspiring against her, Anjola's mother's voice took on a new hardness.

"What good do you think you'll be doing there? Ṣàlàyé fún mi," she demanded. "They won't be able to give you the same caliber of training that any of these other programs would. They'll just be working you like a mule." Her mother, a health care provider herself, was the only other person at the table who could have understood the predicament in which Anjola had placed herself.

And nearly six months in, with this residency program proving to be every bit as grueling as her mother warned, Anjola has begun to question whether she came back to Chicago out of genuine desire or some strange sense of morality.

She had kept the decision to herself for weeks, telling no one but Neil. What had he said again? Something about it never being too late to right one's path. She pulls up her email on her phone, sifting through the exchanges between them that she's read and reread dozens of times.

Hey Jo,

So. You did a big thing. Good job. I mean, I'm sure your family won't be overjoyed if you actually end up doing your residency at Stroger, and you're right—people will make assumptions about your intellect. The whole Yale to Cook County thing is going to be a hard pill for your mom to swallow. But I still think you did a good thing. This whole system is set up to keep us all chasing accolades upon accolades, always pushing forward, never looking back. You were supposed to go to Yale and then Mount Sinai and then what? Go the whole academic medicine route? Get to be chair of diversity and community engagement for some private hospital after you finish residency? Please. I've seen my dad do it—it's a farce.

I think you've righted your path, even if no one else around you sees it that way. Also, the other day I was reading about how Federally Qualified Health Centers really only exist because of the Black Panther Party's free clinics. Maybe Stroger has a stronger legacy when you look at it like that? Besides, Chicago misses you. I miss you.

Keep me posted on how things go.
Neil

When she looks up from her phone, a man stands just across from her, smiling, then nodding vigorously. He wears a pair of washed-out jeans, a Chicago Bulls hoodie with some bleach stains, brown work boots. He starts muttering loudly to himself. Things like: "America ain't shit," with which she wholeheartedly agrees, and "Fuck, I'm high as shit," which is apparent enough, and "It's hard out here, man, money's real tight," which inspires him to sing the reprise from *Hustle & Flow*. Anjola looks away and smiles, resisting the urge to nod along to his gravelly voice. This smile is a mistake. He sees it.

When the seat beside her empties, he comes to sit down. His face and knees angle toward hers.

"Miss, you look absolutely beautiful this evening."

She doesn't want a scene but she doesn't want to talk to him either. Instead, she continues staring past him, at two men seated just across. They, in turn, seem to see right through her.

"Excuse me. Did you not hear me?" His breath is too close, hot and ripe like rotting fruit. She turns her head slightly and fixes her gaze on the train station sign outside. Division. There are too many stops left before Jackson.

"Yo, you got a man or something?" He is loud enough for everyone in her vicinity to hear, but none of them dares to look. She considers getting up and walking to the other side of the train. Years ago she read about a woman on the Red Line who was stabbed to death because she rejected a random man's advances. It could so easily have been her: commuting home from school or work one day, minding her own business, and thus blighting some man's ego. It is her now.

"If you got a man, I'll fuck his ass up." He smiles. A blond mother with a baby in a stroller blocks off the seat to the right, so Anjola can't move. An older couple diagonal from her choose to stare fixedly out the window. No one comes to her rescue.

But their shoulders all jump at the booming "Fuck!" before the softer "All you uppity Black women." Now they all glance nervously in her direction before turning back to their carefully constructed universes. What they are trying to ignore is a decidedly Black affair. She wonders if they think she and this man know each other. It might be convenient now, she imagines, to believe that all Black people are family and that all family matters are private.

"You could at least acknowledge me," the man hisses. He squints, brings his lips closer to her ear, whispers, "Bitch." She holds still, tries to make herself a wall as he lays his head on her shoulder. It is an act so tender and intimate, so diametrically opposed to the language he has just used, that it is more violation than she can stand.

The train pulls into Jackson. She times her exit, slipping through the doors just before they close so he can't follow her. As she stands on the platform, trying to calculate when she might catch the connecting bus, her shoulder begins to itch.

TWO

Saturday, October 20

Though her father would often remind her that her full name, Gbemisola, means "lift me into wealth," Sola is presently feeling pretty low and living pretty broke. She presses her back into the wrought-iron balustrade, just until she feels a slight sharpness beside her spine. Marquise passes her the blunt he has just lit, then leans back onto one of the plush white balcony chairs with a sigh.

"I don't understand why you're sitting on the ground like that."

"I like to have something to anchor me when I'm high," says Sola, pulling smoke from the blunt between neatly pressed lips.

"Personally, I'm trying to get lifted," he says. "Like I'm on a cloud."

As Marquise begins to sing John Legend circa 2005 softly to himself, Sola briefly wonders what might happen if the balustrade were to give out behind her.

"'Quise, this place is so nice. Seriously, thank you for letting me stay with you."

"Please stop saying thank you. It's gross at this point." He closes his eyes and waves his hand lightly. "Besides, you're basically family, so I didn't have a choice."

"Nah, family doesn't love this deep," she says, her mind flitting over the image of her siblings, her parents, the facts of her estrangement. "You're a true friend."

She thought she would feel more when she saw Anjola for the first time in a decade. Deep anger, abiding love, joy, something. She'd been living with Marquise for a month before she found the resolve to text her sister, and by the time she sent the text, she had managed to convince herself that seeing Anjola might do something for her. But she only felt the numbness that she always did whenever they spoke. Anjola was the only sibling she really kept in contact with, not out of keen interest or joy on Sola's part, but because Anjola seemed to insist upon sharing the details of her life. But these details were always boring, like watching a heavy-laden cargo ship traverse the Atlantic in slow motion, wondering if it had even moved at all.

"You know, she's still exactly the same?" Sola says. "Like, she's done *so* much? But nothing is really all that different about her."

"Sorry, but I don't want to talk about your sister," he says. "We did enough for her today. And we already know how that story ends."

"I guess that's true."

"Please, her whole 'He's just a friend' act is so tired. No offense. I mean I know she's family, but yeah, girl, they're not ending up together." He takes another long draw from the blunt.

Sola shrugs, pulling her fingers through the length of the twenty-six-inch, bone-straight Brazilian hair she wears. "So . . . do you think you and what's-his-name are going to end up together?"

"It's Langston," Marquise says, rolling his eyes. "And I can't really predict all that, but I know I like what we have going on so far. And clearly he likes me too, girl, 'cause he's been letting me live here for almost four months. And she, me, her, we do not pay no bills, baby."

She laughs, enjoying the presence of her friend, the crispness of the late fall evening, the weed-addled silence in her head. "See, that's just what I need. A sponsor."

"Ma'am. That's the exact opposite of what you need. You need a whole intervention."

Marquise has always been like this—always ready to tell her about herself. They've been friends since the ninth grade, and while their physical distance has waxed and waned over the years, they've remained close. She doesn't have any other friend who has given her so much grace, who's required so little of her even when she once had so much to give.

"Whatever," she says. "But seriously, a financial arrangement sounds better to me than some bullshit loving relationship. I'm convinced you can't have both."

"I wish," Marquise says wistfully. "It's hard. Honestly, I would let him take me out the game if he actually wanted to be in a relationship. But he wants to keep playing house over there with his wife in Detroit."

"And so here you are, a kept woman," Sola says. They both laugh.

Her head is starting to feel light. She marvels that she's back in Chicago, for good probably. This intangible thing called the internet has made and unmade her life, and she still can't quite figure out the real source of the unfurling.

One evening two months ago, she came home to her LA apartment draped in fur, wearing a long bussdown middle-part wig like Naomi Campbell's, her eyes taped at the temples to mimic her idol's perfect almond-shaped ones. The following day was her thirtieth birthday, and she'd been out with a photographer friend, posing for the shoot she hoped might break Instagram and get her over that 200K-follower threshold. It was harder these days. The beauty standard had surpassed her long and lean physique, favoring a wider hourglass curvaceousness.

She took off her wig and gown and showered before changing into pajama shorts and sitting in front of her laptop to open up her business email. In a matter of minutes, she was watching her partner of ten years having sex with another woman. Sola's eyes welled with tears as she took in the familiar rhythm of his strokes, his face leaning down to kiss lips that weren't hers. She sat there, clicking madly, watching and rewatching, not wanting to believe it was him despite the evidence in plain view before her. He'd sent the email but addressed it to a Steffani. A careless accident, a slip of the S. It wasn't the first time he had cheated on her, but it was the first time he had sent the proof to her inbox.

She wishes someone had been there to stop her, to counsel her, that next day when Aiden came home and roused her from where she lay sleeping on their living room sofa, tear tracks on her cheeks, her breath smelling like old wine.

"I didn't mean to send that email," he said, his hand resting softly against her thigh. She remembers he was wearing the white Armani shirt she'd bought for him, the cuffs rolled up to expose the patchwork of tattoos that adorned his forearms.

"But it made me realize that I'm tired of pretending," he said. "I don't want to do this anymore."

It was like she didn't hear him. She'd gone on ranting about how he'd endangered her livelihood, what could have happened if the video had been leaked, what all the gossip channels would say about their relationship. Why had he kissed her before telling her how sorry he was for everything? It only clicked into place when she saw him walk into their bedroom, yank his clothes off the hangers. He was actually leaving her. She just sat there on the edge of the sofa, suspended in time, thinking of a decade of relationship gone as suddenly as a whisper.

"And, oh," Aiden said, stopping briefly at the door with a garbage bag full of clothes behind him. "I had to borrow some money from our account for the deposit on my place, but I'll get it back to you, I promise." Some money. She hadn't initially thought to ask exactly how much that was. The money they got from YouTube ad revenue and brand deals could range from $10,000 to $20,000 monthly. But their expenses had ballooned over the time they'd been together. Five hundred dollars to rent a room in Compton had become $9,000 a month for a luxury apartment near Venice Beach. They were leasing a Porsche for him and a Mercedes for her. And there were all the expenses they charged to their cards to keep up appearances: designer gowns, expensive watches, first-class flights to supplement what brands gave them for free. But she hadn't been thinking about this question then; what exactly was the sum total of his leaving?

When she later went to check her balance, she found that their bank account was entirely empty.

"I really only had that ten grand to my name," she says, reaching up for the blunt again.

"What?" Marquise asks.

"The money Aiden took from the account. I'd just gotten paid for a brand deal. He took it. I just let him."

"Fuck his Chet Hanks–looking ass." Marquise shakes his head. Sola wants to laugh, but the laughter has no root.

In the days after Aiden left, she had called him incessantly, leaving a litany of voicemails, some scathing, some beseeching. Because who would she be without him? He was her lover and business partner, yes, but he'd also been her family. In all those years of separation from her relatives, Aiden had been a center that held. Without him, she felt that there would be nothing to ground her, nothing to keep her from becoming the tiny, insignificant, floating thing she'd always feared she was.

She didn't post anything for the next week, barely showered, just sat there rewatching every video they'd ever posted, searching for a hint of the thing that had broken them.

But in the days Sola had spent soothing her heart with ice cream, Aiden had only been plotting her downfall. He uploaded a video to his personal YouTube channel at the end of that week. By the time she saw it, it already had over two hundred thousand views. A fifteen-minute monologue about a relationship built around social media, with nothing about his infidelity, nothing about his theft, everything about how Sola was a different person when the cameras were off, claims of emotional abuse, hints at persistent physical aggression. All lies, but a white man dog-whistles "angry Black woman" and the witch hunt begins.

And still, Sola could not bring herself to speak. Her mind seemed bent on excavating the past. They'd started as two angsty college students, eager to leave their families and run to the West Coast. Then they'd become business partners. She and Aiden had started out on interracial YouTube, both in their early twenties at the time, chronicling their newly established life in LA. He, the white, muscled, bearded tattoo artist. She, the bougie, Black fashionista. Both beautiful, both photogenically in love, with nebulous dreams of making it big. Together, they drew in a huge following. People liked Aiden's rough exterior, and Black women adored seeing Sola, dark-skinned and chosen. Even though she had separate YouTube and Instagram accounts where she would upload clothing hauls and style tutorials, the subscriber and follower numbers showed a clear preference for seeing their relationship. Aiden had been able to open up his own tattoo shop, and she'd finally been able to turn to influencing full time. They'd even begun looking at houses together. And then he razed it all to the ground.

Over the next few weeks, her email and Instagram inboxes filled up with messages from followers who wrote to express their judgment, condolences, anger, shock.

> @mellymell122: Hun, you should try to get your man back.
>
> @rogerogilvyiii: Wowwww so you were beating Aiden all this time?
>
> @ttrippsteph: Sis, I'm heartbroken. You both were my favorite couple.

What was worse were the little articles here and there that popped up about her and Aiden, the subtext reminding readers that social media was a highlight reel and that women could be abusers too. The few friends she had in LA wanted to take her out to brunch and pedicure appointments, which she obliged at first, until she realized they were more interested in getting the juicy details than they were in commiserating. She had no real friends, she came to understand. How terrifying, at thirty, to suddenly see that the social circle she had invested in was a black hole, yielding nothing in her time of crisis, this most public of dumpings. It was bewildering to have become this object of speculation and curiosity. It took her three weeks to have the sense to shut their social media pages down. All she could do was remain still, let her mind careen back and forth from the moment he left to the moment they met and everything that happened in between.

And then the rent-due notice had come. Aiden had blocked her, so as not to talk of sending her back any money. Then the pain became a dull ache, a weighty numbness while her mind turned to thoughts of survival. It wasn't just about finding somewhere to lay her head. It was about finding someplace where the embraces were real, where she knew that someone actually loved her.

"It all makes sense to me now," Marquise is saying, his eyes closed serenely.

Sola stands up and lights the blunt again, realizing the weight behind her eyes is gone now. The city rushes on below her, and she likes how anonymous this makes her feel. Rock bottom feels high, like a new start, like a rewrite to the bad ending of a good TV show.

"What makes sense?" she asks.

"You being back," he says. "Sankofa."

"What's that?"

"Girl, have you really never fucked a hotep? Not once?" Marquise's laughter is light and careless. "Let me tell you—the homophobic ones give the best D."

Sola rolls her eyes. "You deserve better. And Black men and I don't go together."

"I *have* better, bitch," Marquise says, gesturing at the apartment behind them. "And I don't have the energy to help you unpack your shit. But just know, your internalized racism is not cute."

He stands up from the chair he's been luxuriating in. "You know the adinkra symbols? The chicken pecking its own behind? The heart shape?"

She shakes her head and he sighs.

"Sola, sometimes you are so tragic to me." He beckons her inside. "Sankofa is like Ghanaian for 'go back and get it.' Like retrieving what you've left behind. Going over the past."

She follows him. In the kitchen he pulls out a large box, its contents hidden by floral wrapping paper. "I saw this at a random vintage store in Old Town yesterday. Don't ask me what I was doing there," he says, pushing the box across the counter. "You remember sophomore year when I got to be Walter Lee in *A Raisin in the Sun*? How that ugly-ass lead costume designer made my clothes all baggy and lopsided?"

While she slowly unwraps the box, carefully undoing the tape, he goes on.

"I never told you how much it meant to me, you sneaking into the design room to take my measurements, staying late after school to tailor the costume so it actually fit me."

She does remember. For two weeks she had gone home late every day, anxious about her mother's wrath but loving her friend more than what she feared her mother might do.

It's an antique sewing machine. A Singer, pitch-black with gold embossment, painted leaves adorning the base and stem and body. It's been a long time since she's sewn. She abandoned her first machine in her parents' basement when she left home, always telling herself she'd get a new one later, always managing to buy everything but.

"Because of you, I was able to go out on that stage and act my little ass off on opening night. Well, partially because of you, but you know what I mean. Like, I knew I looked good. And that made me confident."

Sola runs her fingertips over the leaves, her cheeks warming. A distant dream. She remembers what it felt like to wear a dress she had sewn for herself the summer she was nineteen, the folds in the fabric arranged just so. She remembers how safe this little red dress makes her feel. Safe, even though men whisper lewd things and honk at her on the street. Safe because the projection is hers to determine, because she knows that adornment is the ultimate control over the body.

"Anyway," Marquise is saying, "I got you this because, like, whenever I'm going through it with a man, the best thing I can do is something that reminds me of who I am without him."

She throws her arms around him. "Sankofa," she says. "I like that for me."

THREE

Saturday, October 20

Ola unlocks the door to an apartment that no longer feels like home. He isn't sure when exactly this happened to him. They bought the place nearly two years ago, six months before their wedding, feeling both the giddiness and the groundedness that comes with reaching such an adult milestone. All the natural light was Marisol's favorite part. That and the neighborhood. She liked how young Lake View felt, how close it was to everything that mattered—the proximity to art galleries and brunch spots, the convenience of the train, the swell of activity surrounding every Cubs game.

If there's anything Ola likes about this home, it's the exposed brick—and the size. At any time, they can slip away from each other without question and return to each other's orbit if needed. She has her studio, he has his office (though he will soon cede it for nursery purposes). The guest room usually remains undisturbed. What luxury.

It made him uncomfortable at first. Because he'd grown up in a house where every corner and inch of space was put to use—for sleeping or play, for books or a deep freezer, for hanging up lace or wax-print fabrics or hair extensions—it was discomfiting to have so much square footage lying fallow.

Marisol is into minimalism. Apart from her plants, their home is decorated in cool neutrals. Everything is neatly put away, the tabletops always pristine and clear. She cleans up after him, which irritates him, though he liked it when they first moved in together.

In an act of obstinacy, he now sets his gym bag atop the kitchen island. Instead of going to take a shower, he wanders down the hall to her studio. It is the brightest room in the apartment, and the luminosity of the open door greets him before he hears Sade's "The Sweetest Taboo" set to only instrumentals. What kind of person would do that—strip the deep, rich timbre of Sade's voice from her music? Her voice is the whole point.

Marisol's back is turned to him as he stands watching her from the doorway. She's working on a painting of something imperceptible—deep browns and pinks, circles and pears. He imagines her squinting in intense focus, biting her lower lip the way she always does when something is too mysterious for her to discern. Today she wears all white and stands barefoot. The plain dress billows out all around her, stopping just short of her ankles.

This vantage point, from behind, was how he'd seen her when they first met. She stood perusing the menu in an uncrowded bar in Lincoln Park, wearing a formfitting black dress and ridiculously high heels, her behind wide, her waist evenly small. And her hair. God. He loved her hair before he loved her face, a mass of bountiful golden curls that whispered against the small of her back. Tinder had already done the work of ensuring she was also interested in him. He'd had to listen keenly as she spoke, avoid allowing himself an open study of her body. But in truth, he loved her first with his eyes before he loved her with his mind.

Now Ola announces his presence by knocking on the wall.

"Hello, mi amor." Her voice is a song. Paintbrush still in hand, she walks over to peck him on the lips. "How was the gym?"

"I worked up a good sweat."

"I'd hope so. You were gone for like three hours." She brings her nose to his armpit and inhales deeply. "It's so weird, you definitely stink, but it smells so good to me at the same time."

Ola laughs and reaches for her, but she pulls away before he can lock her in an embrace. He lifts a few sketches up from an antique armchair near the entrance to the room and sits, opting to watch her work.

When he first found out she painted, it enthralled him. Marisol was so unlike him—lighter, freer. She said whatever was on her mind. Sometimes she would show up to their dates with paint crusted in the corners of her fingernails. She was vibrant.

Early on in their relationship, she worked as a receptionist at a law firm while she finished the last year of her MFA program. He liked that Marisol had found a way of blending the pragmatic and the fanciful, that she tried hard to support herself as an artist, despite having come from means. He saw very clearly what his role might be in her life. He wanted to help her, to step into the place where she had rejected her father's provision, to give her the freedom she would need to create her art.

Ola wasn't the least bit ashamed to tell his mother that he was dating a receptionist at the time, though he could hear her dismay in the prolonged silence over the phone.

"Olanipekun."

"Ma."

"At this your big age, with all of your accolades, the woman you want to marry is a small-small receptionist."

"But, Mom, no one's talking marriage yet. I just want you and Dad to meet her."

But he was lying and he knew it. He'd been talking marriage, at least in his mind, from the moment he'd met Marisol. She was too beautiful not to marry. And though he didn't know exactly how he saw himself, he knew that she fit perfectly beside him. "And she's not just a receptionist. She's a painter."

"Ah! Ayé mi ti bàjẹ́."

"Mom, don't say that."

"I must say it o! I really must. The girl is not Yoruba. She's not Nigerian. She's not even Black at all. Me, I don't know anyone from this Argentina place that you say she comes from. And then she has no education. Pekun, does the girl even speak English sef? Ehn? Ṣó n sọ èdè òyìnbó?"

It was his father who took the phone from his mother's hand and calmly said, "Son, bring the girl on Saturday evening for dinner. We'll be glad to meet her." And then hung up.

Marisol had known without his having to tell her how she should present herself at this dinner. She'd drawn all that wild hair into a neat braid, played up her Catholic upbringing, used the terms "sir" and "ma'am" whenever she could, took every slight from his mother in stride. When his mother vaguely mentioned that Ola was attracting all kinds of women now that he commanded a high salary as a financier, Marisol explained that choosing to become a painter was a luxury afforded by her own father's wealth. His mother's cool exterior thawed after that, and by the end of those two hours, she had taken on her husband's more jovial disposition toward Marisol. She hugged Marisol before they left and told Ola on the phone later that night that she was "a very respectful girl."

Ola liked that version of Marisol too, the parent-friendly one, the same way he liked the sultry version of her at the bar where they met, and the fluid version of her who lazily painted streaks of white on his arm right before they had sex for the first time. He liked all versions of Marisol, until now. This woman who came home one day and cut all that gorgeous hair into a short bob, who now only dresses in cotton whites and linen neutrals. All the color now limited to her art. Otherwise, she is all straight lines and clear patterns, unyielding in her rules and regimens.

"So, I've been thinking," she says without facing him.

"About?"

"The baby's name."

He waits for her to continue. She is seven months along at this point, and they have neither a name nor a nursery ready. They've both gone about this pregnancy as though it is simply another fact of their lives, collecting their emotions in neat vessels that they keep separate from one another. He has caught her at times in joyful repose, both hands resting on her exposed belly as she hums to their baby or whispers to it in Spanish. But it's rare for them to share in these moments. He presents himself at every obligatory doctor's appointment and newborn training class, but he notes a distinction between them and the other parents. Everyone else's feelings are laid bare.

"I've been thinking that maybe we should give him an American name."

"Mmm," is all he can say. Because what is an American name? John? Bob? Functionally, by virtue of his having American citizenship, is his name not an American name? Couldn't Marisol be an

American name at this point? What even is America, apart from a thing seized and not ceded to?

She grows uncomfortable in his silence; he can tell because the purple section she's been focused on is now too dark and too thick. "Shit," she says. She turns around to face him, setting her paintbrush and palette on a small table beside her easel.

"I know I said I was okay before, giving him a name from your culture. But I don't know, Ola, I just don't want that to be his struggle. You know?"

"No actually. I don't," he says, his voice stripped of feeling.

"I'm just saying that I see what you go through whenever you call the doctor's office, or when you have to call about the internet service, or how they say your name wrong when they do your boarding pass at the airport."

Ola raises his eyebrows. Somehow, he's surprised she's been keeping a record of all these slights that are simply part of his daily living.

"I can't even pronounce your full name correctly, and I'm your wife." She sweeps a section of her hair out of her face, leaving a small smattering of purple just near her ear.

"But there are shorter Yoruba names with less complex pronunciations." His body flushes warm and his hands grip the arms of the antique chair. He looks down at the platinum wedding band that brands his left hand. Anyone else in his family would probably be surprised that he's here advocating for a Yoruba name. But the pregnancy has made him reflect on lineage, on the importance of having a name with meaning.

He was fourteen when his parents brought his youngest sister home, a tiny, red, mewling thing. For the first week of her life, she was called Baby, her real name a secret that their parents only unveiled the following weekend during the naming ceremony held for her in their living room. Baby had big brown eyes, tiny fists that held love in their grip, and a pitiful cry that made him want to wail in solidarity. Ola loved her instantly. Karen was an ill-fitting name for someone with such profound eyes. He liked her middle name, Nireti, better.

"I mean, if he was going to be a girl, I'd say we could name her after your sister that I haven't met. So-la," Marisol says. "I like that one. It sounds like a song."

Ola chooses not to mention that Sola is only half her full name or that his and his sister's nicknames are just one letter apart. He doesn't know why Marisol is bringing her up. Ola had wanted to invite Sola to their wedding, but his mother wouldn't have it. Weeks after their wedding pictures had all been posted on Facebook, he received a one-word text message from Sola: Congratulations. It was the first contact they'd had in almost three years, after their annual holiday and birthday texts had trickled down to almost nothing. Ola had stopped talking about her long before then, and Marisol had since given up on convincing him to reach out to her.

She's never been able to comprehend the dynamic, though he tried to explain that Sola had abandoned their family and effectively disowned them. Marisol and her sisters are incredibly close—so close that the last time the two of them came to visit, he was relegated to the guest room and the two sisters took his place in their bed. She doesn't have to understand his family's relationship with Sola, but what he doesn't appreciate is how Marisol seems to leverage this estrangement as indicative of something wrong with his culture.

"He isn't going to be a girl," Ola says, turning his gaze away from hers.

"Exactly. Well. He might not be. The point is, honestly, I haven't heard a single name from your culture that I really like, you know?"

"Wow." His eyes widen. "You don't think that's a little disrespectful?"

She wraps her arms around herself, wavering. He hasn't raised his voice, but any expression of strong emotion from him always seems to make her fearful.

"I'm sorry, I'm just trying to be honest," she says. "I don't want the baby to feel othered. I want him to feel like he's just like everyone else."

"But he won't be. He'll have a Nigerian American father and an Argentine mother. He'll be different regardless."

"So then why not grant him this clemency?"

Ola winces. She means that his name is a weight to bear, an onus he should avoid passing on to the next generation.

"We can give him middle names from our cultures." Her voice is soft and low and her eyes search his for affirmation, as though she's just proffered a reasonable olive branch.

"Right."

"I think it's only fair. I mean it's a middle ground and he'll have your last name."

"Okay, Marisol."

"Are you mad at me?"

As she approaches, Ola stands up from his seat and walks toward the open window. It has just begun to drizzle. A man emerges from the café across the street, balancing a coffee, a paper bag, and the task of untying his eager Doberman from a signpost. Ola has always wanted a dog, but Marisol is allergic. And now she is pregnant.

Marisol comes to stand beside him. She reaches for his hand, which he allows her to take limply, to entangle her fingers with his even though he needs space.

"Ola, I'm sorry, I don't know how to say things sometimes."

"It really isn't about how you're saying it, to be honest."

She places his hand on her belly. "He's ours, Ola. Both of ours."

The baby wasn't planned, but they were both open to him existing. Marisol had her IUD removed a few months before they conceived. The hormones made her anxious, she said, and dampened her sexual appetite, which she reasoned was dampening her creative abilities too. She also didn't enjoy the feeling of condoms, which Ola was happy not to use. If a pregnancy happened, they could handle it. But it happened sooner than Ola might have hoped.

She'd given him the news on a Monday evening in March, at a Thai restaurant near his office, pushing a small gift bag with metallic stripes across their table. When he reached through the gold tissue paper and pulled out the plastic stick, the word "pregnant" was still emblazoned on it in digital block text. He tried to search for the right emotion, found a simulacrum of joy and let it diffuse across his features. He'd even stood to embrace her. But his chest had constricted with fear. A baby would anchor them together forever. He hadn't been planning on escape, but now it was a foreclosed option entirely. Perhaps the trouble was that he had never pictured himself as a father. A son, a partner, a brother, an investor, even a dog owner, yes. But this idea of fathering, in the concrete sense and not the nebulous one, made him wind his arms around her tightly, as though steeling himself.

Now, with his hand on her belly, he accepts that these two share an intimacy he will never be able to enter into. Women's work. It *is* possible that Mother knows best. Perhaps, he thinks, this part of him—his name, his culture—is not the best. So much of his life feels like one big assimilatory project anyway: Pronounce your name in a way that Americans can easily understand, avoid cooking with stockfish so the smell doesn't linger in your clothes, forget your language so that it doesn't impair your English. Why would he stop now?

"Right now, he's more yours than he is mine," he says. She opens her mouth to protest and he stops her. "I'm actually just trying to say that I appreciate your perspective. What you're saying makes sense."

"Really?"

"Sure." He even smiles. "Did you come up with any suggestions?"

She turns sheepishly back to her painting. "I like Sylvester."

Ola laughs loudly. "Hell no."

"What about Caleb? Or George?"

"Absolutely not."

Physical intimacy is the common language they speak best. He draws her hair away from the spot on her neck that he loves, plants his lips there and on her ear, draws a finger along her jawline and down her throat.

She exhales deeply as his hand slips inside her dress, his fingers tracing lazy circles around her areola.

"I have to paint," she says, turning toward him.

"I think a break is in order."

Now he is pulling her dress above her head, taking her lips in his, and then her nipple. He pulls back to remove his gym clothes, all the while watching her from above, studying the ways her body has changed. The wider hips, the larger breasts, the swollen belly. He coaxes her down onto the paint-splattered canvas sheet, draws her legs apart, and tastes her. Pregnancy combined with his foreknowledge bring her to an easy climax, her flesh thrumming against his lips and tongue. She smiles down at him in love, her features suffused with pleasure and gratitude. Ola plants kisses along the inside of her thigh. As her husband, his job is to make things easy for her. He is grateful too that she comes for him so dependably, that sex between them is an uncomplicated and linear journey toward a peak. It's the one way that he feels sure of their footing. Now he directs her to her knees, grips her hip bones as he sinks inside her slowly, then quickly, beating his body against hers. She moans. He grabs a handful of her hair, his strokes growing longer and deeper, feeling her undulate around him.

"Whose is this?" he asks between shallow breaths, gratified by his own sense of control.

"Yours. All yours."

At her affirmation, his own orgasm slips through him quickly and loudly. They collapse onto the floor beside each other, breathing heavily, his hand resting on her belly, awaiting a flicker of movement from his unborn son.

"Marisol?"

She turns toward him, presses her palm against his cheek.

"I love you," she says.

He pauses, reflecting on the obvious response. In that moment he mistakes the love she professes for something sturdy, something that can handle the truth about what he's been going through internally for months. "Sometimes it feels like our life is this thing I've just, like, fallen into. And I just keep falling and falling." In his mind he sees himself tumbling through an endless abyss with nothing to ground him. "It's terrifying."

Her eyes are large and sad. "I don't understand. You don't love me?"

He turns his gaze to the factory ceiling above him, unable to meet her gaze. "I just . . . I don't know. I feel stuck sometimes. Don't you think things are different?"

But Marisol is already clambering to draw the canvas sheet over her naked form, rising to her feet, putting distance between them.

FOUR

Saturday, October 20

Karen stands before a full-length mirror and pouts at her reflection. The short neon-yellow dress she wears belongs to Tinu Akinsanya, who stands there fangirling behind her.

"Karen, are you kidding me? You're a babe."

She is not a babe. Tinu is just being nice. As Karen sees it, very many things are wrong with her. Her patchwork skin is the most obvious problem. But her heavy breasts, wide hips, and squat legs have also become a source of internal contention. Especially having grown up in a house where all her older siblings were long and limber in the body. Her mother told Karen that her figure came from her maternal great-grandmother, who was a classically loud and boisterous Yoruba woman, but this did not ease Karen's discontent. The universe has been unfair. Lifelong vitiligo has already been a sentence in itself, but then to be paired with this body that holds fat in unnecessary places . . . Every time she sees her reflection, she feels her flesh warring against her will.

"I think I'd look better in something dark, and maybe a bit looser," Karen says. Her phone chimes and she goes to get it.

"You mean that sack you came here in?" Tinu says. "Absolutely not."

Karen is momentarily distracted by a text from her sister, the first message Anjola has sent in at least three weeks. Typical for Anjola to forget to respond to her. Karen feels a stirring of resentment as she reviews the sea of blue texts unbroken by gray until just now.

Anjola: Hi sweetie. Sorry life has been hectic, residency is kicking my butt. Guess who I saw today though?

Karen: It's okay. Who?

Anjola: Sola!

Karen: What?! No way!

Anjola: She said she's only in town for a couple days. I think she might be trying to lay low.

Karen: Oh wow. Is she okay?

Anjola: She looked amazing.

How's school?

Karen: Yeah it's great. I love my science classes.

Anjola: Dr. Longe 2.0 loading!

When Karen was little, she'd looked up to both her sisters, though admittedly she'd feared Sola as much as she'd pined after her. Anjola was sweeter, but Karen had wanted to be like Sola most. She would try on her clothes and shoes and makeup when she wasn't there, study the way she walked, play and replay the collection of pirated MP3 files Sola had downloaded onto the shared living room computer.

Now, as Karen places her phone back down, she tries to ignore the sinking feeling in her stomach. Her siblings always leave her out, anyway. Sola has never liked her.

"I can't believe you were hiding all of these assets," Tinu is saying.

Karen folds her arms around her belly. "I just feel so . . . exposed."

"Yep. That's the goal!" Tinu claps her hands together. "Imagine, all this time another Nigerian living just down the hall and I had no idea."

None of the acquaintanceships Karen has made over the past two years turned into friendships. At the start of her junior year of college, she decided to be more intentional about it. Or rather, she was made acutely aware of her friendlessness after Ola had come into town for an alumni meeting and offered to take her and her friends to lunch. Her older brother was kind enough not to ask any questions when she showed up alone in a tattered hoodie and sweats, and he filled the time with chatter about their parents and Marisol and the coming baby instead. When Ola dropped her back off at her dorm and told her she was always welcome to come hang out with him and Marisol on the weekends, she decided it was absolutely imperative that she find friends. It was one thing to feel lonely, but another thing entirely to have other people notice it too.

The student clubs fair seemed like a good place to start. The basketball court was dotted with folding tables and displays from dozens of student groups, the room buzzing with excitement. Most of the attendees were first-years, and Karen anxiously walked through the aisles, afraid that somehow she had aged out of this. She feared that people were staring at her, that her body didn't fit there. But at the end of one of the rows, a large group of Black students were gathered, laughing and chatting loudly. Karen recognized Wizkid's music playing from the speaker before she saw the large Nigerian flag adorning the table.

She wandered to the front of the table and began to hastily write her name down on the sign-up sheet when the girl standing on the other side held out her hand.

"I'm Tinu," she said, smiling brightly to reveal a pair of rhinestones on her incisor and canine tooth.

"Karen," she said, shaking Tinu's hand.

"Thanks for signing up, girl. We love having non-Nigerians as well."

"Oh, I'm actually Nigerian too," Karen said, letting out a nervous laugh.

"Sorry! What did you say your name was again?"

"Karen. Karen Longe," she said. "Well, it's Loan-geh." If she was going to play up the whole Nigerian thing, she thought she might as well offer an attempt at the correct pronunciation of her surname. "And my middle name is Nireti."

"Nireti Longe." Tinu repeated her name back to her with proper intonation before smiling knowingly. "So you're also Yoruba."

For some reason Tinu wanted to continue talking with her. They learned they were both juniors and lived in the same dorm. When Karen returned to her room that evening, she opened her laptop to an email from Tinu inviting her to lunch sometime. She replied immediately, suggesting that they meet the very next day, which in hindsight might have been too thirsty, though Tinu didn't make her feel so at all. It was arguably the most exciting thing to have happened to Karen that semester. At the coffee shop, she learned that Tinu had been born in New York but was hastily moved to Lagos during her infancy and had lived there until she was fifteen. She showed Karen photos of the Akinsanya family estate on Banana Island, sprawling and dotted with palm trees. What had it been like to grow up rich in Nigeria? Karen wanted to know. Tinu regaled her with stories of the parties, the Yoruba demons she went to school with, and the girls who would hang out with aristos so they could afford fancy trinkets and keep up with everyone else. In the middle of secondary school, Tinu had been sent to live with an older cousin in Schaumburg so that she could complete her higher education in the States.

Befriending Tinu had been surprisingly easy. She had a breezy way about her, a kind of assurance in her womanliness. And apart from small jokes made now and again about how American or Nigerian Karen was or wasn't, Tinu never made her feel less than. In fact, Tinu's confidence was slowly becoming infectious, inspiring Karen to come out of her shell.

This was why she even agreed to spend this evening at an off-campus party with Tinu. Karen usually spent Saturday nights in her room—if there was an impending exam, she'd be studying, and if not she could while the hours away playing *The Sims*. But finally, she would be going to the quintessential college party. Everyone would be Black, so the vibes would be immaculate.

"I don't know what you're talking about," Tinu says. "Body? Banging. Dress? Fire. Shoes? On point. Skin?" She smiles, sidling up to

Karen in the mirror's reflection. "Beautiful. All we need to do is slick back these edges and we are good to go." Karen obediently sits in Tinu's desk chair, submitting to the cool feeling of the gel Tinu applies with a toothbrush to bring Karen's baby hairs into artful order.

The room stinks of weed. Packed. Hot. Humid. Bodies barely a foot away from other bodies. Which all means that it's a proper party for sure. And the music? The bass is so loud it feels like Karen's own heartbeat.

The two girls slip off their coats near the door, tucking them behind a sofa. Tinu takes Karen's hand and leads her to the kitchen, where she pours a splash of vodka into two red Solo cups.

"Drink. All of it. One time."

Karen does as she is told. It's her first time drinking. She winces at the burning sickly sweetness that now coats her tongue and throat.

"Good," says Tinu, expertly mixing the Absolut with Sprite. "Drink. This one you can sip at." She smiles slyly. "Or just hold it in your hand to look cute."

They dance together in the main room, laughing at Karen's eager dancing when Burna Boy's "Ye" comes on. When Naeto's "Ten Over Ten" follows, they boo the DJ and then go back to the kitchen to get more drinks. By the time they return to the sweltering gathering, the DJ has switched the song to Tekno's "Jogodo." Some girls call Tinu over and Karen finds herself happily alone, unafraid to dance by herself and unbothered about who might be watching her.

A boy draws up behind her, placing his hands on her hips. Somehow she knows, despite never having practiced, how to arch her back, how to lift an accommodating hand to the back of his head. She turns to face her dance partner, who in the dark is actually hot and, by the look of it, is delighted by her body as well, patchwork skin or no. He pulls her in tighter, trailing his fingers down her back until they grip her behind in a way that makes it feel suddenly unlike her own. A bolt of panic courses through her. "Want to go somewhere more quiet?" he asks, his lips grazing against her ear.

Before she can respond, Tinu is beside her, hooking her arm to pull her away.

"That boy is a fucking creep," she tells Karen when they are at some distance. "Apparently he keeps sending Moyo his nudes."

Karen does not know who Moyo is, but she trusts the seriousness of Tinu's voice. Tinu passes Karen another drink, which she downs dutifully, mostly unaware of its taste. She and Tinu hold hands and find laughter again as they dance. A dancehall song comes on, and Tinu takes the cue to bend down low and whine her waist. Karen is pleasantly surprised by the feeling of Tinu's body against hers. When the DJ switches the song to another throwback, Sean Paul and Sasha's "I'm Still in Love with You," which even Karen knows the lyrics to, she and Tinu are smiling and holding hands as they sway. And then they are holding each other. Karen likes how this feels, to be tightly embraced and surrounded by the melody of a song she likes, as well as wrapped up in the tautness of Tinu's body.

"I think I'm officially drunk," Karen says when the song ends.

"Me too. Let's leave before it gets too rowdy."

On the shuttle to their dorm, they slide into the back seat and say nothing, still holding hands. When they finally get upstairs, Karen's door is first. No one else is in the dimly lit corridor.

"I literally had the time of my life," Karen says as she pulls out her key card. Her mind is free of chatter, fully present, calm.

"Same, honestly." Tinu's gaze holds hers steadily, her eyes unblinking.

"I wish every day was this fun here."

"I think we can make it so."

Tinu kisses her. It is sudden but gentle. A tentative grazing of the lips, so light it could almost be mistaken for a warm wind. Surprised, Karen pulls away for a moment, teetering between confusion and desire. She didn't know that a girl could make her feel this way, that Tinu's stare could cause heat to gather between her legs. She returns a more insistent kiss; her arms wind themselves around Tinu's back. Karen has never kissed anyone before, but the mechanics come naturally to her. The two of them stumble into Karen's room. Under the guise of drunkenness, they strip the clothes from each other's bodies. Karen runs her hands over Tinu's flesh greedily, relishing in the smoothness of her belly and her nipples and her thighs. On her small twin bed, they kiss freely, delighting in the friction between them. When Tinu takes parts of Karen's body in her mouth, the press of her tongue pulls deep moans from Karen's lips. She tries to do the same for Tinu later, but Tinu pulls Karen between her legs, and they grind against each other as though there is still music playing, until Tinu cries out and Karen slips her fingers inside her so she can taste the new wetness there. They fall asleep with contented sighs, the sound of the heating system humming loudly around them.

In the morning, Karen awakens with a soft yawn. Her eyes take in all the familiar things in her room, now awash with the yellow light streaming in through the blinds: her Lenovo laptop, her drawer full of natural hair products, her store of cornflakes and evaporated milk for days when she can't bring herself to leave her room. And then her eyes take in the back of Tinu's head, an array of box braids flowing this way and that. Her mind fixates on the slow rise of Tinu's chest as she inhales and exhales, and she thinks a chorus of loving thoughts. She lowers her head to Tinu's shoulder and kisses it.

Tinu turns toward Karen. Her eyes flutter open, and the look in them is peaceful for a few seconds. And then Tinu recoils, so suddenly that she falls out of the narrow bed.

"What's wrong?"

Tinu quickly gathers her clothes from the heap on the floor. "I don't do this," she says. "Not anymore."

"Do what?"

"I'm a Christian."

Karen rubs her eyes and props herself up on her pillow, watching Tinu pull the skintight dress back over her body.

"Um . . . so am I?" Karen says. It is functionally true. She grew up in churches, Pentecostal ones. She still sings songs to herself about Holy Ghost fire. But Tinu stares at Karen.

"I don't want to be doing this lesbian stuff."

It is the invocation of this word, "lesbian," that makes Karen draw the bedsheet up over her chest, as though suddenly aware of her own nakedness. She notices the pounding at her temples then and realizes she has gone to bed with her hair still pulled back so tightly it has begun to ache. She hadn't been thinking about it at all, really, this possibility of being a lesbian. If she had ever questioned her sexuality, it had been because of her internet role-playing forums, where she could pretend to be anything: man, woman, bi, ace, witch, werewolf. And last night, when her sexuality finally found expression in real life, Karen had only surrendered to the thrill of the moment, grateful for how good everything felt.

"Is that what you think I am?"

"You seduced me." Tinu's features are twisted in anger.

"I didn't mean to," Karen says. This doesn't align with her memory of things, but she thinks conceding will be easier. "I'm sorry. We're friends. I just don't want you to be angry." She wants to cry.

Tinu sucks her teeth loudly. "Would a friend do something like this?" Somehow her voice gets even harsher. "You're disgusting." She pulls the fluffy coat from last night over her shoulders.

Karen just lies there with the comforter drawn up to her chin, watching helplessly as Tinu reaches for the door. She turns around to face Karen. "Don't you ever make the mistake of even looking at me in public, much less of opening your mouth to speak to me. Forget my name. Delete my number. I don't know you anymore."

Tinu fights the slow release of the door and closes it behind her with a thud.

Karen is frozen in place. The room feels cold. She reaches up to remove the hair tie so her head will stop pounding. Lesbian. A curse, a byword. Worse than: slut, whore, ashewo. More like: abomination.

She learned that last word early. Once, when she was about eight, she was playing in the basement with her older brother. They were pretending to be DJs, trifling with an old record player, Ola moving the vinyl back and forth under the needle while Karen pretended to beatbox over Boney M. Ola was back from college for spring break, and Karen remembers how thrilled she was to have him home. When he was around, he made the time for her that no one else could seem to find, always paying attention to the littlest one in the house. The music they made was ugly and rhythmless, but they were having fun.

And then, even above their noise, they heard a shrill scream from upstairs, the breaking of glass. He told her to wait, but she ran up the stairs behind him, his long legs climbing three steps at a time while Karen put her small hands out in front to keep from tripping. In the bright light of the living room, her mother was screaming. Something about naked pictures of Sola at school. Sola sat crouched in the corner, covering her face. Her mother had pushed the crystal vase off the entryway table in anger, and then that word: abomination. Glass shards lay everywhere. Ola was holding their mother back from Sola, whom she'd slapped so hard that she'd drawn blood. The image of her sister there, small, fuming, bleeding from the lip, is as vivid to Karen now as it was in that moment.

Karen bites her lip, trying not to cry as she stares out of the bright window. Of course Tinu would be disgusted by her. Having skin like hers, Karen has always anticipated that her sexual debut would not be particularly romantic. The tears flow freely now. On top of being ugly, she has to deal with being a lesbian. And, in Tinu's eyes, a wily seductress of a lesbian. She laughs at this thought, then sobs again. If she is an abomination, she realizes, then she will follow Sola's path. And who better to prepare her for her future position as the family reject than Sola?

FIVE

Saturday, October 20

As Anjola approaches the Promontory—a bar/club/restaurant/community arts space—she takes in how much Hyde Park has changed. Four years ago, the university's shadow visibly loomed over the entire neighborhood. Then, Anjola could have counted on some grunginess to Fifty-Third Street; she would have found the awning signs above most storefronts flickering or barely lit. Now there is light and shine and newness everywhere.

Anjola is directed up the stairs to Neil's party by a big-Afroed, long-earringed hostess with a faint wave of her heavily bejeweled fingers. Even the hostess's disinterest feels classy to Anjola, though anyone else might interpret it as rudeness. As she studies the array of bodies, she imagines the men discussing urban renewal and generational wealth. She imagines the women arguing about the latest study out of Princeton about how Black men are most likely to marry outside their race, and they should too. But no, another woman in Anjola's mind responds—it's about perspective; most Black men are married to Black women. This imaginary conversation has already tired her. This space doesn't seem like the right fit for Neil, but where, she wonders, is the bar for Black men who like to pontificate about Marx and Obama-era neoliberalism while drinking Hennessy and rapping along to Chief Keef?

Under the twinkle of the string lights that crisscross the rooftop, the first familiar face she sees is not Neil's—a disappointment, since she needs to vent to someone about the harassment she endured on the train—but Wesley Kimani's.

Wes smiles at her, and she instantly feels the same openness and good-naturedness she has always felt from him. He's Neil's other best friend. In college he worked at the coffee shop beneath the divinity school building. Anjola would sometimes keep him company behind the counter, watching as girls left their numbers for him on receipts and napkins.

"All the way from Oakland, California!" she says, reaching up to give him a hug. "What are you even doing back here?"

"It's a big night for my mans," Wes says warmly. "But don't worry, I'm not staying. Nothing could ever make me move back to this frigid-ass city. Neil told me you did though. Why would you ever deign to do such a thing?"

"Because this is her home." Neil's voice announces his presence behind her. "And unlike all of you interloping, profiteering, Silicon Valley–ass niggas, she came back to serve her community." He has a way of speaking that makes him perpetually sound like an orator.

"Profiteering?" she says, looking over her shoulder with a smile. "Come on, Neil, Wes is a worker just like you."

"A more highly paid one," Wes says with a smirk, "but a worker nonetheless."

Neil rolls his eyes playfully.

"I'm so glad you could make it," he says, giving Anjola a polite kiss on the cheek.

They usually have more subtle ways of greeting each other. When they were younger, it had been crafty insults, bumps of the elbow, a brief nod or wave when they passed each other in their high school's hallways. So her heart stills in surprise when his lips touch her cheek then. She inhales the earthy scent of his hair—sandalwood, maybe, or patchouli.

"Of course! I'm sorry I'm late. I know how important this is for you."

"You do?" He looks to Wes for confirmation.

"I mean, I've never seen you plan a surprise party for anyone in your life," she says. "I meant to text you on the train that I'd be running late, but then there was this—never mind. I'm here now. You clean up nice, friend."

Over the years she's learned that Neil has a conventional attractiveness that insists upon itself, despite his best efforts. Anjola has seen other women take in the light brown skin and the light brown eyes, the wide lips, the sculpted nose, the slight musculature in his arms, and decide in a matter of seconds that, no matter the state of his clothes or hair, he might be a man worth knowing. He has a jovial spirit, a ready smile, and a pair of on-trend spectacles that lend him an air of wisdom. This evening he wears a white dress shirt, navy blue pants, and brown brogues. His locs worn in a low bun at the nape of his neck, have been tightened to the root.

"Thanks," Neil says. "So do you."

She takes stock of the scene around her. It's an uncharacteristically warm evening. The heat lamps are all off. But from time to time a gentle breeze makes the bodies draw closer to one another. The DJ cycles through a disorienting mix of A Tribe Called Quest and Wu-Tang Clan (Neil), Corinne Bailey Rae and Lianne La Havas (the girlfriend). Anjola can only pinpoint a handful of familiar faces on the roof. Most of the partygoers look clean and fresh, colored and moneyed, shiny like the new Hyde Park. Four years post-college doesn't seem like that much time, but it's been long enough that their social circles have diverged entirely.

"You have so many new friends here," she tells Neil. "It's like ninth grade all over again."

She'd been full of nerves that first day at the Lab School, her impressions of the place poisoned by Sola, who'd told her it would be full of snooty white folks whose ancestors came over on the *Mayflower* or something. Sola hadn't been entirely wrong—though it was not, as Anjola eventually learned, *Mayflower* money, more like two-generations-of-professor money.

After an intense series of standardized tests and recommendation forms and interviews and financial aid petitions, she'd been prepared to fight her way through an equally intense four years of high school. But that first day, she was surprised to close her locker and find another Black face smiling at her, a hand outstretched in introduction. Friendship with Neil had been that easy. He decided they would be friends, and so they were.

"Come on, I'll introduce you to some folks," Neil says. "Wes doesn't even live here, so."

He places a hand on her back and leads her through the crowd, but their journey is quickly intercepted by a group of three women, one of whom excitedly waves him over.

"Neil! I just got a text from Louise. She and Giselle will be here in ten minutes."

"Oh, okay, wow." Neil exhales deeply, nervously. "This is happening, then. Okay. I'm just going to walk around and remind people of the plan." He looks at Anjola as though only just remembering she's there. "Oh, by the way, Anjola, meet Rachel, Nora, Tia—they're Giselle's best friends. They're all local. I'll just leave you all together for a minute."

She watches him leave.

"No drink, Angela?" This is the one named Nora. Anjola does not correct this mispronunciation of her name. Even when she does, more often than not, people hear Angela anyway. If they don't, then they make her name rhyme with Angola, which is not entirely accurate but close enough.

She suspects it was intentional on her parents' part, to give her a Yoruba name that might so easily be incorrectly spoken as a Western one. With each child came increasing capitulation to the assimilatory project, a sequential watering down of their names. Olanipekun, the oldest, a son—once called Pekun for short until he decided that Ola was easier. Gbemisola, the second, a daughter—promptly only called Sola by both parents after observing the teasing endured by her elder sibling. Anjola, the third, a daughter. And Karen, the fourth, another daughter. The three older children would often joke that their parents just gave up with the last one, her name a white flag of surrender.

"No, no drink," Anjola replies. "I have to be up early tomorrow morning to go to church with my mom. I promised."

"That's so sweet," says the one named Tia. "I wish my mom were close by, but she's back in New York. Giselle was actually telling us that you moved back home recently."

"Oh, *this* is the girl best friend?" This is Rachel. She's looking at Tia but gesturing at Anjola. She turns to Anjola fully now. "You know, I don't understand how men and women can be best friends, especially if they're both straight."

"It's an unnecessary title," Anjola says politely. "We're just good friends, we go way back."

"Yeah, but Neil's so cute, I mean how do you do it? I couldn't just be his friend."

Anjola doesn't want to be annoyed, and this Rachel woman, who is clearly tipsy, isn't the first person to have asked. But the fact that she's asking here, at this party Neil is throwing for his girlfriend, feels especially disrespectful.

"We're sorry, she's clearly had too much to drink," Tia says.

"Seriously, ignore her, she's an idiot," snaps Nora, who has a deeper voice and a style that reminds Anjola of Posh Spice, her strappy black heels not unlike the ones Sola tried to make Anjola wear earlier.

Anjola forces a close-lipped smile. "It's all good."

Neil is now standing on a chair near the bar, waving for attention. "Everyone, Giselle should be here in the next three minutes, so please try to keep the noise down. And anyone standing around the entrance, please relocate yourselves. That's where I plan to meet her."

The rooftop is vibrating with restrained excitement. Tia claps happily and Rachel lets out a squeal.

"Sorry," Nora says. "We're just so happy to be part of this. Giselle's such a sweetheart, she really deserves it, you know?"

"Sweetheart" is exactly the right word for her. Anjola met Giselle just a few weeks after she first moved back to Chicago. Neil informed Anjola about this happy addition to his life while he was helping her unpack, insisting they meet as soon as possible. He didn't know that she already knew because Giselle tagged him in her Instagram posts, and Anjola studied his profile often enough that she saw each new post eventually. There were at least a year and a half's worth of tagged photos of them doing things that Anjola never pictured him doing—apple picking or buying ornaments at Christkindlmarket or attending corporate networking events. He'd never posted any pictures of Giselle though, and he'd never mentioned their relationship in any of his emails.

But a few days later, the three of them were all having dinner at Giselle's immaculate apartment in Wicker Park. It was exactly as Anjola would have envisioned: bright, with large, south-facing windows, full of plants and neon decor, with a small, fluffy white dog to match. Giselle insisted on preparing their meal, vegan and colorful. She sat in between Anjola and Neil at the kitchen island that evening, full of questions, her wide green eyes set on Anjola in such rapt attention that Anjola almost loved her too. Anjola hadn't wanted to like her, but Giselle was too sweet not to be liked.

Everyone quiets as Neil rounds the corner, his back to them as he leads a blindfolded Giselle to the center of the gathering. Their fingers are interlaced, his other hand guiding her by the waist. Something about this small intimacy makes Anjola's heart quicken. Giselle wears a tight, light pink dress that works perfectly against her skin tone, never tripping even once in her gold heels, despite being blindfolded. Neil lifts the scarf from over her eyes.

As the guests cheer, Giselle turns around and around in giggly wonder, her brown curls flying with her as she goes. Anjola feels envy like a prickly thing, creeping up her arms and shoulders and the back of her neck.

"I can't believe you did all this for me!" exclaims Giselle, turning to face Neil.

It is then that Anjola notices Giselle isn't carrying a purse. A woman who comes to a social function without a purse is a woman who trusts that someone else will take care of her every need. Anjola's eyes dart between the pair of faces before her. When Neil says, "Happy birthday, Giselle. You're an amazing woman," Anjola expects this. But she isn't prepared for him to continue, though she should have seen it coming. The rooftop quiets again. Neil is still holding Giselle's hands in his.

"I know it may come as a surprise that I want to ask you this. We haven't been together that long, but I've learned not to qualify depth of love by length of time." It's a good line, and as Anjola's heart slaps against her chest, she wonders how many times Neil practiced this speech. That, and how he could ever have neglected to inform her of this plan.

"For as long as you'll allow me, I want to be by your side. I want to spend my life with you."

Neil gets down on one knee and pulls out a blue velvet box. Giselle covers her mouth in shock, her flawless gel manicure sparkling in the low light. Anjola's cheeks flush hot. "Giselle Ivana Winters, will you marry me?"

"Yes!" She nods vigorously. A tear actually falls down her cheek. "Of course, Neil. I love you so much."

As the crowd cheers, Anjola closes her eyes. He hadn't told her he was planning to propose, that she was walking into a surprise engagement party. This is a betrayal. She can't exactly explain to herself why, but she knows it is. Refusing to watch them kiss is the only resistance she has left.

She hears the clapping and cheering around her subside before the DJ turns the music back on. The rooftop begins to hum again, and her eyes open just in time to see Giselle walking over to her group of friends, Neil following closely behind. Anjola doesn't want them to be near her and begins trying to calculate how she can leave without being noticed.

Giselle squeals and extends her arm, wiggling her fingers before the three women. Anjola hears them all prattling about the ring—halo, emerald cut, pink diamond in the center—but her eyes are fixated on Neil. He looks resplendently happy, his fingers interlaced with his fiancée's. Anjola is waiting to see if he'll look at her, but his gaze doesn't leave Giselle.

"She totally knew it was going to happen," Nora says to Anjola once the happy couple is no longer within earshot. "He asked Tia for advice on the ring and then Tia told Giselle, you know how these things go. I mean she always looks amazing, but I'm pretty sure she lost like five pounds in preparation. I just don't know how she does it all. The awesome job. The man. The cute dog. The apartment. I fucking hate her."

So even Giselle knew. Anjola is the only one who's been completely clueless. She winces, pushes her locs over her left shoulder. "How are you friends with someone you hate?"

"Okay, calm down, that was obviously a joke," Nora says.

"Mmm." Anjola turns her attention away from Nora, looking down at her pager in feigned surprise. "Oh, I'm needed at the hospital. Could you convey my apologies to the couple? It looks like it's an emergency."

On the sidewalk outside, Anjola stares absentmindedly at the empty street before her while she waits for her Uber. She doesn't know exactly how she hoped the evening would go, so she's confused by the way her body is reacting—this desire to withdraw, the clenched fists, the hard-set jaw. It isn't because of the engagement, she decides. It's because Neil didn't even bother to ask her how her day had been, that she didn't have the chance to tell him about what had happened to her on the train and discuss how to make sense of it. Or maybe it *is* because of the engagement, not because of Giselle, but because he and Anjola are supposed to tell each other everything. Unable to sift through her emotions, she pulls out her phone.

Anjola: Neil proposed to his girlfriend tonight.

Immediately, there are three dots. They disappear, then reappear again.

Sola: Oh wow. Congrats to them.

Anjola: I guess.

She thinks to type out a message about the train, something that Sola would laugh at, but the three dots appear again.

Sola: ??

Maybe y'all can talk if you feel a way? Idk you'll be alright.

Anjola: I don't even know what I'd say to him honestly, like I'm so mad I can't think.

Sola: Sorry hun. But yeah I'm kind of going through it right now, so I can't really support you like you need.

Anjola: Oh, that's okay.

But she doesn't fully understand. Her sister's texts read as though they're from a very distant friend. Only a couple of hours ago, they'd hugged for the first time in years, fallen into an easy banter, and Sola even implied she was rooting for Anjola and Neil. Now Sola is washing her hands of her again. A familiar ache rises within her. She considers that maybe she deserves the loneliness that always finds her, that no one can really stand to hold the weight of her heart.

SIX

Sunday, October 21

So you're gay," Sola says, her red lips drawn into a satisfied smile.

"I don't know," Karen says with a shrug. "How do you know if you're gay?"

The two sisters are in a booth at a McDonald's. Sola doesn't belong there, seated beneath a picture of a smiling Ronald McDonald in her vintage Chanel tweed jacket, but Karen insisted on this location. They're a twenty-minute drive from Karen's campus, which makes Sola wonder if Karen is concerned about being seen or overheard by anyone who might know her, though Sola gets the feeling that very few people do.

Sola's drive down from the city earlier that morning was pleasant. She had rented a pitch-black Mercedes with tinted windows and an all-black interior for the occasion. Even if her credit card bill kept trying to dissuade her, pulling up in a Honda to see her youngest sister for the first time in years would be unacceptable. If word got back to their mother, that word would have to be that Sola was thriving and successful. She had arrived outside Karen's dorm blasting Aaliyah's "Are You That Somebody" without an ounce of shame. Karen had walked over with her head low, hidden beneath a large gray hoodie. But when she took her hood down in the car, Sola was struck by how beautiful her sister was, how the patches of skin in the upper right and lower left quadrants of her face had lightened to give her almost perfect symmetry. When Sola left home, Karen had only been about ten; she'd had teeth too big for her smile and relaxed hair at that awkward nape length that was always breaking. In the car, instead of hugging her, Sola put her hand on Karen's chin and turned her face toward her own. "Stunning," Sola had said. The smile Karen returned was tentative, though bright nonetheless.

Now Karen is no longer smiling. Sola watches as Karen dips a french fry into her milkshake and then puts it in her mouth, a painstakingly slow process.

"You don't think having sex with another girl is gay?" Sola asks.

"Maybe?" Karen's hands rest upward on the table, plaintively. "But like, what if you didn't think of yourself as gay before? What if it was some kind of fluke?"

"Why does it matter?" But Sola already suspects why it matters: Being gay would make Karen like her, the family outcast. A forgotten resentment begins to simmer within her. This is why Karen reached out, Sola realizes. Not because she has missed Sola, but because she wants advice on being the family fuckup.

"Because maybe if I'm not gay, I can convince her that I didn't mean it."

"Didn't you?" Sola asks, crossing her arms.

Karen pauses in thought. "I did," she says softly.

"Well," Sola says, "whether you're gay or not gay, it doesn't change the fact that that girl is batshit."

"I don't understand why she just flipped like that," Karen says. "And then tried to make it seem like you roofied her or something. Like, bitch, you initiated."

Karen releases the fry she was dipping and watches it sink slowly into the milkshake. "She was my only friend, Sola. Why is life so fucking random?"

"Tell me about it." Sola deigned to buy herself a McCafé smoothie earlier, which she now sips gingerly. She shrugs. "So . . . you texted me for tips on what it'd be like for Mom to hate you or what? If you told her you're gay, I mean?"

Karen looks at her sadly. "Honestly? I half didn't expect you to respond, let alone show up here. You never really liked me."

Sola's defensiveness flags under a newfound sense of shame.

"That isn't true," Sola says. "I've always *loved* you." She sets the smoothie on the table and reaches across to hold one of Karen's hands, an awkward motion. She's never been great at physical expressions of love. Anger, yes. Her bullying of Karen when they were younger had been her way of channeling her own ire into someone smaller, weaker, as her mother had done to her. Now Sola can't help but fear that Karen's lack of confidence is her fault, that she has single-handedly dimmed her sister's light. "I was just angry at the world when we were younger, Karen. I'm sorry."

Karen nods and squeezes her hand. "Before I called? I was thinking of that day when we were little, the glass vase, how Mom busted your lip."

Sola refuses the vision playing at the edges of her mind. Still, the memory asserts itself as a phantom sting on her cheek where her mother struck her all those years ago.

"Yeah?" Sola says. "She busted my ass too, shit." She tries to laugh, but Karen's face is impassive, sad.

"I think she was really mean to you. I would have run away too."

"I didn't fucking run away." She's incensed that this is the story they're all telling themselves. "Actually, I don't want to talk about this right now. Honestly, everything Mom probably told you guys about me is true anyway. I *was* a little slut, I was disrespectful, I was mean."

"Maybe you were neglected? I mean, we all kind of were."

"You don't know the half," Sola says.

"Well. I just want to say thank you." Karen's expression is sincere. "For every meal you cooked. For every time you dressed me up and did my hair. I never forgot."

Sola's eyes well with tears. "Jeez, you've always been good at pulling on the right fucking heartstrings, huh?"

Karen smiles and hands her a napkin. "How long are you in Chicago for?"

"Um, I'm still sorting that out. I want to look into a fashion design program while I'm here," she says, mostly because she doesn't want Karen to know that so far she's just been spending her days wandering about aimlessly and feeling sorry for herself. The thought had solidified when Marquise gifted her the sewing machine, but when she clicked onto the website, she started thinking about how pathetic she'd look going back to school at thirty and then wondering where she'd even get the money from.

"Sola, you have to apply!" Karen's eyes are wide. "They'd be lucky to have you."

She shrugs. "Anyway, so I'm thinking I'll at least be around for a few weeks? A month? Things in LA are kind of messy right now."

"Aiden was a whole entire asshole."

Sola looks up at her, surprised—though she realizes she shouldn't be—that Karen has followed the debacle that upended her life.

"I definitely don't want to talk about that," Sola says. She can't help but be curt. How exposed she feels, knowing that Karen has read through all those articles about her. How embarrassed, knowing that her baby sister has, for years, watched Sola slowly betray herself for a man, pushing her style influencing to the side in favor of trotting out, over and over, the interracial love story their followers were hungry for. Imagine the example she has set, all that time spent relishing the power that being with Aiden got her, all that time forgetting she had any power of her own.

"Okay." Karen's gaze darts away from hers. She pauses for a moment and then looks back up at Sola, her eyes wide with new hope. "Well, if you stay for a month, maybe you could come to Thanksgiving? It's—"

"Hell no." Sola decides without a second of thought. It's as though she's been asked whether neon green can pair well with lavender, or whether it's a good idea for a girl with ass and hips to wear low-rise jeans. Some things are categorically false. Sola ever stepping foot inside that house again is one of them.

"But Mom said—"

"I refuse," Sola says, making the words slow and emphatic so that Karen will feel how deeply that refusal is meant.

Karen nods, but Sola can sense her deflation. She knows she can't leave with Karen feeling any worse than she did when she arrived.

"Why don't you let me take you shopping?" Sola suddenly asks.

"Now?"

"Well, what else are you going to do? Go back to your room and cry?"

Karen laughs. Back in her Mercedes, Sola looks on Google and finds an outlet mall about thirty miles south. She lets Karen choose the music for the ride—a disappointing mix of new age SoundCloud rappers, which feels strangely apropos for the cornfields that surround them.

When they arrive, Sola drives around the outlet before deciding on one store only, Saks Off 5th.

"Outlet malls are where art comes to die," she says as they exit the car, "but we'll see if we can revive something for you yet."

In the store, Karen stands awkwardly with her hands in her pockets. Sola pushes a cart around, throwing in all kinds of things her sister would probably never think of wearing. When they get to the dressing room, she stands outside and hands Karen the items in threes, as they are meant to be worn together. She snaps photos when Karen comes out, hyping her up each time.

"Are you still working on your own designs?" Karen asks her at one point.

"Sometimes," Sola says. "I just started sewing again."

"Good. Your sketches were always so cool," Karen says. And Sola remembers how she used to draw outfits for Karen, frilly pink gowns and posh leopard-print coats.

Karen insists on wearing the fedora and faux fur coat combo Sola has chosen for her all the way to the register.

"That'll be one thousand two hundred and sixty-seven dollars and ninety-eight cents," says the cashier with a smirk.

Karen's eyes widen.

"Don't worry, I've got this," Sola says. "Please, I've spent ten times this in an hour before."

She pulls out her Amex card and places it on the counter. The cashier swipes it quickly.

"Declined."

"Um, what?"

The cashier swipes it again, staring at Sola as the machine beeps.

"Declined."

"Do you have another card you can try?" Karen asks.

"Something must be wrong with y'all's machine," Sola says, fishing for her Chase card.

The cashier sighs heavily now, as if the embarrassment is shared. She waits for a moment as the machine processes. Sola holds her breath.

"Declined."

"This is some bullshit," Sola says, feeling her body flush hot. And yet she knows, somewhere, surely, that she maxed out one of those cards last week on eyelash extensions and a vintage Prada bag she found on Etsy. But the other one should have worked—were it not for the Mercedes rental, she realizes.

"Here, it's okay. Try my debit card." Karen hands her card to the cashier before Sola can stop her.

"Approved," the cashier says, shaking her head.

Sola is silent, her jaw set as she watches the cashier bag all of Karen's new clothes.

"Ola gave me some spending money for the semester," Karen says once they're outside. Sola's features remain steely. The mention of her older brother's name only adds to her shame. Ola has always been an asshole, so the world is an unjust place if he's doing so well that he can just hand Karen a stack of bills while Sola is struggling to make ends meet.

"I think it'll be fine," Karen says. "I've never had such nice clothes before."

Sola opens the trunk. "I just feel really ashamed," she says finally when they're inside the car.

"You shouldn't, you meant well," Karen says as she buckles her seat belt.

"I'll pay you back."

"You coming all the way down here was more than enough. I'll be okay."

On the drive back to Karen's dorm, all Sola can think about is how Karen must be judging her. Imagine, her older sister, the once-upon-a-time influencer, the fashionista, the original flexer, there in a raggedy Saks Off 5th in the middle of nowhere, Illinois, too broke to complete a simple purchase. She feels like a fraud.

Karen switches from mumble rap to Sola's favorite song. When Sola hears Sade crooning along to the rhythmic drums, she begins to smile. Both she and Karen open their mouths to belt out the chorus to "When Am I Going to Make a Living."

They're laughing, dancing in their seats. And it is then, as Sola takes her eyes off the road just momentarily to watch her baby sister crooning, that she decides, finally, that everything will all work out.

SEVEN

Sunday, October 21

Anjola wakes with a start on her family's living room sofa. On Sunday mornings it is customary for one Latifat Omolabake Longe (fifty-seven years old, registered nurse, mother of four, prayer warrioress, elder sister in Christ to many) to blast Yinka Ayefele's *Fulfilment* album from the old boom box in the living room.

"Left, right, tẹ ọ̀tá ẹ mọ́lẹ̀, left right," he sings. Anjola's mother is already dancing, picking up her feet as she rhythmically stomps on her enemies, per Ayefele's synchronic command. She pulls open the venetian blinds, shaking her yansh for the Lord as though it still sits high and wide, and the morning light rushes in around her.

"Good morning, my dear," she says.

Anjola groans, lies back down, and draws the comforter over her eyes. The music, the dancing, the light are trying to force her into a false jubilation she wants nothing to do with. She came home last night to find her bed upstairs covered with lace, Ankara, and damask fabrics and decided that sleeping on the couch would prove less of a struggle.

"Dìde, jàre! Service is in two hours. Or you want to tell me you forgot?"

She wishes she could have. Anjola has never enjoyed going to Sunday service, the ceremony of it all, the three-hour endeavor of listening to God's plans to prosper His children, the tithing and testimony and prayer, then the hour of socializing after. Since she moved back to the city, she has successfully avoided going to church with her mother on most weekends. Medicine sometimes feels like a trap, but in this way it provides escape—she can usually be too busy to attend service. But somehow (Anjola still does not know how), her mother got her hands on Anjola's schedule, pinpointed this day as a free one, and called to cajole her into coming to church.

"I've even picked out a very nice outfit for you to wear," her mother says, pulling the comforter away from her face. "I got it at the Neiman Marcus downtown. What you were wearing when you came in the evening was nice though. You put it together yourself?"

"You saw me when I came in?"

"Yes, of course. I saw it on my phone. Your father put a security camera at the door. This city is just getting more and more dangerous."

Anjola furrows her brow. There is a time for everything, and Sunday morning before service is not the time to try to explain structural violence to her mother. Nor does she have the eloquence. So her mother just goes on believing—in the promise of the Second Coming, in homosexuality as an abomination, in Black Americans as being violence-prone.

"No, I didn't dress myself," Anjola says, opting instead for another untimely topic. "I saw Sola yesterday and she helped." The words slip out before she can stop them, and she braces herself for a discussion more taxing than a theoretical conversation about the root causes of crime in Chicago.

"Mm-hmm," Latifat hums, raising an eyebrow. "So Gbemisola is in town and she's still avoiding me. As if it's my fault she went to go and useless herself for that stupid òyìnbó?" Her eyes bore into Anjola, full of questions. But she can't understand how her mother doesn't see that even the phrasing of that last question would push any daughter away.

Though Anjola doesn't know how to defend Sola in a manner that would prove effective, she can't just listen to her mother berate her. Again, Anjola changes topics, unwilling to venture into this irreparable rift between her mother and elder sister.

"She helped me put the outfit together for Neil's engagement party."

"Wow wow wow. God is so good. So that yellow, gap-tooth boy from your school is now taking a wife? We thank God o. I'm very happy for him."

Anjola laughs aloud at her mother's description of Neil.

"Let me see the picture of the girl he's marrying."

"Which girl?" Her father comes down the stairs then, dressed for service in alligator shoes, slacks, a turtleneck, and cardigan.

"Bàbá Pekun," her mother says, hands already on her hips. "You're wearing English. Why? You didn't see the agbádá that I ironed for you?"

"Woman, if you're still looking for a baby to dress, see one there for you," he says, gesturing to Anjola.

She stands to hug her father, inhaling the scent of peppermint that always seems to follow him.

"So our Anjola-jola has decided to come to service. It is well." He squeezes her hands. "It's always good to have you home."

"Thanks, Dad. No chasing customers this morning?" Her father is a seasoned taxi driver and often misses Sunday service because of his work.

Her mother pulls her away before he can answer. "Forget that one, let me see the picture of the girl."

Anjola reaches for her phone and obligingly pulls up Giselle's Instagram. Her mother glances at it quickly.

"So the girl is short and half-caste, àbí? What does she do?"

"Mom, don't be using words like 'half-caste' and come and embarrass me, please," Anjola says, taking her phone back. "People prefer 'biracial' or 'mixed race.' And she's a magazine editor or something like that."

"It always amazes me how some people in America are paid handsomely to be doing yẹ̀yẹ́ work," her mother says of Giselle. "And then others who are rich and brilliantly educated, they will then turn to be doing yẹ̀yẹ́ work." Here she speaks of Neil, whose family is part of Chicago's Black bourgeoisie, and who works as a social studies teacher on the Near South Side.

"Mom, teaching isn't yẹ̀yẹ́ work. It's important, it's literally the training up of the next generation."

"Important kẹ? For CPS? It's actually poverty."

"I agree with Anjola," her father says, settling down on the sofa beside her mother.

"No matter." Her mother places an arm around Anjola's shoulder. "My own daughter is a doctor. Your husband will come soon as well. Actually, there's someone at service I'd like you to meet."

RCCG Overcomers' Chapel is the fourth Redeemed Christian Church of God that Anjola can remember her mother attending in her lifetime, the second and third interrupted by a brief stint at the Mountain of Fire and Miracles Ministries on the West Side, which had been a bit too Pentecostal even for her mother's taste. Latifat always found something wrong with these churches: an inelegantly dressed pastor's wife, a swindler who sold a friend a jalopy for a car, a Sunday school teacher who slapped Ola (their mother's favorite child, an unforgivable offense even if it did take a village to raise one).

Anjola steps out of the back seat and onto the sidewalk when they arrive, teetering uneasily in the heels her mother has insisted she wear. The outfit is too loud for Anjola's taste: a boatneck dress constructed of black lace and magenta lining so that she and her mother match. Her father is the only one who doesn't look overdone, always an island unto himself, but he offers Latifat his arm anyway. They make an interesting pair—his vintage sweater beside her redolent ìró and bùbá and gold gèlè. Anjola watches as he leans down to whisper something in his wife's ear, hushed and in Yoruba so that Anjola can't understand. Her mother swats his arm playfully, and Anjola just knows that he said something naughty to make her mother's brown skin suddenly look richer and brighter, even in the morning chill. She wonders if this is why they never taught her and her siblings Yoruba, so that they might have a love language all their own.

And they are lovers, her parents. The story, as her mother tells it and her father never refutes, is that they met in Scripture Union at the University of Ibadan. Latifat was full with the fervor of the newly born-again, having recently converted from Islam to Christianity. She was so focused on Jesus that she hadn't paid Gbenga Longe a second thought, quiet and brooding as he was. But Gbenga was patient in his pursuit, opting first to become her friend. Over two years he revealed himself to be exactly the kind of man Latifat had been asking Jesus for—kind, supportive, responsible, faithful. Latifat began to realize that she liked the steadiness of Gbenga's voice, that his lanky gait wasn't so bad, and that most of all, she liked his mind. He was training in electrical engineering, which sounded practical and secure, but he was a dreamer. One day he would go to America, learn more about what it would take to power a country with constant electricity, come back to Nigeria and lead NEPA reform. At this point in the story, Anjola would turn to her father and ask, "And what did you like about Mom?" His eyes would grow wistful. "She has always wanted everything and everyone around her to thrive," he would say. "She makes everything she touches more beautiful. What choice did I have but to love someone like that?" And her mother would smile and smile and smile, the way she does now, secure as she holds on to her husband's arm.

The church is a storefront sandwiched between a Liberty Tax Service and a day-care center. An abandoned field is just behind them, the grass high and fenced in.

"God is so good for allowing us to find this parking spot. See the time!" her mother is saying, locking the car as the three make their way across the street.

Inside the chapel they meet a crowd of people at the door. The usher hands them bulletins but bids them to stay where they are as a woman with a raspy voice speaks fervently into the microphone.

"On this Sunday, God is ready to release an uncommon blessing on your life," the woman says before the church erupts into the sounds of rejoicing. Anjola stands there in rebellious silence.

"But before He releases that storehouse—as I see it so, it's like the blessing is so heavy it's pushing at the door. Hallelujah, thank you, Jesus. Before He opens that floodgate, brethren, you need to give Him a praise offering."

The church erupts again, voices clamoring over one another, voices stepping on shoulders with their arms outstretched toward heaven. Anjola is an onlooker, watching impenitently as her parents close their eyes and raise their hands in vigorous prayer. The voices have no unifying effect, nor are they in melody. They are the din of every man for himself.

"Hallelujah!" the woman cries out again after some time. She leads the church in a prayer of her own, and Anjola finally closes her eyes. When she opens them, she sees her father watching her. His face is blank for a moment, and then he smiles.

They're guided to their seats just before the head pastor walks to the pulpit. His forehead shines as he steps forward in his navy blue suit, its sole button barely clasped over his stomach. His voice is loud and booming as he directs the church to stand for the Bible reading. And as he reads from the fourth chapter of John, easily recognizable by the story of the Samaritan woman, Anjola feels a tinge of sadness come over her. For millennia, people have focused on how many husbands the Samaritan woman has had instead of on the most obvious aspect of her humanness: that she feels undeserving of a love proffered.

When offering time comes, Latifat hands Anjola a check to pass to her father for his envelope. He hands it back to her. Anjola glances at the two of them, her father's brow furrowed in annoyance, her mother's face questioning. Gbenga pulls a wad of cash out of his pocket—presumably tips from cabbying—and stuffs it into the envelope, ignoring his wife's outstretched check.

"But, Gbenga, why do you want to put your dirty money there instead?" her mother whispers.

"Mom," Anjola says in an effort to defuse the growing tension. Her parents have always had a weird thing about money, because her mother makes more of it and has small ways of belittling her father for making less.

"O ṣé," says her father. "But you see, this my money is not too low for God."

To spite her mother, when their row is called forth to dance their money to the offering basket just near the altar, her father does an exaggerated step down the aisle, pretending to draw up the sleeves of an imaginary agbádá. He pulls back just as he reaches the basket and spins around, as though his dance offering is meant to supplement his monetary one. The talking drummer goes wild. The pastor jumps up excitedly from the pulpit. Her mother, who has been doing a small shuffle back and forth, tries to match the vigor of her husband's movements, which amuses Anjola, because everyone in their family knows he is the better dancer of the two. After a bit more shoulder- and footwork, her father finally drops the envelope into the basket before dramatically trust-falling into his wife's arms. Anjola cannot hold back her laughter as her mother chides him to be more serious and act his age.

"God bless you, Brother Gbenga," the pastor says, his arms outstretched toward her father. "The Lord surely receives your offering."

After service her father remains in his seat, peacefully reading over the scripture from the morning's sermon, while her mother makes the rounds, insisting that Anjola follow. Latifat greets this aunty and that, and Anjola stands beside her awkwardly, lost as the women speak in rapid Yoruba.

"Anjola, this is Sister Nike," her mother says, introducing her to a stout woman who wears a velvet headwrap.

Anjola curtsies obediently and tells the woman that it's nice to meet her.

"This one is my third child, she's the medical doctor."

"You've told me," Sister Nike says before turning to wave over a young man standing a few paces away from her. "Anjola, this is my son Dare, he's a financier."

"Kind of," the man says, holding out his hand. "An investment banker. Pleased to meet you."

He's tall. He has large white teeth, an eager smile. His skin is dark and without blemish, his hair cut neatly. From the corner of her eye, she sees her mother beaming. It makes sense—Dare is her mother's type; he almost looks like he could be a long-lost relative of her father's. Anjola shakes his hand.

"Dare, I keep telling you no one knows what that is," says his mother.

"I actually do," Anjola says. "My brother works for a hedge fund. If you can get him on the phone, that type of stuff is all he wants to talk about."

They laugh.

"Actually, Dare, you should meet my son as well. It's good for you guys to stick together, you know?" her mother says. "Anjola can give you his number."

"I'd like that very much." Dare places a hand to his heart and bows ever so slightly. The two mothers are smiling now. They say there is someone they need to go buy chin-chin from.

"You actually look kind of familiar," he says to Anjola once their mothers are away.

Anjola shrugs. She knows that this is a line. "I suppose I look like a lot of people."

"That's impossible. You're very beautiful. And not in a replicable way."

"Ah, well. That's kind of you to say."

"No, it's true of me to say." He smiles again. All the right lines. "Could I take your number? Maybe I can take you out to dinner sometime soon."

Anjola is always struck by this; how forward Nigerian men can be. He's good-looking, but his being the type of man who would attend church on Sunday mornings with his mother and let her set him up tells Anjola everything she needs to know.

"To be honest, I'm actually pretty busy these days."

"I can imagine, residency isn't easy," he says, and Anjola surmises that he knew about her before they even met. Dare slides a hand into his pocket and retrieves his phone. "Well, I'd still love to keep in touch. And you can text me your brother's info as well, I'd be happy to speak with him."

She isn't sure if he seriously intends to connect with Ola, but she also doesn't know how much she cares. His fingers graze her palm as he passes the phone to her. She types in her contact information and hands it back.

"Thank you." His voice is calm, sure of itself even in the face of her obvious rejection. "It's been lovely meeting you, Anjola. I hope I'll be able to change your mind soon."

"Yeah, take care," she says before turning away to go sit down next to her father.

Her father closes his Bible and squeezes her hand. "My Anjola-jola. I hope you still pray sometimes."

"Sometimes, yeah, I do." She isn't lying entirely. She hasn't always been able to muster strong conviction in God, but prayer is the only way she knows of exerting her will over what she cannot control.

"Good. Especially now that your mother is trying to do all this arrangement."

"You knew?"

"Of course. What else does she have to talk about? Anyway. My point is that you'll need discernment. Only the Holy Spirit can give you that." He smiles conspiratorially. "And don't let anybody rush you. Marriage is a serious endeavor."

Anjola throws her arms around her father's neck just as her mother returns with a bag of warm chin-chin. "Ẹ nlẹ́, Bàbá àt'ọmọ."

On the ride home she sits in the back seat as her mother goes on about the latest church gossip and her father feigns interest. Apparently, Ìyá Tunji's wayward, incorrigible son has gotten himself caught up with a gang and is now facing drug trafficking charges, which means there is nobody to help Ìyá Tunji pay her rent. Anjola tunes her mother out. She checks her phone to see whether Neil has texted, but nothing. Not an apology for completely blindsiding her or even a mere thank-you for her attendance. She swallows her irritation and opens up Tinder. She has two new matches and one message. It reads: I knew you looked familiar!

Dare's profile looks exactly like what she would have expected. Photos of him at the Willis Tower, on the lakefront with his bike, at the barbershop, at a Nigerian wedding in burgundy trad attire. She decides not to respond, sliding the phone back into her purse.

Her father turns on the radio.

"Ah ah, Gbenga, must you always drive so fast?"

Anjola leans forward and taps her father on the shoulder. "Daddy, could you just swing me back to my place?"

EIGHT

Friday, October 26

Ola wants to slap his new colleague the way he slapped his classmate in the third grade: with full force, the open palm delivering the anger housed in the back, chest, and shoulders. It would be the kind of slap that came with a comical Nollywood sound effect, after which the new guy would fall dramatically to the floor, clutching the offended cheek in horror. Ola smiles softly to himself, his chin calmly resting in the palm of his hand.

"Ola's idea is old news," says the new guy, his chest proud. "Our investors want us to make bold moves on their behalf."

Ola sits at a long table of white men, the only colored representation among them, tucked neatly at one of its corners. He can feel all their eyes on him, waiting to see what he will say. As though suddenly his ten years of tenure at the company have been forgotten, as though he isn't bringing in more revenue as a portfolio manager than two of the senior partners combined, as though this upstart has them wondering about the exact thing Ola has spent his career working to disprove—that he is sitting at that table for DEI purposes alone.

"I would contend that investors want reliability," Ola says finally, the tension in the room easing as he cuts through the long silence. "And YTS has proven longevity in the market. Our fund's renown is built on a legacy of trust. As in, results. As in, not just chasing after glory stories."

Just bordering on aggressive. Enough to make the new guy look down at the table, loosen his tie slightly, doubt himself.

"It's a bold idea, Chris," says one of the senior partners, "but Ola's right, I think we'll have to stick with what we know on this one." Elsewhere in life, Ola may cower and shuck and jive, but here? Here, where the right mind and the right diction can translate into dollars and cents? He is unstoppable.

After the meeting, Ola walks back to his office with his padfolio under one arm. At his desk, he pulls out his personal phone to read a series of messages from Marisol.

9:01 a.m.: You've been avoiding me.

10:13 a.m.: I called Nour—she said your evening schedule has been clear all week.

11:32 a.m.: We need to talk.

11:45 a.m.: Ola for fuck's sake

He places his things on his desk, pulls up his email, and commences with his pre-lunch ritual. A quick scan for any urgent emails. A momentary perusal of *Forbes.* Tweaking a financial model for a late afternoon meeting. Marisol's texts become obtrusive thoughts. He stares at the computer screen, but he's seeing Marisol instead, the way she draws the canvas sheet over her naked form. She is irate, inconsolable—not that he tries very hard to console her. How could he say something like that to her? While he was still inside her? She feels violated, she says. He is silent. She matches his silence with fury. Where is this all coming from? Over a name? Is he serious? Silence. And then he says that he's sorry. Why? He doesn't know, he says, he just isn't happy. She calls him a bastard. One hand holds the sheet around her body; the other points at the door. *Get the fuck out of my studio.*

How is he to explain? He has spent the whole week avoiding another confrontation with her, putting unnecessary amounts of time into work. He arrives home late, sleeps on the couch in his home office, wakes up early to be at the gym at the crack of dawn. It is too easy to live his life entirely separate from her.

His phone vibrates against the desk. A direct call from his father is a rare treat. He stands to close his office door.

"Hi, Dad."

"Pekun, I'm on the road. I'm going to do some electrical work for a friend in Niles. Then I want to take your mother to dinner at one of those fine-fine restaurants you kids like."

Ola laughs. His father has a tendency to get straight to the point.

"Ah ah, why are you laughing? I'm serious. That your mother, she works too hard."

This is true. His father also works too hard, and perhaps this is why Ola needs to be here. He finds purpose in the office; the strokes of the keyboard, the click of the mouse, they feel like music to him. He may not work with his hands, but he's a working man nonetheless, a good man.

"So you called for a recommendation?"

"Yes, now. But I can't spend more than sixty dollars a plate."

"All right, Daddy big spender," Ola says, smiling into the phone. "I'll text you a couple of places."

"Very good. Sorry to interrupt your workday," his father says before honking loudly, yelling about the noonday traffic like a proper Yoruba man. "Kí ni gbogbo eléyìí? Wọ́n fà bí ìgbín. Is it a driver you call yourself or a snail?"

"Take it easy on 'em, Dad."

"How is Mari?"

Ola sits back down and holds the phone to his ear.

"She's faring pretty well."

"Very good," says his father. "Remember, whoso findeth a wife . . ."

He rolls his eyes. "So you've taken up pastoring now?"

"You see? You don't go to church, that's why you don't know the verse."

But both he and his father are laughing. His father is one of the few people Ola doesn't pretend around.

"My Anjola-jola came to church with your mother and me recently," his father says when their chuckles subside.

"Oh, did she now?" But Ola isn't surprised by this. Anjola has always excessively sought out their mother's approval, almost as though she were trying to make up for something. Ola has never understood why.

"Yes, despite how busy she is."

"All right, Dad," Ola says. "Marisol and I will try to come with you guys one of these Sundays too." Ola knows this is a lie, but he has to at least try to seem responsible like Anjola.

"That's not why I mentioned it," his father says. "Nobody is comparing you. No. How you run your house is your own business. I just want you to check on her. When was the last time you spoke?"

"We texted just last week."

"Not this texting texting, I mean real talk. You know? When you sit down in front of somebody and look them in their eyes." His father leans on the horn again.

Ola smiles. "Okay, Dad. Is there anything specific you want me to ask her about?"

"Not really. She just seemed a bit sad. And you know there's only so much she would tell me. If Sola was here . . ." His father sighs.

"No problem, I'll check on her."

"Very good. You never disappoint me, son."

They hang up without saying goodbye, because they have a way of knowing when nothing more needs to be said. Still, Ola is surprised by his father's words. Is this what it means to be a parent? To so readily forget the things that children fear will follow them forever?

When Ola was in the third grade, at the charter school in Chatham where they still lived, he got into a fistfight with a classmate during kickball. A boy named Reggie Hines. Ola was pitching and Reggie had missed his third kick, struck out, and then refused to budge from home base. Instead he balled up his hands and told Ola that he was an African monkey and he threw like one. The fight that ensued was especially ugly, and Reggie was pulled away with a busted lip, Ola with a cut above his brow.

His father's eyes were sad when he came to pick Ola up and take him home for his weeklong suspension. "I'm so very disappointed in you," he said. Ola said nothing, but he felt a pit in his stomach. He could accept a spanking, but disappointment was too much.

He sat in the front of the taxi beside his father, staring out the window at the dilapidated buildings they passed as they drove to the highway. His father was silent, and though Ola did not look up at him, his rage subsided into shame. Shame was worse than a beating, which his father usually left for his mother to do unless it was a very serious matter. Loud music blared from the speakers. Ola let himself succumb to the rhythmic drums, moving his shoulders along to the music.

"You know who this is singing?"

Ola shook his head.

"This is the great Haruna Ishola." He drummed his long fingers in time against the steering wheel. "He invented this style," said his father. "Apala." After a few moments he added, "You should ask your mother about it. This is the kind of music her father's people would listen to. You know what he's singing about?"

"No."

"So you've really forgotten all the Yoruba you knew." His father shook his head and smiled sadly. "We should be speaking it to you again, both you and your sisters."

"Why?" Ola folded his arms over his chest. "The other kids would just make more fun of me. Next they'll ask if I'm from the jungle."

"Oho," said his father. "So you think we're bush people. I see."

"No, I don't! But other kids think I am. That kid today said I threw the ball like a monkey." Ola drew his hands into fists.

"Mmm." His father nodded stoically. "And so what did you do again?"

"I jumped on him."

"The way a monkey does? Ṣé ọ̀bọ ni ẹ́?"

"No, Dad. You don't understand."

His father chuckled and turned up the music, letting the conversation lie. Ola studied his father as he rolled his slender neck to the rhythm, his beard brushing against his scarf.

Once they pulled up to a grand apartment building, his father ejected the cassette tape and replaced it with another one, filling the cab with soft classical music. Ola looked out the window at the white stone facade behind a gilded gate. His father opened the back door for an elderly white couple and placed their bags in the trunk.

"O'Hare airport, right?"

His father's question was met with silence. Ola turned around to stare at the couple. The old man was squinting.

"He asked if you're going to the airport," Ola said.

"Oh! What a strong accent he has," said the man, nodding affirmatively. "Yes, O'Hare."

Ola furrowed his brow. He hadn't noticed his father had an accent at all.

"It's good he has you here today," said the woman, smiling. "Shouldn't you be in school though?"

Ola turned around, sulking. They drove past a number of buildings like the one the people had come out of, Ola's face pressed to the window.

"Where are you from?" the man in the back asked so loudly that Ola spun around to study him again.

His father paused. "I live in Chatham, sir."

"No, we mean what country," the woman said.

"Nigeria." His father turned up the music just slightly.

"Oh, that's so wonderful. That's in Africa, right? I've always wanted to go. Our daughter is just dying to go on safari. Is Nigeria a good place for safari?" asked the woman.

"No," his father said.

"So how long have you been in the US?" the man asked.

"Five years now."

"That's nice, I'm sure you're liking it a lot better than where you came from."

His father didn't respond.

"I just mean I'm sure you're making a better living driving a taxi here than you were back home."

His father slowed the car to a halt at a red light, his fingers gripping the wheel tightly.

"I hold a master's degree in electrical engineering," he said, more slowly so the man might understand him. Here his father turned around to look him in the eye. "How many degrees do you hold?"

His wife laughed awkwardly and answered for him. "Well, he almost completed his bachelor's in English, but he got pulled into helping out with his father's company a bit earlier than expected."

"Don't you already speak English?" Ola asked, turning to look at the passengers.

The woman smiled, clapping her hands together as though it was a darling question, but the man scowled.

The rest of the ride proceeded silently. After they dropped the couple off at the airport and his father received the fare, he looked down at Ola seriously.

"Never allow these òyìnbó people to make you feel lesser. Ṣó yé ẹ?"

"Yes, Daddy."

"They'll always be looking for the animal in you. They will keep prodding until you strike. And then when you do, that's the excuse they will use to lock you away. You want to show that you have a hot temper like your mother, àbí? That's fine. Temper itself is not the problem. But you have to channel it. Because if you don't learn how to control yourself, if you don't learn restraint, you won't get very far at all. It's only òyìnbó that can be having tantrums left and right and not see repercussions."

It was true that Ola had never seen his father waver. So Ola understood masculinity to be a quiet resolve, an impassivity, a firm standing of one's ground. Where women might find themselves wrapped up in the petty dramas of life (cooking, cleaning, catfighting), men were to see about their work. He watched his father over the years, straight-backed and strong against the tempest his mother could be. And he understood that this was why she loved him, why she could come home after a long day at work and still prioritize making a hot meal for him. His mother took loving care of his father so that he would always be the refuge she could turn to.

Ola spends the rest of the morning and the early afternoon tweaking a set of models for a market trend report that a junior analyst put together. It's just after 3:00 p.m. when his body commands him to find food.

As he joins the line for tacos from his favorite Mexican Japanese fusion food truck on the corner of Dearborn and Madison, Ola pulls out his phone. No additional texts from Marisol. He scrolls down past the main headlines on his *New York Times* app to the set of minor articles at the bottom of the page, where he always finds gold: ethical questions like whether one should leave a sexless marriage, elegant takedowns about the conversion of factory buildings to expensive housing. He clicks a headline about the forthcoming fashion week in Dakar, and though he has never been and never intends to go, he peruses the article anyway, his gaze fixed on a photo of a dark-skinned woman swathed in orange and ocher tones, with undulating mounds of sand behind her. The photography is so stunning that he actually looks at the credit line. Betel Tadesse. At the sight of her name, Ola becomes suspended in time.

He googles her. A constellation of results appear: *Forbes* 30 Under

30. A smattering of links to galleries where her work has been shown—Paris, Cape Town, New York. An Instagram page with over seventy thousand followers.

"What can I get for you, sir?"

Ola looks up from his phone, startled. Betel, his hot mess Betel, has made it big.

Ten minutes later he sits down on a bench, his prized tacos growing cold beside him as he studies images of her. She has added a nose ring, the septum she'd always talked about, to complement the stud in her left nostril. Ola had told her that her nose was too small and delicate to be weighted down by such finery, but he sees now that he was wrong. Her eyes are still bright and doe-like and full of wonder. Betel. His most chaotic relationship. His most bitter of breakups. Yet he cannot stop himself from taking a screenshot of the photo in the *Times* and typing:

To: betel.tadesse
From: ola.longe
Subject: wow!
Date: 10/26/18 Time: 3:32 p.m.

Props to you. This is amazing work.

He attaches the screenshot, and as his thumb hovers over the blue arrow to click send, he tells himself that he only wants to congratulate her, that he means nothing by it, that it is all perfectly innocent. He presses send just as a text message from Marisol comes in.

3:35 p.m.: The baby just kicked.

NINE

Saturday, October 27

Anjola watches Neil lock his bike up against a lamppost that's still lit given the early hour. He hasn't seen her yet, and she relishes having a moment to observe him without his knowledge. He doesn't think there is anything wrong between them. A few days after his engagement party, he texted her as though everything was the same, asking if she was going to make it to their monthly run.

In college these runs had been weekly, Sunday mornings at 7:00 a.m. Outside if it was warm enough. Side by side on treadmills at the gym if it was cold. It had started off as a competitive thing, as so much of their friendship had, Anjola giving Neil the finger as she raced him on the machine to see who would make their distance goal first. But it eventually morphed into a different thing, slow jogs on the lakefront, breathy philosophical conversations about the nature of life and of being. Black bodies braving the concrete, knees rising and feet lowering in tandem.

When she moved back, he mentioned that they should start up again. Looking at him now, the lean torso and the broad chest and the strong legs, she ought to have known that he suggested so with confidence. Any residual leanness in her body could only be attributed to forgetting to eat due to stress. But Neil has gotten stronger. And unlike his younger self, he has been kinder to her on their last few runs, slower than his normal speed, insisting on short breaks when her lungs grow weary and she can no longer talk and run at the same time.

Perhaps this is the new Neil; perhaps maturity means changing the whole nature of their friendship without consulting her first. He wears green joggers and a white hoodie and is tinkering with his bike lock, not a single care in the world. Anjola half expected Giselle to be there too, bouncing her hair up and down beside him with a bright smile on her face. She zips up her windbreaker and announces her presence with the jingling of her apartment keys, which she now places in her right pocket.

“Good morning, Jojo,” he says singsongily.

“Hey, what’s up.” There is no joy in her voice. He looks up at her quizzically before rising. Though she and Neil stand at eye level, without his thick glasses to shield it, his gaze is intimidating.

“I’m good, excited to breathe in this air and see these sights. The usual.”

She looks away and nods. “Ready to get this stretch in?”

“Sure thing.”

They walk toward a grassy area and fold their bodies over. They complete the stretch with a sun salutation facing each other, hands pressed in prayer above their chests. Her eyes are on his, his on hers.

When she first came back, it was moments like these that reminded her of how much this place was her home. How this stretch routine came back to her like second nature, no instruction needed.

It's a five-mile route, from Jackson Park up past Forty-Seventh Street and back down. Standard. She doesn't want to have to talk to him as they get on the trail, so there is only one thing to do. She takes a moment to ensure her bun is tight enough and then she bolts, feet bouncing against the asphalt. He is laughing behind her.

"I thought we gave up this competition thing a long time ago, Jo."

She doesn't say anything. She can't anyway—her lungs are already occupied trying to carry her feet. In a few minutes he is right beside her.

"Hey, you want to slow down?"

She shakes her head. He doesn't even sound breathless at all, which is the most annoying part. Unable to outrun him, she resolves to stay silent as he prattles on about the week before and the one to come. Giselle wants to go on a long vacation soon, now that they're engaged, but he thinks they should wait for the summer. Although if they do, he won't get to teach summer school. And he likes being with the kids. He's reading a book he thinks Anjola might like, about the role of public health in education—has she heard of it?

She doesn't want to answer him. She can't. She is gasping for air. There is a bridge she likes to pass under, brick, with a charming staircase leading up. If only she might make it there. It isn't very far. Can't be.

"Hey, slow down."

She pushes herself faster, feeling her heart banging angrily against her chest, lungs screaming breathlessly. And still he is beside her, running as fast as she is. "Stop." Catching her at the elbow. She almost falls, but he holds her by the waist.

For a moment she relishes the closeness before disentangling herself from his grip.

"You're exhausting yourself." His eyes are wide with concern.

"So?" She is panting, hands on her knees, aware that she's behaving like a child, but unable to stop herself.

"Are you mad at me or something?"

"You're the one who seems to be mad at me." She doesn't want the words to come out but they do, heavy with her hard breathing. "Why else would you let me come to your engagement party and be the only one as surprised as your fiancée?"

"Jo, come on, it's not like that."

"It isn't?"

"With all the planning beforehand and the stress of work, it really just slipped my mind," he explains. "I'd wanted to tell you right before, but you got there late."

"Are you being serious right now?" She hears her voice rise in volume, but she can't find a way to calm herself. "There were so many times over the last few months when you could have told me. I never knew you were even thinking of marriage."

"Okay, but like why do you think I owe you forewarning?"

"Because I'm your best friend? Best friends tell each other about major life decisions." Her voice breaks. "You let me stand there looking like a fool."

"Honestly? You only look a bit foolish right now."

Her eyes grow large. "Neil. Don't do that. Okay? Because a couple of years ago, things weren't so clear-cut between us."

He squints at her quizzically. After a moment his eyes widen with recollection. "My parents' holiday party? That's really what you want to talk about now?"

The Haynes-Stuarts hosted a holiday party every year, the weekend before Christmas, without fail. And without fail, every time Anjola entered their palatial home, one of the so-called Kenwood mansions, which stood majestically on the corner of Forty-Ninth and Greenwood, she was awestruck. How did one own a mansion in the middle of a city? The whole point of a city was the loss of acreage in exchange for proximity to other human beings. To have both was a luxury. Every time she came by, she would find a new extravagance. The driveway was long and laid in brick, not concrete. The main entrance was not at the front but set off to the side in wealthy unwelcome. Around Christmastime they strung twinkling lights around the lamppost and door and windows in tasteful elegance.

Neil's mother was indeed tasteful and elegant. That year she opened the door to Anjola and said—in that almost-Broadway voice of hers, with one arm held out wide and a theatrical flick of the wrist—"Anjola, my dear, you look divine."

She was short, fairer than Neil, with slack hair and hazel eyes. She performed a light hug and air-kisses, thanked Anjola for being there, and motioned for the maid to come and take her coat.

All their guests were in casual dress but still somehow managed to look expensive and important, all wearing deep, rich hues and luxurious fabrics, their skin various shades of brown that shone in spite of the brittle winter just outside the front door. The fireplace was lit. One of Neil's older brothers, Winston, sat at the piano playing jazz. On the far side of the room stood the eldest Haynes-Stuart son, Julius III, who spoke in a deep booming voice befitting his profession as an experienced litigator and aspiring politician.

Neil's father turned his attention away from his colleague. "Anjola, a pleasure to see you, dear." He shook her hand warmly. He always shook her hand and never extended his arms for a hug. She thought it might be because she had breasts. But he was kind to her. And she liked that he had Neil's eyes. He asked after her medical studies at Yale, being himself a well-tenured anesthesiologist. "Well, we're proud of you, Anjola. Keep fighting the good fight," he said finally, reaching out to shake her hand again.

Neil was in the kitchen as she expected, laughing with the waitstaff, drink in hand. His laugh would always be lovely to her, somehow low and tinkling at the same time.

"No tolerance for the bourgeoisie now that you're a teacher, huh?" she asked, sidling up to him and bumping his elbow with hers as though it were just yesterday and not six months since they'd last seen each other.

"Nah, I'm a working-class man now." He smiled brightly at her.

"I don't remember these holiday parties being this fancy growing up," he added a few moments later, ladling some mulled wine into a mug for her. He pointed to the waitstaff stationed just outside the kitchen. "What happened to foil pans of baked mac and cheese over food warmers and people helping themselves?"

"Did you see that in a movie once or something?" she asked, rolling her eyes at this lower-middle-class origin story he'd decided to give himself. "Besides, Lynne Haynes-Stuart would never."

He motioned for her to sit down at the kitchen island beside him and she did.

"What are you reading now?" he asked, and before she could answer he continued. "Have you read that essay collection I texted you about? It's pretty good, I think you'd be into it."

"Honestly, I haven't read much of anything outside of my textbooks lately."

"That's fair. I don't know how you do it. But whenever you have time, you should pick up the book. There's this one brilliant essay. Seriously, Jo, it's genius. A lot of it is about questioning the usual critiques people have of rappers . . ."

And as she watched him go on, his eyes gleaming, his hands gesticulating, his pure joy at discussing an essay, her heart shone for him.

"Um, that's all well and good, you know, that you're reading what intellectuals have to say about the genre and all," Anjola said, "but you still can't rap, so . . ."

And Neil laughed. "I concede that of the two of us, you have better flow . . . but that isn't saying much. Have you written anything new?"

"I wish. No, it's hard to remember to eat sometimes."

"Hey," he said, placing a hand on her shoulder, "don't let them cut you off from yourself. I mean it."

His eyes were steady on hers, and her blood quickened as his palm left her shoulder, heated her neck, now her cheek. Since when had he been so close? In the slowest and sweetest of motions, his lips met her forehead, the tip of her nose, and—

"I'm in a relationship," she said.

She wasn't sure what pained her more as she said the words—the kiss she couldn't allow herself to have, or that Lucas, the boyfriend back in New Haven, was beginning to feel like deadweight.

"Oh." He drew back. "I'm so sorry."

"No, it isn't your fault," she said. "I just didn't know how to tell you. I guess it felt like it didn't matter."

"Didn't matter?"

"I mean, why would it?" She tried to look calm, but her heart was racing. She knew that it mattered to him the way all of his previous relationships had mattered to her. The only difference was that Anjola had been okay with pretending she didn't want to be with him, okay with allowing their friendship to be enough. But now it seemed that Neil was no longer content with pretending. And she felt resentful of his timing; her life in that moment felt so precariously assembled that she couldn't afford to blow it up.

Neil rested his elbow on the island, kneading his eyebrow with his fingertips, sighing heavily. "How long have you been in this . . . this thing?"

"Almost a year."

"Almost a year, Jo? And you think it didn't matter?"

She shrugged, unsure of what to say.

He placed his open palm on the island. "I just don't see how you could keep me out of this huge piece of your life for almost a year and tell me it wasn't intentional."

"I wasn't trying to keep you out, Neil—it just never came up. You never asked."

"Jo." Here he smiled, laughed incredulously. "I literally tell you everything."

She was unsure of what exactly he was offering her, while deep down sure of it all the same. What would she be giving up now in exchange for a kiss? She didn't see how it was worth losing the security of their friendship and the stability of Lucas for a fling that would inevitably fail. Because she'd always known that if she were to try with Neil, to let a deeper intimacy work itself out between them, that she would not be able to bear it when he found her lacking. Perhaps, at this moment, he was genuinely unable to see it, but she knew she was unworthy of him: not pretty enough, not the right cultural fit, too temperamentally prone to melancholy.

"You're right," she said, "I should have told you."

"I guess I'm just kind of confused."

She reached for his hand and held it. "You'll always be a dear friend to me, Neil. I don't want any of this to change that." And because she said this with all the finality she could muster, it was so; both of them silently agreed never to discuss it again.

But as she and Neil stand before each other at the lakefront, she can only think of what might have changed. Whether, now knowing that certain irreconcilable differences between her and Lucas would lead her to end their relationship, she would have decided differently.

And what kind of woman tells her boyfriend of three years that she wants to end things the day after their medical school graduation, after he affirms that he's willing to do long-distance, after he says he wants to finally meet her family, after he expresses his desire to buy a ring? What kind of woman throws love by the wayside as though it is an easy thing to come by? She had undone their relationship months before it ended, the moment she logged in to the matching system and ranked Stroger as her first choice.

Anjola watches Neil silently, the crisp morning wind chilling her arms and legs. She wishes she were still running.

"Is there anything you want to explain?" Neil asks. "Or are you just going to stand there?"

"I just think it's clear why you should have told me."

"No," he says. "In fact, just like you didn't tell me about him, I wasn't obligated to tell you about her, much less run every step of my relationship by you."

She feels a pang in her stomach. "That was different, and you know it."

"How?"

"It wasn't marriage? It wasn't a whole public display? I didn't fucking embarrass you?"

"Embarrass you?" He squints. "Let me get this right. "During" one of the happiest moments of my life, you were there concerned about yourself?"

"Her best friends were there cackling in my face, Neil. Wes knew. Literally everyone knew except me," she says. But she doesn't know what the end of this confrontation is, what she wants exactly.

He shakes his head, laughs that incredulous laugh of his. "Look, I wanted to tell you, it was always just the wrong time, and then it was so close and I just forgot."

"I don't believe you."

"Anjola, I don't know what to tell you." Here he gathers a few of his beautiful locs, grips them in his hand. "It wasn't intentional. I'm sorry. I don't know what else you want from me."

"Why are you even getting married?" She hates that her voice threatens to break.

"What?"

"You're young," she says. "You both haven't been together that long."

"Anjola, you don't have the right to ask me that."

"But if I don't, who will?"

"Seriously?" And he smiles again, but the smile does not reach his eyes. "You know what? I think we should just head back and maybe hash this out some other time."

"No. You head back. I'm gonna finish my run."

"All right, you do that, then."

She turns from him and starts up an easy jog, unwilling to look back.

TEN

Thursday, November 1

Sola has secured a job at a high-end boutique in the Gold Coast, located just a block off Michigan so as to feel clandestinely luxurious. But, despite the lengths Sola has gone to look as though she belongs among the store's clientele, her manager has relegated her to the stockroom. There, she unboxes and tags inventory, reciting to herself a new mantra: Getting one's life together is a slow and grueling process. That and: You're broke now. That and: Don't get fat eating broke-people food. Because all she can think of is the latte she'll buy from the Starbucks down the street once she gets off her shift.

After Starbucks, therapy. Sola isn't excited, but she is committed to pulling herself out of the muck her life has become. Marquise has insisted—a condition of her staying with him. He even provided Dr. Maisie Ali's contact information, insisting that she was an especially good option because she has a sliding scale. Sola had almost said something smart, but then she remembered her mantra: You're broke now.

She's had three sessions so far, and all Dr. Ali wants to do is make Sola dig through the past. Her office is an homage to it, full of the type of excessively Afrocentric decor that Sola finds so off-putting. Her walls are covered in African tourist paintings of giraffes and elephants, her books ended by random fertility statues.

Several hours later, having finally clocked out and now with a latte in hand, Sola hangs up her coat near the door, keeping her sunglasses on. In the back room, she drops herself dramatically onto the couch. Dr. Ali smiles and stands to close the door behind her.

"How are you doing today, Sola?"

She studies the large woven earrings and boubou that Dr. Ali wears, deciding that she must be a regular at one of those African stores where they sell Ankara at exorbitant prices to those yearning for a motherland.

"I fucking hate everything," Sola declares, before taking a long gulp from her Starbucks cup. She is still studying Dr. Ali's dress, envisioning how she would transform it if given the opportunity. Whoever tailored it had done it all wrong. The pattern at the hem deserved more attention, and Sola would have instead used it to hem the bottom of a cropped blouse and the top of a high-waisted skirt, drawing the eye to Dr. Ali's waistline.

"Do say more."

And so Sola tells her about being put in the stockroom, how there was no one back there to admire her ensemble or inquire about where she'd sourced her cape or dainty earrings.

"What would it have meant for you to be seen in that way, Sola?"

"I don't know. It's just what I'm used to. Dressing up and putting myself on display for likes and brand deals." She reclines in her seat, pouting. "Being back there just made me feel like a mule, you know? And I'm not saying you're not a mule working on the floor, because you're still there waiting for your lunch break and somebody else owns your time, but at least you're seen."

"If being seen is so important to you, why did you go on and delete all your social media?"

Sola sighs. They keep coming back to this question, and she doesn't quite know how to answer it. She finishes her latte, savors the last bit of warm sweetness, and sets the cup on the coffee table between them.

"I had to."

"You keep saying that."

"And?" She starts twisting the rings that adorn her long fingers. "It was all Aiden. We were a package deal. Sure, I had my own account, but everyone knew there was an us. I don't know how else to explain it. But after he did what he did, I just couldn't have people out here still putting us together. And like sure, I could have just deleted the posts with him in them, but that would have been a lie too, because even without him in frame I knew he was there, right behind the camera."

"That makes so much sense, Sola," Dr. Ali tells her. "Thank you for verbalizing that."

"Sure."

"Is there anyone else you wish might see you?"

"That's one of those weird questions you therapist people like to ask," Sola says. "I told you to stop asking me questions like that. Give it to me straight."

Dr. Ali nods, scribbling something in a notebook.

"Whatever you're writing there you can say to my face," Sola says.

Dr. Ali looks up from her notebook, smirking. "Oh, I know." Her posture changes slightly, and she settles more comfortably in her armchair. "Right now I'm wondering if you've ever been seen the way you actually want to be? It almost seems like the social media got close but didn't quite cut it."

"I know what you're trying to get at and you're wrong. My best friend Marquise sees me, my ex saw me I guess, until he didn't anymore."

"What about your family?"

Sola closes her eyes. "Some of them, sure. My sisters maybe. Well, the youngest one I was a complete bitch to growing up. Karen? Bruh. Soft. She still lets people push her around. When we were kids, she let me push her around too."

"Hmm. Push her around how?"

"Like I used to slap the shit out of her." Sola shifts in her seat, squaring her shoulders. "You know my mom's a nurse, so even if she babied Karen the most, she couldn't always be there. And my dad, I don't know, his schedule was erratic as fuck. Anyway, when my mom wasn't home beating on me or creating new reasons for why I was a terrible person, maybe I was roughing Karen up a little, you know? Like once when she was like five and I was fourteen, she went in my makeup and wasted a whole bottle of this Lancôme foundation that I had lifted from the Macy's on State Street. Completely wasted. I mean she had smeared it all over her face, her hair, her neck, her arms. And I knew what she was trying to do. She's had vitiligo since she was little. I knew kids called her names, sometimes I did too. But it didn't stop me, I swear I hit her . . . hard. I was just so mad. Because she'd gone into my room and gone through my stuff, you know? I was about to turn and get a belt from my closet to whoop her little ass. But Anjola ran in and stopped me."

"Anjola's your other sister?"

Sola nods and says nothing.

"That sounds like a really charged dynamic."

"Yeah. It was. Anjola and I were closer then, we're closer in age, but she was always protecting Karen from me."

"How'd that make you feel?"

"Betrayed, really. Like I was a monster. Because Anjola knew me, you know? She knew I wasn't a bad person. I was just trying to teach Karen that she couldn't do idiot things and think everything was gonna go her way because she was little and cute. I think I thought everyone was spoiling her? Like, nobody treated me like I was precious. I wanted her to know what life really was. But yeah, I guess I was really mean to her."

"What makes you realize that?"

"When I went to see her, she told me."

"You went to see her?"

"Yeah. She called me last weekend and she was all distressed, and I don't know why. I just had to. And like it was dumb because I ended up maxing out my credit card so I could rent a car. But I could just tell that she really needed me to be there for her."

"Mmm. Why do you think she reached out to you particularly?"

"She doesn't have any friends."

"It seems she and your other sister are close, right?"

"Yeah, but Anjola's like perfect, like the golden child. The whole doctor, went to Yale and U of C, probably still a virgin type of thing. Well, maybe she would be the golden child if it wasn't for sexism or whatever. Because Nigerians love their sons, let me tell you."

"So you think Karen called you because you . . ."

"Have something to be ashamed about. My mother kicked me out of the house when I was in college because she found out I was having sex. So I dropped out and moved to LA with Aiden."

"Oh, Sola, I'm so very sorry that happened to you."

She shrugs, but her fingers are interlaced and gripping one another tightly. "It is what it is. It was freeing, honestly. But yeah, I guess Karen wanted to talk to someone who's already the family reject. Safer that way. I think my mother thinks that without me her family is perfect now, you know? But all three of my siblings are a fucking mess. I'm the resilient one."

"Interesting. Why did you choose that word, resilient?"

"They never went through what I went through. Like they had it mad easy. Karen just had to bat her little eyes. Ola didn't even have to try—as long as he made the right grades, he was good. I can't remember one bad thing my mother ever said about him. Anjola? Please. All she had to do was the opposite of whatever I did. And then? Perfection."

"How would you put what you went through? What words would you use?"

"Terror? I couldn't do anything right. My mother was always upset with me about something. The bathrooms weren't clean enough, nobody told her we were out of eggs, Karen colored on the walls. And the way she would shame me? Once she smacked me so hard I literally busted my lip. Over some silly pictures that went around the school. And they weren't nudes or anything, Dr. Ali. I was fully clothed, I was just trying out some posing, copying the girls on *Next Top Model*, you know? Anyway, I put them on my Myspace and some boys were sharing them around and somehow the principal ended up calling her?" Sola's voice breaks. She runs the backs of her hands over her eyes, leaving streaks of black mascara on her skin. Dr. Ali pushes the box of tissues over to Sola.

"She backhanded me so hard I flew back against the entryway table, broke the crystal vase. She didn't even care what had really happened, you know? Just all this anger, immediately. That's what hurt me the most? Maybe it's true I was a bad child, but like as a mother, aren't you supposed to want to know why? And you know what? Each of my siblings were there and they didn't do shit to stop her. Karen ran to hide. Ola just stood there acting like he was a stand-in for my father, telling her to calm down and telling me I needed to carry myself better. And Anjola? Like two minutes later, this bitch runs to get her report card and show my mother she got straight A's."

"Wow." Dr. Ali's face is frozen in shock, and Sola knows in that moment that she is not crazy and that her family is as unhinged as she has always felt they were. "Why do you think she did that?"

"Because she's thirsty."

"For?"

"My mother's approval," Sola says. But a gnawing feeling in her gut reminds her that after their mother had pinned Anjola's report card to the fridge and gone upstairs to her room to call her friend Funke and complain, Anjola had come back to her holding ice cubes wrapped in paper towel, had lifted the cool mound to Sola's lip and said sorry so much that it brought fresh tears to Sola's eyes.

"I don't fucking know," Sola continues. "But you know what? I know I'm resilient because all I do is bounce back. I get kicked out of the house, I become an influencer. I was molested, repeatedly, as a child, and I still made myself one of the most popular girls in school. Aiden leaves me and . . . well, I come back and start again."

Dr. Ali stares at her, waiting for her to say something else. She stares back. Dr. Ali looks down and writes furiously in her notes.

"Is there anything about what you just said that you might like to expound upon, Sola?"

She sees herself again as a child, on her skinny knees, the deacon's big hands pushing her head back and forth, hears herself gagging and fighting for breath despite her peaceful genuflection, hears the deacon's deep moans. In Sunday school they were taught that God is omnipresent, but perhaps He had relegated himself to the main sanctuary, where the church ladies were having their planning meeting, or the parking lot, where the church fathers prayed a blessing over the new car one of them had just bought. Because He was not in the room in which she sees herself, in the dark, alone, choking. She sees Anjola, from the corner of her mind's eye, peeking through a sliver in the door and then shutting it loudly. Anjola was eight, Sola eleven, and whenever this memory resurfaces, these facts stand beside it in judgment. Yes, she was only eight, but what kind of a person runs away when she sees her sister fighting for breath?

"No," Sola says, "I definitely don't."

ELEVEN

Thursday, November 1

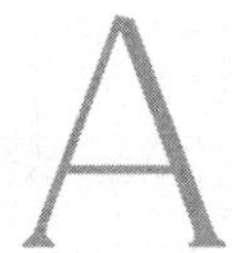

s Ola brushes his teeth that morning, he is surprised to see Betel in his inbox.

To: ola.longe
From: betel.tadesse
Subject: Re: wow!
Date: 11/1/18 Time: 3:29 a.m.

Venus retrograde. Figures.

Thanks tho

He barely stops himself from laughing and spewing foamy toothpaste all over the bathroom mirror. He'd half expected her to ignore him entirely, or to send a one-word reply. But five words from Betel is an in. He leans against the bathroom wall and hastily types, stops only momentarily to convince himself that this is an entirely innocent reconnection between old friends. Besides, conversing with Betel feels for some reason more justified given the growing distance between himself and Marisol. Marisol has given up on repair. She locks their bedroom door at night, so his sleeping in the office is no longer a choice but a necessity. He has to wait for her to unlock the door in the morning so he can get dressed for work. She prepares some of his favorite meals and marks the Tupperwares with passive-aggressive Post-it notes proclaiming, *Do not touch.*

But Ola doesn't entirely mind the silence between him and Marisol. It means she requires nothing of him. No random requests for Sunday brunch double dates, no midnight grocery store runs to fulfill her bizarre cravings, no hints at babymoon vacations to islands in the Indian Ocean (because apparently the Caribbean has become cliché). The silence has also created more space in his mind for Betel.

Before reading her email, he'd spent the wee hours of the morning scouring for mentions of her online, scrolling through her Instagram for evidence of lovers she's had since him. But he found none, just vistas from faraway places and provocative self-portraiture. He finishes typing out a response. He presses send.

To: betel.tadesse
From: ola.longe
Subject: Re: wow!
Date: 11/1/18 Time: 5:07 a.m.

Nice to know you're still insane. Where in the world are you now, B?

To: ola.longe
From: betel.tadesse
Subject: Re: wow!
Date: 11/1/18 Time: 5:19 a.m.

Really? That's what you're leading with?

Nairobi for the next few weeks.

But he doesn't know what else to say, so he lets the exchange dwindle. He leaves for the gym. He comes home again to shower. He only checks his email again after he's finished dressing and is locking the apartment door behind him. Once nestled inside the elevator, he unlocks the screen to read another reply.

To: ola.longe
From: betel.tadesse
Subject: Re: wow!
Date: 11/1/18 Time: 7:33 a.m.

That's it?

To: betel.tadesse
From: ola.longe
Subject: Re: wow!
Date: 11/1/18 Time: 8:07 a.m.

I still think of you sometimes, B.

To: ola.longe
From: betel.tadesse
Subject: Re: wow!
Date: 11/1/18 Time: 8:21 a.m.

Us . . . that felt like a lifetime ago. How've you been? Wall street, bespoke suits, summer in Ibiza type vibes?

To: betel.tadesse
From: ola.longe
Subject: Re: wow!
Date: 11/1/18 Time: 8:40 a.m.

Ibiza is random. But no, close though. Dearborn St. Maybe bougie but not bespoke. Rarely enough time for summer.

To: ola.longe
From: betel.tadesse
Subject: Re: wow!
Date: 11/1/18 Time: 8:45 a.m.

Chicago still? We've gotta get you out.

And I still think of you sometimes too. x

To: betel.tadesse
From: ola.longe
Subject: Re: wow!
Date: 11/1/18 Time: 8:53 a.m.

Please do. I should've come to London. I regret that now.

Across the tracks at the station that morning, he sees the profile of a young woman who almost looks just like Betel (they have the same long forehead; she waits with the same huff of impatience) until she turns and faces him directly, and the similarity is uncanny. He keeps trying to piece together what it all means.

Since that article, he has been seeing her everywhere, her ghost stirring up desire and unease. Like how, when he sees the girl at the station, his heart starts to bang against his chest. Like how, when Betel's next email comes through at work, his body freezes and he has to consciously remember to breathe before he can open it.

To: ola.longe
From: betel.tadesse
Subject: Re: wow!
Date: 11/1/18 Time: 9:31 a.m.

Regret is a choice you don't have to make.

This might be completely bizarre to say, but our breakup fed my art actually. So like . . . thank you I guess?

But I'm sorry for how it all ended.

To: betel.tadesse
From: ola.longe
Subject: Re: wow!
Date: 11/1/18 Time: 9:37 a.m.

I've long forgiven you.

To: ola.longe
From: betel.tadesse
Subject: Re: wow!
Date: 11/1/18 Time: 10:33 a.m.

Cool. Well. Sometimes, I'd wonder whether you actually learned anything from us, yk? Did you?

To: betel.tadesse
From: ola.longe
Subject: Re: wow!
Date: 11/1/18 Time: 12:45 p.m.

Heavy question, but warranted. I took a lot from us ending. Mostly, I think that I learned not to take people for granted.

Because when we were together I took for granted how . . . fun we could be. I didn't realize how hard it could be to find genuine laughter in a relationship. And you were right, I was trying to make you fit a mold that wasn't you. I'm sorry for that.

To: ola.longe
From: betel.tadesse
Subject: Re: wow!
Date: 11/1/18 Time: 3:54 p.m.

Thanks for owning that, it means a lot.

This feels really wild to be writing in email cause I've imagined it in my head over and over again. That we'd meet at an airport or a cafe or something and we'd finally hash things out properly like adults.

Anyway, in those "fantasies" (I can't come up with a better word, you're better at words) I always tell you this thing that's true: no one else has ever made me feel how you made me feel. I regret nothing.

He spends the last couple of hours at work reading that email over and over again. Ola remembers that when they were together, it was as though the world was made anew, made more vibrant. And yet he and Betel were toxic, their relationship marked mostly by fucking and fighting and laughing in between. She could be volatile, and Ola's feigned attempts at impassivity only heightened her anger. They broke up ostensibly because she was moving to London for an art fellowship and he refused to go with her. At least, that was the story he would tell after. On dates when women would ask him why his last relationship ended, Ola learned that the best story was a short one.

But reality had been messier. They were both nearing the end of their graduate programs. Yes, she had won an art fellowship in London, and, she argued, Ola could work for a hedge fund there. He pretended he would think about it. But he had never planned to go. At some point over that period, he even allowed her to think he was leaning toward going. It gave him some sense of control amid the perpetual rush between them; it prolonged this dance they had been dancing for a year and a half. Betel was overly impassioned in all things, unpredictable, needing him. Ola liked being the one to rein her in.

Toward the end of their relationship, she had come to his apartment one night, a week before graduation. High heels, slip dress, winged eyeliner, staggering gait, full regalia of the woman wronged. Pounding at the door in the middle of the night, and when opened, demanding to know why. Why he had strung her along until the final hour. Why he had never introduced her to his mother. Why he only saw her as a behind to bend over or a mouth to suck dick with. How he had never really cared about her anyway, given that he was a selfish piece of shit.

Ola had been sitting on the living room couch, pretending to be impassive, despite that all-too-familiar thud of his heart in his ears. And finally, with Betel screaming in his face at the top of her lungs, Ola rose to the occasion. One fist slammed against the wall. Again and again and again.

Had she forgotten, he asked, about all the times he'd gone out of his way to make her happy? All the times he'd bought her groceries, attended silly gallery showings with her, tolerated gatherings with her confused socialist friends, helped her pay her rent? Did she not realize that he was tired of taking care of her? He was yelling. Did she not know that she was fucking exhausting? Why would he condemn himself to spend the rest of his life with a crazy bitch like her?

She jerked back as if slapped. Turned. Lifted the coffee table above her head. Hurled it through the center bay window. He heard the glass shattering before he could make sense of it. Disbelieving that Betel, only about five feet tall, was capable of this, even as he rushed to the broken window, glass cutting his foot as evidence, to see the cracked windshield of the car parked below on the street.

Worse still, a neighbor called the police. Ola spent his first night in jail keeping vigil, near tears. First catastrophizing about school and his parents and future employment. Then wondering, of course, about what led him there. Blaming her, and then deciding that no makeup sex could be worth this. Swallowing down all those feelings, the confusing aspect of his body wanting hers, even then, and what that said about him. He had to make this simple for himself. He had to decide that she was not the kind of woman who would help him get anywhere he wanted to go.

In the morning, they released him. He saw her for the last time when he came outside. Her face unwashed, her lips dry, pleading, explaining that she would borrow money from her parents to pay for the window repair and the car damage. Her hands clasped together in profuse apology, of the crying and beseeching sort. "We don't work," he said, turning away from her. Only that.

A chime from his phone.

> Mom: I hope you people aren't traveling for Thanksgiving o. I'm not working. I want us to spend it together as a family.
>
> Ola: Okay, we'll be there.
>
> Mom: Very good. I love you.
>
> Ola: Love you too.

Ola notes the date. It's three weeks before Thanksgiving, and his mother usually isn't the planning type. He also can't really remember the last time she wasn't working on a holiday. Perhaps the coming of her first grandchild has led his mother to redouble her efforts to bring the family together. Ola almost types out a message to Marisol about it before he remembers they're fighting. Wherever his mind may be, he knows he must repair things with his wife.

He decides to start with flowers. After work he heads to the florist in Ukrainian Village where Marisol procured her wedding bouquet. He knows that she'll appreciate the sentiment.

He wanders around for a few minutes, looking at the various flowers, most of them unfamiliar to him. He puts his hand out to touch one with leaves that open around vibrant petals in a crescendo of color. He looks at the different vases lined up on the shelf, and they remind him of spring break during his senior year, when he'd come home for a weekend and given his mother a Waterford vase. It was Ola's reward for helping a fraternity brother pack up a family home in Lake Forest. It had never been used, its grand, curved body latticed into perfect diamond shapes. He'd known she would love it and she did. He recalls the way her face broke into a wide smile when he presented it to her, the care with which she placed it on the entryway table. "No flowers?" she'd remarked playfully. He spent the later part of the afternoon making music with Karen in the basement, Ola's heart warmed by how much Karen delighted in him, how she copied his every move, how she clung to his side and constantly begged him not to go back to school. Then, above the sound of Boney M., he heard breaking glass. He ran upstairs to see Sola cowering beneath the entryway table, her hand covering her head as though to block their mother's blows. It was frightening to see Sola so reduced, but even more frightening to see his mother so enraged. All he could wonder was what Sola had done to drive their mother to this point.

"Mom, calm down," he said.

"Calm down? Ask your sister why she's parading her naked body around her school." His mother had turned to him, eyes pleading. "It's an abomination, what she's doing, it's very wrong. Pekun, kí ni mo má ṣe pẹ̀lú ọmọ yìí? Wo. Speak to her. Ọkọ mi, jọ̀ọ́."

His father was, as always, out working, and Ola understood that this was his mother's way of asking him to stand in his father's place. And he thought he knew how to do that, what exactly his father might have wanted to say and how. So he turned to Sola and said, "You can't be going around acting like this, you're a reflection of our entire family."

Then Sola, bleeding from the lip, turned to him with the most intense look of hatred Ola had ever seen. He shifted, heard a piece of crystal crunch beneath his slippered feet.

When the shopkeeper interrupts this memory, Ola can't bring himself to admire the vases any longer. Instead, he wonders why he often thinks of Sola when guilt is brewing inside him.

"Hello, sir," says an elderly man with a thin-lipped smile. "How can I help you?"

"What type of flower is this?"

"Protea. Just come in."

"I'm looking for an arrangement for my wife. An apology bouquet or something I guess."

"Then protea not so good. Maybe hyacinth instead." He points to a cluster of white and blue flowers. "I can make you something nice. What size you want?"

Ola draws his gaze away from the hyacinths and back to the protea, the audacity of them, the furiously bright petals, their apparent sharpness to the eye and their softness to the touch. They remind him of Betel.

"Actually, let's go with the protea. She'll love them."

"Whatever you say, boss. What size you want?"

"Uh, large?"

"You sure? Will be like three hundred dollars."

"Sounds good."

"Must be very big apology." The man guffaws, then winks. "I hope you no make another lady pregnant."

Marisol sits at their dining table, her back turned to him, head bowed in concentration over her sketchbook. It is well past her usual bedtime. Ola places the bouquet on the kitchen island while he contemplates escape. Surely she has heard him enter, hang his keys up near the door, remove his shoes as mandated. And yet he is still thinking of how he might avoid what is to come.

Suddenly her honey-colored curls fly as she turns to him. She stares wordlessly.

"You've been avoiding me," she says eventually.

"Yes," he says. "And you've shut me out. Which I suppose is fair."

"Those flowers are supposed to be for me?"

He nods.

She looks at them thoughtfully, her head slightly tilted to the side. "They're strange."

"You don't like them?"

"I mean, they're beautiful, but they're irrelevant," she says. "Are you ready to have a real conversation, or do you plan to keep running away?"

He walks over to the table and glances down at her sketch pad, unable to discern anything from the page.

"I'm sorry," he says, taking the seat opposite hers. "I'm ready."

She leans forward, resting her head in her hands. "Why did you say that? That you feel stuck?"

He doesn't know. In the time that he spent avoiding her, he ought to have devoted more mental energy to coming up with an explanation. All he knows about what he wants has come to him in images. Images of what it might be like to take up more space at home, of a life with no routine, of mornings with Betel, who he would not put on a pedestal, who would not require his best behavior at all times.

"When I asked you to marry me, I didn't think it was going to be this complicated," are the words he uses.

One hand instinctively flies to her stomach, as though to protect the baby.

"Complicated how?"

Ola breathes in deeply, trying to find words that feel true, justified.

"I guess I've been thinking about how I'm showing up in life. What's really me and what isn't, you know? Like when I was a kid, I was always trying to pretend to be Black enough. And now at work it's like I have to try and pretend to be white enough. Do you have any idea what that's like? To constantly have to wear a mask? I don't want to pretend in my marriage."

"I'm not asking that of you."

"Really? Okay. Let me tell you some things that are true, then." His index fingertip is pressed against the table, housing all his frustration. But her eyes are wide and expectant, waiting. "I don't want to fucking take off my shoes at the door. I think this house is too fucking empty. It's literally always cold in here. I hate your hair that short. I hate how you never wear any color anymore. I don't know if I want to raise a Black kid in this neighborhood, but I do know that I don't want to give him some white-ass name."

"Wow," is all she says.

She stands, sways heavily to the kitchen, and puts the kettle on. Neither of them says a word. He is still at the table as she picks out a bag of loose-leaf tea, does her whole ceremony with the strainer and the milk frother. As Ola watches her, the protruding stomach overlaying the counter, he thinks of what Betel might look like with his baby inside her. This house, with Betel in it, would be awash with color. There would be expletive-laden music playing, Betel twisting her hips to the rhythm. And their baby, a lovely brown-skinned thing, would have a name like Abel or Ayo or Seyi or Haile. Sure, he would still be a bicultural baby, but the baby could at least be certain that he was Black. And because Betel was the way she was, attuned to everything cool, adept at traversing the various streams of Black diasporic cultures, the baby would be sure of himself. As Marisol approaches the table again, all Ola can think is that this child they are having will be just like him: unrooted, in-between.

"You've been really unkind," she says, her measured voice drawing his gaze up from her belly to her eyes.

Ola shrugs. "I've just been wondering where I'm showing up honestly, you know? And like, I try to tell you things and you can't handle it. So I don't know how I can bring my full self to this marriage."

She takes a long sip from the mug. When she sets it down, her eyes have tears in them.

"Ola, fuck you. Do you even know how much stress I've been through these past couple of weeks? You said those words to me and then you froze me out completely. And then for you to come and blame all of it on my hair or what colors I wear or make it about some kind of philosophical treatise about how you show up?" She shakes her head incredulously. "Seriously, fuck you. I deserve an apology."

He nods, looks down at his hands. That familiar guilt rises up in him again. He can't talk to her, not really, this is true. But he thinks of all the other truths he dare not utter: how he's been fantasizing about Betel, how he is already regretting the son he doesn't yet have, how he doesn't think he can really be the father this boy will need.

"I apologize."

"And I never asked you to pretend for me. I'm not staying the same and I don't expect you to either, but I do expect honesty. If you're not happy because you're pretending, that's on you."

He sighs. "You're right."

"Of course I am."

"I'm sorry," he says again. He feels himself shutting down. He doesn't want to lose her, not because she is easy to be with, but because he feels he can handle her without losing hold of himself. He finds safety in the coolness that emerges between them in the heat of argument, believes that this is why their marriage will endure. Standing and walking around the table, he turns her face toward his. "It's me, it isn't you. I'm the one who needs to sort my shit out. I'm sorry." And then Ola kisses her forehead, and she releases her hands from fists.

Lying beside Marisol later that night, her back nestled against his chest, he thinks of how peaceful things can be with her. With Betel he might have had London and Amsterdam and Jaipur. He might have had days full of laughter and color and heavy food, nights of hard partying and rough sex. But he might not have had peace. And yet he turns over to reach for his phone on the nightstand.

To: betel.tadesse
From: ola.longe
Subject: Re: wow!
Date: 11/2/18 Time: 1:45 a.m.

We weren't so good for each other, B. But I do miss us.

TWELVE

Thursday, November 8

Karen rests on the counter at the student-run coffee shop, eyeing the croissants and sweet pastries beneath the glass enclosure. The last time she spoke to Sola on the phone and told her how acutely she felt Tinu's absence, Sola told her that a job could be a good way to "forget about that trifling bitch and make some money." It wasn't the empathy Karen had been hoping for (and in hindsight this wasn't surprising, since Sola could hardly talk about her own breakup), but she didn't think that getting a job could hurt. And though her new job doesn't actually pay that well and hasn't exactly made her forget about Tinu, it does fill her time and provide a way for her to talk to new people.

It's a Thursday morning, one of her slowest shifts. Greg, the barista on schedule, puts in his headphones and tells her to call him should anyone come and order. Karen watches him retreat to the back room, his long ponytail swinging behind him.

She pulls out a library book—a pristine copy of Okri's *The Famished*

Road—and leans over on the counter as she opens to the last page she was reading.

"Hi there."

She looks up to see her African Religions professor smiling down at her. Dr. Jones McBride is arguably the most beautiful man she has seen in her three years on campus. Karen knows she isn't the only one who feels this way. On the first day of class, the cool Black girls in their red sorority jackets stopped whispering from the row behind her when he came up to the lectern to introduce himself, silenced by the weight of his voice. He wears his hair in thick sponge curls, is vain enough to have a tiny gold nose ring in his left nostril, and has warm-hued skin that the sunlight seemed to love when it beamed through the windows of their lecture hall that day.

Karen stands there awkwardly behind the counter, waiting for him to order. Later she will sit alone in her dorm room with her eyes fixed on the vintage Angélique Kidjo poster on her ceiling, recalling this conversation with deep embarrassment.

"Uh, a cappuccino please," he says.

Karen nods and, unable to find words, instead points to the digital display by the register.

Of course he only carries cash, she thinks to herself, shakily taking the five-dollar bill he holds out to her.

"I love that book," Jones says excitedly as she opens the register.

Karen squints at him. "Why?" Her voice sounds like crossed arms, but it is the only way she knows how to engage with people she finds attractive now. Defensively. Begrudgingly.

She places his change neatly on top of the book between them. He doesn't seem put off by her in the slightest.

"For so many reasons. I think it's kind of radical. A sort of fever dream. In the way it subverts reality—"

"Is it a subversion if it is Okri's reality though?" She grows self-conscious. "I just mean, is it radical if this is what he knows, you know?"

Jones's eyes light up. "Nah, I feel you. I mean, these are great questions. There's a kind of tension here, between what he knows and what we know, you know? Like, yes, perhaps this exists within his cultural imagination. And yet he is still operating within Western strictures—by this I mean he wrote the book in English, had to send the book to a white man to publish it—that deny his reality as truth. And so to insist upon your reality even in a world that denies it, to tell a story that will only be seen as magical, not realistic? I think that's subversive. But it's a good question."

"I guess." Her mind tires from trying to follow his train of thought and come up with a response while also taking in the sight of him up close. She usually sits in the second-to-last row of their lecture hall and might have gone unnoticed were it not for her hand jerking compulsively into the air at any question posed to the class. A vestige of her star-student, perfect-attendance upbringing. She is nervous when the words finally come to her. "I think maybe there are just two realities. There's his, where this is kind of what life is like? And then there's yours, where magical realism isn't real."

Greg comes out on his own and interrupts them to ask for Jones's order. Above the hiss of the steamer, Jones smiles and says, "You should come by my office hours sometime. I have to be there, and it gets boring, but I like arguing with students."

When she arrives at the lecture hall, their midterm papers are splayed out in the front of the room, Jones standing guard over them like a watchful priest.

"Hey, Karen," he whispers softly as she approaches the throng of students gathered around the table. Still thawing from the cold outside, she waves hello before rummaging to find her paper. She immediately flips to the back page to see a B+ circled in bright red ink, underneath which Jones has written *Come see me* in neat cursive. She glares at him and shoves the paper into her messenger bag, stalking to her seat near the back of the hall, a respectful distance away from Tinu's regular spot in the front row.

Karen settles into an empty chair beside the Deltas and pulls out her notebook as Jones switches to a new slide. The girl next to her—Rachelle, Karen remembers, outspoken, pretty—smiles before turning her attention back to the front of the room. The other two are whispering just loudly enough that Karen can hear them.

"The things I would let that man do to me," says one. Karen's eyebrows rise.

"I know! All these dusties on campus need to come and take notes."

"Y'all are so thirsty," Rachelle whispers back.

The first one rolls her eyes. "Don't try to act like you're above it all just because you like to eat the box."

The three of them laugh, but Karen keeps her face neutral, pretending that she hasn't heard anything at all.

As the slide changes behind Jones, she studies the image of the San Lazaro feast day procession.

"In Cuba, San Lazaro might be the most popular saint," he explains. "Many Cubans, and Santería devotees in particular, envision him as a homeless beggar. Every year on the seventeenth of December, thousands of people make the pilgrimage to Rincón to pay respects, praying for health and miracles of all kinds. Remember that I told you last week that Santería is a religion of living memory.

Somebody who did the reading last week—can you tell me which orisha San Lazaro reminds you of?"

Still thinking of that B+, she wonders what it feels like to be him, standing there, passionately lecturing about his life's work. Why doesn't he see how much she loves this material, how much it lights her up, how it provides an escape from the mind-numbing chemistry problem sets and physiology lab reports? This is the only subject in which she can see herself. As he cold-calls on student after student who offer up the names of incorrect deity after incorrect deity, Karen decides she will give him a piece of her mind.

"Ṣọpọna," she announces out of turn.

"Careful," says Jones, smiling up at her. "Tradition holds that even uttering the name can bring about unforeseen calamity. He is often referred to as Obalúayé or Babalú-Ayé instead."

Tinu politely raises her hand in the front row. "Isn't this witchcraft? I don't think you should be lending these subjects credence in the classroom."

"Why the fuck are you in an African religions class, then?" Rachelle interjects. The classroom is silent with awe, and perhaps gratitude. Karen cringes internally, wondering how the weight of Tinu's religious baggage is only becoming apparent to her now.

"That's enough, Rachelle," Jones says, his words punctuated with stifled laughter. "Next class, let's have a quick discussion about 'witchcraft,' as you've called it, Tinu."

That whole afternoon before Jones's office hours, Karen sits in the library, staring at a benzene reaction formula in her organic chemistry textbook while her mind rehearses all the things she wants to say to him.

Inside his office, Jones sits easily behind a grand oak desk, his feet propped up confidently on the tabletop. He looks up from the book he's been reading with raised eyebrows.

"Karen. I wasn't sure you'd come."

"I came to speak to you about this." She reaches into her messenger bag to lift out the offending sheets of paper, now crumpled from her reading and rereading.

"Ah." He takes the paper from her and sets it down on the desk.

Karen sits and then takes in her surroundings to avoid looking directly at him. "I just don't think the grade you gave me was fair," she says, peering down at her hands. She watches her fingers entangle and disentangle themselves again and again. They are like a familiar mosaic, the digits of her left hand primarily brown, the ones on her right primarily white apart from a speckling of brown near her knuckles. When she isn't feeling insecure, she is fascinated by herself, enthralled by the way her skin rejects social and biological mores. Sometimes she likes to think that she is gradually defying categorization.

"I worked really hard on this assignment. I guess I was wondering if you could walk me through your reasoning."

She looks up finally and Jones is staring at her. Not at her arms, not at the colorless ring around her mouth, not at the small patch of hair above her forehead that turned white last year. Directly into her eyes.

"It was a brilliant paper, actually." He shrugs and leans back in his large chair. "I really enjoyed reading it."

Her eyes widen. "Then why did you give me such a low grade?"

"B+ isn't a low grade."

"I guess. I just usually make A's and this paper—I guess I was just surprised. I tried really hard on it."

"I know. I could tell."

Karen feels her skin flush warm. "I even called my dad to weigh in on it."

Her father had found the paper exciting. On their call he jokingly promised he wouldn't tell her mother she was using school fees to learn about juju instead of focusing on her pre-med classes. Karen could always count on him to delight in anything she chose to do, and to make fun of her in the process.

"Why?"

"He spent his childhood in Òṣogbo. He sometimes snuck out to join the Ọ̀ṣun festival parade when he was young."

Jones stands to face the bookshelf behind him. Karen is grateful for the break from his probing stare. It is a lot of psychological work to be talking to someone so beautiful up close.

"You might enjoy reading this," he says, placing a large white book on the desk with a thud. "And I really do think your paper was brilliant. You're a skilled writer."

Her body warms again.

"What are you majoring in, Karen?"

"Biology and chemistry."

"Ouch." Jones places his hands over his chest. "You're breaking my heart here."

She offers a faltering smile, unsure if he is flirting with her, unsure if she would like for him to be. "My mom wants another doctor in the family."

Jones drums his hands on the desk. He picks up her paper and flips to a specific page, then reads her words out loud. "Absolutely stunning writing."

"Thank you." She's unsure of whether to keep pushing on the point. "I guess I'm still wondering why my stunning writing only earned a B+?"

He takes out a pen from his drawer, crosses out the grade on the last page, and writes an A+ in bright red ink. "How else could I have gotten you to come to my office hours?"

"What?" Her lips part, but she doesn't know whether to laugh or storm out of the room.

"It was always an A in the formal gradebook," Jones says. "Look, I know we need Black doctors. But we also need Black anthropologists and ethnographers. And I'm in need of a research assistant."

"Really?"

"Really. You have such natural aptitude for the subject matter. I think it could be the beginning of a solid thought partnership."

Her smile widens, her mind suddenly invigorated with new life. Finally, the chance to invest her time in something that genuinely interests her, and she'd get to work under Jones's tutelage. She knows she has a tiny crush on him, but it isn't the distracting kind. It doesn't feel the way hanging out with Tinu did: all-consuming.

"Yes. I want the job."

His smile is brilliant. "Great. It would be about ten to fifteen hours of work a week. And I think I can pay you better than that coffee shop does."

As she emerges from his office, she only feels the profuse gratitude that comes from being seen.

She makes her way to the shuttle stop, eager to catch the next ride to the library, but she is caught behind two girls holding hands. Their affection for each other takes up all the space on the narrow sidewalk. She observes them, envying how cool they look together, how brazen they are in their desire for each other.

They are free. That's the thing she wants. She doesn't know if she's into women, but she wishes that she were allowed to decide for herself. She wishes that if she were queer, it wouldn't cost her alienation from her family. How is anyone supposed to know if they're gay when the cost is so high?

Safely nestled in the back seat of the shuttle, she pulls out her phone and dares to ask Google the question she has been avoiding for weeks. "Five Signs You're a Lesbian" is the first result she clicks on. And by the time she reaches the end of the article, she feels an overwhelming urge to hide. According to the website, she is at least 80 percent gay.

But maybe, she thinks, the whole article is moot since she hasn't really tried with men. In middle school when the few friends she had all became boy crazy, Karen couldn't understand. And in high school she was too busy trying to pretend she didn't hear the comments other students would make about her skin, so she didn't have the energy for romantic fantasies of any kind, really.

But in all that time, Karen had never suspected herself of being gay. Now Tinu, Sola, and Google are all gathered in accusation. She considers Jones, and even if he doesn't make her body warm the way being near Tinu did, there is something about him that confers a degree of happiness to her heart. As she exits the shuttle and makes her way across the main quad, a sense of calm comes over her. She might not be gay after all. There is still Jones.

THIRTEEN

Thursday, November 8

Ola burrows down into the plush seating, perhaps out of shame, perhaps out of exhaustion from holding his spine upright. He reviews the email exchange he and Betel have been having for the past week. He examines each message like a precious, secret thing, studying the relative lengths of their responses, the absence of exclamation points, the note of desire underlying their easy banter. She's just asked him if he has WhatsApp, says she wants to send him something. His mother has told him to download it time and time again so he can chat directly with his aunts and uncles in Nigeria, and he has explicitly refused for that reason. But after noting the suggestive tone of Betel's email, he finally installs it. He has time to kill, he reasons. He's waiting for Anjola at a gastropub in the West Loop, and she's running nearly twenty minutes late. Because Marisol is still anxious about things between them, he quickly shoots her a text message saying he'll be home later than expected. A minute later, Ola is looking at a stunningly clear image of Betel, posed for a photo she claims to have just taken upon checking into her hotel. She sits at a windowsill, her hands gracefully resting on each side of the window frame flanking her body, almost like a figure in an Egyptian hieroglyph. She is nude—her nipples are large and indecent and beautiful. His eyes sweep over the familiar contours of her shoulders and breasts and thighs.

"Sorry I'm late. Getting over here was so annoying."

Ola quickly sits up and turns his phone over onto the table, looking to see Anjola slide into the seat opposite his before he can stand to hug her. She seems almost as flustered as he feels, and though she looks tired in the eyes, there is a frenetic energy about her.

"Maybe it's time for a car?"

"Yes, with my resident salary. I'll be sure to go look at a Maybach this weekend." She pours herself a glass of water.

"Marisol and I barely use the Volvo. I can ask her what she thinks about lending it to you."

"No need. Today was just annoying. Most of the time it's fine." She is being curt with him, avoiding eye contact. She looks down at the menu. "What have you had here that's good?"

"The trout's pretty good," he says. "So's the fried chicken. I mean it's not Harold's or anything, but it's good. Also it's on me, obviously, so get whatever you want."

"Thank you, big brother," she says, pouting slightly. She pushes the menu to the center of the table and downs her glass of water. "So . . . what's up?"

"With me? Oh, I'm good, yeah." Given the eight years between them, he struggles to figure out the right angle with her at times, whether she needs stern fatherliness or jovial brotherliness. Perhaps this, he reasons, is just a product of growing up, the exigencies of adult life shifting the nature of their relationship. He shrugs.

"How's work going?" he asks.

"It's tough," she says. "I can't really lie. But that was expected."

"Well. We all have to live with our decisions."

"What do you mean by that?" She crosses her arms. "Just because I'm not wasting my life helping billionaires get richer, my work is . . . what? Something I have to stomach?"

Before he can respond, the server comes and takes their orders. Once he leaves, Ola holds a hand to his heart.

"I'm sorry. I didn't mean for it to sound that way," he says, choosing to ignore her slight against him. "I wasn't referencing the whole . . . ranking situation. Just that . . . yeah, it's a tough job."

He doesn't envy Anjola. But he's glad that someone else fulfilled their mother's voracious need for a child who's a medical doctor. Their mother also encouraged him down that path, but his mind had been set on business from an early age. And having analyzed the years of potential life lost to study in comparison with the pay doctors received, he knew he would only be doing it for clout. Sure, Anjola had her MD from an Ivy, but at its highest, her earning potential would still fall far below his own.

"But, Ola, you only think that because I'm not clearing mid-six figures a year like you. But I actually love what I do." She turns to look out the window and Ola takes the opportunity to study her, the dry skin between her fingers, the bony angles of her wrists.

"Yeah, no, of course. We all just want what's best for you," he says. "I don't really know how to do this without being honest . . ."

"Is that so?"

"Well yeah. So in all honesty, Dad asked me to check on you. I guess he's concerned, mental health–wise? He said you seemed sad. I don't know, to me you look drained."

Her expression softens and she brings her hands away from her chin. "Dad's such a sweetheart," she says as she finally looks at him. "And yeah, I definitely am drained. Sad? I don't know. Do you know what it's like when you don't even have time to feel your feelings?"

"Can't say I do. I think I just avoid mine voluntarily."

She smiles. "That works too. Anyway, I'm glad I'm back here in the city, like I don't regret that. But it's also disorienting, being in the same place I was when I was younger. And I feel pulled in a lot of different directions, you know, work-wise, dating-wise, Mom-wise?"

Ola laughs. "Yeah. I definitely get the Mom-wise."

"Do you?" she asks, raising an eyebrow.

"Absolutely. Also, is it just me or does it seem like she's doing a lot for Thanksgiving this year?"

"Literally the absolute most, Ola," Anjola says. "She's texted me like seven times in the past three days asking me if I'm coming."

"Did you respond?"

"I'm busy!" Anjola lets out a low groan and runs her hands over her eyes. "Let me respond now." She digs for her phone in a large canvas sack and begins typing.

"Oh, has Sola reached out to you at all?" she asks, looking up from her phone.

Ola furrows his brow. "No, I haven't heard from that girl in like a year."

"She was in town a few weeks ago. I got to see her briefly."

"Yeah? How was that?" Ola isn't exactly surprised that Sola would pass through Chicago without reaching out to him, but it still hurts. He tries to tell himself that this casual disregard of hers is merely accidental, but some part of him insists that it isn't.

"It made me really happy. I've missed her, you know?"

"I can imagine." He smiles wryly, trying to put his hurt feelings aside. "You both were a devilish little duo. Terrorists."

"We were not!"

"Literally, yes you were. You forgot that time you both went and put ground crayfish in my hair cream?" he asks, eyes widening from the ridiculousness of the memory. "I went to my first day of senior year smelling like ass."

"I remember!" Tears are forming at the corners of her eyes; she is laughing so much she can hardly get the words out. "Because you were so stingy with your summer job money."

"Can you imagine?" Ola does a poor imitation of a Nigerian accent and points emphatically at his chest. "My own money."

Anjola is doubled over, and a warm feeling suffuses through Ola. The woman sitting before him finally bears some semblance to the sister who left for medical school four years ago, the lightness of her younger self. He finds himself wishing he had reached out to her sooner, wishing that they had more of this, feeling how it makes him lighter too.

"*And* you two were snitches," he says, lifting a glass of water to his lips. He smiles and shrugs.

"It didn't matter because Mom never saw you as anything less than perfect."

"I mean, but I am though." Ola pretends to dust off his shoulder. "Anyway, as for her pushing you and whatever else, I just try to remember that everything she does, everything she nags about, it's all coming from a place of love."

"I think *she* thinks that," Anjola says. "Like she introduced me to this guy who . . . It's weird, actually—he's almost your if-our-parents-hadn't-left-Nigeria counterfactual. Anyway, I don't know, do you ever think that she's just got a file somewhere where she's mapped out all our lives for us?"

He beams at her, delighted by her choice of words, by how precisely they convey a shared experience. The food comes. Neither of them attempts to say grace.

"This guy sounds cool if he's my 'counterfactual,'" he says, making air quotes. "Why don't you want to give it a chance?"

"Mmm." She pauses to shovel some shrimp into her mouth. He realizes how hungry she must be, that her work may be leading her to neglect basic self-care.

Anjola continues. "I mean he's a good-looking guy, it's just that he's trying *so* hard. And I can't see why."

"Any guy who wants to be with you should definitely be trying hard."

She pouts thoughtfully. "Yeah, maybe you're right."

"Do you want me to vet him for you?"

"Absolutely not. Although"—she pauses for a second—"Mom did mention that you might like one another, since you both work in finance. He seemed receptive to the idea."

"Sure thing. Send me his information," he says. "But finance sounds reasonable. It's not like she set you up with someone who works at a Western Union, right?"

She shakes her head slowly as she chews, completely missing the joke. "He's an investment banker. But why is it that you and Mom only think about money?"

"It's not even like that," Ola says. "All I'm saying is that you could just go on one date with the guy. Besides. Marriage, if you want to be married one day, is primarily an economic institution. More women could benefit from looking at it that way."

"And that's why you chose Marisol?" Her voice has an edge to it, a hint of challenge.

"Not exactly," he says, putting potential disrespect aside. "But did I take it into consideration? For sure. Anyway, Mom's not asking you to choose him or marry him."

"Maybe," she says with a shrug. "Anyway . . . since it's honesty hour . . . I saw the picture on your phone, Ola."

He chews his bottom lip, trying to find an excuse. Lying to his sister would be a wasted effort, and perhaps a betrayal of the openness they've just found.

"I can't say I'm not ashamed," he says finally.

"Who is she?"

"An ex." He places his elbows down on either side of his plate and presses the heels of his hands against his eyelids. "It's nothing. It's silly. I don't know why she sent me that."

Anjola's eyebrows rise; her lips part just slightly. "Look, I really don't want to be in your business. I don't want you to think I'm judging you. But . . . this doesn't seem like the best idea. Isn't Marisol due in like two seconds?"

He doesn't know how to explain why the impending delivery makes it feel all the more justified. These are things he is not allowed to say. How might he express the terror he feels about bringing a child into this life, into the indoctrination of school and work and saving for retirement and running to catch up with time as it compounds itself toward death? Would Anjola understand him if he said he feels trapped—that his home, his office, his commute are a gilded cage—but looking at an image of Betel's naked body is almost like looking down a path toward freedom?

"I didn't mean for it to turn into this," Ola says. "But I do miss her."

"I see. What's she doing for you that your wife isn't?"

He hasn't considered it in these terms. He can't say anything because, all things considered, Marisol goes beyond just doing, often anticipating his needs before he can. But there is something else. He looks at Anjola thoughtfully, gauging whether he can trust her with his feelings, whether what he says will reorder their relationship somehow. He takes a deep breath. He leaps.

"I just. I guess with the baby coming . . . I've just been thinking about where he'll fit in in the world, you know? Like with having a mother who isn't Black. Maybe with us growing up and not being as tapped into Nigerian culture—whatever that's supposed to be."

Anjola's face is open, free of judgment, as she waits for him to continue.

"Betel, my ex, sometimes I think about whether the kid would be better off with a mom like her, you know?"

"Damn."

"Yeah, I know, it's messed up. But you know how growing up it was like, oh, maybe you're not capital B Black enough? And now, you know, I meet Nigerians who are so clearly Nigerian, and I think—what's this kid going to be? Half his mother, half me, and I'm just not always sure where I stand really. I don't know if any of that makes sense."

"It makes sense." She nods slowly. "It sounds like you're thinking about his cultural inheritance? Maybe you're even worried about him experiencing what you did, not knowing where exactly you fit in the world?"

"Exactly," Ola says, feeling comforted by her understanding, grateful that she hasn't met his vulnerability with judgment.

"What it means to be Nigerian to Mom and Dad compared with a kid growing up in Lagos today? I bet it's entirely different. Honestly, Nigerian isn't even an ethnic identity. I think about this sometimes. How this country we all claim is this thing some white men carved up on a map. Like, people go on and on about how Nigerian they are, but that wouldn't have meant anything to our ancestors from three generations ago. Sorry. I'm getting off topic here. But I'm just trying to say that maybe what you're looking for is something no one really has, because it's all always changing. And also, you're not the only one like you, you know? Maybe this in-between thing is a culture in itself."

"That's incredibly wise," he says, impressed to hear such nuanced perspective from her. "And you're right. Maybe I'm too fixated on what it felt like when I was a kid, you know? How it felt like I was the only one?"

"Right. But you're not. I mean for one, you have me, and you have Karen . . . and maybe Sola, I don't know. But also, I think you could try to find some friends who are like you, or just who might be able to help you as you raise him. Like, maybe talk to that guy Mom set me up with from church." Anjola waves her hand dismissively. "And this ex or whatever she is—it isn't about her. It's about you."

"True," he says, picking up his fork again, as though weighing her words in his hand.

"Because otherwise, what are you hoping will happen here? Are you like actively trying to get divorced?"

"Whoa, Anjola. Relax." Ola lifts his free hand, a motion of surrender.

She pauses. "Sorry."

"I don't want a divorce, I'm not a cheater. This is just a friendly exchange between exes that went a little sideways. I'm going to end it, okay?" He smiles softly. "Don't come and chop off my head."

He knows that Anjola is right—that every instance of contact with Betel is an escalation toward an increasingly untenable future. And yet he can't imagine going back to the drudgery of his daily life without her.

"Good." Anjola laughs and then tilts her head thoughtfully. "Also, please don't be offended by this, but . . . I didn't know you dated Black women."

"Nope." Ola shakes his head. "We're definitely not doing this today."

They finish the rest of their dinner with affable conversation, keeping things light. After he pays the bill and they wait outside for the Uber he has insisted on ordering for her, he tells her she should come hang out with him and Marisol sometime.

"I'll certainly try," she says, reaching up to give him a hug.

He knows that this is her way of equivocating, that he shouldn't expect her visit anytime soon, but he forces a smile anyway, waving goodbye as her car door closes.

When he slides into the back seat of a cab, he is grateful for the solitude. He looks down at his phone, unsure of what exactly to say to Betel. He opens the image again, hearts it, considers sending a hasty message that explains that he doesn't want her to get the wrong idea, types it out, deletes it. He sets the phone down and fixes his gaze outside the window. Remembering how Sola would tease him about his secret girlfriends when he was in high school, Ola smiles. "I don't understand why these girls like you anyway," she once said, "you're like medium ugly." What would Sola tell him to do now, he wonders? Would she like Marisol or Betel more? He imagines her saying something about his being destined to be a deadbeat and snickers at the thought. He turns the phone over again, types out a message.

> Ola: Hi Sola. I just saw Anjola and she mentioned you'd been around. If you ever come through town again, I'd love to see you. Don't be a stranger.

He watches as three dots appear, disappear, appear again. Each dot glimmers successively, and he feels hope rise in his chest. Then, suddenly, the cloud is gone. He shifts and resets his jaw, tries to tell himself he doesn't actually care.

Dare is so exclamatory in his messages that Ola expects to be greeted by a man with permanently raised eyebrows and a saccharine grin when they meet that weekend. Upon entering Kola Café, a Nigerian restaurant on the border of Edgewater and Uptown, he is surprised to encounter a man who is less eager than he comes across over text. Swaggy even, Ola thinks, as he observes that Dare stands two inches taller than he does, has a clean fade, and sports brown wingtip shoes. Ola follows him to a table near the television where three other men sit. Wale, Nwosu, and Jérome, he learns, shaking hands with each of them. He takes the empty seat beside Jérome, whose eyes are glued to the soccer game on the television screen above.

Ola learns that Dare knows Nwosu from J.P. Morgan, where they both work, Jérome knows Wale from their soccer league, and Wale and Nwosu met at a party in the suburbs last year.

Their waitress comes over then and deposits a hot platter of Suya and a few bottles of German beer on the table. She smiles bashfully at Dare when he thanks her by name and asks her to bring one more.

"I take it you come here often," Ola says when she leaves, feeling slightly envious that he hasn't elicited the same reaction from the waitress.

Dare shrugs. "I have to eat. No one is cooking for me at home, shey you get?"

Ola nods, afraid to attempt any response in pidgin that would expose how American he has become.

"Me, I'm bringing my wife from Nigeria in the spring," says Nwosu. "This buka food e no reach."

"I don't think all your little girlfriends will like that," Jérome says, playfully wagging a finger. They all laugh.

Ola gratefully accepts his beer from the waitress and reaches over for a piece of Suya.

"How long have you been married, Ola?" asks Wale, taking note of Ola's wedding band. "And does your wife cook well?"

"Almost two years now. And she does, but not Nigerian food. She isn't Nigerian."

"I don't know how you guys do it," says Dare. "Me, I have to be with a Nigerian woman."

"How Nigerian?" Ola asks.

Wale interjects, "If she can't pronounce *pi* and *gbi*—I don't want it. If she can't go on her two knees to greet my mother—I don't want it. If she doesn't have a deep freezer stocked with my favorite soups . . ."

"You don't want it," say Nwosu and Dare in unison.

"Can you imagine that this guy was born and raised in America and he has all of these stipulations?" asks Jérome.

"No, but the real irony for me," says Dare, "is that Wale will do long-talk like this and then bring us one òyìnbó woman to meet."

Nwosu and Jérome burst into uproarious laughter, but Wale only smiles wryly. Ola decides that even if he doesn't feel Nigerian enough, he still prefers what he has become to Wale's obvious, overreaching, overexaggerated performance.

"Anyway, I don't need all of that," Dare says. "She doesn't have to speak Yoruba. She doesn't have to be an excellent cook. As long as she's well brought up and has a hustler's mentality, I'm good." He motions for the waitress to come back.

Ola chooses not to mention that Anjola is far from a hustler. Accomplished, yes. Brilliant, yes. But she is less striver than do-gooder. Still, he thinks a man like Dare might be a good counterbalance for Anjola's inclination toward a life of service and low compensation.

"How is married life?" Jérome asks Ola. "You and Nwosu are the only married men at the table, and Nwosu basically lives like he's single."

"It's good. I mean it was fine at the beginning," Ola says. "It's been more stressful lately."

"Maybe you should find a likkle side ting, that's what my cousin in Indiana did," says Wale earnestly. "His wife has no idea and he says their marriage has never been better."

"Na true you talk," says Nwosu. "Sometimes a man just needs to log in to a new computer. It makes life sweeter."

Ola shakes his head outwardly, but a part of him turns this piece of advice over and over in his mind. Surely not all married men do this; surely his father didn't do this. And yet, were he to review his message exchange with Betel, the evidence of his wrongdoing would be everywhere.

"If you don't mind my asking," says Jérome, turning to Ola, "what made you choose your wife? Like how did you know she was the one?"

"It's hard to explain, honestly. She was just everything I needed. Things were easy."

"No wahala," says Nwosu, nodding approvingly. "I keep telling you, Jérome, just find a babe who doesn't talk too much or bring too much trouble."

"Yes, Jérome. Please let this Véronique woman go. Do you want your future children to be loud and uncouth like her?" asks Wale.

As the men fill Ola in on Jérome's on-again, off-again saga with an Ivorian home health aide who lives in Naperville, his mind tunes in and out. He makes emphatic sounds at correct intervals and nods when Nwosu looks to him for agreement, but he is thinking of how happy he is to not be on the dating market. And yet, while he is free from the indignity that comes with looking for romantic partnership, he hasn't reached any sort of pinnacle. Marriage brings indignities of its own.

At around ten they settle the bill. Outside, Wale, Nwosu, and Jérome go to their cars. Dare and Ola walk together toward the train.

"We should do something active next time," Ola says. "Ask your guys if they'd be down to play squash."

"Definitely," Dare says. "Even if they aren't, I'm definitely interested. And then we can talk shop."

Ola grins. "I'd like that, man. Hey, if you ever want to leave that IB nonsense alone and come do serious business, I'd be happy to help."

Dare laughs at this. As they mount the stairs to the elevated train platform, Ola almost wants to tell Dare that he has his blessing with Anjola, but he knows that he actually holds no sway there. Still, he likes the idea of having Dare as a friend. When the train pulls in, they take seats beside each other, and as they begin to discuss their market predictions for the close of Q4, Ola decides that Dare might have something to show him. He's a man who knows who he is.

FOURTEEN

Thursday, November 8

In the back row of the lecture hall, Karen looks down at her phone to see a message from her brother. The notification suffuses her with the warm feeling of being remembered by someone you love.

Ola: You don't call, you don't text, do I ever cross your mind at least?

Karen: 😁 Sometimes. You're my elder. You're supposed to reach out to me.

Sir.

Ola: That's not how this works.

In fact, you only reach out to me when you're looking for pocket money.

Karen: lmaoooo. You're my big bro. That's how it should be.

Ola: Sure. Did Anjola tell you that she saw Sola recently?

Karen: Yeah. I saw her too, actually.

Ola: Wow. Well, she left me on read.

Karen: Sheesh!

Maybe she just needs time.

Ola: She's still around?

Karen pauses, unsure whether she should admit that Sola is still staying with her friend in Logan Square. The two of them chat a few times a week now, sharing brief updates, although Karen is always the one to reach out. She doesn't mind though, happy to have a window into Sola's life, to know that Sola is on the other side of the phone and willing to respond. But if Karen were to tell Ola about Sola's proximity and it got back to her, Karen might lose the connection they've been building.

Karen: Umm . . . maybe?

I'm in school, I can't be keeping track of the three of you lol

Ola: I don't understand why this girl always acts like I'm her enemy.

Karen: I mean . . . idk. Wasn't it always like, you and Mom against her?

Ola: No. I was just trying to help rein in her reckless behavior.

And, we were all kids.

And, it's been a decade.

Karen: Maybe just let her come to you?

Idk.

Respectfully, I don't wanna be involved.

Ola: Fair. Have either of you told Mom or Dad that she's been around?

Karen: I haven't. I don't think you should.

Mom would lose it

But I think it would actually break Dad's heart.

Ola: You're right. I'll just take this one on the chin.

Jones is pointing to the projected image behind him.

"All right then. So what's a witch according to Evans-Pritchard? And what does witchcraft have to do with religion in this context?" He looks to Karen, though she is not raising her hand, and smiles. "What do you think?"

"Um"—she can feel the classroom watching her—"I think a witch is someone who has the ability to harm people through unclear means. They're often people on the margins. Based on the reading it almost seems like a political category, right? Like, if someone has more resources and they don't share, then they attract envy, and the envy causes the witchcraft, but the witchcraft is . . . in a way . . . justified?"

"Yeah," says Rachelle, turning to Karen. "And it doesn't really seem like it has anything to do with these people's religion, whatever it is, like maybe it says something about what they believe is spiritually possible, but . . ."

"Well," says Jones, "you're on the right track, Rachelle. Part of the function of the religious order in these societies is to uncover whether witchcraft has occurred through the use of ritual or oracular divination, but—"

"Okay, but how are all of those things not also witchcraft?" asks Tinu.

"Maybe like in the same way that you wouldn't say a Catholic priest is a demon for exorcising one?" offers a student in the third row.

"That's a good analogy, Theo," says Jones.

"Yes, but Catholicism has all of this organization and intricacy," says Tinu.

"But so does Zande religion," says Karen. She wasn't planning to speak again, but the excitement of the debate makes the words pour out of her anyway. "Isn't it like kind of messed up to reduce all that complexity?"

"Is that supposed to be complexity? Witch doctors?" Tinu spins around and looks at Karen, her face layered in a false calm, her eyes betraying the anger brimming underneath. "It sounds like backwardness to me."

Rachelle groans loudly, "Girl, are you trying to be a spokesperson for the colonizer or what?"

The class breaks out in laughter and scattered applause, but a pang of anxiety shoots through Karen on Tinu's behalf.

In the hallway afterward, Karen is clipping her messenger bag closed when she feels a tap on her shoulder. She turns around to see Rachelle standing in front of her, smiling. Karen smiles back.

"Yo, you seem really cool and . . . like you know a lot in there," Rachelle says.

"Thanks," says Karen. "But that's only because I'm failing everything else."

"I find that hard to believe."

"Oh, believe it."

"Well . . . would you be down to study for this midterm together? My friends never do the reading. I don't really want to study with them."

"I'd love to!" Karen says, suddenly aware of how eager she must sound. As she hands Rachelle her phone to get her number, Karen is conscious of its cracked screen and dirty case. By comparison, Rachelle seems almost exceedingly put together. Her natural hair is dyed fire-engine red to complement her sorority jacket, the curls defined to collar-length perfection.

"Your hair is . . . everything," Karen says as Rachelle returns the phone.

"Thanks. Not gonna lie, it's lowkey my hobby. I have hand-in-hair syndrome like real bad."

"Who could blame you?"

"So . . ." Rachelle tucks a lock of hair behind her ear. "Study sometime this weekend?"

"Sounds good, I'll text you."

They stand there looking at each other and smiling. After a few more awkward seconds, Rachelle turns to go and Karen watches her receding figure, the self-assured sway of it. She tells herself that whatever she feels has nothing to do with this unobstructed view of Rachelle's behind, or with how she just got a cool girl's number, or even the possibility that Rachelle might think Karen is cool too. But the feeling itself, whatever its genesis, she recognizes as unmistakable happiness.

FIFTEEN

Friday, November 16

It is 10:00 a.m. on a Friday and Sola is on the first shift at the store. There aren't any customers, so she opens up her Finsta and begins clicking through some of the stories from the eighty-seven accounts she follows.

Her nails are filed to long stiletto points, and the tips click loudly against the screen. She's trying to pretend that she isn't exactly seeking him out, that if an update appeared, it wouldn't be because she looking for it. He doesn't post as often now as he did when they were together. His life, she is certain, must be way less interesting without her in it. She watches a video in which a makeup artist rails against Blac Chyna, who is apparently launching a bleaching cream for Nigerians at $250 a jar. Sola finds herself more intrigued that Blac Chyna has thought of Nigeria at all than by what it says about colorism and the exorbitant price of the product for a Nigerian market.

Sola has never been. At this point she is willing to hand over her

Nigerian card if she has one. She spent her teen years imbibing as much AAVE as possible, not necessarily due to proximity but because she was hiding. She still remembers the African booty scratcher jokes and the conversations with her school friends in which she'd desperately try to pretend that she wasn't African at all. She'd even gone so far as to help bully a fresh-off-the-boat Ghanaian girl in the ninth grade to prove the extent of her disassociation from all things African.

What an interesting turn of events, then, that Nigerian is now in thanks to Wizkid and Davido and the rest. She finds herself unable to keep up. She can't really do the accent, the Yoruba and pidgin in their music sound like gibberish to her, and she finds all the comedic videos about African parents mildly irritating. Why turn toxicity to humor?

There's a new story update from Aiden.

Just then, the bell rings over the door as a customer enters. "Good morning! Welcome to Two Saints," Sola says in response. She does not look up from her phone. Her heart is racing. She clicks his profile photo, now emblazoned by a pink ring.

"I'd like to return this jacket." She hears the woman's voice, but she is transfixed by her screen, where Aiden's white hand holds a brown one, the ring finger weighted with a large diamond.

"Ma'am?"

Sola slams her hand on the countertop and finally looks up at the woman. "Bitch, you can't see I'm busy?"

The woman purses her lips; her skin flushes a few shades redder. After a moment, she calmly says, "I'd like to speak with your manager."

"Oh, really?" says Sola. "Well, she's not here."

"Then when will she get here?"

"Only God knows, to be honest." Stacey-Ann is due in approximately forty minutes, but she can tell the woman is in a rush.

"All right then. Well, you and your manager will most certainly be hearing from me soon." The woman turns to leave.

Sola is just about to win when Stacey-Ann waltzes through the front door, cheerily greeting the woman and asking her how her shopping experience was with them today.

"Are you the manager?" she asks.

When she gets back home later that day, Marquise is on the living room sofa watching *Dreamgirls*.

"Would you have fucked Jimmy Early?" he asks by way of greeting.

Sola allows herself to fall gracelessly onto the chaise longue. "Absolutely not, but if I did I wouldn't have been like what's-her-name and actually fallen in love with him." She reaches over for some of Marquise's popcorn.

"Nuh-uh, bitch," he says, snatching the bowl to his chest. "'Cause I see you came in this house and didn't wash your hands. Tryna get off the train and put poor all up in my popcorn."

Sola laughs loudly.

"In other news," she says airily, the last few waves of her laughter subsiding, "I'm jobless again."

Marquise presses pause on the remote, turning to look at her with concern.

"I called a customer a bitch today," she explains, pulling up Instagram on her phone, "because she was distracting me from this."

He takes the phone from her and his eyes widen. "Oh wow. Well."

"What do you mean 'well'?"

"I mean 'well' as in like, well—y'all are broken up, well—if that's what he wants, shit, let him have it, well—I guess you're not over it because you let all of this fuck with your pocket. Again."

"Wow."

Marquise shrugs. "I have a lot more to say, but for me the biggest problem is you came back here unemployed today."

"Fuck you."

"No ma'am, fuck you actually. I have a job."

Sola stands to leave, shuts her bedroom door. She paces back and forth, still smarting from Marquise's words. Because of Aiden, she lost her job today; because of Aiden, her influencer career is over; because of Aiden, a book of half-finished dress sketches sits on her nightstand. Because of Aiden, she's alone. She knows she needs to figure out how to regulate her feelings somehow, but Dr. Ali keeps recommending goofy things like writing Aiden an unsent letter, like that's supposed to help.

Other things that Dr. Ali recommends do help, though. She writes so much memory in her journal that her fingers hurt sometimes. She meditates every morning on the balcony, no matter the weather, learning to escape the clamor of thoughts in her head. She keeps in touch with Karen, resisting her natural urge to sever ties, because Dr. Ali says it's good for Sola to experience what it means to be in relationship with someone who's had to forgive her.

Sola's eye catches the sewing machine on the small table at the end of her bed, pitch-black and gleaming, its presence accusing her of neglect. As she goes to sit before the machine, she hopes it will forgive her too. She begins pulling the denim fabric for a dress she is working on through its tread. The loud, bullet-like hum of the needle calms her, another form of meditation.

Before long Marquise knocks on her door. He enters with a bottle of merlot and two glass goblets. He sets them down on the dresser.

"What are you working on?"

Sola's eyes light up. She shows him the design she's been laboring over, how the dress will eventually feature accents of Àdìrẹ fabric at the pockets and the collar. The boning of the dress will be overlaid with the same indigo fabric, and instead of denim, the center will be constructed with blue mesh so that the boning will look almost like a cage, a metaphor for how one's origins can ensnare. She tells him she wants to submit the sketch, and the first iteration of the dress, as part of a scholarship application for the School of the Art Institute. Though she's been going back and forth about it internally, she's decided that submitting the application might be the win she needs right now. He nods approvingly.

"I'm sorry about earlier," he says. "I meant what I said, but I shouldn't have said it like that. It's just been a day. Tell me why Langston spent two whole hours on the phone this morning complaining about his wife like I ain't got shit else to do? So I told him that I am not a marriage and family therapist. Now he's over there butthurt. Anyhoo. You need to figure out how to let Aiden go. There's nothing there for you anymore, babe."

"I was with him for ten years," she says, trying to keep her voice level. "I never even got a promise ring. But that tacky bitch is the one he asks to marry him?" Scorn is easier to reach for, is better than Marquise knowing the truth: that she wishes she could reverse time and go back to when her life still made sense because she and Aiden were together.

"Girl, I always told you he was tacky himself," Marquise says, opening the wine bottle and pouring her a glass.

"I know I shouldn't care—"

"No, that's not what I'm saying. I'm saying you can care, you can take however long you need to process, but you can't let him fuck up your money more than once. No ma'am."

She lifts the glass to her nose, her nails awkwardly curled around the stem. "You know what, let's go out tonight."

"With what money?"

"It's a manifestation technique," she says. "Tonight I'm finding a sponsor."

"Well shit, cheers to that." He lifts his glass.

The Velvet Room is as swanky as it sounds. Because they're on the North Side, there are only two other Black people at the lounge. Sola is in a skintight black dress and a white fur coat, Marquise in figure-hugging denim, a bandeau bra, a white blazer. They fit neatly into this dimly lit space overrun with well-dressed bodies. The lounge is buzzing with chatter and the insistent sound of swing jazz, because white people love to listen to Black music that Black people don't listen to anymore. As she and Marquise strut to the bar, Sola briefly imagines herself at sixty, walking into a department store and hearing Young Thug playing over the speakers as suburban moms pick out new Spanx in the lingerie section.

A chandelier hangs overhead, and the liquor bottles are shelved above a wide mirror, the display ensconced in gray damask curtains. Marquise hails the bartender, and Sola orders a martini for herself before making Naomi Campbell eye contact with a wealthy-looking man farther down the bar.

While she has never been a sugar baby herself, she knows a few friends who have done it successfully. They have conveyed it to Sola as an exact science. To attract a high-value man, a rich man, one has to think like a rich woman herself. Flirtation is a kind of art, elegance a performance, wealth an aura.

Marquise is prattling on about how Langston has been ignoring him for the past few hours. "It's like fine, bitch, you ain't gotta text me back as long as that two grand keep hitting my account every week."

"He sends you two thousand dollars? Every week?" Sola's mouth is agape. "What is he, an architect up front and a drug dealer on the side?"

"Girl, I don't question God when He blesses me." He shrugs and sips his Moscow mule.

Sola glances at the man across the bar again. His hair is white and straight and coiffed neatly to the back. She guesses he's in his early to midsixties. He wears thick-rimmed black glasses: a look that was in style in 2013 but is now outdated. She wonders if that was the last time he had a wife.

"What do you think of my guy at the end of the bar?" she asks.

Marquise smiles. "He's giving older doctor. He looks sweet. Like he has money but doesn't know how to construct an outfit. I'd guess surgeon."

"Ooooh, we love a surgeon." She runs her fingers through her hair.

Sola glides over to the other end of the bar and sits in the empty seat beside his. She says nothing, but smiles when he builds up the confidence to look in her direction again. She doesn't break eye contact, not for a moment.

"I want to buy you another drink," she says finally.

The man nearly chokes on whatever he's currently drinking, sets the glass down, and wipes his lips with the back of his hand.

"*You* want to buy *me* a drink?" He smiles. He has blue eyes, kind eyes, and for a moment she wonders if he sees her more as a little girl than the sensual being she is trying to embody. She laughs the thought away as quickly as it comes. She is Black. She is herself. No one saw her as a little girl even when she'd been in the middle of being one.

"Yes," she says, turning her gaze to the bar now to study her reflection in the mirror. "If that's all right with you."

The man's name is Charles Wasserstein, and he drinks single malt scotch. He wears a very subtle cologne, which Sola appreciates, because loud cologne is the mark of a poor man trying to make himself feel rich. He isn't a surgeon, but he does own a med-tech company, which sounds even better to Sola. He grew up in upstate New York in the '60s; his parents had been hippies, had made him memorize parts of Dr. King's "I Have a Dream" speech when he was eleven. Sola sips quietly at her second martini and listens as he soliloquizes about Chicago's unjust police system. As he speaks, she wonders if white men would also subject Naomi Campbell to protestations that reveal their white guilt.

When she tells him her name, he makes a quip about the solfège scale, which she forces herself to smile at obligingly. He likes talking about himself, is delighted that she is taking an interest in him at all, and so when he asks her to tell him more about who she is, she knows that it is only a ploy, that he wants her.

"I'm not that interesting," she says, folding her hands neatly in her lap. "I grew up outside LA. I tried my hand at modeling for most of my twenties. And I moved here a few months ago for a job in fashion merchandising." These are not entirely lies so much as they are distortions of truths lived and not yet lived.

"You're very interesting to me," Charles says, reaching out to place a hand over hers. She can feel the heat from his palm seep through her dress and onto her thigh. But his eyes look sincere. It is amazing to Sola how earnestly men believe in their pursuit of sex from women, how willing they are to pretend at love in exchange for that pleasure.

"That's so sweet of you to say." She clasps his hand between hers for a moment before pushing it back into his own lap. "You're so kind. You must be someone's dad."

He throws his head back in laughter, exposing a set of large, pristinely white teeth. "Don't say that, you make me sound so old."

He is, in fact, a dad. A father of three. Two girls, one boy. The girls are grown women now; his son is still in high school and lives not too far away, in Evanston, with Charles's ex-wife. As she listens to him, Sola becomes more and more engrossed in the story, happily envisioning herself as any of the characters, a member of this family without any extreme dysfunction, moneyed and secure.

"Anyway, Susan's been a real pain about Frankie being over so much," Charles is saying, his eyes looking far away. "But I promised him I'd take him and a few buddies to Sint Maarten for Christmas." It amuses her how casually he throws about his wealth in words. New money buys labels. Old money tells stories.

"That sounds amazing, I'd love to go to Saint Martin."

"Sint Maarten. We'll be on the Dutch side." He turns to her and grins as though he's discovered the come-on to end all come-ons. "I'd be happy to take you with us. Seriously."

"I'd be happy to come along," she says. "As long as *we* won't be surveilled."

It seems her plan is working; Charles begins to blush profusely. She's never really tried to pick up an older man in this way, at least not intentionally. There's something protective about the fact of a male partner that she misses. Charles seems harmless enough, but she doesn't feel entirely invulnerable.

Now he's telling her about the house he bought in Wicker, his eyes gleaming with excitement. It has a pool, it's more space than he needs just on his own, but he couldn't help wanting it. Sola wonders what that is about—that human need to consume more and more, to take up space and then the space beyond that. She might attribute it to whiteness, but it is so familiar to her that she can't be quite sure.

"I'd love to see it," she says. She knows that this is off script, that a lady seeking to be a rich man's consort shouldn't give it up on the first day, not if she wants him to keep her around. But she so wants to feel his wealth up close, to be inside it, lying comfortably on the pillowy cushions of his abundance. It doesn't mean she is going to sleep with him.

Charles places a hand on her exposed knee, stroking it with his thumb. "Then you should come home with me."

"Only if you remain on your best behavior," she says, lifting up an index finger in warning.

She glances quickly to the other end of the bar. Marquise is flirting with the bartender, biceps flexing as he strains over the bar top. As Charles settles his tab, Sola sends Marquise a quick text:

Don't wait up.

Outside it is beginning to snow. Sola stands beneath the heat lamp, her teeth chattering unglamorously as Charles attempts to hail a taxi. He stands an inch or two shorter than she does in her heels, which shouldn't matter because he seems to have wealth, and that is her only desire for this arrangement. But something about being so cold makes her wish she were standing beside a man who might wrap her in his arms and rest his chin on the top of her head, the way Aiden would even in the summertime.

"Why not an Uber?" she asks, aware of how petulant she sounds.

"It's my form of protest," Charles calls back as he waves his hand vigorously at a taxi down the street. "Driving a cab's an honest profession. The gig economy is turning it all to shit."

Here he opens the cab door. Sola rolls her eyes as she gets in. Barrington Levy is playing, and she is grateful for the warmth and how the sound transports her somewhere else. She folds her arms and closes her eyes, sinking into the seat beneath her.

Charles is tapping his hands against his thighs, humming off-key to the music. "Picture us swaying to this on the beach in December," he says. "A nice vision, huh?"

"Mm-hmm," she says. She decides that she will not be sleeping with this man. A quick tour of his house. At most a kiss. Maybe a hand job, but only if something concrete might be offered to her in exchange. Jesus, is she becoming an ashawo for real? How can she explain to him that she wants to lie freely in his sheets, wants to swim in his pool in the nude, and wants the trip to Sint Maarten, but all without his actual presence?

"You're still so cold," he says, drawing over to her side of the car. He drapes his arm over her shoulder. It's the closest he has been all night. There is the faint scent of something hot and piquant, subtle and cigar-like. He kisses her cheek.

Sola thought she was in control before, at the bar. But now, nestled together with this man in the back of a taxi, his hand stroking her shoulder, she is beginning to feel like she's the one who's been bested.

"I'm not trying to sleep with you tonight," she says, opening her eyes slowly. "I just wanted to make that clear." Not the right card from the coquette playbook, but it's worth stating her boundaries now.

The light is green, but the cab comes to a halt. Her body jerks forward against her seat belt. Charles's forehead nearly meets the plexiglass before he holds his hands out to protect himself from the force. The music cuts off abruptly.

"Gbemisola." The driver's head spins around. The voice, the possessiveness with which it says her name, the neat beard, the wide forehead, the plaintive eyes. All are unmistakable. Her heart drops.

"Daddy."

The sad, scared look in her father's eyes is the same one he wore when he came to get her from school on 9/11. She was thirteen. She remembers she was called away from her seventh-period Spanish class with Mrs. Ramirez, where she sat in the back with her friends listening to Destiny's Child on a Walkman and refusing to learn her verb conjugations. The class was already half empty, and the teachers refused to tell them what was going on. So she and the other girls were even louder and more obnoxious, screeching as they played MASH and discovered that Sola was destined to marry Lil' Romeo. After her name was announced on the loudspeaker, she smacked hands with her friend Felice, laughing loudly on her way out. Outside of home, within school bounds, she moved with all the bravado and ease that she couldn't muster under her mother's watchful eye.

When she neared the office, she spotted her father sitting on one of the benches, his legs and arms folded patiently. Though she was sure he'd already seen her, she wiped her lip gloss off with the back of her hand, unknotted her uniform shirt so that it was no longer cropped.

"What's going on?"

He'd wrapped his arms around her. This show of emotion, and the fact that he had nothing to say about her attire, filled Sola with panicky delight.

"Is Mom okay?" The delight felt like butterflies in her stomach. In her father's silence, his nose breathing heavily in her hair, she found herself wishing that her mother might not be okay. First, she'd felt glee, then she felt wicked for having had the thought at all.

Outside, the sun was brilliant and high overhead. For the first time in a long time, she walked with her hand in her father's, and he explained that two planes had crashed into a pair of skyscrapers in New York, that Chicago had shut down in fear, that the whole world was watching with bated breath. When they got to where he'd parked the car and she saw that none of her siblings were in it yet, that her father had come to pick her up first, she threw her arms around his waist. Sola had felt special then.

Now they sit across from each other in a booth with red vinyl seats. The diner is off North Clybourn, one that stays open late for people like them. Truckers, strippers, graveyard shift workers, cabbie fathers and long-lost daughters.

"How have you been?"

Sola shrugs, averting her eyes. She studies the menu again, decides for the third time that she will have a bacon and egg cheeseburger with fries. It will be worth the consequences. A heavy, greasy meal to undo the knots in her stomach.

She fidgets with the paper wrapping from her straw, ripping it into tiny little pieces. Her father places a hand over hers. It is heavy and warm.

"Gbemisola."

She looks up at him, staring at her with those large, sad eyes of his. Minutes earlier they were full of fury. Her mind keeps replaying the whiplash she felt as he careened the car over to the curb, stomping heavily on the brake.

"Let go of my daughter. Now."

"He can't be serious," Charles looked at her, smiling incredulously. His front teeth were particularly large, and, shining in the darkness, they looked like fangs. He placed a hand on her thigh. "Don't worry, I'll take care of this."

Sola sat there in stunned silence as Charles peered through the plexiglass. "Are you drunk, man?"

Her father laughed, shifting into park. "I said, let go of my daughter."

Charles looked back at her, eyes widened in shock as her father unclicked his seat belt.

"You shameless nonentity. See someone your age chasing after a small girl like this."

Something inside her broke. Because if anyone were able to still see her as a child, it would be him.

"Do you care to explain?" Charles asked her.

She did not. Her father was opening the door, gripping Charles's arm, pulling him from the car. Sola drew her body into a small ball, buried her head in her arms. From inside the car, she could hear Charles yelling threats, promising to sue for assault and battery and loudly repeating the taxicab medallion number.

"You'll never work in this city again, you fucking ape."

Her father got back into the car wordlessly, his shoulders hunched over in what Sola read as shame. After a few silent minutes, he turned the Barrington Levy track back on as though nothing had happened.

"This was what I liked to listen to back at UI," he said softly. "Your mother liked Boney M., Abba, all the danceable ones. Not me."

In the diner, her father looks at her in a direct and pitying way, as though having just rescued a starving, rain-drenched cat. Which is something she can absolutely picture him doing. Even in his anger he has a gentle, gracious way about him. She's saddened to see that his hair is nearly gone now, that his beard has gone fully gray, both a testament to how much of his life she has missed. But what really ages him, as Sola sees it, are his tired, sunken eyes, the heavy bags beneath them. She feels guilty that for the last ten years she spent money on expensive bags and gowns when she ought to have been like her own parents, dutifully sending money back home. Her father shouldn't still be driving a cab. If she'd helped, perhaps he could have gone back to school as he always talked about. It is apparent to anyone who knows him that he is a dreamer.

She clenches her jaw. How has she been? The waitress comes and saves her from having to answer such a stupidly loaded question. The woman gazes down at Sola admiringly when she asks for her order, and Sola becomes aware that her attire doesn't suit her surroundings. Her father places an order for a tuna sandwich, and after the waitress walks away, Sola scrunches up her nose.

"You and tuna sandwiches," she jokes, hoping to alleviate the inherent awkwardness of the situation.

"Some things have to stay the same," he says, still looking concerned.

She wants to explain to her father why she was with that man, but nothing she can come up with feels like it would assuage the concern she reads on his features.

"How long have you been in town? How long are you staying?"

"A couple months now." Sola shrugs. "And I don't know how long."

He raises his eyebrows, folds his arms.

"So you decided to come back and you didn't tell us."

Sola folds her own arms and glares back at him. "Would you have cared?"

"Gbemisola. Don't say that."

"Okay." She resumes the tearing apart of the straw paper, lowering her eyes to focus on the ministrations of her fingers. "What would you rather I do, then?"

Her father shakes his head heavily. "You're still angry with me. After ten years."

"I don't think about you much," she says honestly, biting the inside of her lower lip and looking away. It had been almost too easy to numb herself to all of them, insisting to herself that they simply did not care about her and she was free to do the same.

"How can you say that?"

"You were never there."

He squints in confusion. She doesn't know how to explain to him the violence she endured while he was out driving trucks and taxicabs, the heavy load that had been placed upon her head. Being the eldest daughter in a Nigerian family was already a burden to bear. It was worse given that she was like him, full of her own dreams, her own delusions of grandeur.

"It's true I wasn't there that day."

That was just one symptom of the whole problem, really. He had never been there when she needed him.

"It wasn't just that."

"From what your mother told me—"

Sola puts up a hand, halting his speech.

"I'm sure she told you whatever she needed to make herself look good."

"But, Gbemisola, I called you every day until you blocked me. I reached out to your old friends. I sent you emails. You never responded."

"She made it *real* clear that I would never be welcome home again."

He places his hands on the table, palms open beseechingly.

"Ọmọ mi. Jọ̀ọ́. You are always welcome in my house." His eyes look near tearful. His voice breaks as he repeats it more slowly. "You are always welcome in my house."

She will not allow him to render her a small girl again, will not catch herself feeling so broken and dependent as to wish for him to come and save her.

"But we both know that it isn't your house, don't we?" Because no matter what he could contribute financially, her mother contributed more, and there were both small and large ways in which she asserted this fact.

He looks pained. Before he can speak, the waitress comes and deposits their plates in front of them, smiling much too brightly for the hour and occasion.

Sola takes a fry and dips it in her ketchup as her father lowers his head briefly to pray. There is no God, she wants to say. She is a shame, an apostate, and now a hyena, circling a dying thing, wanting to say whatever might hurt him more.

But her father offers a close-lipped smile. “We haven’t done the best for you. I’m sorry for that,” he says, leaning over with sincerity shining through his eyes. “But not a day has gone by when I haven’t prayed for you. I don’t care where you’ve been, or with whom, Gbemisola. I want you to come home.”

She picks up her burger and takes a large bite of it, allowing ketchup to smear over her upper lip. The knots in her stomach ease, and she nods in satisfaction. Broke-people food, she decides—the best of all.

SIXTEEN

Saturday, November 17

Sustenance," Karen says, walking into the study room. She holds up a bag of pastries from the café.

"Aw, this is so thoughtful of you," Rachelle says, shifting her headphones onto her neck. She rubs her palms together before selecting a chocolate muffin. "What's your zodiac sign? No. Let me guess. You're really smart. You're quiet, which probably means you reflect on things a lot. And you're a sweetheart."

Karen settles into the seat across from Rachelle, struck by how highly her new friend seems to think of her. She momentarily wonders if Rachelle thinks she's pretty, then questions why it would matter.

"I don't know how much I believe in that stuff," Karen says, "but let's see if you get it right."

She watches Rachelle drum her fingertips against her chin. Her fingers are arrayed in gold rings, and her nails are painted a bright, unyielding orange. Karen finds herself wishing she could wear that color, one that expresses a fearlessness, an insistence on being seen. Rachelle's whole being implies a lightness of spirit.

"You're a water sign," Rachelle decides. "But definitely not a Scorpio. I'm going with Cancer."

"Pisces," Karen says, opening up her computer to a study outline she put together over the past few nights. "You were close."

"I love that. I'm a Sag."

"What does that mean?"

"I'm blunt as fuck."

"You . . . actually are," Karen says. "But in a funny way." She wants to use the word "charming," because Rachelle's bluntness does have a disarming effect, does make Karen feel as though she has known Rachelle her whole life. But she's wary of coming off as too flirtatious. She wouldn't be able to stand the loneliness if she lost this friendship too.

They lock eyes, and Karen notes for the first time that Rachelle's irises are a slightly lighter shade of brown and that her nose is dotted with freckles.

"It's the Trini in me," Rachelle says. "We're honestly the most unserious people."

"Oh, I hadn't realized, I thought you were—"

"Regular Black? My dad is, but he didn't raise me."

"Isn't that term kind of offensive?"

"Not to me. Does it offend you though? If so, my bad."

"I'm Nigerian . . . so it's not my place to say, I guess."

"I had no idea! Usually y'all don't—no offense—assimilate that well."

Karen furrows her brow, unsure whether she should actually take offense.

"I just mean usually when I meet Africans, they just look very

African. Even if they're super Americanized. Like this girl in my high school, Nnenna, she tried to act like she wasn't, but you could still see the African all in her face and in how she carried herself." Rachelle grins and adds, to Karen's surprise, "I loved it."

"So I don't carry myself well?" Karen asks earnestly, aware that she is reaching for affirmation but wholly unable to stop herself this time.

"No, you definitely do. You're just kind of quiet, you know? Usually Nigerians are mad loud and overconfident. Like that girl in the front row of class. I mean, yes, her accent gives it away, but still."

Karen's cheeks warm. Because she has decided to blot Tinu from her life completely, she avoids adding anything else to that particular topic. Instead she pulls a textbook from her bag and places it on the table.

"No offense taken."

Rachelle is fun to study with, focused yet playful, and they have an easy way with each other. Karen finds that she isn't nervous around her. By the time they finish working through Karen's study guide and trying out the sample questions, it is well into the afternoon.

"So, since you're Jones's favorite student and all . . . do you think any of the witchcraft stuff is going to be on the exam?" Rachelle asks.

"I'm not!" Karen protests, afraid that Rachelle may be reading more into things than she would like. "I'm just his research assistant."

"Exactly," says Rachelle. "But I can't blame him. You'd be my favorite student too." She leans her elbows onto the table, dimples appearing on her cheeks.

Karen struggles to keep her face neutral. She looks away, deciding she has misread, misheard, misunderstood. If she allows herself to suspect that Rachelle is into her and she's wrong, what then? More rejection, more aloneness, more of this feeling of being misplaced in the world.

"Oh shit, I'm almost late for photography class." Rachelle stands suddenly and begins to pack up her things.

Karen withdraws her hand into her lap. "On a Saturday?"

"Yes, we have these annoying weekend composition sessions. I'm sorry. I would have said we should get lunch."

"Almost dinner at this point," Karen says, glancing at the time on her laptop. "But that's okay. Another time?"

"I'd love that," Rachelle says. She looks Karen in the eye and nods once, as though underscoring her words. And then she waves goodbye, leaving a warm vanilla scent in her wake.

Karen sees a missed call from her mother and a text asking whether she wants a ride home for her upcoming Thanksgiving break. Karen pockets the phone, intending to call once she's outside the main library building. But even then, she can't bring herself to call her mother back. Because what if her mother won't recognize her voice anymore, now that she's been messing around with girls and wondering whether she's a lesbian and failing organic chemistry and arguing against Christianity in class? She sends a text. She will take the train.

SEVENTEEN

Sunday, November 18

Anjola rolls over in plush sheets that aren't her own. Sleepily, she stretches her arm over the face of the man lying beside her. Mistaking this for a sign of affection, he begins to plant kisses on her palm and wrist.

"Good morning, olólùfẹ́ mi," Dare says, placing a large, smothering hand over her hip.

She doesn't know what "olólùfẹ́ mi" means and she isn't sure that she wants to ask. Instead, she blinks her eyes open to study his face. There is nothing wrong with him, she thinks. He looks almost like an Instagram model, with his perfectly lined beard and smooth skin. Here is a good-looking man who can afford the space for a king-size bed in one of the most expensive zip codes in Chicago. Here is a tenacious man: He stuck around for weeks despite her attempts to blow him off under the guise of a busy schedule. Here is a responsible man: He ordered her an Uber Black in advance of their date and left his platinum card with the waiter before they sat down at the restaurant. Her mother likes him, her brother likes him, but she knows that her considering them while she lies beside him is the surest of signs that she does not.

In the daylight, his wealthy bachelor decor is even more ostentatious. From his bed she can see his walk-in closet, fine suits beside finer suits, a wall of clean shoes, a display case of watches. This place has no soul, she thinks, glancing at the faux stag head above his headboard. It's the type of style Neil would probably describe as Don Draper–adjacent, Brooks Brothers–aspirant. If she and Neil had a different kind of friendship, she might have taken a photo of the stag head and sent it to him as some kind of false trophy, pretending to be proud of herself. If they had any kind of friendship at all, they would have spoken something, anything, to each other in the past three weeks. And then she wouldn't even have been here, trying to fill the yawning silence between them by spending the night in Dare's bed.

The sex was not good. Everything that was supposed to make it good was there. Dim lighting, early 2000s R&B, a large dick. At the restaurant, he'd asked if he could order her a ride home, but as soon as she said that she wanted to see his place instead, she'd known that it was a bad idea. Minutes later, they sat nestled together in the nook of his huge L-shaped couch, talking about nothing she can remember. She could feel his arm around her shoulder, his warm breath just near her ear, the light ridges of his abdomen against her back, though it didn't excite anything within her. So she leaned up to kiss him and unbuckle his pants, and still nothing. When he pulled away to unzip her dress and whisper that he was so grateful this was happening, she thought she might feel something then, but by the time he put his mouth between her legs, she knew that all the wetness came from him and not from her. And still she thought she might feel something when he was inside her, something to awaken her mind to the sensory experience of living, but no, all the feeling came from him. She gritted her teeth in the darkness, drawing her body through the machinations of sex it did not really seem to want, and still felt only a growing numbness.

Now Dare is running his fingers through her hair, kissing her cheek, and she envies his vitality.

"This your hair," he says, chuckling to himself. "I've never really liked dreads, but yours are absolutely beautiful." She says nothing as his fingertips trail the length of one of her locs from her temple to her waist.

Nearly six years ago in the dead of a Chicago winter, Anjola, Neil, and his then-girlfriend had gone to see a Doc Films screening of *Marley* for Black History Month. It was a Thursday night and Valentine's Day, and she had nothing to do. While third-wheeling with Neil and Ashley was less than ideal, it had been more enticing than another evening spent in the library practicing physics equations. Neil had been obsessed with Bob Marley at the time, and he was going through a phase—a regurgitation-of-ideologies-from-prominent-male-figures-of-the-African-diaspora phase. At the beginning of college, it had been Mandela, then a hard pivot to Malcolm X, followed by Marcus Garvey, and now he'd begun embracing the "I and I" philosophy of Rastafarianism, smoking weed on Sunday mornings instead of going to church with his parents, and toying with a vegan diet. Ashley was the elephant-necklace-and-harem-pant-wearing sort, a white girl who hung out at the Office of Multicultural Student Affairs and thought she loved Rastafarianism too, since all humanity needed was to embrace unity in a spirit of "one love" to "get together and feel all right." Anjola forgave him for how little she saw him that winter because she knew that this phase would pass, Ashley included.

They all sat at a table in the Pub afterward, discussing the film over beers.

"I think I totally misunderstood the movement," Anjola said. "Like I really thought it was some weird vibe-with-the-earth-and-the-moon, smoke-weed-all-day situation. People don't talk enough about the Pan-Africanist vision there too."

"See! This is what I've been trying to explain to you, Jo. Marley was way more of a movement leader than you think. If you ask me, the film didn't touch enough upon the Cold War politics that were at play at the time either. Like the anti-imperialist sentiment promulgated by his music was a huge threat to the existing power structure."

Before Anjola could make fun of him for using the word "promulgated" aloud, Ashley interjected.

"I don't think it was just about that though," she said loudly, as though it were not just the three of them and she wouldn't have been heard otherwise. "I think their vision of our oneness and the importance of breaking down divisions across color and class was a threat, too." She turned to Anjola and smiled. "And also, what's wrong with vibing with the earth and moon?"

She momentarily felt as sorry for Ashley as she did for herself. Yes, Anjola was single, but Ashley was there fighting for her boyfriend's attention on Valentine's Day.

"Nothing, baby." Neil kissed her on the cheek. "I'd happily vibe with you beneath any moon."

Anjola excused herself to the bathroom. By the time she got back, Ashley was gone.

"What happened?"

"She wants me to go to a DU party with her, I told her I'd meet her there in an hour or so."

"Neil," she said. "What kind of guy brings his girlfriend to see a Bob Marley documentary on Valentine's Day?"

"If she wants to be with me, she's gotta learn how to hang."

Anjola laughed. "So, when you date white girls you bombard them with Black shit as part of . . . a hazing process?"

"One hundred percent. What other way is there to go about it?"

They were several drinks and twenty missed calls from Ashley in when Neil looked up at her suddenly with brightened eyes.

"I think we should both get our hair locked this weekend."

"They're cool," she said, "but I'm not really about that Rastafarian lifestyle."

"It's not about that. I just think they'd look good on you, and, respectfully"—he glanced up at her Afro puff, the ends littered with fairy knots—"it seems easier than whatever you've got going on right now."

"Rude."

"Sorry!"

"You just want locs because you're going through your little bougie Black stand-for-the-people moment."

"And you don't want them because you're stuck in your little child-of-immigrants, class-mobility-and-palatability-seeking moment."

"Fuck you."

"Okay, okay, I'm sorry." He had stopped smiling. "I mean it, I'm sorry. But we both know that locs aren't only for Rastas. You should consider it. If not this weekend, maybe next weekend."

She did think about it. In between lectures and lab sessions over the following week, the thoughts became intrusive. What would it be like to have hair that she didn't have to fret over? She'd stopped relaxing her hair only at the end of first year because all the other Black girls were doing it. But nearly two years later, Anjola couldn't help but feel somewhat dissatisfied. Her hair was as unruly as her mother had warned her it would be, refusing to do as commanded by the girls on YouTube with looser curl patterns. Even when she spent hours blow-drying it, upon meeting Chicago's humidity it would shrink in rebellion. Anjola studied online videos following other women's loc journeys, and when she finally discovered Sisterlocks, she felt like she'd found a cheat code. They were natural but elegant, a matrix of neat and obeisant coils. All Anjola desired was hair that did what she wanted it to while not labeling her as under the thumb of some white oppressor. Her locs would be beautiful and she wouldn't have to think about them too much.

They took a bus down to a shop in Grand Crossing the following Friday. Neil's appointment only took one day while hers took three, but he came back and forth with her every day that weekend. Perhaps it really was because he liked to finish what he started, as he claimed. But when her loctician installed the last loc and made a joke about needing the kind of boyfriend Neil was for herself, they both said nothing to correct her. Later, on their walk back to the quad, it had started raining. In front of her dorm, he'd held an umbrella over both of them before he reached out to touch the hair at her nape, the warmth of his fingertips covering the parts in her hair now vulnerable to the cold. She faltered for a moment before also running her thumb along the curly ends of one of his starter locs.

"What are we doing?" she asked.

"Having a moment." He smiled. "I'm glad you did this with me."

"Me too."

"They look so beautiful on you," he said.

Anjola looked away. She knew that his words invited risk, that their friendship was too lovely a thing to let herself ruin. "I'd better get inside, catch up on my problem sets."

She remembers that when she'd gone upstairs, she had stood at her quad-facing window to watch Neil leave, his hands jammed into his pockets, shoulders hunched over against the wind. Turning to the mirror, she took in the tiny wires of hair that framed her face. Despite everything, she was comforted that she now shared her hair with Neil, a thing that could intertwine them together across space and time.

Her hair slips through Dare's fingers as she stands from his bed.

"What's wrong?"

"Nothing. I should just get home and get cleaned up before my next shift."

Instinctively, she uses her free arm to cover her breasts as she crouches down on the floor in search of the black dress she wore the evening prior. Here is a perfect man. Not factually perfect, but outwardly perfect. And there she is, still unable to find the feeling required to commit to being fully present.

"Oh," he calls as she walks into his bathroom, "your brother invited me to your family's Thanksgiving dinner since my mother is going back home. Is that okay?"

Anjola pauses mid-pee-stream, everything clenching, everything uncertain. Then she decides that enduring his presence at Thanksgiving will be easier than having to disappoint her brother or mother or even Dare himself. "Uh, yeah, that's totally fine," she calls, releasing her bladder.

"Are you sure? I don't want to make you feel uncomfortable."

"No, my mom would definitely love that. It'll be good," she says, trying more to convince herself than him. It's only dinner, not marriage. He will eat with them and then that will be the end of it. She stands to flush and wash her hands. "I'm glad you and Ola are becoming friends."

When she comes back into the room, he stands to envelop her in a hug from behind.

"Can I treat you to breakfast?" he asks.

Anjola disentangles herself, but she lets her fingertips linger in his for a moment, so as not to offend.

"That's kind of you." She pulls her dress over her head. "Maybe another time."

On the sidewalk outside, she breathes in and out deeply, creating clouds of vapor to stop herself from crying. She thinks of Neil again, how he's pulling away from her life, and how she probably has caused it. It is normal for her and Neil to have their misunderstandings from time to time, but never silences as prolonged as this one.

When they were teenagers, best friendship was Anjola taking the right earbud and Neil always taking the left. They would sit together on the wooden bench in the main hallway after school, listening to *Lupe Fiasco's Food & Liquor* on Neil's iPod. On the few weekdays when he didn't have basketball practice and she didn't have science club, he would wait with her for the two hours it would sometimes take her father to come pick her up. Neil's older brother Julius had gifted him the iPod that year, and Anjola had been mystified by the clicking sound it made when she ran her finger over the circle in the middle, by the many worlds of music that Neil could listen to at any given moment. She had built up the courage to ask for one for Christmas, but her mother had refused on the principle that it was a waste of money. So instead of creating her own music collection, she learned Neil's. She learned Anita Baker, Teddy Pendergrass, Bobby Womack. She learned Bob Marley, Peter Tosh, and Lucky Dube. She studied his corps of conscious rappers: Common, Mos Def, Talib Kweli, Nas. And then Lupe, the great ethnographer of their city, the West Side's griot. They listened to *Food & Liquor* so much that she would hear the phantom melodies of "Daydreamin'," "He Say She Say," or "Kick, Push" as she drifted off to sleep.

One day, as Lupe crooned about sunshine and moonlight and starry skies, Neil took her hand. In the quietest of gestures, his fingers whispered themselves between hers. From the sure sturdiness of his palm against hers, she could feel how purposefully he wanted to be there beside her. Her heartbeat slowed. The song kept looping. Slowly, together, they found themselves outside of time, outside of 03:55, outside of whatever would await them when the loop ended.

The realization came over her as calmly as the steady rise and fall of her chest. Neil liked her. He *liked* her liked her. She was fourteen and she didn't know what kissing was like, or what it felt like if a boy put a card in your locker for Valentine's Day, but she knew definitively in that moment that he liked her. Neil Haynes-Stuart, her best friend, the classroom charmer, the future Senator Obama—he liked *her.* Anjola wished she could understand what about her perpetually disarrayed hair and off-brand sneakers, or her inability to speak up in their rhetoric class without her voice shaking, or her flat chest and skinny legs, would make him want to take hold of her hand.

The music stopped playing. He let go and the momentary panic she felt was quickly replaced by the pleasure of turning her head to see a beaming Neil. "I got tickets to this festival. It's on Saturday. Lupe's going to be performing," he was saying, sounding nervous as he held one ticket up as proof. "Will you come with me?"

Was it a date? If she didn't ask, then it could be a safe thing that only they knew, outside of the labels and definitions the world placed on things. Still, she couldn't pretend not to be ecstatic, her lips uttering a repetition of yeses.

"Okay," he said, placing the ticket in the palms she held open to him. "Julius can give us a ride back and forth so you won't be on the train too late. We'll get to yours at eight. I'll call you when we're outside."

She hugged him, her arms crossed around his neck, her cheek momentarily resting against his. There was the honk from the taxicab outside.

Her father's concern about the embrace he'd observed through the main hall's glass doors was hindrance enough. He told Anjola on the way home that evening that Neil was a good boy and he liked that Neil was not too proud to try eating ẹ̀bà and okra soup with his hands when he came to visit their house. Still, Anjola was too young, had too much future ahead of her to be entertaining boys. They could be friends, that was all.

Worse still, her mother, reeling after learning that Sola had circulated sexy photos around her college prep school, had issued a moratorium on "carrying on" with boys. Anjola didn't dare to ask either parent for permission to go to the concert.

Wednesday turned into Thursday and into Friday, and she still couldn't conceive of how she might be able to go with Neil. But she liked this feeling of possibility, how it made her want to take more care in styling her hair in the morning, how it inspired her to borrow items from Sola's closet that accentuated her nascent hips. She liked what this new thing, this not-date, this safe secret, did to her heart. She liked that, in those three days, he started waiting to walk with her between classes, offering to carry her books. Something had shifted between them, and she couldn't bear to say the words that would shift it back.

But when Saturday morning arrived, her stomach was in knots, and by evening time she could barely move from her bed. She just lay there, looking at her Motorola Razr as it lit up over and over again, the image of the handset rising and falling like a wave. By eight, she heard the doorbell ring. Of course, she thought, of course Neil would come to the door to get her, would never assume that she intended to stand him up, even if she hadn't picked up to confirm she was ready. When Sola called from downstairs that Neil had come to see her, Anjola was near tearful. At the sight of him waiting right by the front door, smiling, holding a bouquet of white flowers, she was despondent.

"I can't go," she said, standing before him with her head hung.

"I don't understand."

"I'm not allowed," she sighed. She finally lifted her head to look at him, to confront the deep sadness his features held. "I wanted to go, but I'm not allowed."

She couldn't make out what his face meant, if it was anger or confusion or betrayal or hurt. Hurt.

"Okay," he said. He held the flowers out to her, and she laid them on the entryway table where the vase had been. When she turned back around, he was already down the front steps, his shoulders hunched over as he retreated to the car.

"What was that about?" Sola asked, emerging from the adjoining dining room.

"Lupe Fiasco's performing. He wanted us to go." Anjola bit her bottom lip, trying not to cry.

"Well"—Sola shrugged, ascending the stairs—"they're nice flowers."

Anjola sank down into the living room couch, her mind holding fast to the image of Neil's face. He hated her now, she was sure. She hated herself too, hated that she didn't know how to explain it all to him. Instead, her mind turned over the same thoughts: that she was only good enough to be his friend, that she would only mess things up if they ever became anything more. He deserved to be with someone who wasn't afraid of being called an abomination for going out with a boy.

When she saw him in the school hallway the following Monday, she readied herself to apologize profusely, to explain as well as she could, to say that she hoped they would remain good friends. But Neil just waved and made his face a smiling plane of inscrutability. "The show was amazing," he said, coming to stand beside her open locker. "You would have loved it." And she saw that though his lips curved into a smile, his eyes looked worried, and she understood that he was afraid of having pressured her, having assumed the wrong thing. She thought to correct him, to say the speech she'd spent all Sunday rehearsing, but decided against it. She saw that they both wanted the same thing, even if by different paths—to just be friends again.

Anjola draws her phone from her bag and types out a quick text, hoping that once again, Neil won't need her to explain.

Hey. I'm sorry.

Her chest tightens when she hits send. She inhales the cold morning air deeply, chilling the inside of her nostrils. Her coat is inadequate for a November morning with no alcohol in her system to numb the pain. She wonders if Neil is angry at her, then wonders whether he understands why she was angry in the first place, or if he even cares.

She gets into the car and gratefully welcomes the warmth that envelops her. The driver is playing "Glory to Glory to Glory" by Fred Hammond, which is the only reason she remembers that it's a Sunday morning. When she looks down at her phone, Neil has already responded.

> It's all good, Jo. I know you've been busy. And I know you wish me the best.

Thanks, I really do, she types back quickly.

Outside the window a man bumbles dejectedly between cars, toting a pair of socks in one hand and a shopping basket full of hats and gloves in the other. Anjola studies him for a moment before reaching into her purse for cash. When she lowers the window and lets in the cold to offer him money, he insists on giving her something in return. She accepts the white knit hat with CHICAGO emblazoned in red lettering just as the light turns green.

When she looks down at her phone again, there is another message from Neil.

> Super short notice but my mom has an extra ticket for this Thanksgiving luncheon at the South Shore cultural center today. You free? Maybe we can chat there.

Her chest tightens again. She pretends for a moment to weigh a decision that was instantaneously made in her mind.

Lucky you, I have a golden weekend.

And it's been too long since I've seen the esteemed Mrs. Haynes-Stuart.

Send me the deets.

She doesn't know why she's surprised to spot Giselle first, gliding elegantly through the French doors with Neil just behind her. Their fingertips touch in a private moment of affection that Anjola feels wrong for observing. She is slow to get out of the car, simultaneously desiring to catch up to them and to avoid them altogether. As she studies Giselle's appearance—the bright smile, the hair drawn up into a classic chignon, the effortless sweaterdress and heeled boots that she walks in so easily without faltering—Anjola can't help but wonder if beauty is what she lacks. And then she is ashamed, reasoning that this is only a projection of her mother's and sister's voices, prodding her to get her eyebrows waxed and shave her armpits more regularly and learn to "spruce up" because no man wants a woman who doesn't take good care of her appearance.

Anjola is wearing a white collared shirt beneath a black sheath dress, along with a pair of oxfords. Were Sola around and aware, perhaps she might have helped Anjola find an outfit that looked less academic. She can't remember if she's ever been inside the cultural center before. It is as lovely as she might have anticipated from the outside, this relic of Chicago's golden age. She is taking in the latticework of the glass ceiling above her when she hears Neil's mother calling her. She tries to make her way over with as much confidence as she can muster. The three of them stand near the center of the front vestibule, looking very much like a perfect family. His mother greets her with a warm hug.

"You're really repping the city now," Neil says, pointing up at her head.

She takes the hat off and smiles awkwardly.

"I bought it off the street and forgot to check it at the door."

"It's so good to see you, girl." Giselle smiles too brightly and offers a hug, perfunctory and light.

Anjola follows them into the main room, a large bright area with an ornate, chandeliered ceiling in baby pink. The French windows make the outside look lovely, despite the bare trees and the bitter wind blowing against their branches. The event, Anjola comes to understand over the next half hour, is a fundraising luncheon for members of the Midwest chapter of the Black sorority to which both Giselle and Lynne belong. Anjola is there in place of Neil's father, who was called into the hospital for an emergency.

They are seated at a round table with two friends of his mother's, also alumni of Chicago State University. Lynne obligingly laughs when she introduces Anjola as her date. After one of the servers comes to take their orders from the fixed menu, the elder woman's husband leans back in his seat and stares at Anjola, hard. He is the only other dark-skinned person at the table, she notes, and he wants to know where she went to medical school.

"Yale, huh? That's quite an accomplishment." He leans forward now, his forearms resting on the table, hands clasped together. "And where are your people from?"

"Nigeria," she says.

"That sounds about right."

Anjola looks down at her hands, feeling her chest tighten again. She has been in several iterations of the conversation to follow, and they never end with good feelings.

"It's just always funny to me how Black immigrants make up the majority of the Black student population at these Ivy League schools," he begins. "Seems to me like all these quotas and affirmative action policies were set up to benefit everyone *but* we Black American folk."

She nods silently; she has no desire to speak.

"Now see, for a Black American male to get into an institution like Harvard or Yale, his ancestors would have had to have survived several generations of slavery, Jim Crow, the civil rights era, the crack epidemic, the war on drugs." He takes a sip of water. "What else? A century of disenfranchisement, redlining, stop and frisk."

"You're not wrong," Anjola says.

"I know I'm not wrong," the man says.

"Actually, you're a little bit wrong." Neil pushes up his glasses, folds his hands neatly on the table. Giselle has been looking back and forth between them with a bemused expression on her face. When Neil speaks up, Anjola sees Giselle place a protective hand on his thigh.

"I mean for starters," says Neil, "Black Americans aren't a monolith. We didn't all endure the same struggle, and even if so, not to the same degree. There's a whole class and color dimension that you're missing."

"Young man, that is beside the point." He turns back to Anjola. "I'm just wondering what you all survived that should make you beneficiaries of policies set up to benefit our people."

"Africans on the continent also survived a legacy of colonization and forced labor. I mean, Africa is literally still being robbed today," Neil says.

"Yeah. But they came here on a plane. We came here in shackles."

"That's enough, Walter." His wife, Annette, looks embarrassed, though not altogether in disagreement.

"No, it's okay," Anjola says. "It's true. My parents did choose to come here. And you're right, my forebears weren't part of the Black American struggle." The tension leaves her shoulders and chest as she continues speaking. "And you're right. I did leverage a lot of privilege in being a child of educated immigrants, along with the opportunity provided me by the efforts of Black Americans. But for me the work is about using everything I've gained to make some kind of difference."

"Well," says Walter, "that's all well and good, but most of y'all come here to make money to send back home."

Now Lynne speaks up. "Walter, everyone at this table is done with this topic of conversation." She places a reassuring hand on Anjola's shoulder. "I've known this one since she was a teenager, she's like a daughter to me." Anjola looks up to see Giselle's eyes widen at this statement.

"I was just having a dialogue," Walter says, leaning back in his seat.

Giselle graciously interrupts. "Now, Miss Lynne, Miss Annette, when was the last time either of you strolled?"

Anjola tries to enjoy herself for the remainder of that afternoon's festivities, but it is hard to stay outside her own head. She picks gingerly at the plate of salmon, roasted potatoes, and asparagus in front of her, ignoring the hunger pangs in her stomach. She has the unsettled feeling of being in a place where she does not belong.

The day has been too much. Perhaps because it began with her waking up beside Dare. She knew the sex wasn't going to be good, that she didn't want him to come to Thanksgiving dinner, and yet she resisted nothing. She realizes that she keeps trying to bargain herself into the life designed for her and then making small compromises to inch outside of it. It is a halfway kind of living, and she has no idea what a full life might look like anymore. She has spent so many years keeping her head down, trying to do her work, promising herself that pleasure is on the other side. And there Neil sits just beside her, and still he is beyond reach.

"Hey," she says, leaning over to whisper to him, "I'm probably going to head out soon."

"Because of this dude?" He motions obviously with his hand.

"No. My shift tomorrow is ridiculously early in the morning, I need to make sure I get enough sleep."

He doesn't look like he believes her. "Okay, let me order your Uber back, it's the least I can do," he says. "I can wait with you out front."

He insists even when she tells him it isn't necessary. Anjola bids everyone else farewell, and Giselle looks up at Neil questioningly as they stand from the table, touching her hand to his hip. He kisses her on the forehead and tells her he'll be right back. Anjola tries to unsee this tenderness.

"How's the new school year been?" She speaks to him but trains her eyes on the attendant at the coat check.

"Amazing. I hit the jackpot this year. The kids have been so engaged."

"You are the jackpot," she says quietly.

"Yeah?"

"Absolutely." She reaches out to grab her coat from the woman and thanks her. "Those kids are lucky to have you."

He teaches at a school in Woodlawn, only a few blocks south of the building where he earned his master's in education. With two degrees from the University of Chicago, he might have gone to teach anywhere in the world, but he says he finds his purpose here, serving Chicago's Black and Brown youth.

"I've been wanting to touch base with you." He takes the coat from her, holds it up for her to put her arms into. This is the problem with him. These small acts of kindness make her blood stir, and it's derailing her entire life. "And I'm sorry it's been so long. Things have just been hectic."

"It's okay, it's good we got to hang out today."

"But I wish we'd had more time to catch up." He reaches out to help with her zipper. This time she pushes his hands away, ashamed. She is not a child. He shouldn't have invited her; he shouldn't be in the vestibule waiting with her. He should be inside, sitting with the woman he loves out loud, their hands clasped together in premonition of their future matrimony.

"I know this is kind of unorthodox." His hands are in his pockets now, barring themselves from touching her further. "But you still are my best friend. I can't imagine getting married without having you involved in the ceremony somehow." Neil smiles and lets out a heavy sigh. "I was wondering if you might be willing to be one of my groomsmen. Or—groomspeople I guess?"

She wants to say no, say maybe, say she will think about it and needs some time. But she resists the part of her that wants to run. She is good at performing under pressure.

"Of course, Neil." She smiles. "I want to be there for you in whatever way I can."

He holds open the door to her Uber when it comes, closes it behind her. She turns to watch him standing there in the cold as the car drives off, and when he is safely out of sight, she gives in to the heaving in her chest. A rush of hot, angry tears fall down her cheeks.

EIGHTEEN

Thursday, November 22

3:22 p.m.

Karen watches her mother lift up a bag of yellow onions. "Bá mi gé àlùbọ́sà yìí."

Karen nods, using context clues to decipher that she is being asked to chop them. Her mother is trying to teach her Yoruba now, twenty years too late. But she plays along as though the effort isn't futile, as though a childhood of linguistic assimilation can simply be undone by small efforts like these on her mother's part. She retrieves the big knife from the drawer and proceeds to pull out the cutting board, only for her mother to shake her head in disappointment, the crocheted curls she wears shaking too readily along with it.

"You American kids don't know how to cook," she says.

Her mother takes a smaller knife from the drawer and a large onion from Karen's hand, then deftly removes the skin and minces half the onion within her palm in easy strokes. "We didn't have cutting boards in our house when I was young."

"Then why do you have one now?" Karen takes another onion from the bag and places it on the cutting board as originally planned. Her mother shoots her a warning look, dropping the minced onion into the pot so that the palm oil crackles in protest. Karen's eyes begin to water as soon as she cuts the onion in half.

Thanksgiving is going to be an event, it seems. Her mother has asked her father to pull out the extension on the dining table so that it can seat eight instead of six. She has even purchased a gauche runner with stitched depictions of pumpkins and squash to go on top of it. And she is cooking a veritable feast. They did most of the American food the evening before, interesting attempts at dressing and mac and cheese that Karen is sure no one will enjoy, and now her mother insists on making a few Nigerian dishes as well.

Karen doesn't know what to make of it, really. For the past few years, Thanksgiving has been a minor affair. Either her mother was working or her father was trying to profit from the airport runs, or this sibling or the other couldn't come home for whatever reason, and it would just be her somehow, eating leftover rice and stew and watching old Rankin/Bass Christmas specials. This sudden burst of festivity makes Karen anxious. She's also tired of being on her feet. And she's pretty done with her mother's commentary on her culinary ability. In Latifat's eyes, only one of the Longe children learned to cook properly, and Karen is sure that Sola will never be cooking beside their mother again.

"Okay, if you can't chop onion," her mother says, walking over to the stereo in the adjoining living room, "help me blend the pepper and tomato. And then slice the plantain."

She sighs as she watches her mother remove a CD from its paper casing, annoyed as Tope Alabi's crooning takes up all the peace in the room with its loud piety. She fills up the blender and quickly turns it on so the noise might compete with the music. Her mother is dancing anyway.

"Who all is coming to dinner?" Karen asks when the blender finally goes off.

"Me, you, your father, your brother and his wife." She rarely calls Marisol by name, and Karen isn't sure if this is because it feels strange in her mother's mouth or because her mother still doesn't like her. "Aunty Funke"—and she smiles brightly now—"Anjola and a guest."

"What kind of guest?"

"Àlejò ọkùnrin. The male kind, the kind you should be looking for on your own campus."

Karen laughs hoarsely.

"I don't know why you're laughing," says her mother as she takes the blender from Karen's hands. "It's not good to be single for too long. Don't be like Anjola and only be facing your book all the time."

"Should I be like Sola, then?"

Her mother sucks her teeth loudly, which is all that needs to be said on that matter.

The oil sizzles angrily as her mother pours all the red from the blender into the pot. Karen watches as the stew pops up and then quiets.

"I don't think I ever want to get married," she announces, and then instantly regrets it.

"Ah ah, God forbid. You will marry in Jesus name."

"Amen," she says, hoping that might close the discussion entirely.

Karen wonders who Anjola is bringing to dinner. The last time she saw her sister was just before the beginning of the school year, and Karen had been the one to ask Anjola if she could come visit her at her new apartment in the city. They fell back into an easy familiarity over the day, watching *Osuofia in London*, ordering Senegalese food from Bronzeville, their backs touching as they both fell asleep in Anjola's bed. She knew then and knows now that Anjola loves her. She just wishes for more care sometimes. And she does wonder where her sister has found the time to be dating someone seriously enough to invite to Thanksgiving dinner when she seems unable to find the time to call Karen and ask her how she's doing.

She and Aunty Funke will be the only single people at the dining table, Karen realizes, and at least Aunty Funke once had a husband, even if she is now divorced. All the couples will be sitting around blissfully, asking her prying questions about her romantic prospects back at school. And what will she say? Would Thanksgiving dinner be the most appropriate time to tell her family that she's starting to like girls? She can picture the fallout, can already feel all the air being taken out of the room as her mother begins to quote from Romans and then asks Karen where she learned all these dirty things from. And she can imagine her father, looking away from her in shame, saying nothing. This is what she will do at dinner, she decides—say nothing.

She lowers the heat on the plantain and unlocks her phone, reviewing her texts with Rachelle. They've continued to sit next to each other in class. And they've texted. But they haven't gone out for a meal, mostly because Karen is too afraid to ask, even though she keeps replaying this imagined scene in her mind, what she might wear, how she might remark to Rachelle how beautiful she is. Awkwardly, she types out a long message about class, then deletes it, opting for something simpler.

Karen: Happy Thanksgiving!

Rachelle: Happy Thanks-taking!

Karen: You're so right. Stolen land.

Rachelle: Ignore me. It's not like America is giving it back.

Karen: I'd never ignore you ☺

Rachelle: Thanks for studying with me. I got an A-. Let's do it again for the final?

Karen: Definitely.

Rachelle: I can buy you dinner as a thank you.

Karen: No need! It would be a pleasure.

Her father comes through the front door then, shaking snow off his boots. Karen pockets her phone, smiling to herself. He puts a reassuring hand on her shoulder before walking over to the stove, where her mother stands inspecting the contents of the pots.

"No ọgbọnọ for today?"

"No. You know òyìnbó doesn't like to eat anything that draws," says her mother.

"Which òyìnbó is coming? Mari? She won't eat the ẹ̀gúsí you're preparing either."

"She's not white," Karen interjects. "She's from Argentina."

"What's the difference?" her father asks.

Karen smiles and shrugs. Her father walks over to the stereo and changes the music, for which Karen is immediately grateful. Music is no small matter to her parents, and in their house, controlling the sound system is a question of age and seniority. Being the youngest, Karen could only select the music when no one else was around. She likes her father's taste in music though. While her mother's song of choice is any Yoruba gospel hit, her father keeps a collection of CDs and cassettes of West African classics from the '70s and '80s that feel to Karen like a kind of musical transportation. She feels special, more worldly, for knowing them.

Moments later her parents are grooving together to "Come On Home" by the Lijadu Sisters, their hips swaying with a slow familiarity. Karen stirs the pot of stew and the pot of boiling meat, then returns to watch them through the pass-through. They are smiling, laughing as her father lifts her mother's arm and spins her around.

Sometimes their love makes Karen sad. It seems like the kind that has no duplicate, forged by divine, expert blacksmith hands. It's the kind that traverses sea and country and still endures, the kind that makes four children and struggles to eke out a living and still tries to make time for itself when it can. Their love did not take them on vacations to faraway places, could not afford fancy dinners. But it showed up every day in small moments like these. Karen doesn't know where she might find anything like that for herself. Not everyone finds this, she thinks; it is not guaranteed.

Aunty Funke arrives first, enveloping Karen in a warm hug and the scent of Robb when she opens the door. Karen isn't sure exactly what her mother likes about Aunty Funke, with whom she seems to have very little in common. Her mother takes care to don the latest

TJ Maxx fashion, wears her MAC foundation for trips to the grocery store, and keeps a collection of shoulder-length wigs in color 30 for various occasions. Aunty Funke, by contrast, usually goes about plain-faced, seemingly unbothered by the acne scars littering her cheeks, and keeps her hair in a close-cropped TWA.

"My precious daughter," she says, pinching Karen's cheek as though she were still a child. Because Aunty Funke could not have children of her own, her husband left her for another woman. Karen only knows this because she pestered her mother about why Aunty Funke was so often in their house when she was young. They are family, in a way. Karen came to realize, only years later, that this level of friendship between an unmarried woman and a married one was rare in Yoruba culture. Unmarried divorcées were usually regarded with suspicion by married women, seen as potential husband snatchers who must be kept at bay. But Karen also understands that her mother doesn't see Aunty Funke as a threat.

"It's been too long," Aunty Funke is saying, slinging an arm around Karen's shoulder. "You should have been calling me, now." She leans in conspiratorially. "Me too, I want to hear the latest gist on campus. Did you find any bọbọ́ yet?"

Karen shakes her head, announcing to her mother, who is getting ready upstairs, that Aunty Funke has arrived. Aunty Funke chides her before ascending the stairs. She and her mother have the kind of friendship that forgoes the sitting room.

Karen goes back to the dining room, a small space made even smaller now that the table has been elongated, and resumes setting it, retrieving the gold-rimmed plates her mother keeps in the china cabinet for special occasions. She looks up at the wall in front of her: all their family photos in gold-toned frames. From left to right: her parents' wedding photo, a solemn church affair, her mother in a full lace gown and her father in a tan suit, their faces uncharacteristically unsmiling apart from the mirth around her father's eyes; a photo of Ola at two, wearing a black suit, grinning happily for the photographer; a photo of Ola and baby Sola, Ola looking miserable and holding Sola as she wails with her mouth wide open; a photo of Sola and Anjola, holding hands and wearing white dresses and standing in front of a mall Easter Bunny; a photo of Karen as a baby in her father's arms, only a bundle in a blanket as he leans back on the door of his taxi parked right outside their house, looking down at her serenely. The next row is all their high school graduation photos. Karen looks horrible in hers.

For the first time, she notices that Sola's graduation photo has been taken down. In its place: a framed calligraphic rendering of the Prayer of Jabez. Has the rupture been so complete? She remembers staring at that photo for so long after Sola left. Every morning when she sat to eat her breakfast of Cheerios at the table, she would gaze up, take in her oldest sister's thin neck and slanting eyes, and think about how unfair it was. How could someone have been so pretty? She was, in Karen's view, the perfect amalgamation of their parents' best features. Where Ola's forehead was too wide, Anjola's eyes set too far apart, and Karen's skin an ever-changing patchwork, Sola had emerged as smoothly as a bronze sculpture and as proportionally as the Vitruvian Man. Why hadn't God taken his time with each of them?

Now the photo is gone. Her mother most likely took it down while Karen was away at school. Which means that she's actually done with Sola. She stares at the prayer through narrowed eyes. Does her mother really think God is on her side?

Her father comes down the stairs, wearing his typical dark blue jeans and sweater combo.

"If you don't have to dress up," says Karen, taking in his regular-looking attire, "then why do I?"

"Ehn, I'm the man of the house, now." He begins to help Karen set the table. "That your mother, she thinks she can just boss me around anyhow."

They smile at each other, at the unspoken truth. Her mother does boss him around anyhow indeed, but he only allows it because of how fiercely he loves her.

At the table, her father sits at one end and her mother at the other, her back to the door. Ola and Marisol sit to the left of her father, which Karen knows Ola did purposefully so as to put as much distance between their mother and Marisol as possible. Aunty Funke sits on her mother's right, and Anjola and her guest sit on her mother's left. They arrived a bit late and had rightfully been given the worst seats at the table, close to the prying elder women. Karen is happy to be nestled safely in between her father and Anjola, both of whom only pay attention to her from time to time to make small jokes but otherwise leave her to the meandering thoughts and wonderings of her inner life.

Karen helps herself to another serving spoonful of jollof rice and then reaches over to take a few pieces of the dòdò her mother made her fry. They are slightly burnt, and as she puts one in her mouth, she recalls her mother's rant in the kitchen earlier, about how at Karen's age she had both procured a medical degree and a husband and could not only fry dòdò but also make any dish her mother-in-law called on her to make. "What am I raising?" her mother said, which had made Karen feel something like a failed effort. Why hadn't life required her to learn how to fry plantain to golden, crispy perfection? But also, what kind of person just went and fried plantain as a hobby?

From the bits and pieces of conversation she can glean from the other end of the table, Anjola's guest is a man she met at their mother's new church, and he seems more like their mother's type than Anjola's. He bent and touched a finger to the ground in greeting their parents, which seemed to Karen obsequious and extravagant, even if it was custom. He was the one to suggest that someone lead them in prayer, which their mother had smiled at delightedly, and now he is walking their mother and Aunty Funke through his five-year plan, alluding to buying a home in Highland Park in which he and Anjola might raise children. Karen nearly laughs aloud. Anjola pinches her thigh.

Ola is advising their father about the gig economy now, something about whether to invest in up-and-coming rideshare stock portfolios. It is so silly that he does this, Karen thinks, watching as their father nods silently and dips a morsel of pounded yam into the ẹ̀gúsí stew in front of him. Sometimes Ola can be the worst. The worst parts of him show up at times like these, when he seems to constantly swagger about in his fancy shoes and knowledge of finance, as though he is too big for them now. She watches as her older brother squares his shoulders, slides his hand up Marisol's back, and strokes her neck with his thumb.

"Have you both decided what you'll name the baby?" Karen asks. Her father winks at her and smiles.

Marisol opens her mouth to speak, but Ola interrupts her. "We're still thinking it over," he says.

Marisol looks down at her plate of food. White rice, stew, a leg from the turkey that otherwise remained untouched, and a small forkful of stuffing. Karen feels sorry for Marisol whenever she comes around their family. Their glamourlessness is unbefitting.

"Isn't he due in like five weeks?"

Now her mother interjects from the other side of the table. "In our culture, parents don't share the name of the child until eight days after its birth."

"I know," says Karen, "but I'm going to be the kid's aunt. I'm family."

Marisol smiles at her. "Actually, we're thinking we might give him an English name," she says. Ola lifts his hand from her neck.

"Is that so?" asks Aunty Funke, her eyebrows raised in disapproval.

"That's cool," Karen says quickly, nodding. "I mean, my name's Karen, so you know these two can't rightfully object."

"Nireti! Ah ah. Your mouth no wan tire for this night," her father says, playfully pulling at her ear. Everyone at the table laughs, including Marisol, who has either been working on her pidgin comprehension or simply wants to be included in the joke.

The slow chime of the doorbell breaks up their laughter. Her mother furrows her brow, glancing at the waning smiles around the table. "Who else is expecting a visitor?"

NINETEEN

Thursday, November 22

4:05 p.m.

Ola's nose is assaulted by the heavy scent of frying oil and spices. The just-opened door releases a wet warmth onto his and Marisol's faces, and he finds distinct notes amid the aromas: fried plantain, fried assorted meat, bay leaves, curry, and thyme heated in palm oil. On the other side of the door, his mother's face beams up at him with pride, the vellus hairs on her forehead dotted with beads of sweat.

"Happy Thanksgiving, Mom."

"Happy Thanksgiving."

She reaches up to hug him and Ola can also smell the muted scent of her favorite perfume in the crook of her neck, the loud scent of fried onion in the blond ringlets she wears. After a brief moment she pushes Ola inside, opening her arms for Marisol too.

Though Ola has brought Marisol to his parents' house before, it is his general preference not to. She doesn't quite fit there, and perhaps he feels that he no longer fits either. House Longe is a three-bedroom foursquare structure that always feels too full, too hot, too loud. He can't shake the contrast between her, her origins, and this teeming box that is his childhood home. He briefly recalls her family's sprawling estate, how the housekeeper had been the only other Black person during their visit that weekend, how Marisol's father had turned up his nose at Ola's new-money stench.

Ola now feels the urge to wrap his arm around Marisol's back, but his mother's presence stifles him. He glances around the house. It is unglamorous, yes, but alive. Adding to the heavy mixture of scents is the loud sound of King Sunny Ade playing from the living room. He sees his father dancing, his back bent low and his arms held wide as he turns in a circle. Karen mimics him, and the sight of her beaming face strikes a tender chord in Ola's heart.

Marisol is handing the box of pecan blondies she made to his mother, who promptly lifts the lid and looks at them quizzically.

"Kí le l'éyìí?"

"They're pecan bars, Mom," Ola says. "They took her a lot of time."

His mother purses her lips and then gives Marisol a side hug. "Thank you so much. Our darling wife," she says, with what Ola knows is a forced smile. His mother turns to place the box on the entryway table beside a porcelain vase filled with orange and yellow flowers, and Ola knows that if he doesn't remember to offer the blondies to people later, his mother will forget them entirely.

"How's my grandson?" she asks, reaching out to pat Marisol's belly. "Mari, I hope you have stopped all that your exercise o. You need more fat on your body. Please eat well, my dear. We want our baby to be strong like his father."

Ola notes the look of vague discomfort that passes over Marisol's face, but before he can think of what to say, his mother has taken her by the hand to give her a preview of the dinner spread for the evening. He walks past them, through the dining room and into the kitchen, where his mother's best friend, Aunty Funke, stands guard over a pan of frying puff puff. Ola greets her with a warm hug and dodges more discussion about the baby when Karen comes over to take him by the hand and pull him into the living room.

"Dad, show him your 'Penkele' dance," Karen whines. Ola smiles at how his baby sister's style of greeting is to thrust him into whatever is going on at the family's center. He puts his arm around her shoulder and Karen leans against him.

"You just move however your body wants to move," their father says. He sways his shoulders along to the drums, but his face takes on a pained look, both of his hands settling onto his head as he sings along to the chorus. Karen is smiling, waiting for her father's cue to join in again, but Ola senses something pleading, something beseeching in his expression.

Ola wishes that he could discern the meaning of the words, but most of it is lost on him. His parents always remind him that he spoke very good Yoruba as a child, as a toddler, before the three of them left for America. Ola sometimes wonders about what happens to a person when their language, their whole world of knowing, becomes supplanted. His mind turns over the words to the chorus again, searching for some clue about the place his father has just gone to.

"You people should come and eat o," their mother calls from the dining room. "Dinner is ready."

Karen looks up at him and flashes a conspiratorial smile. "What if we pretended the food was trash?" she whispers.

"Why would we do that?" he whispers back.

"Ummm, revenge?" she says, feigning a tearful voice and placing a hand over her heart. "If you could see what I went through in that kitchen today."

Ola wraps an arm around her neck and guides her to the table, King Sunny Ade's voice echoing behind them. "What if we didn't gaslight Mom and give her a heart attack and I made it up to you some other way instead?"

Karen holds up an open palm, her eyes unblinking. Ola pretends to be reluctant before retrieving a fifty-dollar bill from his wallet, smiling as he places it in her hand.

Their father seizes both of their shoulders from behind. "Chief conspirators one and two," he announces with a smile. "Are you two planning a coup? If so, don't forget me o." He releases his hold on Karen and claps an arm around Ola's shoulder. "Son, happy Thanksgiving."

"Happy Thanksgiving, Dad."

Ola goes to stand beside Marisol at the other end of the table.

"Everything good?" he asks in a whisper.

She wears her hair in a tight bun, covers her body in a knit dress that extends well past her knees. Her lips are fixed in a tight smile, as though she fears that if she lets her face drop, she may offend.

"Definitely," she says. He places his hand in hers and interlaces their fingers together. Ola feels pleased with himself in that moment. For nearly two weeks, he has avoided answering Betel directly about her offer for him to join her in South America, leaving it as a mere suggestion in his mind, a foregone conclusion in hers. There's something nice, he thinks, about the security of being there, holding Marisol's hand, while another version of himself exists in Betel's mind, planning a trip he'll never take. It is a way to be beyond where he is, wider, larger than the circumstances that contain him.

Anjola pushes open the front door and Dare follows just behind her.

"Happy Thanksgiving, everyone!" she calls, lifting a CHICAGO knit cap from her head and black gloves from her fingers. Dare, ever the gentleman, helps her take off her coat. They go around the tight table, Anjola kneeling to greet Aunty Funke like a proper Yoruba daughter, Dare half prostrating before Ola's parents like a proper Yoruba son-in-law. Ola is happy to see them together, and he says so when Dare comes around to shake hands with him. But when Ola winks at Anjola, she looks away, and for a brief moment, he wonders if she is actually happy. Marisol shifts beside him, the hem of her dress rustling against his calf.

"This is Marisol," he says, "my wife."

"So great to meet you," Dare says, gesturing at her belly. "And congratulations to you two. Or should I say three?"

"Let it be three o, in Jesus name," their mother says, before motioning for Anjola and Dare to come sit in the two empty seats beside her.

"Who will bless the food?" Dare asks when everyone is seated. Ola watches at least four sets of eyes turn to his father, who looks back at his mother with amusement. She is looking to him to sit in his authority as the man of the house and lead them in prayer.

Dare speaks up. "I'm happy to," he says. Their mother nods and everyone bows their heads.

"Heavenly Father, we thank you for this delicious meal in which we are about to partake. Thank you for blessing us with one another's company. Thank you for the lovely hands that prepared this meal. We pray that you will allow us to be a blessing to others in the same way that you have blessed us so abundantly. In Jesus name."

"Amen," joins the table in unison.

Ola shifts in his seat to look properly at the spread before him. Pounded yam, ẹ̀gúsí soup, ayamase ọbẹ̀ ata, jollof rice, fried rice, white rice, fried plantain, baked macaroni and cheese, one gleaming turkey, a sad bowl of stuffing.

"You remember some of this food, right? From the wedding?" Ola asks Marisol in a low voice. Their white wedding had been a huge, half-a-million-dollar affair in Miami, replete with a five-course meal, two peacocks, and one celebrity DJ. But Ola's mother had asked them to do their traditional wedding there in a hotel ballroom on the North Side. The spread had been similar. His mother had taken care to explain the dishes to Marisol's parents, but Ola wasn't sure that they really enjoyed any of them. Worse, he wasn't sure that they were happy to see their daughter join her life with a man whose people ate food with their hands.

Marisol nods. "Yes, of course, I really loved it," she says politely.

Ola's father takes the turkey into the kitchen and carves it up, as though finally willing to stand in his role as man of the house.

"So, Karen, how's school?" Marisol asks, lifting a spoonful of macaroni and cheese onto her plate.

"It's fine," Karen says quickly. "How's painting going?"

"Good. There's this one piece I'm almost done with. It's a self-portrait—here, I can show you." She passes her phone to Karen to share an image of the painting Ola has seen her laboring over for weeks, a pregnant figure standing before a dimly lit window as darkness closes in all around her.

"You're so talented," Karen says, handing the phone back. She turns her attention to the other end of the table, and Ola knows that Marisol will, in some way, take this as a rejection. He doesn't know what to say to draw her into conversation with everyone. But it's better that the table's focus is on the potentialities of Dare and Anjola, he thinks, than on Marisol's pregnancy. Because that's what will happen: she'll only be interesting to them insofar as she is a vessel for the generation to come.

Their father returns with half of the turkey in slivers. He sets the plate down again, and Marisol is the only one who reaches for a piece.

"So, Dad," Ola says, "have you gotten a chance to look over the investing prospectus I sent you? I really think if we're aggressive, you could cut back significantly on work in the next five years."

His father shrugs and unravels two mounds of pounded yam from plastic wrap. The shrug irritates Ola, its carelessness, its fundamental disregard for him and his siblings, who will have to care for their parents when they can no longer work. Do their parents think that someone will swoop in and save them? Are they counting on it being him? Ola exhales, tries again.

"I really found some promising investments," he says, spooning white rice and ayamásè onto his plate. "Rideshare stocks are incredible right now, honestly anything related to the gig economy is too. You and Mom really need to be thinking about retirement. Daytrading is a crapshoot—"

His father shoots him a look.

"I mean, it's not the most secure investing strategy, but if you decide that you want to invest, I could see to things personally. Or we can ask an IB guy to weigh in," Ola says, gesturing at Dare. "Anyway, we can start small, Dad. Maybe two hundred dollars a month, we can do a lot with that."

"We have the house, Pekun. I'll be okay."

"But, Dad, you and Mom can't just keep refinancing the house when things get hard," Ola says, his voice growing more and more impassioned. "You have to consider your health and your age. You both can't just work until you die."

His father shifts his jaw and looks away. Ola knows that he has pushed too far. Marisol touches her palm to his thigh and squeezes an affirmation. Ola slides his hand up her back, runs his thumb back and forth across the bone at the base of her neck.

"Have you both decided what you'll name the baby?" Karen asks. At the mention of the baby, the whole table turns toward them.

"We're still thinking it over," he says.

"Isn't he due in like five weeks?" Karen asks.

Marisol mentions something about potentially giving the baby an English name. She shifts uncomfortably beneath his hand, and he lifts it from her neck. Instead of the name issue, Ola is thinking about Karen's invocation of time. The baby is actually due in four weeks, an impending deadline he has found ways to forget. Not only does the baby not have a name or a nursery, he also has no real place yet in his father's heart. Ola looks at his own father and wants to ask, reminds himself to ask later, about how he should prepare for the enormity of this new thing set to enter his life. Ola watches him, his eyes creased with mirth as he goads Karen, and wonders whether he has been talking about the wrong thing entirely. Instead of preparing an investment prospectus for someone who doesn't want one, he should have been asking his father about how to be a father.

The doorbell rings.

"Who else is expecting a visitor?" his mother asks. "Maybe go and check the security video on my phone."

Karen says it's likely their neighbor, whose youngest son was a friend of Ola's in elementary school. The last he heard, both of Mrs.

Das's sons were serving sentences for credit card fraud. As Karen moves toward the door, their mother is waxing on about how violent the city is becoming, even there on the North Side, how she never thought that it would be like what Chatham was turning into when they left all those years ago. His mother is still talking, her back to the door, but the rest of the table has fallen silent. When Ola looks up from his plate, curious about the sudden solemnity that has befallen the room, he sees a vision from the past standing just there at the front door. Her skin shining like bronze, slick hair inching down to her waist, eyes widening with uncertainty.

"Sola," he says.

How could he have forgotten that one of them was missing?

TWENTY

Thursday, November 22

4:47 p.m.

Sola stands before the house on North Hermitage Ave., its facade in pebbled gray feeling familiar and strange at the same time. She shrugs her puffer jacket more tightly around her neck as the wind picks up. It will be warmer inside, she knows, and still she is suspended just there at the front steps, struggling to ascend them for what will be the first time in a decade. When they sat together at the diner, she told her father she probably wouldn't come to Thanksgiving. It would be too tense, she'd said—it would be better to just leave things as they were. She'd taken up a new job as a sales associate at the Forever 21 on Michigan Ave., and between shifts over the days since she'd seen her father, she would replay the series of events in her head, the broken look on her father's face when she had told him that the damage done was irreparable.

In the years before, the holiday season had come with a tinge of loneliness. Whether it was just her and Aiden in their first apartment in Koreatown, or them and all their friends on a tradition-bucking trip to Bali, there had always been a measure of sadness. It was as clear to her then as it is to her now: What was missing was *them*. The rest of the Longes: Ola's pretentious laughter, Anjola's gentle graciousness, Karen's random outbursts of sass, her father's music, her mother's cooking. She thought of taking a trip to one of the African stores in Uptown, buying ingredients for the ẹ̀wà àgànyìn she'd been craving for weeks, eating it alone on Marquise's couch while watching old episodes of *Moesha*. Or she could have gone with Marquise to his grandmother's house in Roseland, had a solid soul-food dinner replete with the baked macaroni pie and collard greens she had come to love. Instead, she chose to be here, staring at her childhood home in the cold. She brings her finger to the doorbell and her heart stills.

Karen looks as stunned as Sola feels when she opens the door. She steps into the warmth, her heartbeat now echoing in her ears.

"I can't believe you're here," Karen says, holding out her hand for Sola's coat.

She is leisurely in removing it, turning around slowly as she takes in her surroundings. The living room still has the same shaggy brown carpeting, a dark ring near the tiling by the front door. The corduroy sectional and armchair set are still there, sagging in the middle where Sola used to sit when she would braid her younger sisters' hair. The television has been updated, which is likely their father's doing, but it is still nestled between bookshelves, heavy and loaded with cookbooks, books on electrical engineering, nursing textbooks, *Prayer Rain* by D. K. Olukoya, *The Watsons Go to Birmingham*. She realizes Karen is staring at her.

The last time she was home it had been raining, such that the water spot near the window grew and the room had an earthen, damp odor to it. She can still smell it when she closes her eyes. She had been crying, her mother screaming, flinging Sola's journals at her in accusation. Sola had been sure that her mother wanted to kill her for a long time, but that day her death had felt so imminent that a part of her wanted to surrender her body, lie out on the living room floor and allow her mother to pierce her with the arrow-like words she had been reading aloud from Sola's journal. *Afterwards, when Aiden is still inside me, it feels like home*, she had written. *I feel safe.*

Sola cannot hear the word "ashewo" now without shuddering. Still, to this very day, it can propel her mind back to this scene, her mother proclaiming the word so frequently it felt like a chant.

It was the spring of her sophomore year at IIT. Sola was living at home then. The few dorms offered to students were so scarce and so expensive that it made the most sense. Although she'd made good enough grades to enroll at a few schools farther away, her mother had argued that it would be a waste of money for Sola.

Meeting Aiden that spring semester had felt like a kind of freedom after a long imprisonment. He was in the year above her, wore ripped jeans and a genuine leather jacket, and though generally brooding in appearance, he smiled brightly whenever he was with her. He had been her respite, an escape from years of feeling like a domestic servant and not a daughter.

Perhaps it was the heaps of unwashed laundry and dirty dishes that had finally driven her mother to sit on Sola's bed and read through her journals that day when only the two of them were home. By the time she came downstairs to the living room, where Sola sat on the couch, her mother was already seething and sweaty, toting the set of composition notebooks as ammunition. Moments later, after her mother had run out of journals to throw and words to wound, she'd gone upstairs to yank Sola's clothes off hangers and throw them in a suitcase. "I'm not raising any slut in this house," her mother had said, her accent rendering the words slow and destructive like a blunt knife. Sola had never come back home, until now.

Now her youngest sister is looking at her with disbelief.

"Dad invited me."

Karen nods and sweetly takes her by the hand, leading her to the adjoining dining room where the conversation has stilled entirely.

"Hello, everyone," Sola says in a small voice, feeling the least confident she has felt in years. "Happy Thanksgiving."

Her mother turns around slowly. She looks Sola up and down. But her father, seated at the head of the table, beckons her toward him. Sola smiles back at him, feeling safe for a moment. Her eyes meet Ola's then, which widen in surprise and dart from her face to their mother's. Sola has never had much respect for Ola, and now she has even less. Ola is the kind of brother who would give her extra dishes to wash, would tell on her if she refused to fold his boxers, would command that she bring him his plate at the table because he had seen her mother do it and it seemed to him an acceptable way to behave. He had never protected her. Even now, he searches their mother's face for direction as to how to react to Sola's presence. Anjola's face looks almost fearful, eyes drawn wide, lips parted.

"I'm so glad you came," says her father, standing up from the table before her mother can say anything. "Nireti, go and bring your sister a chair. She can sit here beside me."

Sola feels their eyes on her as she makes her way to where her father stands, welcoming the embrace she'd bristled against less than a week earlier. Being beside him steels her somewhat. She sits directly across from Ola now and grins falsely, pushing her contempt for him back down her throat.

"Is this the wife?" She extends a hand toward the woman. "I missed the wedding invite I guess, but welcome to the family."

"Marisol," she says, letting out a nervous laugh as she shakes Sola's hand. "Thank you."

"And with a baby on the way!" Sola says as she begins to scoop some ẹ̀gúsí onto her plate, ignoring her mother's stare from the other side of the table. "No one told me the first Longe grandchild was so . . . imminent."

"Ehn, what do you expect when you choose to abandon your family?"

Sola allows the false smile to fade, stares back at her mother scornfully. This version of events is already grating at her spirit.

"Would you have come if we'd invited you?" Ola asks.

"Absolutely not."

Karen laughs aloud and then covers her mouth when she catches the look on Aunty Funke's face.

"You stuck around all this time?" Anjola asks, leaning with her elbows on the table so she can look at Sola past Karen's large Afro puff.

"Yep," Sola says, reaching over for a mound of pounded yam.

Anjola says nothing.

Sola feels herself the center of the entire table now. All eyes are on her as she turns to look past Anjola to the man seated beside her.

"And you are?"

"Dare." He lifts a hand to wave at her. "I'm Anjola's boyfriend," he says in a voice that sounds like it is reaching for security. Sola watches Anjola's eyes widen and then look down at her hands.

"I take it you're her senior sister," Dare says.

"I am," says Sola. "But I'm not entirely convinced that you're her boyfriend."

Sola turns her attention away from the charade to her right and back to the spread of food in front of her. The fried rice glints at her beneath the chandelier lighting, each grain covered in an oily sheen. Her mother's secret, the one that only Sola knows, is the half stick of butter added to the pot of fried rice at the end. Perhaps the kindest thing she gave Sola, even if it was a form of labor, were lessons in Nigerian cuisine. She remembers the time they spent together in the kitchen as the soft, calm hum of two workers in synchrony.

Her mother sucks her teeth loudly.

"Latifat," says her father, his voice raised in warning.

"Gbemisola, won't you greet me?" asks Aunty Funke, looking at her with the same derision her mother does. They are twins in their misery.

"Preferably no, Ma," Sola says, unraveling her iyán from the cellophane it is wrapped in.

"But that is very impudent," Aunty Funke says.

"Gbemisola," her father cautions.

Sola looks back at Aunty Funke and grins falsely again. "Good evening, Ma."

"How could you be here for a whole month and not tell me?" Anjola sounds hurt, but Sola only shrugs.

"Why?" Sola asks. "So you could make it all about you?"

"You see? I've always told you she was jealous of you, Anjola," her mother says.

Sola had expected common decency. Not arms wide open, not love overflowing, but at least the respect they might show a stranger. Instead, it's this same stupid bullshit. All this animosity. And for what? She wasn't wanted, so she left. And now they expect her to apologize for giving them what they asked for? Absolutely not. But she's more than willing to fire shots back.

Sola swings her head in her mother's direction, boldly looking her in the eye. "Pardon? What is there to be jealous of?"

Karen nearly chokes on her water.

"Where is your own medical degree?" asks her mother. "Where is your own husband? You stay there on the internet, carrying on, trading your virtue for likes."

Sola purses her lips, blinking slowly. She has no rebuttal. If these are to be the markers of success in her life—an advanced degree, a husband, the performance of virtue—she has failed perfectly.

Her father clears his throat. "Everyone at this table will partake in this dinner with civility."

"What type of rubbish civility are you talking about?" her mother says, looking her husband up and down.

"Gbemisola is part of this family," he continues. "You all will make her feel welcome. That is my wish. Don't drive me to anger in this house tonight."

Sola is shocked by the authority with which he speaks. She mostly remembers his quiet acquiescence to her mother's wishes. Where did he find the power to command a room with his voice? Something about this softens her. She remembers that someone wants her there, and that is a kind of security.

"And Sola," he says, turning to her, "while you are in this house, you will show respect to your elders."

"That includes me," Ola says, picking up his glass of wine. He is the only one drinking at the table.

"Well, then." Sola tilts her head. "Respectfully, your hairline is crooked. You should ask Anjola's friend here for tips."

Ola laughs loudly, though Sola doesn't buy it. He lifts an arm to place around his wife's shoulders and she smiles, resting a hand over her belly. Sola realizes then that she has hardly heard his wife speak. She has the sneaking suspicion that it might be because the wife is uncomfortable around Black people. It wouldn't surprise Sola, for her older brother to choose a woman who has an aversion to his people but would make an exception for him.

"I see a barber on the West Side, I'll text you his info," Dare says in that voice of his that just strains for attention.

"The West Side?" Sola says, her eyes wide. "Oh, Ola's too afraid to go."

"I'm not afraid to go," Ola says. "It's just easier to go somewhere close by."

"Ah! You should be afraid o!" says their mother. "These Akátá people are just shooting jẹjẹjẹ everywhere like they have nothing to live for."

"Mom," says Anjola. "You can't say that."

"Why not? It's true." She turns to Aunty Funke. "Ṣé mo n parọ́ ni?"

"Rárá. Lóòtọ́ ni."

"But you both are acting like just being Black American means someone is going to pick up a gun," Anjola says.

"Yeah, like aren't they shooting people in Lagos?" Karen adds. "You guys are always talking about armed robbers back home."

As Anjola and Karen launch into an argument with their mother and Aunty Funke about their anti-Black prejudice, Sola, who is grateful to no longer be the center of attention, begins to eat her food in peaceful silence. It has been a long time since she has eaten ẹ̀gúsí soup that tastes proper, and as the rich oiliness and saltiness hits her tongue, she closes her eyes in pleasure. When she opens them, her father is smirking at her. A look that says: *See, I told you*

you should come home. Sola smiles and voluntarily reaches for his hand.

"Ẹ̀n lẹ, bàbá àt'ọmọ," her mother says jeeringly. Greetings to father and child. The dinner proceeds with strained bits of conversation over a heavy soundtrack of pained silence.

"So, Karen, what are you studying in school?" Dare asks.

"I'm pre-med."

"Oh wow, you all are very accomplished." He looks toward their mother and does a singular nod, as though to commend her for her efforts.

"Thank you, these three bring me so much pride," her mother says.

Sola ignores her mother and continues to relish in the plate before her, sinking her teeth into a perfectly soft piece of ṣàkì, the tiny pockets on the rough side of the tripe bursting with flavor. She has missed this. It's been a long time since Sola ventured to make any Nigerian food for herself. Part of the point of leaving home was to shed former parts of herself, to embrace a new way of being.

"So, Anjola," Aunty Funke asks, "do you think you'd like to stay in Chicago after you've finished residency?"

"I'd like to. I think so." Anjola's voice rings with nervousness, matching the fidgetiness of her body that Sola observes from the corner of her eye.

Sola stands to wash her hands, trying to do it quietly, hoping not to draw attention to herself.

"Clear your father's plate," her mother says in that commanding voice that she seems to reserve for Sola, which, at thirty years old, still makes her feel like a small dog. Sola bristles, looks around at the faces all staring back blankly. She grits her teeth, reaching to take her father's plate.

"Actually, take anyone's who has finished. Then bring the dessert Mari made. It's on the front table."

No one says anything, all of them watching Sola to see what she will do. She knows that they recognize this as a kind of gauntlet. It is her mother's way of showing her eldest daughter her place, which has always been one of dishonor. Had Karen been asked to clear the table—no, commanded to do it—it would've made sense because she is the youngest in the house. No one would bat an eye. But for the prodigal daughter to return home and be re-rendered a domestic . . . Sola is going to do it anyway, but as she reaches to get Ola's plate over the tray of struggle macaroni and cheese, she looks up at the wall behind him and drops it.

"You took down my photo?" She turns to her mother, who is now speaking with Dare about his future plans and hinting at ways that they might involve Anjola.

Her mother furrows her brow. "Yes. Obviously."

"Why would that be obvious?"

"Hmm." Her mother claps her hands together, chuckling bitterly. "Didn't you go and disown yourself for that òyìnbó ráda ràda?"

"Oh, I disowned myself? That's the story you're telling?"

"Yes, now!" Her mother's voice rises. "Instead of facing your studies you were there opening your legs káàkiri káàkiri."

Ola's wife gasps.

"Wow." Sola is livid. "You're really still this wicked, ten years later."

"Will you shut up that your dirty mouth?" Her mother stands from her chair. "Gbemisola, how dare you? I said, how dare you? You just show up at my house without apology? Do you know how much shame you've brought me? You were there parading your body all over the internet. In ten years you couldn't even send a simple text message to apologize, to let us know how you were doing. Can you imagine?" She turns her face to Aunty Funke, speaking of Sola as though she were not there. "She went and ran away from home, I had to be going on Ingramgram to even know whether she was still alive, and now she expects me to welcome her with open arms?"

"Eeyah." Aunty Funke has the nerve to shake her head with her mother and utter the words, "That is very wrong."

Sola turns, stunned. All around her the faces are blank, accepting, as though this is a truth they have heard many times. Heard enough times that it's met with a slight indifference, despite their mother's emotion.

"Ran away?" Sola repeats slowly. She will not allow this retelling of events, not in her presence. "You literally kicked me out of my home. So you mean you just conveniently forgot the whole scene with you throwing my journals at my face, flinging my clothes into suitcases?"

Sola feels what the weight of this admission has done to the room around her. Her siblings sit with mouths agape, forks and water glasses suspended in midair.

Now her father speaks, his voice quiet and stern. "Latifat, is that true?"

"Gbenga, you didn't know the dirty things she was up to," says her mother. "That child has always been incorrigible."

"So you mean you were the one who sent my daughter out of my house?"

"Yes, now. You think I should have allowed her to stay and turn everything upside down? To mislead the younger ones?" She sneers at Sola, raising a finger. "Wòó, if you don't want to confess your wrongdoing, that is between you and God. But you will not stand there in my house and make me out to be a monster."

"I don't have to make you out to be anything." Sola looks at her mother, debating her next words. "You've done that on your own."

She turns into the kitchen, exits through the entryway into the living room so as to avoid drawing closer to her mother. Even though Sola has grown bold enough to find her own words that might cut like a blade, she knows a raised hand will still make her flinch.

Her father is calling for her as she slips her jacket on and makes her way back outside into the cold. She stands on the corner, seething, wondering how her siblings could just sit there and watch. Why did no one, still, even to this day, try to defend her? Anjola didn't raise a single word of protest for her. Karen, the same Karen for whom she drove miles to help in a crisis, couldn't muster even a single objection. They are all a family worth disowning. By force or by choice, she was right to have left them behind before. Except for her father, she thinks; his only sin has been loving her mother so much that he has been blind to all her flaws.

TWENTY-ONE

Thursday, November 22

5:03 p.m.

Ola refills his glass from the bottle on the buffet table, a Bordeaux he had gifted his parents two years ago that he'd also known they would never drink. Pouring slowly, methodically, he tries to forget the look in his father's eyes, a kind of heart-stricken love as he stood and beckoned Sola to the table. How his father had embraced Sola, had bidden Karen to bring a chair for her, his guest of honor. Was it envy Ola felt?

As Sola lowered herself into the seat across from Ola, he read, unmistakably, a self-satisfied smugness in her features. He glanced at his mother then for a reaction he could understand, something that didn't leave him in the dark. Shock. Then anger. These made sense to him, these were logical, this was how one regarded a family member who had abandoned them and then just showed up without warning.

So he understood from his mother's frank expression that Sola was not welcome. But there she was anyway, settling in comfortably beside their father, looking at Ola brazenly and then speaking to his wife without uttering a single word to him. She mentioned the missed wedding invitation, yes, but made no apology, no mention of the times he'd reached out and she had ignored him, no acknowledgment that he was even there, besides that his wife was pregnant. All this hostility, and for what?

"Would you have come if we'd invited you?" he asked, which perhaps had been rude in lieu of an apology.

"Absolutely not," Sola replied. A jolt to his chest. And then Karen snickered, a betrayal. It wasn't that he expected his money to buy Karen's loyalty, but was he so wrong for expecting that his love might? He looked to his mother again, her brewing anger stronger than anything he could conjure up himself, but at least an emotion that made sense. He stood to get more wine.

With his back to all of them now, he takes a long gulp from the glass, trying to drive away the bitter taste in his mouth, the panicky feeling Sola's presence has stirred up in his chest. Sola is interrogating Dare; Aunty Funke is complaining that Sola hasn't greeted her. Ola pours again, more quickly, wonders if he should offer anyone some for a second time, then decides against calling any more attention to himself. He slides back into his seat beside Marisol, who issues to him, just briefly, a questioning look. And in turn, he smiles, interlacing his fingers with hers, squeezes. All is well.

She doesn't look convinced. He turns his gaze to Anjola, who leans on the table and asks Sola about sticking around and not informing her. He feels for Anjola in that moment—the sibling she loves most has betrayed her anyway. Why? Because, perhaps, Sola is incapable of loving anyone but herself, he wants to say. But then the thought feels damning, feels like something someone could say about him.

His mother offers an alternative explanation: envy. He turns this over in his mind. Is that what it is? Sola's been jealous of them? It would make sense, would explain her reticence to engage over the years, her inability to be happy for others. The shame of not being a success. Which, by all counts, he and Anjola are, Karen on her way. Sola the one blight on the family name, and not for lack of opportunity. They've all had the same parents, the same educational opportunities, the same access to nutritious food. Something in her nature must be off, then, worse even than whatever lurks inside him. And whatever is wrong with her is something their father is surely blind to. Even now, whatever spell Sola has wrought over their father seems to be losing its power: the raised finger, commanding that she respect her elders.

"That includes me," Ola says, his tone goading, his lips smirking. One thing he remembers about Sola as a child: a temper worse than his but with none of his charm. It's why their mother had to discipline her the most.

But Sola doesn't take the bait. She tilts her head just slightly and her eyes leave his, her gaze hovering just above them. "Well, then. Respectfully, your hairline is crooked."

He is overcome with embarrassment that Sola has sidestepped his jab and issued a strong right hook to the body. He isn't even sure why it hurts so badly. Something about vanity, something about how she knows his teenage insecurities, how he never felt cool enough for the Black girls. When Ola places an arm around Marisol's shoulders as though to say, *Regardless, someone loves me*, Sola just shrugs, and so, feigning imperviousness, unable to find a retort of his own, he laughs along.

How Thanksgiving has become a roast session he does not know. Now she says that he is too afraid to go to the West Side. A ludicrous accusation. He sips at his glass of wine in a show of ease as his mother orders Sola to take everyone's plates. They are all falling into familiar patterns. Their mother commands Sola to serve him, the elder brother, and she does, standing to reach for his plate. But beside him, Marisol silently lifts a hand as if to stop Sola from taking it. Of course. Of course there is something wrong with this. He can suddenly see it from Marisol's point of view. All this dysfunction. Yes, perhaps his mother has gone too far. But when he looks back up at Sola, she seems to be focused on something else entirely. Her missing picture, not irrelevant, Ola thinks, because even he knew that something was kind of fucked up about his mother taking Sola's face off the dining room wall.

"You were there opening your legs káàkiri káàkiri," his mother says. Ola's eyes widen. This is nasty work. There are plenty of unkind things that he could say about Sola, but to shame her here, at the Thanksgiving table, in front of everyone? In front of her father and brother and two strangers? It's a low blow. Even Ola can't respect it.

Nor does he respect the classless show to follow: his mother standing up, screaming at the top of her lungs about how Sola abandoned them and never reached out and then turning to Aunty Funke for backup. This is not what mothers do. This is bullying. This is, for Sola—it dawns on him as he remembers the last time their mother was worked up like this, the crystal vase—how it's always been. A quick glance at Marisol, who wrings her hands in her lap.

And then it gets worse.

"You literally kicked me out of my home." Sola's voice is full of resentment, loud.

What to make of this, of Sola's rebuttal about their mother throwing her clothes into a suitcase? Ola looks now to his father for the emotion that would most make sense. The furrowed brow is anger, yes, but the thin-drawn eyes are despondence. And Ola does recognize that despair in himself before he looks away from his father and comes back to his own bewilderment. All along his mother had let them think their sister had made herself an enemy, had hated them. She had let them be without Sola for ten years. And for what? Self-righteousness about a young woman having sex? How has he not seen, all this time, his mother's capacity for cruelty? And only for Sola. And why?

Because she dares to exist as her own person, with no half steps, no teetering along parallel paths as he and Anjola and Karen have done. Sola fully plunging herself headlong into a life of her own making, refusing her mother's dictates for her. And still the things their mother accuses her of pale in comparison to the things Ola has done.

"Latifat, is that true?" No impassivity today. Though his father's voice is soft, his words land like bellows. "You mean you were the one who sent my daughter out of my house?"

His mother simpers, tries to cajole. Not respectable behavior. Shameful, actually. Ola watches Sola make her exit, ignoring their father as he calls after her, her body a blur of motion through the front door. And then his father fixes a look on his mother worse than betrayal. The look of love inverted, of sweetness turned rancid, of rotting fruit.

If Sola abandons them this time, it would only be fair. All her hatred, for Ola especially, is well deserved too. He was the dutiful son always taking his mother's side, currying his mother's gratitude and his sister's servitude. His very sense of morality has been shaped by their mother in the form of the knife he always stuck into Sola's back. How has he never stopped to consider what it must have been like for his sister? This dysfunction, as he sees it clearly now, had simply been to Ola the logical ordering of their family's universe. And what does this say about him? Who is he because of it?

He turns to Marisol as though looking for explanation. Surely she must see through him now. But she fixes her gaze down at her hands, clasped tightly in her lap, her body held rigid, except for when her shoulders jump at the slamming of the door behind his father.

She is terrified, he realizes. Karen pushes her chair back from the table, free to extricate herself in ways Marisol is not. He watches Karen turn into the living room, hears the sound of her feet running up the stairs. Dare coughs and looks away from him. Anjola sits with her head in her hands. As the oldest, Ola knows he should for once, finally, do something, say something to his mother, make some attempt at repairing this disaster. But they are not his priority any longer. Ola glances at Marisol again. He owes her, at the very least, the dignity of departure.

They walk toward the parked Volvo without speaking. He reaches for her hand to hold. She swats him away, continues on down the sidewalk in quick steps, remaining just feet ahead.

"What is it?" he asks.

She turns back to him beneath the lamplight, her irises golden and flaring. "I'm sorry. You're waiting for me to say something?"

"I don't . . ." He pauses, his fists flexing in the cold. "I don't know what that was. I don't know what to say." He raises his ungloved hands to his lips, blows heat against them.

"Try."

"I want to tell you that it's never been like that before."

"But?"

"But it used to be like that. When Sola was here, whenever my father wasn't around, it could often be like that. But Sola should have always been here, so really my mother is . . . well . . . She's a problem. All right?" He pauses again, trying to find the right words to explain the heavy feeling that has come over his heart. "And I guess, if I'd really tried, I would have known my mother was probably *the* problem. If I'd cared enough. And I didn't."

"That was insane in there," she says, her hands flailing, the color coming back to her cheeks. "I mean, my family is batshit, sure. But that was . . . ruthless. Love doesn't do that." Absentmindedly she pulls the tie holding back her hair, and he can almost feel the tension leaving her forehead—hair loose, free to speak. Of course, of course she has always been exceedingly prim and proper around his mother, and he had judged her for it. But Ola sees now that loving him left her no choice, since all his life he has hung on to his mother's every word and judgment.

"I kept thinking about the wedding after she mentioned it," Marisol continues. "Like why your mother was so against inviting her, you know?"

"Right. And then I shut you down when you tried to ask."

"I always thought it was weird," she says. "Because how do you just lose a sibling who's like still alive and just go along with it? And as for your mom, like how could you let go of your kid like that?"

"Right," he says again, not knowing what else to say. He has failed as a brother. And by enabling his mother's cruelty, he sees now that he has failed as a son. Holding back tears, he clears his throat, looks down at the ground.

Now Marisol takes his hands in hers, holds their cold against her warm cheek. “I’m sorry. I don’t want to make it worse.”

And if he could speak without his voice cracking, he would tell her that she isn’t, that everything she is saying he needs to hear. Seeming to understand, she links her arm in his, pulling him against her. They walk to the car.

“I liked her though. Your sister?” Marisol says. “Full of fire.”

TWENTY-TWO

Thursday, November 22

5:49 p.m.

It's the sight of her father rising slowly from his chair that will cement this moment in Anjola's memory. It's the fury in his eyes, his fingertips pressing down against the dark wood of the tabletop.

Anjola wants to tell her mother that her sister never misled anyone. When they were younger, Sola taught her how to put on winged eyeliner, how to do the Harlem shake, how to add just a tiny bit of powdered milk to her garri to bring the sweetness out. Before she left, Sola had only been a loving presence in their lives. Anjola opens her mouth to speak, but her voice betrays her, leaves her without sound.

Anjola looks back and forth from Ola to Karen, hoping for either of them to speak up because words have failed her. Where would she begin? Does she announce that she mostly remembers Sola as sorrowful? Does she tell them about all the times she woke up in the middle of the night to hear Sola crying on the bed below hers?

Does she tell them about the memory she always tries to tell herself is a false one? The one that never fails to make bile rise in her belly—the one where, through a sliver of light in a dark-filled room, Anjola saw a man almost as old as their father use her sister's body in a way that choked the child in her? Does she tell them that they only made it worse, with all the responsibility they heaped on Sola's head? What child could survive that? But the words don't come as words. They come as a wave of rising heat over her body, a quickening heartbeat, a dry mouth. She tucks her trembling hand beneath her armpit, folding her arms over her chest.

"Dúró. Sola. Please don't go." Their father's hand is extended and he edges around Karen's chair. But Sola has already zipped up her coat, pulled the door open, thrown her body to the night's wind by the time he can repeat himself fully.

The room stills in stunned silence. The scraping of a fork. The soft thud of a glass cup against the tabletop. The sound of her father's voice as he turns back toward her mother. She looks away from him and folds her arms.

"Latifat. You call yourself a mother?"

Anjola's jaw drops. Her mother says nothing at first. Then she looks around the table, at all the sets of eyes bearing witness.

"Gbenga, a má sọrọ̀ later. Ẹ jọ̀wọ́, nítorí Ọlọ́run."

"No," he insists. "I'm talking to you now. Don't you have anything to say for yourself?"

Her mother looks away from him. She lets out a long sigh. Anjola hears her father behind them in the kitchen, grabbing his keys from the key hook. In a moment he, too, is on the other side of the front door, leaving them all with his fury in his wake.

No one goes after Karen when she runs up the stairs.

Anjola looks around the table, at her mother, at Aunty Funke and Ola and Marisol and Dare, trying to interpret their faces. Aunty Funke stands to retrieve the box from the front table. She places a pecan bar on her plate.

"This is very nice," Aunty Funke says, turning to Marisol. "You made this?"

Marisol nods and smiles hesitantly, but Ola's eyes are full of sadness. A silence ensues again. Dare resumes eating, drawing his fork through the mound of pounded yam to pull apart pieces that he then dips into his soup. There is something about his eating pounded yam with a fork that Anjola cannot abide, that she knows her father would not respect. It annoys her that he seems to feel none of the urgency to leave that she does.

"We need to get home," Ola says hoarsely, standing up from his chair. "It's getting late. I'm going into the office tomorrow."

Anjola waves goodbye to them as they both leave, still unable to speak, still regretting Dare's presence as she waits for him to finish his food. Her mother is sitting there, staring down at the pecan bar on her plate, looking all too sorry for herself but not quite sorry enough for what she has done. Aunty Funke leans back in her chair and gulps heavily from her glass of water.

"A wonderful meal," Aunty Funke says, "very delicious."

Anjola's face involuntarily makes a look of disgust.

"I'm ready to go too," she announces, struck by the clarity of her own voice.

Some part of her hoped that when she made it outside, they'd all be waiting for her—Sola, her father, Ola, Marisol, a congregation of indignants. But when she and Dare finally open that front door and step into the night, there is only wind and chill and the sound of merriment from the house next door.

"Well. That was. That was really something," Dare says when they are on the sidewalk.

"It was," she says. She has nothing else to say to him. This dinner was harder, more vulnerable than lying naked beside him a week ago. She's embarrassed, angry that he has seen her family like this, splayed open before a perfect stranger.

"Do you need me to help you get back to yours?" he asks, placing his hands on her shoulders and squeezing them. "Do you want to come back to mine?"

He reaches for her hand. She shoves it into her pocket.

"I'm going to just order a car," she says with a wave. She turns away before he can open his arms for a hug, before he can insist.

"Thanks for having me," he calls behind her.

Anjola swiftly turns the corner. She paces the adjacent block, her mind looping the same scene: Sola's confession, her father rising from the table, her mother's refusal to admit wrongdoing. She feels sick. She leans her back against a brick wall, pulls out her phone.

Anjola: I'm so sorry to bother you, but can you talk?

Neil: Of course. I'll call you in a few.

And she waits, waits for what feels like an eternity, phone in her right palm, her eyes staring down at the screen. Her exposed hand grows numb in the cold. The screen lights up.

"Happy Thanksgiving, Jo." There is mirth in his voice, the sound of brightness, happy chatter, celebratory music behind him. Nineties R&B.

"Hey, happy Thanksgiving."

"What's up?"

"I'm sorry for interrupting," she says, trying to stop her voice from wavering. "It sounds like a good time over there."

"It's all good. What's wrong?"

She inhales deeply, lets the words tumble out on the exhale. "Sola came to dinner tonight."

"Whoa." The background noise becomes more distant, more muted from his side of the phone. She hears a door close.

"Yeah. And somehow my dad knew she was coming? But my mom didn't. I saw Sola like a month ago and I didn't even know she was sticking around. I didn't even know she spoke to him still."

"Your dad?"

"Yeah. So, you can just imagine how intense that was. Like, I'm shaking, Neil." She lifts her left hand out of her pocket, still trembling, and holds it out as evidence to herself.

"Take a deep breath."

"Okay." And she does.

"Tell me more." His voice is tender in her ear.

"You know how we all thought it was Sola who left? Like how I told you I felt abandoned by her all these years?" Her voice breaks. "It was my mother. *She* kicked her out. *She* made us all abandon *her*."

"Oh my god."

"Like how is this even my family? All these fucking secrets." Anjola pauses. "I just don't know how I didn't know. I wish I'd known. I wish she'd told me."

"But what would you have done if she had?" asks Neil.

"I don't even know." She switches the phone to her other hand so she can put the numb one in her pocket. "I just feel like this is all my fault somehow."

"I really don't understand how you could come to that conclusion, Jo."

She rubs her palm up against her nose, sniffles. "I feel like I was always trying to make up for what happened to her? For her behavior, for her absence? But all I did was make her look bad. My mom literally said she kicked Sola out so she wouldn't mislead me and Karen. Do you know how insane that is? And like, Sola is so not that, Neil. If any one of us is a problem, it's me."

"Hey, hey, hey," he says. "Stop. Stop that right now."

"But—"

"No." His voice is stern. "What your mother did to Sola is the cross she has to bear. I won't listen to you blame yourself for this."

She wants what he says to feel true. But some part of her needs to accept blame, needs to feel like this thing that happened to her family couldn't possibly have gone on without her complicity. She knows how much she has sacrificed in an effort to keep her family stable, how much teenage rebellion she denied herself, how much perfectionism she's taken on. It would only make sense if the fault lies with her somehow.

"I just need a hug," she says from her child self.

"I'm sorry, I wish I could give you one. I'm in New York with Giselle's family until Sunday. Rain check?"

She clears her throat. "Of course, I should let you get back to them."

"Look, before you go," he says, "promise me that you won't blame yourself for this. Just give it some time. It'll all come together, okay?"

"Okay," she says.

He hangs up. She walks back toward her parents' house. The lights are still on downstairs. Through the window into the dining room, she sees her mother sitting alone at the table, staring into space. Anjola turns and walks down the empty street.

TWENTY-THREE

Friday, November 23

When Latifat awakens the next morning, Gbenga is not there. Her eyelids open to the morning light that slips through the curtains, spilling onto his side of the bed. Her head is throbbing, a dull but persistent ache that seems to migrate from her temples to her frontal lobe. She yawns and sits up, her breasts spreading wide and announcing their heaviness with an ache in her upper back. She has often mentioned getting a breast reduction while dressing on mornings past. Sometimes Gbenga watches her, ever ready to chide as she opens her mouth to discuss the potential merits of a tummy tuck or liposuction, cooling procedures to freeze away the obstinate fat that clings to her sides. "Olólùfẹ́ mi," he sometimes says with a smile, "I love you as you are now."

Gbenga. Who could predict that he would embarrass her the way he did last night? Imagine, he invited Gbemisola to come to their house and heap disgrace upon her head. In front of Funke, even, who everyone knows is àmẹbọ and will probably go and be telling all the ladies in their susu group what transpired at dinner. Which, speaking of, she has not yet heard from Dunni, who still owes $200 for this weekend's pot. Latifat makes a mental note to call her as she stands from her side of the bed, crosses over to the bathroom, where she lowers herself heavily onto the toilet seat, cradling her throbbing head in her hands.

She and Gbenga are supposed to be a team. They don't keep secrets from each other. Well, he hasn't kept secrets from her. There are things a woman has to keep to herself, ways to maintain an air of mystery after thirty-six years of marriage, necessary omissions made in order to keep the peace. Gbenga never would have understood driving Gbemisola out of their house. But he also couldn't have understood the intricacies of a relationship between mother and daughter. He has always tended to overlook Sola's flaws, to handle her gently like a piece of glass, perhaps because she is pretty and lepa-shandy (a younger version of Latifat, some might say). But Latifat had seen Sola for who she really was then: a problem.

Is it wrong for a mother not to like her child? She delighted in Sola when she was young and small, high-voiced and giggly, of course. She'd been a sweet girl, obedient, kindly. But by the time puberty struck, Latifat knew that she would be trouble. Elevenish-twelvish was much too early for a child to become so disobedient, not while she still lived under her parents' roof. Sola would always be challenging her mother, refusing to heed any kind of instruction. It wasn't just that Sola became a stubborn teenager (because Latifat could relate to this, having been strongheaded herself when she was young). It was that Sola had none of her mother's tenacity or dedication in the classroom to make up for her strong will. Latifat might have been able to understand all the abandoned chores had Sola brought home strong marks like Anjola did. But instead Sola suddenly brought home C's and D's where she had once been at least a B student. And then how many times had Sola intentionally oversalted the soup before Latifat had to knock her upside that her head like Hausa calabash and show her who the true woman of the house was? Sola had become slack in every arena of life, and as Latifat saw it, love simply did not allow its beloved to become wayward.

So when she'd gone to read through Sola's silly little notebooks, she was looking for something, anything, that might give her a foothold toward understanding. But all she found was luridness, enough to make Latifat see red. She knew that if she didn't act fast, Sola would become a blight on her household. And she'd worked too hard to make this family what it was.

When she packed her daughter's suitcases that day ten years ago, she intended for it to be a teaching moment. The girl was only twenty years old, and she was there giving her sex away to common riffraff for free. Yes, Latifat had acted out of anger. But it was only because she wanted her daughter to walk the straight and narrow path, to keep her legs closed and her eyes trained on her studies. Latifat couldn't have dared to imagine that her daughter would never come back home.

"Ayé mi," she says to no one but herself, standing from the toilet seat and pulling up her pajama pants. Last night, the table was silent after Sola walked out of their house again, and then Gbenga looked at Latifat like she was àjẹ́ for real, a cackling witch ready to transform into a bird and take flight. Her Gbenga, who was sweet like a dried date, gentle as a dove, was so angry with her then that she felt herself having fallen from grace. She quickly brushes her teeth, rinses her mouth, makes her way down the creaky staircase.

Karen is laid out on the couch, an old blanket covering her body, the television playing infomercials without sound. Latifat can never understand why her littlest one likes to do this—to lull herself to sleep before wordless images and awaken to QVC commercials in which white hands with freshly French-manicured tips market emeralds and rubies. She started doing it when she was little, while waiting for her father to return from his late-night shifts, after which Latifat would hear him carry her into the small bed she slept in beside her elder sisters. When Karen became too heavy to carry, he would rouse her from her sleep, gently enough that, were Latifat not a light sleeper herself, she might not have heard him. That Karen is still there on the couch means that Gbenga has not yet returned.

The dining table is a mess, none of the food packed away. Latifat stretches and yawns, preparing her heavy, aching body for the morning's work of ushering last night's leftovers into Tupperware containers, discarding the food remnants on dishes into the trash, and placing them into the sink for Karen to help her wash. Ideally, the children would have all stayed to help her clean up. Gbenga should have told her that Gbemisola might be coming. Yes, she would likely have protested, it was true, but at least she would have been prepared, mightn't have let herself get into the embarrassing shouting match that Sola had led her to. After Gbenga left, the table had been so silent, all the eyes around it watching her in judgment

But none of them knew. None of them knew what it was like for her in the days and weeks after she had thrown Sola out. How that pit of dread sat in her stomach, unmovable. How she would wake in the morning with hope rising in her chest that today would finally be the day that Sola would respond to one of her phone calls. How she would come home from work, exhausted, yes, but not too exhausted for the guilt that plagued her when she looked into her husband's eyes.

That Anjola had been the one to inform her and Gbenga that

Sola was alive and well in Los Angeles was already an insult. But then for Latifat to come across a video of Sola gallivanting with that tattooed ingrate who had disvirgined her and who Latifat knew would never restore her daughter's honor by making her a wife? It was as though Sola believed she was in the right. It was as though she refused to remember that she had a family, a mother who cared about her. Every single time Latifat went on YouTube or Instagram to try to glean details about her daughter's life, it made her love feel like defeat. Of course she hardened her heart against Sola; she had left her mother no other choice.

But of course, no one else cared to try to understand.

She scrapes the pan of mac and cheese into the dust bin, studying how the inside is still sloppy and wet though the top has crusted over. A metaphor for her life, she thinks, their house on North Hermitage Ave. a thing fought for, one child a doctor, another on her way, her first son a successful businessman. It all looks good on the outside. And yet she accepts now that the inside has been rotting. Her children don't seem to understand her, not really, nor she them, but the good three have had enough respect to listen to her for the most part. At least Gbenga has always been a friend to her spirit and to her mind. Now she isn't sure if he might ever forgive her.

She raises the house phone in the kitchen to call him, dialing his number from memory, gets his voicemail, places the receiver back on its cradle. She returns to the table to clear more dishes, the framed print of the Prayer of Jabez staring back at her in accusation.

That had perhaps been too much. Even after a decade of silence between her and her daughter, she admits that removing Sola from the wall went too far. Even Gbenga said so the day he first realized she'd done it. "She may come back home one day," he said. "She's still our child." But Latifat had been so incensed by yet another phone call gone unanswered that she had finally reasoned the rupture was final. Now, for the first time in her life, she feels like a bad mother.

She has an unsettling feeling in her stomach. She can't tell if it is because she has disgraced herself in front of the people she loves most or because her husband has not come home. He always comes home in the morning, even when he goes on late-night taxi runs to clear his head. He is so angry with her that he is ignoring her calls, has let early morning come and go and left Karen sleeping sweetly on the couch, waiting for him.

She slaps Karen's arm, quickly rousing her. "Can you call your father from your phone?" Latifat asks as her daughter yawns and props herself up on her elbow. "He's not answering my call. Good morning."

"Good morning." Karen squints and pulls her phone out from beneath the pillow where she lies. "It went to voicemail," she says after four rings. "Weird."

"No bother," says Latifat. "Go and brush your teeth and then please come and help me with these dishes."

Karen rolls her eyes, covers her head again with the blanket.

"I want to make pap for breakfast, would you like some?"

"No thanks."

She can't remember which of the children it is that likes pap. She is a bad mother in that way too, unable to keep track of their changing food habits, dietary restrictions, and whims of taste over time. When she has time to cook, she prepares what she and her husband like, and enough of it in surplus for anyone in the house who might also want to partake in the meal. No one goes hungry in her house, unless of their own choosing. Which they have sometimes chosen, refusing her cooking in favor of American fast food. This is another problem with her children: They can't seem to appreciate her as fully as she deserves. A mother's work is a never-ending, unrelenting sacrifice of time and energy and selfhood. How many of their classmates had mothers who worked eighty-hour weeks as nurses, came home to cook and braid hair and do laundry and clean, and then took on the spiritual work of praying over them? And each of them does sincerely need her prayers.

Olanipekun is lost. She told Gbenga that they should send him to boarding school in Nigeria for junior secondary school, because by the time he was a teenager he had started playing all that yo-yo-yo music and using dirty pictures of blond women to touch himself, but Gbenga still refused. Why? Latifat did not know. She knows that the Ola of today is well-off and good-looking, and Latifat does take pride in him, but she isn't fooled. She's his mother. What good can come from a boy having so much money and no guardrails to lean on? She can tell that Ola doesn't pray or read his Bible or go to church. She knows that his marriage is in shambles even if Ola himself cannot see it. Her heart is already saddened for this child who will be born to two parents who do not understand each other.

Anjola is brilliant, Latifat thinks, but she has never seen anyone hold herself back the way Anjola does. Of course Latifat has had to push her. Push her to complete the private school applications, push her to study medicine, push her to find a good husband. Gbenga would sometimes say that she was too hard on Anjola, especially with sending her to high school on the other side of the city, but Latifat knew that pressure would build diamonds. Yet there is only so much a mother can do. She can't make Anjola confident, can't convince her to put on makeup and nice clothes and carry herself like a woman who knows that she is going places. If Latifat had it her way, Anjola would be training in psychiatry or dermatology and making a big life for herself in New York. But Anjola doesn't see that she deserves the world.

And Karen. Her baby who prefers not to be seen. She and Gbenga had to force her to go to university outside the city; otherwise she would have been content to live at home. It isn't Karen's fault, it's true, that by the time she turned four, her beautiful brown skin began to form pink, splotchy patches. Latifat is just still thanking God that Karen did not become an àfín in full. Still, she knows that it can't be easy to move through the world in her daughter's skin. But of what use is it to now go and add voicelessness to this her vitiligo problem? As Latifat sees it, Karen has even more of an imperative to meet life with boldness, to seize her own destiny. Instead, she cowers with her books and her internet and refuses to go out and experience the world.

Latifat used to think she was at fault for how her children turned out, but now she knows that most of this is beyond her. So she prays for them fervently, asks God to watch over and guide them where she cannot. And what does she get in return? See the way they all abandoned her last night, each of them disloyal and ungrateful, and that Gbemisola, the most ungrateful of them all.

But they are all her children, Latifat thinks, as she puts a pot of water on the stove to boil. She runs the corn flour and water mixture she left to ferment for a few days through a sieve, presses down on it until only a thick white paste is left behind. It's enough to feed a whole family, she realizes. Perhaps she carelessly assumed that Ola and Anjola and Karen would still be there in the morning, looking to her for what they might eat. This is another problem, Latifat thinks—she hasn't figured out how to cook in small portions. Now that it's just her and Gbenga, the deep freezer in their basement is overflowing with leftovers.

"What a complete mess," Latifat whispers as she pours her pap into a bowl. She comes to sit in the living room and eat. Karen stands to clear the rest of the dishes from the table.

"O ṣé, ọmọ mi," Latifat calls.

"It's fine," Karen says.

There is a knock at the door. Latifat puts down her bowl of pap and goes to find a sweater with which to cover herself. She looks through the peephole to see two police officers on the other side. The cold makes her shrug the sweater even more tightly around her breasts as she opens the door.

"How can I help you?"

"Are you Lati-fat Long?" one of them asks, a young woman who seems like she might be around Anjola's age, with light brown hair that she wears in a bob.

"Latifat Longe," she repeats, correcting their pronunciation. The final *T* of her given name is silent; the *E* in her surname is not. "Yes."

"Can we come in, ma'am?"

They sit awkwardly in front of the television, her bowl of pap now sitting coldly on the coffee table. She can hear Karen in the kitchen, washing the dishes, trying not to be a disturbance.

"Ma'am, we're so sorry to have to drop in on you like this."

"That's all right." Latifat offers a small smile. "What's going on?"

The female officer looks down at the carpet; Latifat's eyes follow hers to a stain from a Ribena spill Karen left when she was a toddler. They've long given up on trying to get it out.

The male officer clears his throat, clasps his hands together.

"Ma'am, your husband's taxi was found on the 5400 block between South Indiana and South Lafayette Avenues early this morning at around seven fifteen a.m."

Latifat's breath quickens, her heart racing. "And?" she prompts them.

"A man was found in the taxi, ma'am. We think he was robbed because there wasn't any ID on him. He was shot. We believe it was your husband."

Was. Past tense. It doesn't register at first. The officer has blue eyes. Latifat stares into them without blinking. Blue eyes always seemed to Latifat to be more cold than feeling. In the kitchen, Karen drops a glass onto the floor. Something in Latifat breaks at the sound. Her hands jump to cover her mouth.

Karen rushes in, eyes wide and white, her fingers covered in soapsuds. "There must be some mistake," she says. "That's not possible."

Panic takes over Latifat as though it is a possessing entity. Her hands fly to her head, snatching off her nightcap so they can properly grip at the strands of hair.

"Ayé mi tì bàjẹ́. Mo kú," she exclaims, not caring that the officers cannot possibly understand what she is saying. "Mo gbé. Mo ni, mo gbé o! Mo dáràn."

Karen sits beside her, wrapping an arm around her waist. But Latifat cannot be comforted by this. So Gbenga has left her, just like that? Someone has taken him from her so callously? It cannot be so. She shakes her head violently. No. Not before he could be made to understand why she and Sola were the way they were. Not before she might hold him one last time, not before she would be allowed to say goodbye.

"We're so very sorry, ma'am," says the female officer, sliding her card onto the coffee table. "When you're ready, feel free to give us a call, we'll try to provide as much detail as we can."

"Olugbenga mi." What manner of world was this? "My own husband. Gbenga, so you've left me just like that?"

It could not be so, it could not be so, it could not be so. Latifat slides to the floor, begins to wail loudly and roll backward and forward on the carpet. She does not care that there are white people in the room. She does not care that her own daughter might barely understand her. This shouting and working out of the body is the only natural expression she has for this kind of news. She will not perform solemnity with socially acceptable sniffles and tears. Heaven and earth and down below will bear witness to her grief. There will be no silence about it. Karen, though, has enough Western composure for the both of them, stands to open the door so the officers might leave them to their shock.

"One last thing, ma'am," the man says, turning to look at Latifat on the floor with visible discomfort. "We'll need someone to come and identify the body."

TWENTY-FOUR

Friday, November 23

Nothing in life has prepared Ola for this, how cold it feels in the hospital basement, the way the hairs on his arms stand on alert. He would have worn a sweater, but he hadn't the presence of mind. He has been moving slowly since the call half an hour earlier, but it's as though he's on autopilot. The call roused him from his sleep, his mother's voice on the other end wailing that he should help her, go to the morgue and identify his father's body, because she couldn't bear to see her husband as a dead thing. Ola assented and, as though he was operating his body from above, ordered a car, stood up quietly from the bed where he and Marisol lay, gathered his wallet and keys, and made his way to the hospital. The programming allowed the news to register, but it did not allow Ola to give in to feeling, not even enough to remember a sweater. He stands there in the morgue hallway, in front of a glass barrier, in his pajama pants and slippers and an old UIUC T-shirt.

He wraps his arms around himself, the seconds feeling like hours as he waits for the attendant to bring out the cadaver. His father. Apparently. His father is now a cadaver. This is a hard thing to accept, this purported death of his father, who only hours ago had been seated at the head of the table with a bright smile on his face, looking every bit the patriarch.

The attendant brings the gurney closer to the window, looks to Ola to gauge whether he is ready. Ola nods. She pulls the sheet down, just to the body's collarbones. The body lies in sweet repose, the eyelids shut, the brows relaxed, the lips pursed in gentle concentration. They are, Ola realizes as he stares at the body, his father's cheekbones, his father's beard, his father's receded hairline. This is unmistakable. Ola nods, says the words, "That's him," pulls his arms more tightly around his own living body. The attendant covers his father up again. Ola turns toward the elevator.

He goes home first, intending to shower and put on warmer clothes. Natasha Bedingfield is playing on blast; he can hear it even from outside. Marisol is in the kitchen by then. At the door, he watches her for a few moments, studying the way she kneads the dough, the skill of her hands, the deft movements of her palms against the sticky white expanse between them.

"I'm making medialunas," she yells above the music. She tells Alexa to lower the volume. "It's a type of Argentinian bread. I think you might like it."

Her smile fades when she studies him further, his back against the wall.

"What's wrong?"

"Um, I have to go to my parents'. My dad." Composure fails him. His chest starts heaving.

She drops the dough, wipes the remnants off on the apron worn over her belly. His cheeks grow hot, his hands draw themselves into fists. Ola realizes she has never seen him cry, and this realization makes him want to stop. He tries wiping away his tears. He turns from her as she approaches him, faces the door and buries his head in his arms as she places a soothing hand on his back. But the sobs rack his whole body anyway, loud and bitter and so unbefitting of him as a man. Marisol attempts to wrap her arms around him. Ola recoils from her touch at first. Then he succumbs to her embrace.

His mother is mute when he and Marisol arrive. Karen and Anjola are sitting on either side of her, their hands holding hers. She looks up at him through reddened eyes, and he nods, unable to find the words yet unwilling to put anyone else through any additional suspense.

"I know it was him," his mother says. "It's like I knew when I woke up this morning that he was no longer with us."

He and Marisol sit down across from her. Marisol places the bouquet of flowers she took from their kitchen at home onto the coffee table. "I'm so very sorry for your loss," she says.

"Why couldn't they just rob him and go?" his mother asks, each of her words punctuated by sharp breaths. "Why did they take my husband?"

Ola almost begins to cry again, just from looking at the state of his mother. His father was not supposed to die in that way, he thinks. Such a man was not supposed to have met his end being gunned down in the street.

Anjola shakes her head, her voice thin. "He was just here. Literally just yesterday."

"Mo sọ fún bàbá yín, that he should stop that his taxi driving. In this day and age, it's just too dangerous. But he was too proud to allow me to be the one to take care of him."

The room grows silent.

"Ah, Gbenga! See what you have led me to," his mother says suddenly. "Mo ti dì opó."

"Has anyone told Sola?" Karen asks, looking around the room.

Ola is struck then by how accustomed they have all grown to her absence. Each child has been summoned but her. And the loss of his father, along with his casual rejection of his younger sister at his mother's bidding, feel like accusations in and of themselves. Sola should be there, and had Ola not been so acquiescent to his mother, he might've thought to fight for her. And had he thought to fight for her, things wouldn't have become so bad, last night wouldn't have gone the way it had, his father would have had no cause to leave the house.

"She should know," their mother says. "Why shouldn't she already know, when she's the one that killed him?"

"Come on, Mom." Ola kneads his forehead with the free hand that isn't clasped tightly within Marisol's. "Don't say that."

"Why shouldn't I say it? She came here and upset everything, upset him so much he went to do that his unnecessary late-night driving to clear his head," their mother wails. "See what it has come to? Gbemisola has killed my husband."

Anjola shakes her head, standing to place a reassuring hand on Ola's shoulder.

"I'll call her," she says.

They are all still seated there when Sola arrives, as though frozen in time. He stands to answer the knock at the door, his belly in knots, because who knows what their mother might do, how the situation might devolve.

Sola looks pitiful, her hair wrapped in a black scarf, her skin bare and replete with dark undereye circles and acne scars. She wears a puffer jacket, leggings, and a velour sweatshirt. It is the most dressed down he has seen her since they were teenagers. Ola is surprised by himself when he extends his arms wide for his younger sister, drawing her into an embrace. He feels her stiffen for a moment before relaxing in his arms, and he wishes, if anything, that he had hugged her so many more times before this. It transpires wordlessly. He makes space for her between himself and Marisol on the couch.

"How could this happen?" Sola asks finally, breaking the silence that has fallen upon the Longe home.

Their mother crosses her arms. "Ehn, sọ fún mi."

"What do you mean I should tell you?"

Karen interjects, her voice clear and her eyes dry. Of the four Longe children, it seems to Ola that she is holding it together the most. He is supposed to be like Karen.

"They found him in his taxi early this morning. He'd been shot. And robbed."

"But what was he even doing out so late, and on a holiday?" Sola asks.

Their mother sucks her teeth and buries her head in her hands. The room falls silent again. Anjola goes to the kitchen to put on a kettle for tea. Ola turns to Sola and studies her again. Their father had been right to invite her home for Thanksgiving dinner. Ola wants to say so many things to her in that moment—how sorry he is for letting life bully her the way it did, for how he treated her yesterday evening, for how confused he was by her presence and how grateful he is for that presence now. But the words will not come. His throat feels like it might be closing in and his eyes are so ready, so willing to spring forth tears. He reaches out and takes Sola's hand. She does not pull away from him.

TWENTY-FIVE

Monday, November 26

Only three days after learning that her father was shot, Sola finds herself back at Forever 21. It's a Monday afternoon, and her outfit—all black—has at least not gone to waste there in the fitting room she is manning. She feels the customers' eyes on her. Not with impatience but awe. She wears a short pleated skirt with buttons hiding the zipper at the hip. A black silk blouse. A genuine leather biker jacket. Black tights, black heeled oxfords, black eyeliner, heavy. Picking up worn clothes from the floor of each stall, she thinks about how mundane this is—the trying on of clothes. A woman waiting in line with her teenage daughter asks Sola if the things she's wearing are on sale at the store. No, she says simply and without apology. Even if her outfit could be found in this bargain basement trash heap, how could she explain that what really makes her clothes beautiful is that she has imbued them with herself? They have been tailored, worn, and loved by her, such that their extravagance has become as comfortable as her sadness.

This sadness feels so familiar to her that she questions whether it has always been there. Though she has never lost a father before, at least not in this way. There was the severing of ties, because she reasoned that if her father could, for most of her childhood, allow her mother's behavior, then he could not also love her. She had assumed that all his calls and texts were an empty show of affection, false concern. But how she wishes she could go back to that day she blocked her father's number. How she wishes they had had more time together, or just that there had been so much less resentment during the time they had apart. He hadn't known, had loved her mother so much that he couldn't begin to fathom the truth. And of course, her mother lied, wanting to remain flawless in her husband's eyes, a jewel of inestimable value. Perhaps sadness suits Sola. But this heavy load she has been carrying (still with her back straight, her posture impeccable) is now unsupportable. Now that she knows her father had loved and wanted her all along, when she had thought no one really loved or wanted her at all, she feels herself about to buckle.

His death raises all these questions about the assumptions she's held her whole life. Like, what if she had told her father about Deacon Titus and what if he had believed her? And wouldn't he have? She realizes now that the same man who stood up for her at that Thanksgiving table was the one who would have sought out justice for her. That he has died not knowing is one thing. But that he has died at all, and in that way, is another thing entirely. And there she is at work, of all places, this grief hers alone to bear because bills must be paid.

All the fitting room stalls are full. Amid the lull, she unlocks her phone. Ola has added her to the family group chat: *House Longe* 🏚. And why does her heart swell when she sees the notification? Perhaps because only they can begin to understand. Her siblings, her fellow bereaved.

Ola: Hey S, I'm sorry this has taken so long.

How are you?

Sola: No prob. Not great. You guys?

Karen: I don't even know how to function

Ola: Very much agreed.

Anjola: Sola, we have to choose a casket for the burial next weekend. Mom doesn't want to come. Will you come with us?

Sola: When

Ola: This evening. The funeral home closes at 8. I can drive everyone. Pick up at 6:45?

Sola: OK pick me up at the Water Tower.

Ola: Alright cool. Will text when I'm close.

When she places the phone back down, relief washes over her. She will finally be in the company of people who know her somewhat, people she won't have to smile for. A customer clears their throat, motioning to the empty stall when she looks up at them.

"Sorry about that," she says as politely as she can. "How many items?"

When she emerges that evening onto the sidewalk, the chill biting through her nylons, she isn't sure which car is Ola's. The window of a gray sedan lowers to reveal Karen waving. Sola walks toward the back and around to the street side. Volvo, she notes. Understated but European. In the warm belly of the car, Karen sits beside her. Anjola looks back at her from the passenger seat. No greetings uttered as Sola clicks her seat belt in.

"Is this where you work?" Ola asks, his eyes glancing at hers in the rearview mirror.

She nods, then wonders if she actually heard derision in his voice or if she just expected to hear it. This is another thing Dr. Ali has helped her realize, that sometimes she is primed for the fight even when none is brought to her. She looks down and sees she is still wearing her Forever 21 lanyard, quickly pulls it off. Karen's face is kindly toward her, and perhaps this is what inspires her to announce, "Yeah, I'm waiting to hear back about design school. So . . . I'm working retail to avoid being a broke bitch."

"What about all your influencing stuff?" Ola asks over the sound of the ticking blinker. She watches him raise a hand in thanks to the driver who lets them in, feels the smooth movement of the car, and is reminded briefly of their father. A split-second ghost. Karen looks over at her with a raised eyebrow.

"I don't want to do that anymore," she says. She doesn't know if Ola knows about Aiden or if Anjola knows or if Karen has told them. She doesn't see it mattering. Their father is dead.

"Well," he says, "we're glad you're here. Thank you for coming."

"Sure. I mean, I didn't do it for you," she says. But this is bait none of them take. The silence castigates her somewhat. She shifts lower in her seat.

"Nice car," she says.

"Thanks," Ola says. "I wanted an Audi. But, uh, actually, Dad was the one who insisted I go for the Volvo." He imitates their father's accent: "Volvo is sturdy and reliable. Audi is just for shakara."

Karen laughs, Sola smiles, but Anjola is silent. After a moment she turns to look at Sola from the front seat, her hair all over the place, heavy circles under her eyes. The two of them, Sola thinks, are inverse mirrors, classic case responses to grief: keeping it together, falling all the way apart.

"How did you and Dad get back to talking?" Anjola asks.

Sola shrugs, knowing she will not tell them about the rich white man she tried to make her sugar daddy. "By chance. I actually ended up getting into his cab one night," she says. "We had dinner together."

"How odd," Anjola says.

"So . . . if not for that, you would have never tried to talk to us?" Ola asks.

"Well, not you," she says. She isn't trying to be hurtful then. It is just true. She would have never tried to see Ola. Maybe Anjola, eventually, when she had the time and energy to deal with her.

"But yeah, honestly, why would I have?" Sola asks. "I guess I always thought you all knew about what went down between me and Mom."

"We didn't," Karen says.

"But it's not like it would have changed anything," Sola says.

"We'll never know now, will we?" Anjola says with a roll of her neck, turning her gaze to the front.

"Nope," Sola says sharply. "We won't." But she feels guilty when she looks over at Karen, her face overcome with so much sadness that Sola regrets her tone.

At the red light, Ola turns his head just slightly. "Thank you for coming," he says again.

At the funeral home, the four of them stand huddled in the front vestibule. A kindly young man comes to introduce himself. Fred Novak. He hands Ola—the man, the authority—his business card. Poor-fitting blazer, navy blue slacks, a tie with Mickey Mouse all over it. He catches Sola looking. For the kids, he explains. She nods, thinking that hopefully kids aren't frequenting funeral parlors, before she realizes that he means his kids at home. She wonders if their father ever carried little vestiges of them when he was out and about. Mementos. Whoever shot their father took his wallet, she remembers, so she'll never know if he carried their photos around. As Fred leads them into the casket showroom, she decides to believe that her father kept their photos on his person, her photo especially, even if her mother took it off the dining room wall.

Fred is showing them the standard options. Interiors customizable. Oakwood, cherrywood are fine choices, pine if they prefer to save; beech is rarer but beautiful nonetheless. Sola runs her fingertips against the glossy exterior of a deep green casket. Seeing the siblings standing there in silence, Fred offers to give them some time to think it over.

"I never imagined doing this before," Karen says after Fred leaves. "I don't know how to explain it. I just never imagined anyone in our family would ever die." She looks at Sola. "Even when you were gone."

Sola says nothing, just keeps looking around that room of caskets, trying to find one better suited for their father than the one she just touched. All these caskets on display, plain and ornate, money still the final arbiter of whose death is most dignified. She turns toward her siblings and, taking in their bewildered faces, realizes that she has had more experience in burying loved ones than they have.

"For a long time, all of you were dead to me," she says, then regrets saying. She tries again. "I wish I could take that time back now."

"Me too." Ola locks eyes with her, his face a picture of sincerity. "I wish I could take it back too."

Hearing him say this, she feels a rush of emotion come over her. Does she hate Ola less now? She doesn't know. All she knows is that she is grateful for him, and for Karen and for Anjola, because they also know what losing their father is like.

"I keep being afraid that something's going to happen to me," Anjola says. "I keep looking over my shoulder, thinking today might be my day."

"Same," says Karen. "Like suddenly it's like dying is possible now. Being killed, I mean. Before it was just this thing on TV."

"Yes! And I've lived in some wild places," Sola says. "Like in LA, Aiden and I rented this spot in Compton for a little while, and there would be random gunshots." She notices their ears perk up at the mention of Aiden's name, but she quickly moves on before any of them can ask about him. "Anyway, there's nothing scarier than Dad going that way. It brings it closer."

Anjola says, "I'd always imagined your life was glamorous out there."

"Not at first, but eventually," Sola says. "At the beginning it was tough. Temporary housing, low-wage jobs, credit cards and payday loans. We were just good at making everything look good before it got good."

"Isn't that the American way?" Ola smiles and Sola is surprised to find herself smiling back. But when she looks at Anjola, her face is so downcast, so sad, that Sola feels her stomach drop.

"I wish I had known. We all could have done something," Anjola says.

"Enough," Sola groans. "This is about Dad, okay? I'm fine. I've always been fine."

Ola touches Anjola's shoulder. "I agree. Caskets. Let's focus. Also, no need to worry about the cost. I've got it."

"Why else do you think Mom asked you to lead this part?" Karen asks with a smirk. This time Anjola laughs too.

"I like the cherrywood," Anjola announces. "It's kind of classic, right?"

Karen shrugs. "Honestly, anything but the white ones, they just seem so . . . pious?"

"I like this emerald-green one behind me," Sola says. "The cherrywood is nice. But this one reminds me of him. The color is quiet but heavy, you know? Deep."

"Let 'em know! My sister is a real designer, not a fake one," Karen says. Sola tries and fails to resist smiling.

"Yeah, that's fine," Anjola says. "I'm not opposed. It's nice. Unique, but nice."

"Great," Ola says quickly, as if grateful not to have had to decide. "That's perfect. Easy enough. I'll go let Fred know."

Sola looks at Anjola, her sister's face again a composite of sadness and anger, which is confusing because if anyone should be angry, it is Sola. But before she can ask why, or even consider whether asking would be worth it, Fred enters the showroom, beaming. "I hear we have a sale."

In the car again. Sola in the back with Anjola now. Karen up front with Ola. She turns the radio to some AM classical station.

The little weirdo, Sola thinks, with her wide-ranging music tastes. Anjola turns to her, her face overcome with guilt as she whispers below the sound of violins. "I'm sorry. I'm sorry that I never told. I'm sorry I never tried to talk to you about it. I think it would have changed something, a lot of things, if I had. So, I'm sorry."

Sola shrugs, unable in that moment to hold both her father's death and her sister's betrayal. Putting aside the ill timing and their other siblings being within earshot, she also refuses to go back to that place in her memory. Is Anjola only sorry because she thinks that, by some odd calculation, it has cost her a father? It's an apology Sola doesn't really trust.

"You're good," Sola says quickly. Isn't that what Anjola has always wanted? Absolution. To be good at the expense of everything else. Her goodness a boulder between their mutual understanding. Fine, Sola absolves her. Let them be free of each other.

Karen turns around in the passenger seat, her eyes wide. "Sola, if you're not too busy this week, do you think you could talk to a caterer about the food for the repast? You're better at Nigerian food stuff," she says.

And though she has seven shifts this week, a scholarship application to complete, and a microblading appointment, Sola nods. "Of course, I've got it," she says. Because maybe, some part of her wants to be good too.

TWENTY-SIX

Saturday, December 1

Anjola has heard often enough that Chicago police do not solve murder cases. Especially not if the murdered are of color. Black and Brown bodies turn up dead on street corners and in alleyways, in warehouses and crack houses, on lakeside beaches and in taxicabs. This is the way of the world. She doesn't expect them to find out who killed her father or why. Sometimes the facts of his death occur to her like a news headline: *Olugbenga Longe. Husband, father of four. Immigrant. Chicagoan. Murdered by unknown assailant as part of taxicab robbery.* And then Anjola remembers that he is hers, her father, that this has happened to her as much as it has to him. Then she feels like crawling into a small ball and turning off all the lights and disappearing completely. She oscillates between moments of hyperactivity and swaths of slow emptiness.

Anjola has been given two weeks off work for bereavement, which feels both generous and like not enough time. She spends most of that first week beside her mother, trying to help her plan a funeral befitting their father. These are things she has never anticipated having to learn. This somber affair that they have emptied out her parents' savings account for feels like a betrayal, a final form of assimilation. Anjola can tell because her father's siblings said so on the phone when her mother called them—a chorus of *You people should bring our brother back home, you know we can't come to America by Saturday, you never helped us get papers, how could you have allowed him to die the way he died, you people in America just throw bodies into the burial plot like refuse.* Had he met a different end, he might have been both mourned and celebrated in Nigeria, the story of his life heralded like joyous news. He would have been danced into his grave and whatever lies beyond.

She feels sorry for her mother. Her father's people back home, people Anjola has never met, has only heard stories about, spoken to on the phone on occasion, feel they have more claim to her father than her mother does. Her mother had to insist, despite the cultural norm that a man's body be buried in his homeland, in front of his own house, that her Gbenga must stay close to her overseas. Anjola lay fully awake beside her mother that night, listening to her cry. Her mother whimpered to God: America had taken so much from her; none of it was supposed to have transpired in this way; they were not supposed to have been in this country for so long, such that even her own children were foreign to her now; they were not supposed to have made this place both a homeland and a burial plot.

He is interred two weekends after Thanksgiving, a proper Christian funeral, everyone donning black, the turnout greater than Anjola could have anticipated. There are other drivers from her father's taxi association, family friends, church members, even some of their neighbors. At the church, so many people come to pay their respects that some have to be seated in the overflow. This surprises Anjola, and then she is ashamed of herself for only now understanding how many lives her father touched.

It all passes as a blur—the preacher's words, Ola's eulogy, all the people who come to shake her hand at the church service. But her mother insists that the five of them and the pastor be the only ones present at the actual burial. Anjola finally understands why when the casket is lowered into the ground. It is so her mother can express her grief in its fullest form, uncaring of who sees her. The Longe children are singing in unison, not a hymn, which might have been more appropriate for the occasion, but the refrain from a simple song their father had loved to lead them in during praise and worship when they were young.

We plead the blood,
the blood
of Jesus.

Her mother's sobs form a grating underscore to the refrain, and Anjola cannot foresee how her mother might ever move on from his death.

Anjola watches as her father's casket meets the bottom of the plot with a soft thud. Here he will lie in this graveyard full of strangers. The Longe children stand in birth order, Ola closest to their mother, then Sola, then Anjola, then Karen. Their mother wails loudly as the siblings continue singing, each casting a white rose into the pit. Sola is the one to lift their mother off the ground this time, wrapping an arm around her waist and leading her down the front cemetery path. Their mother is too delirious with grief to resist her.

They hold a repast in their house, returning home from the cemetery to a whole slew of visitors that Aunty Funke has been kind enough to entertain while the Longes buried their father. Anjola is amazed by the sheer number of bodies in the house. When she was growing up, six people had felt overwhelming enough; now she wonders how the house isn't bursting at the seams. A bead of sweat runs down beneath her breast.

"Karen, can you go turn down the heat?" Anjola asks as she takes off her coat and adds it to the heap near the door.

Her sister nods and disappears into the basement. Ola wanders off to where Marisol sits in the dining room. Sola helps her mother to a seat on the living room couch that the guests have cleared for her. Anjola goes into the kitchen for some ice.

Neil is there helping himself to a plate of rice when she enters. She stops just short of the refrigerator, watching him, waiting to see if he can feel her presence before hearing it.

"Jo," he says, setting his plate down on the counter. He rushes toward her and envelops her in a hug. Anjola breathes in his scent, which is different from how it has always been. Before it had been a dependable, clean, soap smell. Now it is refined with an edge, wood and vetiver.

"You came."

"Of course I came. I knew you probably wouldn't be able to answer my calls, so I reached out to Karen."

Anjola places a hand to her forehead. "It's just all been a lot. Where's Giselle?"

"She's out of town for the next few days. She has a few meetings in New York."

She nods, edges beside him to stand in front of the open freezer and close her eyes. The cool air kisses her nose and sweeps down her neck.

"I know I've already said it over text, and I'm sure you've heard it a thousand times, Anjola. But I'm so sorry for your loss. Your dad was a really good dude. Upstanding, really."

She chuckles. "A good dude. I like that."

"Can I get you anything? There's this amazing purple juice in the dining room."

"Zobo," says Anjola. "It was his favorite. Yes, actually, I'd love some."

As if the day can't get any worse, Dare finds his way into the kitchen, clearing his throat to announce his presence. Anjola effectively ghosted him after Thanksgiving, but she can't be bothered to figure out how he learned of her father's death. She understands now that bad news travels on its own.

"Babe, you haven't been picking up my calls."

"My father died," Anjola says, closing the freezer door to face Dare.

She knows that allowing Dare to come to their family's Thanksgiving dinner had been a mistake, that she ought to have heeded that unsettled feeling she had when he first mentioned it. But she'd wanted to feel like her life was going somewhere, like she was attaining proper adult milestones, the way she suspected that Neil might feel about Giselle.

"I know, I just want to support you," Dare says, reaching out to grab one of her hands.

Anjola lets it lie there limply. She wants to end this thing with him, whatever it might be called, right then.

"Sorry to interrupt, Jo," Neil says, his voice soft behind her. "I've got your zobo drink."

She turns around, mustering a close-lipped smile for Neil, whose eyes meet hers and then look up to study Dare behind her.

"Dare, this is Neil, my best friend," Anjola says, gratefully accepting the cup. "Neil, this is . . . Dare."

"Hey. It's unfortunate to be meeting you under these circumstances." Neil extends his hand in greeting. Dare shakes it firmly.

"It's really a shame," says Dare, shaking his head dramatically from left to right. "Chai! The way that Bàbá died. I still can't believe the way he went."

Anjola wraps her arms around her body, turning the words over in her head. A shame. Her father's death, a shame? There are other words she might have chosen. An injustice, a loss, a sorrow, a divine theft. But a shame? She feels hot. She takes some of the zobo in her mouth, letting the cool sweetness settle beneath her tongue.

"Uh, yeah," says Neil. "He'll be missed."

"I really pray they catch the murderer, it's just too much," Dare goes on, looking at Anjola. "The way these Black Americans are just going around and killing people in this city."

"Excuse me?" Neil pushes his glasses up the bridge of his nose, a move that signals to Anjola that he is ready to disabuse Dare with all the lofty words at his disposal.

"Oh," Dare says as though suddenly aware of his company. "I just mean that, well, you know. Statistically, most murders in this city are committed by Black people." Dare reaches out to wrap an arm around Anjola. She shrugs it off. "I just mean, there's so much gang violence and everything."

"What statistic is that?"

Dare shrugs, pushing his hands into the pockets of his expensive suit pants. "I didn't mean to offend you, brother."

Anjola's eyes widen. Neil clenches and releases his jaw, as though waiting, deciding. "Don't you think that statement was a bit . . . contextually lacking?" he asks, turning back to Dare.

"Oh, come on," says Dare. "Look. The fact of the matter is that it's most likely, given where he was when he was killed, that an African American killed him."

Neil's gaze is steady on hers as he says, "Maybe this isn't the right discussion to be having at a time like this."

She feels Dare glancing between them, sensing something.

"Why?" Dare asks, spurred on. "Is it because you don't have any empirical evidence of your own?"

"You know what?" Neil looks at him incredulously. "You should probably think about that, why the first thing your mind jumps to is that Blacks are violent. I don't know," he says with a shrug and a raising of the hands. "Maybe we deign to give you the benefit of the doubt. Maybe you for some reason have no fucking clue about the forces Black Americans have contended with every day for generations."

"If it's about racism, then why do Africans come to America and do so well?"

"Dare. Just stop," is all Anjola can muster. It is too much work to find intellect now.

"How do you mean?" Dare asks.

"Now really isn't the time."

"Baby," he says, reaching for her hand.

She pulls her hand away, places it behind her back as she leans against the counter. But the word has already been used. Neil looks at her silently, observing her for confirmation. Amid the latent grief she finds embarrassment, and then anger.

"I think it's best if you leave, please," Anjola says, looking up from the floor and directly at Dare's face. "You're upsetting me."

Dare opens his mouth to protest.

"You heard her," says Neil.

"I definitely heard her too." It is Sola's voice. Anjola turns around to find her sister's gamine figure leaning against the doorframe, her arms folded in judgment. She's still wearing the hat she had on for the service, a dainty number perched delicately atop her wand curls, with black netting to cover one of her eyes.

Neil smiles at Sola, and they greet each other warmly as Dare exits the room, his shoulders squared in anger.

"It's all just been such a mess," Sola is saying to Neil. "Shit, if I'd known coming back was going to be like this, would lead to this? I would've tried harder to get my ex to stay."

"Oh, so that's why you moved back without telling anyone? Because things ended with Aiden?" For weeks, Anjola has been wondering why Sola had neglected to inform her that she was living only a few miles away. She thought it might be because Sola blamed her for all the things Anjola blames herself for. But she has tried apologizing and Sola still refuses her. So Anjola decides that if Sola insists on punishing her by keeping her out of her life, then she will accept it, and that she will be punishing too.

"Partially why, yeah," says Sola, reaching for the cup of zobo behind her. "You wanna hash this out another time?"

"Not really," says Anjola, looking away. "I mean, you can just keep doing what you've been doing, you know? Acting like you don't have any family."

Neil promptly excuses himself from the room, forgetting the plate of food he was making on the counter. Anjola picks it up, having found hunger too.

"It was never about you, you know that, right?" Sola says.

"Which part, the leaving or the coming back?"

"Both."

"Fine." Anjola looks squarely at her sister now, her nostrils flaring slightly. "But then you could have said that. All this time you could have said something." Because while Anjola cannot wrap her mind around her mother's overt lies, Sola's omissions also seem to be entirely without reason. Even if Sola could not conceive of the lengths to which Anjola's mind would go to blame herself, even if Sola had been totally unaware of the self-flagellation that underscored every email and text Anjola had sent over the years, Sola ought to have trusted her with the truth.

"Look, my life is literally a mess right now." Sola stands in front of her, an unflinching expression on her face. "I didn't really know what my plans were when I came back. And honestly, I guess, everything that happened with Aiden made me feel kind of ashamed."

Aiden is irrelevant, Anjola wants to say. He has only ever been a distraction, a paltry form of escape. But she sidesteps.

"Dad knew you were living here before I did. Karen knew. Did Ola know too?"

"Hell no. And believe me, neither of them finding out was intentional."

"You and I are supposed to be close," Anjola says, immediately regretting the plaintive sound of her voice.

"Okay, well, yeah. Maybe we aren't, then." Sola shrugs. "What now?"

"You're an asshole."

"All right, cool. Well, you keep standing there and worrying about where I've been and for how long, but our father is still dead, your mother is in the next room literally falling out, and you can't seem to figure out your own life. Like, you're letting Mom pick out the men you mess with?" Sola's lips form a cruel smile.

Anjola slams the plate down on the counter, fracturing the china, grains of rice falling between the cracks. The sound shocks them both.

"This is all *your* fault," Anjola says. She regrets the words as soon as she says them. In the silence that follows, she finds shame. She watches as Sola folds her arms, scrunches up her nose, how her eyes look down at the floor and lose their confidence entirely. Her sister is not as invulnerable as she makes it seem.

"I'm sorry," Anjola says. "I shouldn't have said that."

"No, you shouldn't have," Sola says. "But out of the overflow of the heart, right?"

Sola turns back into the living room. In the empty kitchen, Anjola wonders at the state of her heart. Fragile, yes. Liable to lash out, to wound. All this time she has spent trying to perfect every imperfection within herself, and yet she missed the ugliness that took Sola only an instant to bring to light. She begins moving the pieces of broken plate and rice to the trash.

It's much too late when Aunty Funke finally leaves their house, the last of the guests to depart. She insisted on staying behind to clean. The other aunties, friends of their mother's from church or her university days, are staying in a hotel nearby and promise to come back tomorrow. Ola and Marisol have gone. Karen is upstairs in her room, sleeping soundly in her church clothes. Their mother still sits on the couch, staring blankly at the television screen.

Anjola bends down to remove her mother's black shoes from her feet. Lifting her mother's swollen legs onto the coffee table, she presses a thumb to an ankle, studies the pit that forms when she lifts her finger.

"Are you having any chest pain or shortness of breath?" Anjola asks.

Her mother waves her away. "I don't have DVT, I'm fine."

"Then make sure you do a bit of walking, okay?"

"O ṣé, Doctor," her mother says, clearly intending to ignore her.

Sola sits carefully on the edge of the armchair, like someone who feels their presence is an imposition, as though what Anjola said to her earlier in the kitchen has taken root. She sees it in how Sola holds her body. Anjola goes over to her and places a hand on her shoulder.

"I'm sorry for what I said earlier," Anjola says. "I didn't mean it."

"You did."

"No. I just, I knew it would hurt your feelings."

"I see. Because it seems to you that I'm just not hurt enough?" Sola looks up, her gaze direct and unwavering.

"Sola, I'm sorry."

"Yes, you keep saying that. What is it that you want from me?"

"To stop keeping me out of your life? I'm not your enemy, I'm your sister. I'm on your side."

"Anjola, I'm really supposed to trust that? Are you even on your own side?"

She stares back wordlessly, blinking, trying to understand.

Is she on her own side? It feels, resoundingly, that the answer is no. For as long as her memory allows, she sees that she has put everyone before herself as though this were some Christlike way of being. But how has all this suppression of her own desire, permitting herself only half measures toward happiness, profited her? It hasn't made her family more whole, hasn't undone Sola's suffering. It is breaking her own heart. She sees now that it's her martyrdom that Sola doesn't respect. And why would she?

But before Anjola can respond, their mother stands up and begins to mount the stairs. She seems all out of tears, and this silent mourner of a mother frightens Anjola. The wailing made sense, as heart-wrenching as it was. But this person who is now moving emptily as though she is a ghost herself is nothing like the mother she knows.

"You go home," says Sola. "I'll try to take care of her for the night."

TWENTY-SEVEN

Saturday, December 1

Ola's and Marisol's footsteps echo softly in the hallway, the cement walls failing to absorb the sound of black, funereal leather shoes, wood soles against wood floors. When they reach the front door, Ola pulls away, his back resting on the opposite wall. She turns to look at him wordlessly, one raised eyebrow a question.

"I think I need to take a walk," he says. She nods, and he turns back toward the elevator, listening to the even sound of his steps.

In the wake of his father's death, he has seen the women in his family step up in ways that have exposed him. Sola has handled the catering, the finagling of people in and out of the house, the fitting of countless Tupperware containers in the fridge. Anjola worked beside their mother to organize the funeral service, sobered herself enough to handle details he thinks he would buckle under the consideration of. (Imagine having to determine what clothes to dress his father, the corpse, in? Or what time exactly his father, the corpse, should be lowered into the ground?) Karen has the natural gift of knowing what kind of comfort everyone has needed—a squeeze on the shoulder, a held hand, a gentle word. Marisol has put plates of food and cups of water before him at regular intervals, keeping him alive at this time when he should really be taking care of her. Together, they have all exposed him for his uselessness.

He wants to go back to work. Without it, his time feels rhythmless, structureless. But he has already tried and failed at that. The Monday after his father died, Ola knelt at the door, lacing up his shoes. Marisol stood beside him in her nightgown, telling him that he needed more time, that he should stay home. But it was a text from his mother that ultimately convinced him.

Because Ola was responsible for arranging the funeral pamphlet, his mother had sent him an old photo. It was of her and his father in their midtwenties. They stood beside each other in their graduation robes before a university building, holding their diplomas, their faces unsmiling, the proximity between them the only indicator that they were two people in love. Looking more closely at his father's face in the photo, Ola was struck by how alike they looked. People had always told Ola that he and his father were essentially twins who had come in different generations. But in that moment it dawned upon Ola that he was undeserving of his father's face. If he was the closest image left of his father in the world, he was also a travesty.

So instead of going to work in the week before the funeral, Ola hacked away at the eulogy, buoyed by some resolution to do right by his father. On the third day, another message from Betel came in. He turned his phone over and silenced it, tried to go back to the eulogy, picked the phone up again.

Betel: Did you decide? I'm heading out tomorrow.

Ola: I don't think I'll be able to make it.

Betel: You're definitely making a mistake sir 😉 👀

Ola: I make a lot of them.

Ola knew that the truth would be kinder. But he also knew that if he told Betel he was married, that there was a baby on the way, he would cease to be elusive, no longer a fantasy to her.

As Ola walks in increasingly large loops around their building, he considers the inescapability of his present life. Wife, apartment, job, baby. He wonders how his father had four of them, and then why his father never left. Ola has heard enough stories about Nigerian men who have left their wives beleaguered with children in America and returned home to start up again. Deplorable, yes. But why does Ola feel like he can understand them? It's his father's long-suffering nature that confuses him. There must be some kind of missing gene, something that helped his father reach a state of contentment that Ola himself lacks.

He has been walking outside in the cold for so long that he can't feel his toes or his fingertips. Seeking warmth, he's drawn into O'Flannigan's Pub. Sliding into a seat at the end of the bar, Ola orders a whiskey neat and rubs his palms together. Around him, the bar is full of mostly younger men, mostly white, mostly in casual dress. He shrugs off his wool coat and undoes the button of his suit jacket. When the whiskey comes, he draws in a long sip, enjoying its sickly warmth in his mouth and throat. A group comes to sit in the three empty seats to his right.

"I was talking to this one girl on Tinder. She was kind of dumb," one of them is saying loudly. "And she actually drove all the way from Nowheresville to come see me."

Ola looks over at them as he finishes his whiskey. The boy is maybe in his early twenties, his cheeks dotted with acne scars. No one should be driving out of their way to see a guy like that, he thinks. He cannot fathom how—Ola glances down at the boy's shoes—a guy wearing white Air Forces that look like they've only ever been walked through gutter water is opening his mouth to talk about any woman this way.

"She wasn't even that cute," he's saying.

"Did she not look like her pictures?" asks one of his friends.

"Yeah, but like twenty pounds heavier. Anyway, I didn't fuck her, I fell asleep on her. I've got plenty other options actually worth the effort."

Ola orders another whiskey, pushes the empty glass back across the bar top, trying his hardest not to look like he's listening.

"Something's wrong with these girls, man," says the second boy. "Like they're sending nudes and driving to see dudes for free? At this point, the market is oversaturated with pussy."

"Flooded. I'm swimming through that shit, bro," says the third. They let out hooting and howling laughter, filling the space with themselves.

Ola downs his new glass of whiskey, the burn now a comforting warmth, a slight release of the pressure that has been brewing behind his eyes. He isn't a big drinker, but he doesn't know what else to do with himself. He thinks the whiskey will help drown out their voices, render them slow and viscous. They're guys and they're dumb and they're young, he thinks. He has been young and dumb too, and he has played the game of disparaging women when they weren't there to defend themselves.

But now he is considering whether his father ever did such a thing, whether that was ever a stage his father had to pass through on the way to becoming a man, and if not, where Ola learned it from. How could he have let himself, when all the women he knew—his sisters, his mother, his wife—have proven themselves again and again to be so much more resilient than he? Is he really any better than this boy with the beat-up Air Forces? Ola doesn't know if he's given any of the women in his life their due respect, certainly not Marisol.

He pulls out his phone then, his head swimming.

Ola: I shouldn't have reached out to you.

Betel: Umm, what?

Ola: I'm sorry. It was a mistake. I've just been lonely.

Betel: . . . I think you're panicking, we just need to see each other in person.

Ola: No. Sorry for leading you on.

I don't want this.

Betel: Wow.

Ola: I'm sorry Betel. Genuinely.

Betel: Fuck you.

He deletes WhatsApp before he can read whatever else she is typing and places his phone on the bar top, breathing in heavily. He orders another, downs it, places his head in his hands. The liquor has done its job. He can still hear the boys beside him, but their words are unintelligible now.

But the whiskey cannot numb the overwhelming sadness he feels. He realizes now that he should have stayed home with Marisol, let himself cry while she cradled his head in her lap. He picks up his phone again.

Ola: I don't feel well. Could you come get me?

Marisol: Sure. Share your location.

It is the immediacy of her response. In his mind he first pictures her sitting in her coat on their living room sofa, phone in hand, waiting for his message. But no. Surely she took the coat off, he thinks. Surely she went and made herself some chamomile tea. Surely she changed into her pajamas. In fact, he realizes, she has never just been waiting for him. She has always been fully capable of caring for herself. She never trapped him. He has entrapped himself in his need for her.

Because Ola's head is buried in his arms, resting against the dark wood bar top, he sees her feet first, laced up in thick snow boots. She places a gloved hand on his arm and squeezes. He sits up and hugs her, resting his heavy head on her shoulder.

"I wish we could be friends," Ola says, his words slurred.

"We can," she says haltingly. "You just have to see me."

She settles his tab and helps him put on his coat. Outside, he leans back against the brick exterior of the bar. He breathes in and out slowly, trying to allay the bout of nausea that has just come over him. Marisol holds his hand. The three boys emerge, boisterous, wearing too few layers for the cold. How empty their lives must be, Ola thinks, with nothing to anchor them.

TWENTY-EIGHT

Saturday, December 1

Anjola doesn't go home after she leaves her parents' house. This is premeditated enough that she elects to take the long ride on the Red Line from Rogers Park, then transfer to the 6 bus downtown. She has plenty of time to think through what she is about to do, what she's about to ask for. Bus rides are comforting for her, this one in particular, the way it speeds down Lake Shore Drive, how austere the lake looks on her left, frozen over and enveloped in snow.

It is close to midnight when she arrives at Neil's. For a moment, she entertains the thought that he might not be home, but she presses his buzzer. There is no answer. She presses it again. Waits. He might be asleep. She presses it harder, again, and again. Finally he answers, his voice heavy and slow through the intercom.

"Hello?"

"It's me," she says. "Let me up."

He is waiting for her at the door when she makes it up the three flights of stairs to his apartment. She is panting softly. He leans against the doorframe, squinting as though his eyes are newly adjusting to a flood of light. He wears the shorts that he must sleep in and a yellow hoodie that he hasn't zipped up all the way. She knows he has put it on to cover his own nakedness, and something about this makes Anjola feel ashamed.

He lets her in, takes her coat and her hat and hangs them up in the closet, yawns and even offers her a cup of tea. As though she were a stranger, there on some kind of business matter.

"What's up?"

"I came to apologize for earlier," she says, sitting awkwardly in the armchair in his living room. He is in the kitchen, putting the kettle on. She takes in the large bookshelves that partition his living and office spaces. A basketball lies in the corner, looking unused given the wintry weather. She has an urge to go over and pick it up. She does.

"You didn't have to come all this way." Neil sets down a couple of mugs on the coffee table. He slides some coasters underneath them.

"Since when do you use coasters?" Anjola asks, dribbling the ball lightly beneath her hand as she sits down. She is aware enough of herself to know that this is a distraction, a way to avoid looking up at him.

"Um, well, Winston gave me this coffee table as a gift for finally getting my own place a couple years back. Coasters were the condition."

Neil leans back into the sofa, blowing lightly on his tea. She feels his eyes studying her. Waiting for her to explain further.

"I appreciate you coming to the funeral," she says finally, setting the ball down on the floor beneath her. "I appreciate all the ways you support me."

"I mean, it's the least I could do, really. The least." He clears his throat, places the mug back on the table. There is a lack of ease about him, even amid the grogginess, a rigidity she recognizes as his gingerly approach to her grief. "I really should have done a lot more."

"I'm sorry about what Dare said, and he isn't my—"

"That's not on you." Neil brings his hands together, places them awkwardly in his lap. "You've got enough on your plate. Seriously, you didn't have to come all this way."

"I wanted to."

He nods. There is silence. In the silence she picks up her cup, forces herself to sip at tea that she doesn't want because it gives her something to do with her hands, something to do with her body, which feels increasingly out of place. She's still wearing her church clothes. The plain black dress and loafers make her feel matronly and childlike at once.

"Well. I mean, it's kind of late. I mean you can stay here for as long as you like, I can sleep on the sofa, I can order you an Uber home, it's up to you."

She folds her arms around her body. "I don't want to go."

He motions for her to come sit beside him. She does and, still under the auspices of seeking solace for her grief, lays her head on his shoulder. He has a soft smell to him, like a recently roused baby. He draws an arm around her, runs his hand down the length of the large braid she has made of her locs.

"I'm so sorry, Jo," he says again. "I don't know what else to say. I just can't even imagine what you must be going through."

Anjola says nothing. She wraps her arms around his waist, settles into his body. He kisses her forehead. She is aware that this comfort she presently feels is costly. She knows she should let him go, that she should rise up from that sofa and call herself a ride home. But she feels safe only here. She feels understood and held only here. If she could, she would go back in time and undo every single thing she did to rob them of moments like this one. She wants to better align her life with her desire, to be a bolder person. And had she stood up for Sola . . . but Neil's hand is warm against her arm and he squeezes, drawing her mind away from these places it likes to go. She notices the rise and fall of his stomach and then, closing her eyes, listens to the slow echo of his heartbeat.

"Was it ever going to be me, Neil?"

"Like how?"

She sighs. "I mean like, you and Giselle. Did we ever really have a chance?"

He lifts his arm from her shoulder, pulls back from her. His eyes are sad looking, almost nervous.

"Don't do that, Anjola," he says. "I know how hard things are right now, but don't play about this."

"I'm not. It isn't a game." She reaches out to him, takes his hand. He lets her, then intertwines his fingers with hers. A voice in her head tells her she looks desperate, is making a fool of herself entirely. She ignores it.

"It is though. Because you know it's always been you."

She feels in that moment a new way unveiling itself, that former path of self-denial eclipsing itself behind her. She thinks she must be at the helm of the rest of her life, their life. There can be no going back.

Neil stands abruptly, walks a few paces, places his head in his hands. He is facing away from her. She senses that he is afraid of her, afraid of what is now astir between them. But Anjola is not at all afraid. She stands, touches him softly on his back.

His breath is sharp against her fingertips. "Look, I want to do right by you," he says, turning to face her.

"What if this is right?" she asks. "What if what we want is just the right thing?"

"You're grieving, Anjola."

"I think that death brings life into sharper relief." She takes another step toward him, encouraged by the look in his eye.

He winds his hands around her waist, pulls her body against his. Their breathing slows. She traces her finger along one of his eyebrows. For a moment, she thinks that this could suffice, this moment of clear desire between them. But Neil kisses her then, gently, questioningly, as though he doubts any of this is real. She wraps her arms around his neck, pulling him in closer as she deepens the kiss. His lips are softer, more pillowy than she'd imagined. The hardness is everywhere else on his body, she finds, as she traces her hands over his jawline, his shoulders, his abdomen, down to where he has swelled in his shorts. He lifts her up.

Later, on his bed, as he removes her clothes, asking if it is okay, she is surprised by the tenderness of it all. He reaches into his bedside drawer for a condom, and she gently pushes it away. Because she wants to feel him, because she's on birth control, because she gets tested regularly, she says, and doesn't he? It doesn't take very long, the dexterity of his fingers and his lips bringing her to her climax much sooner than she expected. She is so overwhelmed that tears begin to fall when he enters her. She tells him she loves him just as he spends himself, and afterward, as they lie together with their limbs entangled beneath his sheets, he says it back.

Neither of them falls asleep for a while. They just lie there holding hands. Neil stares up at the ceiling, Anjola at the wall beside his bed. Her eyes make up figures in the darkness that look the way she imagines electricity might, like the sparks of delight that had traveled up her arms when she'd come before. Eventually, Neil pulls her in closer to his body and falls asleep, his lips parted, his breathing slow and heavy and hot against her ear. She thinks then that he might really love her, that all of this might really be true.

The next day, she wakes up to the morning light shining disrespectfully through Neil's large bedroom window. He isn't there beside her. She goes into his closet, fishes out one of his college T-shirts to cover herself. She finds him in the kitchen making some semblance of a breakfast. It smells sweet, like cinnamon. She sidles up beside him in front of the stove to see oatmeal in the pot.

"I'm not that great of a cook," he says after she greets him and kisses his shoulder. "Oatmeal's the best I can do on an impromptu basis."

"You're better than me. In my house it would have been cornflakes in spoiled milk."

He laughs at that, and for the first time in months, it feels like they are normal again; ease has been restored. She watches as his smile fades, and she begins to look around the kitchen for bowls. She can't explain the calm she feels in his space, the casualness with which she opens the cupboard doors as though she lives there as well.

"We need to sort this out," he says, turning off the stove.

"Do we?"

"I'm engaged, Jo."

"Can't we just pretend a little longer?"

They fuck again, on the couch this time, with Anjola on top, kissing him greedily. They eat afterward. Anjola does the dishes. Then they attempt sex in Neil's small shower, as though trying to make up for lost time. They fail so miserably that they fill the bathroom with laughter, opting to wash each other instead, a kind of lovers' baptism. They spend the whole day in that apartment, breathing each other in, acting as though the facts of their lives aren't what they are.

"I thought you didn't want me," he says to her when she is sitting on the edge of his bed, putting her tights back on.

"I didn't know how to say it."

"I don't believe that," he says.

"You're right. I didn't know how to let you love me."

She stands and he zips the back of her dress for her.

"Things would have been different," he says. His palm settles on her shoulder, near her neck, where her skin is exposed. She exhales.

"They're already different," she says. "You know now."

Neil says nothing. He walks her downstairs when her car comes, kisses her at the door, flooding her stomach with butterflies anew.

Having done this thing she has long wanted, having proven to herself that she is not wholly self-sacrificial, she opens her phone to text Sola. Because even greater than her anxiety that Sola might still be angry with her for what she said is the need for this thing with Neil to exist outside her own head, inside the mind of someone who might understand her.

Anjola: I spent the night at Neil's, I'm just leaving now.

Sola: With y'all two? I'm gonna need you to spell it out for me.

Anjola: We slept together. A lot.

Sola: As in?

Anjola: We had sex.

Sola: Wow. I didn't know you had it in you.

Anjola: Me neither.

Sola: How was it?

Anjola: Possibly the best I ever had.

Sola: Possibly?

Anjola: Definitely.

Sola: I could have guessed his stroke game was strong.

Anjola: LMAO

Sola: Damn. Well. Is he gonna break up with old girl?

Anjola: I don't know.

Sola: I see. You know you're grieving still, yeah?

Anjola: I thought you'd be proud of me.

Sola: Are you proud of yourself?

Anjola: Yep.

Sola: Then that's all that matters.

Anjola leans back in her seat, feeling all that good give way to anxiety. It is a humming in her head and a knotting in her belly.

It's late when she gets home. Someone left flowers in front of her door, a vase of now-wilting white lilies. Her heart leaps excitedly as she approaches, but she chides herself for even daring to imagine that Neil sent them. She opens the door and sets the bouquet on her kitchen counter before reading the card. They are from Dare, and they express condolences, not undying love.

She strips in her bedroom, puts on an old T-shirt from the laundry basket. In bed, she buries her head in the pillows, wondering what might become of her life. It's odd, to be on such a sure path and still have no idea where it leads. Her father's death means a lot of things, but this feeling of life being so starkly out of her control lingers most.

She rolls onto her back, stares at the ceiling, thinking over Sola's messages. How quickly the joy has turned to dread. She writes Dare a text, explaining that she has appreciated getting to know him but is no longer interested in pursuing anything romantic, ends it without punctuation, clicks send. She marvels at how terrifyingly easy life can be when she allows herself to do what she really wants.

TWENTY-NINE

Sunday, December 2

Sleep eludes Sola. She rolls over around 2:00 a.m., exhausted but unable to keep her mind from turning. She yanks her phone off the charging cable on the bedside table and then pulls the comforter over her head so that the light from her screen doesn't rouse Karen, who sleeps peacefully above her, snoring ever so slightly.

In her email inbox, mostly junk. Holiday sale announcements, a hair supplier in China has a discount on premium bundles, H.E.R. is performing this week. She nearly clicks the button to delete all of them before she sees the email from the School of the Art Institute. An invitation to interview. She blinks and reads the email a second time. They're impressed with her application. They want her to interview with the department chair. Surprise lifts her heavy heart. And pride. Lying there, she imagines telling her father the news before he leaves for work in the morning, how happy he would be to see her accomplish something that matters to her.

In the covered darkness, she scrunches up her face. For the first time since she returned to her parents' house the day after Thanksgiving, Sola feels her chest begin to heave. She turns onto her stomach, sliding the phone beneath her pillow, burying her face into it so she doesn't feel the tears on her cheeks and nose.

Her eyes are still swollen when she wakes up in the morning. Her mother is sitting at the table in front of a cup of tea.

"Good morning," Sola says, placing her hands atop one of the dining room chairs.

Her mother doesn't return the greeting, just watches her for a moment, her lips pursed in judgment.

"So, Gbemisola, you've been crying."

"I guess."

"It's good. Because the way your eyes have just been dry, me I was thinking maybe it was you that killed my husband self."

Sola rolls her eyes, but she bites her tongue, which is no small thing. It is the kindest gesture Sola can think to offer her late father, to stay in watch of her mother the night after he is buried, to swallow her hurt and attempt to show her mother some measure of kindness.

"Can I make you anything for breakfast?"

Her mother clears her throat. "No o, I'm fasting."

"What are you fasting for?" Sola asks, the words slipping from her lips like water. "He's already dead."

Her mother chuckles, to her surprise, and Sola feels some of her anxiety subside. As expected, she finds a tub of oatmeal in the cabinet above the microwave, begins to make herself a bowl.

"You were your father's favorite," her mother says when Sola sits down at the other end of the dining table.

"Dad didn't have favorites. You did."

"No, I don't have any favorite o. You were just a troublemaker."

Sola shrugs. "And you were . . . unkind, so. I guess we both got what we deserve."

Her mother's hand trembles as she picks up her cup of tea. She closes her eyes.

"What are you even doing here, Sola? Everything had been going so well for us."

"At your big age," Sola says, lifting a spoon of oatmeal to her lips. She has found a kind of calm amid the tension. "You're still looking for someone to blame?"

They sit there in silence. Her mother stares at her as she eats.

"How do you stay so thin eating such heavy food?"

"What's the point of the question?"

"I don't know o, I thought to be lepa-shandy like you, they eat salad morning, noon, and night."

Sola ignores her, finishes her breakfast, goes to put her bowl in the sink. "Do you want any of this food the funeral guests brought?"

"No. Who even knows what my enemies put inside it?" her mother says. "Maybe sometime later this week you can cook stew for us."

Sola stands at the sink, uncertain, unable to decide whether this is her mother's way of offering an olive branch or if it is a trap.

She spends the early evening in the basement, pulling cardboard boxes away from spiderwebs. Though she suspects that her mother threw everything of hers away, she decides it's still worth the search. The old sewing machine is easy to find, since it sits, strangely enough, beside her father's old record player. But where are the sketchbooks? When she was younger, she envisioned making headbands that would be smaller versions of the million-pleat gèlè style that Nigerian women wore. If she can just find that book, she'd have something else to work with, something she might be able to bring along to her interview to show how long she has harbored this dream.

Her phone chimes and she pulls it from her back pocket to read Anjola's text. Sola tilts her head to one side, volleys off a response. One part of her is impressed that Anjola has finally let herself have something she wants; another part of her is doubtful. Anyone can turn to sex to stave off their sadness, but she doubts it will bring Anjola the happy ending she really seeks. Sola's thumb hovers over the letters, wondering if she should say anything more, if Anjola even deserves her concern or advice after what she said to her the day before. Yes, Anjola had apologized. But still, those words coming from her had been so pernicious that Sola had—once she got over the shock—actually respected her for them.

You know you're grieving still, yeah?

Which is to say, at this time, give yourself grace, view yourself with circumspection. We are all in pain. She knows that Anjola will understand exactly what she means.

Sola silences her phone and places it face down. She cuts into another box and opens it to find her framed high school graduation photo. She picks it up and smiles, taking in the chin-length hair perfectly bumped at the ends, impressed by the wonder she wrought with Walgreens eye makeup and blush. She places the framed photo aside and looks at the random scraps of fabric that had once been folded neatly. At the bottom of the box, her hand touches the sketchbook. Her heart leaps as she reaches to grasp it.

"Good," her mother says, almost making Sola jump. "You found the things I packed away for you." Her mother's face feigns hardness, but her eyes are sad. "When you're ready, you can carry your load and go." She turns back up the stairs.

Sola stands there holding her precious book of drawings, this missive from her teenage self, stunned. Had her mother always expected that she would come home?

THIRTY

Sunday, December 9

Karen sits upright, her back glued to the wall behind her. The practitioners are all wearing white. There are about twelve of them, ranging from their twenties to their forties and fifties. Her eyes scan the room back and forth, trying to take all of it in. Jones is seated on the floor beside her, his tape recorder nestled easily between his fingers. Since she agreed to be his research assistant earlier in the semester, she has been tasked with a large literature review project on Ifá initiation ceremonies. It has been surprisingly difficult to find academic information on the subject that doesn't just brush over the intricacies of the practice. But she understands why—some things are best left in spirit, in the minds of the people who experience them, and cannot adequately be conveyed in text.

Still, Karen fears she isn't doing enough. She didn't return to campus after Thanksgiving break. There is nothing for her there and everything for her at home. A grieving mother, a fragile family, a house full of her father's things. She went into his closet yesterday, lifted one of his scarves to her nose. How beautiful, how obscene, that her father's scent still lingered there after his death, a mixture of the peppermints he liked to eat and the Classic Match cologne he often wore. She cried then, as she now cries at things that were once commonplace: shootings reported on TV, the mail that still comes to the house with his name on it, all the family photos with him that hang in various corners of their home.

The practitioners are dancing. Karen tries to take notes, but as the drumbeat picks up, her mind careens back to the day they got news of their father's death, how grief had suddenly seized her mother's body. She considers whether emotions can be seen as spirits that visit once in a while, whether there is a sacrifice she can make to appease whichever god can take away her grief.

"So what did you think?"

She and Jones are sitting at a counter in a pizza shop not far from the train station. She chews slowly on the pepperoni slice from the personal-sized deep dish they share.

"Honestly, I don't know," she answers, without looking at him. Her eyes are trained on the window in front of them. "It almost feels like it isn't my place to be thinking anything."

"What makes you say that?" he asks, regarding her carefully.

Karen shrugs. "I guess, being on the outside of it, like why is what I think important? It's not like I really understood anything."

Jones smiles. "It didn't seem like you were as outside of things as you say you were."

"Why not?"

"I don't know how to describe it. There was a moment there where it felt like you were really in it. When that woman fell and you stopped taking notes and—"

"Oh," she says, growing conscious of his having watched her without her knowing. "I'm sorry."

"No need to apologize!" he says. "Sincerely. And remember, I have the recording as well." He lifts the tiny tape recorder up for emphasis. "But yeah, I mean, in any case, I think you're asking whether an outsider perspective is useful here, and I think it is. But also—another thing about ethnography—being an observer means that you become part of the spectacle too. Your presence changes things."

"Exactly. So what's the point? Like, if I'm not part of this community, why would my attempts at understanding matter? Like why do you even do ethnography at all?"

Jones chuckles and Karen smiles up at him, feeling more at ease.

"Why are you laughing at me?"

"You just have this brilliant way of coming down on things, like reducing years of scholarship into these little quips. It's charming." She watches his laughter subside, feels infused by its warmth. "These are good questions and they've been a subject of debate for a while. It seems like you're getting at a question of objectivity. Like, surely a Santero would be better at taking meaning from that ceremony than you or I would, right?"

"Yes! That's what I'm trying to say."

"Understandable, but I actually don't agree. Being an observer gives you a different sense of meaning making. And I think the process of trying to understand what isn't yours doesn't have to impose a hierarchy of expertise, it *can* be a collaborative process. You can ask the people you're studying about how they make sense of things, you can consult scholars from those communities."

"End rant," Karen says with a smile.

Jones laughs again. "For what it's worth, my maternal grandmother was a Santera."

"Is that like a straight person saying they have a gay best friend?"

"I sincerely hope not. I just meant that—"

"I'm just kidding," Karen interrupts, setting her pizza crust down on her plate. She wants to ask him if he practices himself, but it seems too personal. "I think your grandmother being a Santera, or even me being Yoruba, it like only matters how much we think it matters. Or maybe how much it changes our understanding of what we see."

Jones rests his head in his hand thoughtfully. He doesn't say anything, just watches her. Ordinarily this kind of scrutiny makes her self-conscious, but she senses something adoring in his gaze. Her body flushes warm again.

"Are you into me or something?" she blurts out.

Jones doesn't seem the least bit discomfited by her question. "I adore your mind, actually," he says. "But I don't mean that in the romantic sense."

"Oh," Karen says, a bit crestfallen. It would have been nice, she thinks, for someone who looks like Jones to have thought of her in that way.

As if sensing her dismay, he says, "I think you're striking, it just wouldn't be appropriate."

Karen nods. And then, because she doesn't know what to do with the awkwardness of the situation, she adds, "Well, that's good. Because I don't even know what I'm into anymore. Actually I hooked up with this girl in class earlier on in the semester—Tinu? And then she freaked out and now I don't even know if I'm gay or straight or what."

Jones widens his eyes and clasps his hands together. "You and

Miss 'Saved and Sanctified' in the front row? Yoooo. I never would have guessed that."

As she laughs, she realizes that this is the most fun she has had in weeks.

"Not to belabor the subject," says Jones, "but I hope you know that one encounter with someone doesn't define your orientation. You *do* get to do that for yourself. It took me over a decade to own and understand my own queerness."

Her eyebrows rise at this admission, but she doesn't inquire further. She is surprised to find that she feels—rather than disappointment that Jones is not secretly in love with her—the satisfaction that comes with mutual understanding.

"You're right. There are a lot of things I need to figure out for myself."

"Actually, unrelatedly but relatedly—I think you should consider applying for a Fulbright," Jones says. "They'll fund a year for you to do independent research after you graduate. You could go to Cuba, or Nigeria, or wherever else you'd want to be. And I'd be happy to write you a letter."

Karen's eyes widen. But she doesn't know how she can possibly think of this when they need her here. Her whole family is torn apart, and who will put it back together?

"I don't know, my grades aren't that great," she says with a shrug.

"Try not to worry about that," he says, placing a hand on her shoulder. "Just think about it. Promise me you'll consider it."

She nods. And in that moment, she begins to contemplate what it might look like if she put off medical school for a year or two, how life-changing it might be to live in Nigeria for a time, conducting her own research. Having never been there—this nation of her provenance that her parents spoke of with a mixture of nostalgia and disappointment—she accepts that her imaginings are a bit romantic. But she can picture herself living somewhere remote, waking up every morning to the cockerel's crooning. She would insist that people call her Nireti instead of Karen, would wear bright Ankara every day and have her hair braided in artful styles for a low price. Perhaps she might finally find a place of belonging.

THIRTY-ONE

Sunday, December 9

Ola lifts a small blue stuffed unicorn to his nose. He expects it to smell the way being here feels—soft, powdery, light—but it smells like nothing. Marisol stands some distance away, frenetically pulling onesies off their hangers and dumping them into the shopping cart that the store attendant gave her. She approaches Ola and takes the unicorn from his hands.

"Oh, that's cute, he'll love that," she says, as though their baby is already a real person with real preferences, adding the unicorn to the growing heap in the cart.

She moves around him, touching a plush gray teddy bear for just a moment before adding it as well. He finds her bewildering. The baby is only weeks away now. She walks with a waddle, often holding a hand on her back to support the load at her front. Her breaths are sometimes heavy and labored. But today she has energy. He has none. Or at least not enough to match the flurry of movement coming from her. He feels none of the urgency that inspired her to rouse him this Sunday morning with a cup of coffee and a reminder that he'd promised to come with her to this boutique in Andersonville selling sustainably crafted baby things.

Ola lifts up a jumpsuit meant for a one-year-old. It has tiny brown pinstripes that sit proudly against ivory linen. It costs $150. The first item Ola ever bought for $150 was a silver Fossil watch, its face black with bold white numbering. He'd saved up money from his summer job at the local library between eleventh and twelfth grade, where he shelved books all day. He borrowed plenty of reading material about personal finance and wealth consciousness—*Rich Dad Poor Dad, The 9 Steps to Financial Freedom, Think and Grow Rich.* While his sisters chittered downstairs, he would hole himself up in his room reading, and then he would play around with compound interest equations, not because he loved math but because he loved the idea of money. It had a mind of its own, a fickleness to it if you didn't treat it with enough respect, but the reward of loyalty if you handled it with care, put it in the right conditions under which it could flourish.

He walked into the Macy's on State Street with exact change, confidently pointing out the specific model he wanted to the store clerk, even though her eyes studied him warily.

A hundred and fifty dollars is almost nothing for him now. Not so little that he has no memory of its worth, but little enough that he knows it will be nothing to his son. That the baby will have both nice things and generational wealth brings Ola a mixture of pride and sadness, that he will do more for his son than his father could do for him.

Ola walks back over to where Marisol now stands with the store attendant, presenting the jumpsuit to her.

"This will look great on him when he's old enough," he says.

She smiles, almost looking relieved that he is taking any interest at all. Since the funeral he has been moving about emptily, unable to will himself into feeling much of anything.

"Yes, I love this," she says, touching its hem before motioning for him to add it to her cart. "Which one do you like?" She points to a display of cribs above them. Before he can answer, she says, "I think the white one will go best with the mural I painted, no?"

He doesn't know how she found the time, the energy, the will to paint a mural in the new nursery. But one day last week he wandered into his old office and found that one wall had been painted over in creams and browns and verdant banana leaves. And he knew that he had already proven negligent in his role as a father. The room had no furniture yet.

"The white is nice, but I kind of like that one with the light wood over there." The crib he points at has high straight spindles leading up to a curved bough.

"You're right, Ola, it's really cool. It's kind of modern-looking."

"For that one, we can add a wooden plaque with your baby's name engraved on the front," says the store attendant, opening up a binder with a laminated photo example.

Ola holds it and nods. "That would be cool."

"If we'd already decided on a name," Marisol adds.

The attendant raises her eyebrows. "Oh! Well. Some people don't name their babies for months after they're born."

"Really?" Ola asks, handing the binder back to her.

"She's just trying to make us feel better." Marisol lets out a short laugh that sounds as though it hardly has any air.

"I think we'll just go without the plaque," Ola says quickly, watching Marisol cross her arms and walk a few paces over to the changing table models. He follows, stands close behind her. She moves away. She doesn't ask his opinion on the changing table, simply points out a white one and tells the store attendant to write it down. The air has shifted between them.

She only turns to him again when it is time to pay.

"That'll be just under eleven thousand dollars today. Wowza. Are you folks paying in cash?" asks the store attendant with a wink.

"Not today." Ola lets out a hoarse chuckle, trying not to look too alarmed. He pulls out his card and hands it to the attendant.

"We may be able to get everything to you by tomorrow evening. Your address is pretty close."

"Maybe you can work from home for the next couple of days," Marisol says to Ola as he signs the receipt. "That way we can start putting things together."

"I hope you mean he'll be putting them together while you sit back and watch," the store attendant interjects, gesturing to Marisol's belly. "You're doing enough as it is, young lady."

"No doubt about it," Ola says, placing his arm around Marisol's shoulders. She stiffens beside him.

But outside, the cold forces them to huddle together as they wait for their ride home. Neither of them felt like driving, but Ola insists on an Uber because he can't imagine subjecting Marisol to a twenty-minute walk to the train, even though she tells him that she takes hour-long walks every day when he's at work. Snow falls thickly around them, blanketing the sidewalk, chilling the tips of their noses.

Her arms are wrapped around his waist, her head tucked against his chest when she says, "He deserves a name, Ola."

"I know. Of course."

"I haven't wanted to bring it up. I know how much you've needed to be there for your family. But we have a family too."

"I'm sorry," he says. "I've been avoiding it."

Their car pulls up and he opens the rear passenger door for her, closes it, slides in on the other side.

"I'd like for us to choose a name today," she says, reaching out to hold his hand. "We can sit down at the table, make lists, both try to be open."

"I think we can do that." Ola nods. "In our culture there's this way we honor our ancestors, especially if a child is born soon after the passing of an elder."

"I really loved your dad, he was a great guy." Marisol sighs. "You know I had a lot of respect for him. But I can't agree to name the baby after him, his name was quite difficult to pronounce."

"What happened to being open?" Ola pulls his hand away from hers. "And naming him after my father wasn't exactly what I was suggesting."

"All right. I just . . ." She falters for a moment. "Your father made a lot of sacrifices for you guys, right? He left his country, he worked so hard, he stopped speaking to you in Yoruba, he let you marry someone like me."

"Where are you going with this, Marisol?" Ola tries not to raise his voice, briefly meeting the curious gaze of their Uber driver in the rearview mirror.

"My point is, where would you be now without your father's sacrifices? I want our baby to own art collections, or galleries, or his own Fortune 500 company. I want him to move through the world with pride."

"You don't think I move through the world with pride?" He glances out the window at the wet, snowy mess on the street. "Do you know what my name means, Marisol?"

"Something about wealth, right?"

"Olanipekun means that success and wealth have no limitation." He looks directly at her. "Names aren't about just copying whatever's top ten in the US right now or what the other ladies in your Lamaze group think is quirky enough."

"I'm not in a fucking Lamaze group, Ola, it's a prenatal meditation circle."

"Okay, sure," he says dismissively. "But my point is that a name is about deciding something about a child's destiny. It's about an origin story, it's about who the child belongs to. Like, I take more pride in the name my father chose for me than I think you could ever understand. And because of what it means, I would choose my name again and again and again, no matter how many people butcher it."

Marisol runs a hand over the raised leather on the empty seat between them. Her eyes have tears in them. "I don't want you to be mad at me."

"Look, at the end of the day, you're the kid's mom. I get it. You'll inevitably end up doing more for him, not even because I intend it, but because that's just the way of the world." Ola shrugs. "So you can have final say on his name and that's fine. But please, don't assume that my name is a source of shame, and don't make his name some shit that's cute just for the sake of being cute."

Marisol lifts her hands to her cheeks, wiping away the tears from under her eyes. "Okay, baby, I'm sorry. I still want us to choose his name together." She reaches out to grab his hand again and he lets her, the tears from her fingertips moistening his palm.

The driver clears his throat, announcing their arrival. Ola dutifully helps her out of the car, holds the front door of their building open for her, helps to remove her coat when they get inside. She wordlessly puts on a kettle for tea, goes to the fridge to retrieve a pot of soup to heat for their lunch. They don't have much to say to each other, but as Ola watches her, he imagines that these roles of domesticity they rely on, while sometimes stifling, are also their own language of care. He pulls out his phone and sends a Slack message to his boss: Working from home over the next few days, sorry for the short notice.

THIRTY-TWO

Wednesday, December 12

There are times when Anjola thinks that medicine was a mistake. She is usually too exhausted to think thoughts like these, but in the two weeks that she has had away from work for bereavement, her mind comes often to this point. She tries to remind herself that intern year is the hardest, but at times medicine feels like one long grueling road at the end of which there is no light.

Her first day back at the hospital ends just four hours into a twelve-hour shift. Anjola has to call in child protective services because she suspects a four-year-old is being abused at home, and then, unable to contain herself, Anjola slides to the floor in the main hallway and begins to bawl. The chief resident sends her home and mandates another week of leave.

In her empty apartment that afternoon, she strips her body of the hospital scrubs and steps into the shower. She neglects to use a cap, letting hot water run in between the interstices of her locs and down her face, her back. She opens a bottle of some kind of fruity tropical shampoo, and as she lathers up, she considers why all hair products marketed to Black women are named after sweet things or foods from warm places: coconut, mango, honey, avocado, smoothie. And then as she rubs her generic shower gel over her face and body, she considers whether she might benefit from a trip to an island far away. The idea comes to her with such force that she quickly rinses off, wraps a towel around herself, and makes her way to her desk. She is looking at pictures of Aruba, Turks and Caicos, even Seychelles when she hears a knock at her door. She glances through the peephole and sees that Neil is on the other side. When she opens the door, he pushes his glasses up on his nose and draws his lips into a satisfied smile.

"I wasn't expecting you to actually be here," he says.

"Then why'd you come?" She beckons him inside and closes the door behind him.

"To leave you this." He pulls an envelope from his back pocket. "Giselle was late in putting the engagement dinner invites in the mail, so she put me on hand delivery duty for local folks."

"She couldn't just send an email?"

"Come on now, you know how she is."

Her eyes lower. In the eleven days since they first made love at his place, they have had three four-hour-long phone calls, good sex in her apartment twice, and only one instance of Neil having to comfort her while she cried about her father's passing. Not for one second of those eleven days has she allowed herself to consider that Neil would still intend to go through with this wedding. She stares at the off-white envelope he extends to her, then takes it from him. The cardstock is thick, expensive-feeling, would be lovely, even, if it did not also feel like the weight of his betrayal. She places it on the small table to her left.

"I'm still trying to figure it out, Jo."

"Of course."

He touches a hand to his forehead. "I know I'm a shitty person."

"No," she says. "That's not true." She reaches for a hug. He kisses her, gathers her hair in his hands.

"Did you put on a leave-in?"

She shakes her head no. He goes into her bathroom and retrieves another fruity-smelling concoction, as well as a small tube of oil that she bought months ago. He motions for her to sit down in her desk chair. He separates her hair into quadrants, braids the length of three, sprays conditioner on each section of hair before rubbing it from her roots down the shaft. The feeling of his fingers against her scalp as he oils it sends a thrill of goose bumps up her arms.

"So, Aruba?" he asks.

She has the urge to ask him to come with her. She suppresses it. "Yeah. Anywhere warm where people go to forget their problems. I need to get out of here."

"I'd miss you," he says.

She doesn't say anything for a little while. He continues moisturizing her hair. There is safety in the silence between them. His fingertips lightly massage her temples.

"Work was really bad today," she says.

He asks her why and she tells him the story of the four-year-old, all her blue-black bruises, the mother's silence in response to Anjola's questions. "I had to call in the social worker and then they separated them," she says. "It was bad."

Neil stands at the kitchen sink, washing the remnants of jojoba oil from his hands. He doesn't say anything. She turns from her computer to look at him.

"I don't know if I did the right thing," she says.

His eyes look sad, disappointed even. "I don't know either."

She watches him turn to dry his hands, and because she knows him, she knows that he is weighing his words, hesitating.

"What would you have done?" she presses.

"I mean, the child welfare system is basically carceral," he says, carefully refolding her kitchen towel. "But I mean, I get it." He shrugs.

Anjola places her head in her hands. Her mind replays the scene again and she sees the young mother, frightened into silence, the screaming little girl, her eyes wide and bewildered, angry tears streaming down her cheeks.

"I'm a mandated reporter," she says when she looks up at him finally. "And as a teacher, so are you."

"I understand," he says. "I wish there'd been another option, but . . . I mean, you did have that legal obligation."

"And?" she asks, still sensing that he has more to say.

"And . . . I would only call in the state as a last resort. But I get it. For you maybe that was the only resort. And as a doctor, you aren't as much of a fixture in your patients' lives the way a teacher might be."

"But?"

"But sometimes I wonder, like, Anjola, some of the things you told me about your family back in high school? If any of our white teachers had heard and had the same prejudices about your family that they do about Black Americans . . . they could have called DCFS on y'all too. And where would you be then?"

"Wow." She stands to walk toward her living room window, tightens her towel beneath her armpits. "That's so fucking low."

He sighs deeply and walks up beside her. "I'm sorry. I didn't mean to make it personal. I was thinking aloud."

"About how I'm a fuckup of a doctor?" she asks, turning to look at him. "Don't worry, I know."

"No, you're not. That's not what I meant. You're well-meaning. But yeah . . . I do think DCFS only perpetuates harm."

"So what exactly should I have done, then?" she snaps. "Sent the kid back home to her abuser?"

"I don't want to argue. Let's just drop this. You're right."

"Well, I'm sorry that I'm not the radical comrade of your dreams," she says. "I'm sure Giselle would have made a much better decision in my position."

He takes in a sharp breath as though wounded. They stand there at the window, side by side, their hands resting on the sill, centimeters away from each other but not touching. Even in their cold silence, she knows that she doesn't want him to leave. She inhales and exhales deeply in cycles, trying to calm herself.

"I just got really defensive," she says. "I didn't mean it, not that way." She goes to sit on the couch and he follows.

"You did," Neil says. "And it's okay. I fully acknowledge the messiness of our situation. And I don't want you to hold back from me."

"In my mind this should be so clear? And I guess because it isn't for you, it makes me feel like I must not be enough."

He looks hurt. "Anjola, no, that couldn't be further from the truth."

"Then I really don't get it," she says. She believes that he loves her, but she cannot understand how anything still keeps him from her. It is impossible that he would love Giselle more, she thinks, and she cannot fathom his loving them both equally.

"I think I'm struggling with duty," he says, removing his frames and setting them down on the coffee table. "Duty to her. To my word. I made a promise."

Duty she knows well. She understands in this moment that this is why she loves him, that this is what they share, and that this is also what hinders them. She resists this knowledge.

"But, Neil, what's your promise to her worth if you love someone else?"

He is quiet. They sit there for some time. Even amid the tension, he clearly wants to be close to her, draping his arm over her shoulders.

"I don't like the kind of person this makes me," he says, breaking the silence. "Like, as much as I like getting to show you how I feel about you, I don't like being the kind of person who cheats on their partner."

This strikes something tender in her. She knows that if he were someone who could be entirely at ease with cheating on his fiancée, he would not be someone she would respect. But she needs him to overcome this.

"Going through with it isn't going to make it any better. It isn't going to change what we've done," she says.

"I want to do the right thing." His eyes are sad again. "I don't want to hurt either of you."

She doesn't want to hear this. She wants to hear that he loves her so much that he is willing to risk bringing Giselle pain. She wants what they have to be worth his allowing himself to be in the wrong. She also knows that he has to decide this for himself. So she pivots.

"Do you know how full of wrongness life is?" she asks, trying and failing to suppress her frustration. "At this point, who even cares? Like, is it wrong that some dude shot my dad for petty cash? Probably. But everyone's living by their own warped calculus at this point."

"Jo, are you talking to anyone about your father's passing?"

"Fuck off."

He takes her head in his hands. Her eyes well with tears.

"I really want to support you," he says. "Just let me know how."

They sit there like that for a moment. She kisses him and kisses him and he surrenders. Finally, he undoes her towel. His lips find her nipples and she moans, back arching until her clit grazes against the swell in his jeans. He reaches down and strokes her lips with his fingers. A violent heat comes over her.

"Can I?" he asks.

"Please," she says, but her voice demands it.

He shifts lower on the couch; his face hovers between her legs and he stares at her in wonder, as though this is his first time seeing her in this way. A moment later she feels his tongue pressing against her. She sighs contentedly, then groans when he adds a couple fingers, bucking her hips against his mouth. When she comes, the pleasure washes over her body in small waves, in pinpricks that even reach her fingertips and toes. He kisses her stomach and lays his head there.

She asks him to fuck her, and he doesn't hesitate to gather her up in his arms and carry her into her sparsely decorated bedroom. She watches from her mattress on the floor as he strips his clothes, her mind recording the goldenness of his skin and the strength in his thighs. When he enters her, she closes her eyes, focusing on how filled up she feels, the rubbing of his stubble against her jaw, the scent of him. He comes inside her, loudly, his voice almost a roar.

He kisses her and then lies down beside her, holding her body against his. It is dark outside now. Bridgeport is silent at night. All she can hear is his soft breathing against her ear. She likes this. In a way, she likes that he has made her no promises.

THIRTY-THREE

Monday, December 17

Karen rises on a Monday morning to receive a cryptic text from Tinu offering something like an apology and a request to meet, because she wants to explain. Karen starts to type a response about not being available, but the part of her that aches for understanding accedes.

She hasn't been to this ice cream shop since she was a teenager, when she would divert her route home from her magnet high school downtown and end up here, gorging on sundaes by herself. She enters and the bell rings behind her, and she is hit with the familiar smell of fresh cones and sweet cream.

Tinu is there waiting, her arms crossed protectively. Karen stands before the booth, unsure of what to do, and she opts for a stilted wave. Tinu waves back.

At the counter, Tinu insists on paying for Karen's butterscotch sundae, makes a show of retrieving a heavy credit card from the tiny Dior bag on her arm. Back in the booth, Karen takes a spoonful of the sundae and waits for Tinu to speak. She lost her appetite before she came in, she realizes, but she needs something else to focus on apart from the tense silence between them.

"I never really explained to you why I was sent here to finish high school," Tinu says. Karen shrugs. It is quite a normal phenomenon, as she understands it, for Nigerian kids who have papers and money to get to study in both countries at some point.

Karen watches her look down into her lap. Tinu has taken out her weave over break. Without it, she looks smaller.

"No, you didn't."

Karen makes divots in her ice cream, pushes butterscotch syrup into them, not looking at Tinu but listening.

"Have you heard of Tongues of Fire Ministries?"

Karen hasn't. Of all the Nigerian churches her mother has shuffled her to over the years, that isn't one of them.

"My father is a big pastor back home," Tinu says. "Like really big. In Nigeria, some pastors are almost like heads of state."

Karen waits for her to continue.

"I've never really liked boys," she says. "It's always been easier for me with girls. When I was in secondary school back home, I kind of fell in love with this girl. We tried to be secretive about it, but someone reported us, and one day we were caught in the dormitory. Especially because of my father's standing, the school was really quick to tell my parents. And really anyone who was willing to hear. Everyone at school knew, even people outside of my school who knew my family knew. It was humiliating. My parents didn't flog me. But they pulled me out of school and locked me in my room, alone, for like six months. They wouldn't speak to me. I was only allowed out every evening for family prayer, and sometimes my father would sit me down afterwards and make me talk about it, this spirit of lesbianism.

Sometimes he would speak to the spirit itself, not to me, telling it about how evil it was and how it must leave his daughter."

"Wow."

"Don't feel bad for me," Tinu says. "The girl I loved, Olamide, was sent to one of those small-small churches for conversion therapy. I heard she was raped, repeatedly."

Karen studies Tinu's face, and it is blank.

"After those six months, my parents just decided to send me here to finish high school. They had a family friend in Schaumburg who was willing to let me live with them."

"Do you talk to your parents now?"

"Not really."

Some part of Karen wants to reach out and hold Tinu's hand, but she knows better now. She looks out the window instead, studies the piles of snow on the sidewalk, one portion of them stained yellow. Listening to Tinu recount her experiences feels like a betrayal of the shame and confusion Tinu left her to contend with all on her own.

"My life has honestly been fine. My parents still send me money even if they don't talk to me like a human being. I like our school, I've made friends, I feel normal again."

Karen is surprised to hear Tinu say this. Every time the two of them had run into each other, there had been so much tension that Karen assumed Tinu was a chronically unhappy person.

"I was in London over Thanksgiving break a few weeks ago. Can you believe I was actually out there forcing myself to hook up with guys? And I hated every second of it. And I kept thinking of you, how happy we were when we were hanging out, it just made me reflect on how being normal isn't worth being miserable."

Karen is struck by Tinu's complete unawareness of the happenings of her life. Happiness has been so far from her for so long that she has no expectation of meeting it again. In lieu of happiness, she'd give anything for a kind word from a friend. She thinks then of Rachelle. Beyond a text message inquiring about Karen's whereabouts and a "sorry for your loss" card in the mail, she hasn't spoken to Rachelle much at all. Karen doesn't know why she thought that Tinu might have asked her how she's been doing, but she understands in that moment that they never would have worked out, as friends or anything else. Tinu fails to imagine that Karen has a life of her own.

"You lashed out at me," Karen says, her arms prickly with heat.

Tinu nods.

"You made it sound like I had pushed you into what we did. But, like, you wanted me too. And that was my first time. You made me feel like garbage after."

"I'm sorry."

"Then you made me feel like I was hurting you by existing somehow."

Tinu purses her lips, nodding, shifting uncomfortably, growing impatient with the apology required of her.

"Why did you ask me to come here?"

"I just wanted you to know that I was sorry. Nothing I said that morning was true."

"Okay, thank you for providing that context," Karen says curtly. She understands that this is all about Tinu's desire to unburden herself.

"That's it?"

Karen is thoughtful for a moment, trying to decide on the right words. She considers how Tinu has assumed the primacy of her own story.

"I don't know what you were expecting," she says. "But if you're wondering if I'm grateful for you asking me to come here so you can trauma dump, I'm actually not."

"That's not why I asked you to come."

"Okay, because it feels like you just assumed I'd forgive you or something. And I don't know what even got you to this point, but I do know that you didn't care to think about whether I'm in a space to hear all of that. You don't know what I've been dealing with."

Tinu pouts a bit. "I'm just trying to be better. And I wanted to apologize for how I treated you."

"Cool." Karen slings her bag over her shoulder and stands from the table.

"Karen, please."

Wordlessly, she picks up her barely touched sundae, throws it in the trash, and walks out the door.

The sidewalk in front of their house is littered with trash. Old Doritos bags and empty soda cans have found their way into the leafless hedges; Styrofoam containers sit happily on top of the drain covers on the sidewalk. As she turns the corner, she shrieks as a rat scurries past her foot. There are too many rats in this city. When she finishes college she will move far, far away. Maybe she'll do her Fulbright research in South Africa, though she knows little about it. As kids, she, Sola, and Anjola watched *Sarafina!* over and over again on VHS while Ola was at basketball practice. Then they would act out some of the scenes. Anjola was always Whoopi Goldberg's character, Sola was Sarafina, of course, and Karen was her close friend. Sola was an abysmal singer, and it was never long before they were all howling with laughter. Karen smiles to herself.

As she enters the front door of her parents' house, the melody to "The Lord's Prayer" from the film plays in her mind. She takes off her boots near the door and begins to hum.

"You sing well, you know?"

Her mother is lying on the living room sofa, her hands settled on her stomach. It is humid inside. The aroma of seasoned rice fills the room.

"Thanks," says Karen.

"Where were you?"

"Out doing something for school."

Her mother's eyes are closed. Karen comes to stand near her, reaches down and strokes her mother's hand. It is the first time her mother has been downstairs since the burial. Last week, Sola came back to prepare a meal for them in bulk, then Karen took a portion upstairs to their mother, only to later find the tray of food untouched. She tried again the next day, with the same result. Karen doesn't want to be resentful, but her mother's mourning is taking up all the space and it feels like there is no room for any of her own.

"Dad would want better for you," Karen says, dropping her messenger bag at the end of the coffee table with a loud thud. She regrets saying anything as soon as the words leave her mouth.

Her mother opens her eyes suddenly. "What do you mean?"

"I just know," says Karen. "He'd want you to take good care of yourself."

She goes into the kitchen, surprised to find Sola there at the stove, quietly stirring a pot of fried rice and shrimp. She is wearing an apron, which feels too distinctly American for the food she is cooking.

"I'm surprised you're back again so soon," says Karen.

"Yeah, girl, me too."

Sola wears leather pants and boots and a cropped red sweater. Karen studies her from head to toe, the way her straightened hair falls down her back like water, the French tips that grace the ends of her long fingernails.

"Where are you going after this?"

"I got a meeting with the department chair at the Art Institute," Sola says. "For the design program?"

"I'm so happy you applied!" Karen says. "You've got this."

Sola smiles in response, then dishes out some of the fried rice and gives Karen the bowl to take to their mother.

"Did you eat today?" Karen asks, setting the bowl down on the table and handing her mother a spoon.

Latifat says nothing. Karen watches her mother hoist herself up, disturbed to see how gaunt she has become, how grief can erode a body. It's different for Karen. She can't stop eating. In the middle of the night, she often comes down to the kitchen to find expired Kit-Kat bars or Pepperidge Farm cookies that have long gone stale, then gorges until her stomach hurts and her mouth tastes so sugary it begs for water.

Sola comes out of the kitchen just as their mother puts a spoonful of rice into her mouth. Karen watches as she swallows and then makes a jeering face.

"Gbemisola, after I trained you for how many years," her mother says as she chews, carelessly allowing a few grains of rice to fall from her lips, "you still can't cook simple rice?"

Both sisters stand before their mother in stunned silence.

"Okay. What's wrong with it?" Sola asks calmly, in the voice one would use to pacify a small child.

"No salt! Any idiot can salt rice. I mean what's wrong with you?"

A subtle thing about Sola—when she's wounded, her eyes seek comfort from the ground. It's her tell. Karen watches Sola look down, just for a moment, and feels her sister's spirit bow. Then Karen thinks about what Jones said about the outsider's sense of meaning making. From her place at the family's periphery, she has learned to watch and observe well enough. But she knows now that it hasn't left her unscathed, that she no longer wants to be a bystander.

"You can't talk to her like that!"

Their mother looks up at Karen in surprise. So does Sola.

"You never even say thank you." Karen's eyes brim with tears. "She comes all this way to cook for you, to keep you alive, and you never say thank you."

"It's okay," says Sola.

"Ehn, who told you I want to be alive?" Their mother's eyes are also welling with tears. "She came and killed my husband for me, why would I want to be alive?"

"How could you even open your mouth to blame her for this?" asks Karen, her voice breaking. "It was you. *You* caused all of this. *You* lied about why she left. For years, Mom. How could you lie like that for years? Don't you have any shame?"

"Wòó, Nireti, má jẹ̀ kín fọ́ etí ẹ. I'm still your mother."

"Come slap me, then! All you like to do is beat and yell. It's like we're not even real people to you. Just pawns you keep pushing to whatever you think success is."

"Is it a crime to want good things for your children?"

"That's what you call what you've been doing?" She is now delirious with anger. "Honestly, I don't know how Dad ever loved you."

She has gone too far. The stricken look in her mother's eye says it first before her body does, swaying uneasily as she stands and leaves the room. From the half bathroom in the hallway there is the sound of running water.

Karen is crying, overwhelmed by sobs that start stomach-deep. She feels Sola's arms around her, her hand on Karen's cheek, coaxing her head down to rest on her chest. "It's okay," Sola is whispering, "we'll be okay."

She is safe in her sister's arms. Her breathing slows.

"You'll be good," Sola says after some time, using her thumbs to wipe tears from Karen's eyes. "We'll all be good."

Perhaps out of respect to their mother, still within earshot, they say nothing else. But Sola takes both of Karen's hands and squeezes them, and she understands that Sola is grateful. A moment later, Karen watches Sola shrug on her puffer jacket and leave.

In her room, Karen stares up at the ceiling. Everything has gotten so bad so quickly, and she starts to wonder with church logic whether God has withdrawn his hand from them, whether they have been completely abandoned to their misery.

Her phone lights up. Jones has texted her a link to the Fulbright website.

> The application is due by the end of next week, which is daunting, but I really think you should do it. I can write a rec letter for you.

She opens up her laptop to look at the website again. They will pay for her to go away for a year and do research after she graduates. Nothing appeals to her more in that moment.

The knock at her door is so soft, so questioning, that Karen isn't sure that she hears it. When she opens the door, her mother stands before her, her eyes downcast. She enters silently and sits at the foot of the bottom bunk, hands clasped in her lap. It's hard to see her mother so reduced in this way. Karen stands on the other side of the room, her breaths slow and shallow.

"I just wanted her to be excellent," her mother says. "I wanted that for each of you."

"But at what cost?"

Her mother is nodding, trying to hold back tears. "We could have been happier."

Karen doesn't know what to say. Watching her mother, Karen realizes she will never fully understand her. And still she comes to sit beside her, studies the skin tags that dot her cheeks and the backs of her hands. She has no way to account for the set of experiences that have led her mother to behave the way she does, but she knows that her mother was once a child herself.

THIRTY-FOUR

Monday, December 17

As Sola leaves the train station, she tries not to think about the scene she left at her childhood home. But when she recalls Karen trying to stand up for her, she has to pause in the middle of the sidewalk and take deep breaths to stop the tears from falling. That someone else, apart from her father, has tried to advocate for her. That this person would be Karen.

Outside the front doors of the SAIC building, she shivers in the cold, shaking off all the feelings of sadness and unworthiness that are so familiar to her. Unsure whether this will be her first chance or her last, she must offer a stellar performance. Inhaling deeply, she squares her shoulders and struts through the automatic doors, buoyed by the certain click of her heels against the vinyl floors. As she waits for the elevator she tries not to look too in awe of where she is, but she is struck by the school's lobby, how its clean lines and brightly colored modernist furniture contrast with the building's art nouveau exterior.

It's as though she has stepped out of the old world and into a newer one, more full of promise.

Feeling a restored sense of hope after her interview, Sola is disappointed to find that Marquise isn't home when she returns. Unsure of what to do with this feeling of good-things-to-come, cheeks flushed and chest hot, she emerges onto the frigid balcony. From her inner coat pocket, she retrieves a joint and lights it, smiling again as she recalls the dean's commentary about her design.

Finally, something is beginning to work. Sola thinks back over the past few weeks, how everything has fallen apart around her. Chaos is a lot on the body. She has to give herself props for making it to her lash and nail appointments, that her lace is still melted properly, for never going more than one day without a full-face beat. Letting herself go is not an option.

Neither is letting herself off the hook. She knows her father's death isn't her fault. Nor is she to blame for the way her mother treats her. But she also sees the many ways she betrayed herself through the falsehoods she had come to believe—that she was unworthy of loving, of protecting. Forgiving herself then, she forgives them too.

Inside, lying on the sofa, she stares up at the exposed beams on the ceiling high above her, thinking thoughts of ascension until she begins drifting to sleep.

She is awoken by the slow trill of her ringtone. It's Ola. She thinks of the last time she saw him, the day of the funeral. In her mind's eye he's still at the pulpit, delivering the eulogy. Fine, sharp, British-cut suit. Quality leather shoes with wooden soles. That same crooked hairline, only that time, endearing in its familiarity.

"Hello?"

"Hey," Ola says hesitantly, as though surprised the call hasn't gone immediately to voicemail. "Hey, Sola. I was thinking of you. How are you?"

Her mind is clear, so she says without hesitation, "Since when do you think of me, Ola?"

"Awhile. More often than you'd think."

She doesn't know what to say to this, though his words warm her. After a pause, his words hanging in the air, she changes the subject. "Hey, I know we didn't talk much after the funeral, but . . . I wanted to give you your flowers. You really ate up that eulogy."

"I did what now?"

Sola laughs. "You need new friends. I mean it was a really good speech."

"Oh. Thanks." He sounds so hesitant and uncertain that Sola wishes she could pass the joint she was smoking earlier through the phone. "Actually. I guess I'm also calling because . . . I just wanted to thank you too. I mean, for showing up. For Dad, for Mom, especially after everything."

Her voice is mirthful and light. "My therapist thought it might be good for me to confront the past. So . . . I'm trying to not run away. You were a shitty big brother, FYI." And then she giggles at her own admission.

"Sola, are you high?"

"Yes, but I still mean what I said."

He is silent but for his heavy exhale.

"Hello?"

"I'm sorry," he says. "I didn't know how bad it was. But I could have tried to know. I want to make it up to you."

"Make it up to me how? Please." She doesn't intend to dismiss him, but his words make no sense to her. This is a debt none of them can repay. It's why she hasn't really been waiting on an apology from him or Anjola or their mother even. No matter how much or little they do, her forgiveness can't be earned. Only freely given.

"I'm good, Ola. I've always been good, even when I didn't think I was. God's got me." Sola turns over onto her side, hoping that he has understood this as her pardon. "Make it up to your wife, make it up to that baby you've got coming."

"How do you mean?"

"Like be there for them. You know why you were a shitty big brother? Because you always did whatever was easiest for *you*. You know how you kept talking about not being able to fill Dad's shoes in the eulogy? This is how you do it. You make your wife and kid the priority."

"Sola, I didn't call you for a lecture." And though his voice is soft, she suspects that some part of him has taken offense.

"But, Ola, you don't even know what you called for. It's okay, just let me read you," she goads, her voice taking on a singsong quality. "You have the money, the resources that you need to be a present father. So do that. Dad would have done it if he could. He wasn't absent by choice. So don't confuse absence for masculinity or some weird shit like that."

His silence she takes as permission to continue. "Wifey seems nice. I mean, nobody knows why you decided to marry this non-Black woman, though I'm sure we can guess. It doesn't matter. If she's not deranged or praying on your downfall, try to be a good husband, you know? Honestly, I'm sorry for the girl. She has to be married to you."

"Wow," he says, but he is laughing on the other end of the phone. "You know I'm your elder, right?"

"So?" Sola smiles, deciding that she now understands him completely. All this time she had thought him unscathed and resented him for it. He's been overcoddled, for sure. But isn't that a different kind of load to bear? Learning this late that love takes kindling and stoking work, diligent effort, that it isn't just handed to you? The same way she's had to learn, this late, that she even deserves love at all? She forgives Ola because she knows now that he is just like her: messy, unsure of his place in the world, striving to make it to somewhere only God knows.

"Also, even though you weren't a good big brother, I actually don't think you're a shitty person," she says. "So, if you want, I'm willing to let you try to be my friend."

"Yeah?" he asks, and Sola begins to take comfort in what she had never before imagined. She pictures him smiling at her through the phone, passing back the imaginary joint. "Nothing would make me happier."

THIRTY-FIVE

Wednesday, December 19

Karen sits in the armchair her father loved. Her mother lies calmly on the sofa, and from time to time, there is the sound of tinkling laughter. Their eyes both follow the figures in the Yoruba film with rapt attention. They are watching a poor man leave his wife at home and go to a ritualist for a solution to his poverty. As the husband amasses wealth and houses and cars, his wife is nowhere to be seen. Her friends and family come looking for her, and at the end, the woman's mother unlocks a secret room in his house to reveal that the husband and ritualist have turned the wife into a zombielike being, eternally bearing a calabash atop her head. Inside the calabash are stacks of crisp naira notes. This is the source of his wealth.

"Ah! Ọlọ́run má jẹ̀," says her mother, snapping a finger above her head. "This is why I always tell you and your sisters to pray for good husbands, but you all will just be looking at me."

When Karen was younger, film scenes like these would terrify her. She would watch with chill and confusion at scenes of ritualists standing before carved statues, chanting in Yoruba for long stretches with subtitles that only read *[incantations]*.

But now Karen turns to her mother with a smirk. “You mean so a man won’t use juju to sacrifice us for money?”

“It can happen o. You don’t know the things I’ve seen in this life. The world is a strange place.”

“Sure.” But Karen now lives in a reality that insists on more logical explanations for things. Surely her mother has never seen a woman turned into a money-generating zombie. But what if this were a metaphor for the free labor that men often extract from women in relationships, and would that make its meaning any less true? She considers, for a moment, the possible limits of her own belief.

“Do you think these types of things can happen here, Mom?”

“Of course. Some of these witch doctors have power that can cross borders,” says her mother, nodding emphatically. “One really really has to be prayerful.”

Karen resists the urge to prod her mother with more questions, but internally she wonders about the hierarchy of gods, their alignment with the hierarchy of peoples. Realizing that this could be the subject of her research proposal, she pulls out her phone to type a few notes. As her mother rants about the many inadequacies of a homeland that has not been hers for over thirty years, Karen thinks of her religions class, and then of Rachelle. Karen taps to her text messages, isn’t sure what to say exactly, then pushes herself to write the first true thing she can think of.

Karen: It really made my day when I got the card you sent.
Thank you.

She is surprised to see the three dots appear instantaneously.

Rachelle: You're so welcome! How've you been?

Karen: Up and down tbh. I've been spending a lot of time with my mom. I need to come up with more reasons to get out of the house. Lol.

Rachelle: I hear you. I'm at my auntie's house and they're driving me crazy.

Karen: Haha. If it wasn't for this fellowship application I've been working on I would have gone crazy. How did the rest of the semester turn out btw?

Rachelle: What fellowship? And good enough. And I got into the winter photojournalism seminar. So I get to go back to school in a couple weeks . . . yay?

Karen: The Fulbright. And wow! Proud of you.

Rachelle: That's amazing, I'm sure they'll pick you. And yeah, I'm excited. But it's been a while since I've done any good photography.

Karen: Thank you! And I'm sure it'll just take some practice.

Rachelle: Actually . . . wait!!

Karen: ??

Rachelle: You should let me photograph you.

Karen: Okay, why not?

Rachelle: and also audio record? It's like this digital journal project thing.

Karen: Sure. It would make me really happy to see you again.

Karen is pleased with her own lack of hesitancy and she smiles to herself.

"Who are you smiling at?" her mother asks over the sounds from the movie. "Your boyfriend?"

"No, Mom. It's my friend from school. She's a girl." Though she still can't imagine telling her mother about it, she realizes that if she were gay, there might be a kind of autonomy for her there. She would be free to go about things at her own pace, without all the expectations people have for how straight relationships should progress.

Rachelle: That's sweet. How's tomorrow?

Lincoln Park Conservatory at noon?

Karen: Sounds good. Is there anything in particular I should wear?

Rachelle: Wear whatever you want. You always look good.

Karen: !! Okay, see you tomorrow.

Her coat is cobalt blue, stark against the Edenic scene at the conservatory that surrounds her. It's the coat she got with Sola earlier in the semester, a loud, shaggy, polyester number. When she saw it in the closet that morning, she knew that this was its day, that it would not have very many days because she would rarely find the confidence to wear it. She also wears the black fedora that Sola chose for her, and from time to time, she lifts her hand to touch its rim or the wine-colored feather nestled in its band. She sits on a bench by the rubber trees, busying herself on her phone, trying not to look like she's waiting.

"Yo! This coat is crazy. I love it!"

Karen looks up and Rachelle beams down from above her. She wears a black peacoat, an oversized gray sweatsuit, Air Jordans, her camera.

"You said I could wear anything," Karen says. Standing to hug Rachelle, she takes in the scent of vanilla, soft notes of frangipani, something like pepper. "And that's . . . a really good perfume," she says when they part.

"Thank you." Rachelle is still grinning, then she lifts her hands to her cheeks. "I cannot get over this look. This is so dope."

Karen almost mentions Sola's assistance and then decides against it. Instead she says, "Thanks, I was kind of like, when else am I going to wear it, you know?"

"Girl. Every day! You should wear it forever."

Karen, imbibing the joy emanating from Rachelle, chooses not to darken the moment, to say she fears she might not be attractive enough to wear it. And besides, she reasons, the coat *is* hers.

"So what's the vision?" she asks instead.

"All right so, it's supposed to be like a candid conversation? I'm going to take pictures while I record," Rachelle says, lifting up a small device. "And if there are any questions that make you uncomfortable, you can skip them. And it's okay if there are some that you want to answer but might take awhile. Cool?"

"That works," Karen says with a nod.

"Great. So, first question." Rachelle switches on the recorder. "What motivates you?"

Karen shrugs. "The will to live? I don't know. I suppose I want to make my family proud or whatever."

"Why?"

"Mmm. Maybe because they're who I belong to? I guess. When do you stop belonging to your family? You don't, right? Or maybe only if things go badly. Maybe I have this feeling that I owe them something. Maybe it's that whole child-of-immigrants thing."

"Yeah. That makes sense. Do you think that's fair?"

"I'm not sure how much that matters," Karen says, entirely unbothered by the soft clicking of the camera shutter. "Sorry, not in a rude way, but I mean, like maybe that's not the thing I want to question? It's more, why is there this assumption that having been born here is this opportunity that I should be in my parents' debt over? Why doesn't anyone think about what our parents take from us by choosing to raise us here, you know?"

Rachelle is nodding. "That's good. Say more. What do you think they take?"

"Belonging. Having a real stake in where you come from because it's yours. Music."

"Music?"

"I don't know how to explain it. And I could be wrong," she says, "but I guess I mean like a harmony with life? Like, not needing to code-switch. Everything just flowing. Ease of understanding."

"Young Karen the Philosopher. That should be your rap name. Like when are you dropping the album?"

Karen laughs, covers her mouth with her hand. "If I had an album to drop, this would be the perfect promo."

Rachelle directs her to walk into the Fern Room, and Karen is wholly at ease as Rachelle continues taking photos of her.

"So. What do you think life is currently teaching you?" she asks.

"With my dad passing away and everything?" Karen looks up at the glass paneling above her, contemplating Rachelle's question. "It's still wild to me that he's not here. My mind really can't comprehend it." The shutter is clicking rapidly, but she continues looking above, her eyes fixed as her mind wanders. "It's like, I'll hear a song or something and think, 'Oh, Dad loves this song,' and then I'll have to correct myself. 'Past tense. Loved.' Like even though I saw them put him in the ground, I'm still confused as to why he's not here."

Rachelle straightens, lowers the camera from her face. "I'm really sorry, Karen."

"Thanks. But yeah. I think life is teaching me that it's senseless really. It can mean whatever meaning you give it. It can mean nothing at all. But you don't know how long you get to be here, so I guess choose a side?"

"What side are you on?"

"Meaning." She nods once, resolvedly. "The side where I know that I'm here because I want to be here. I know that I like being alive. I like when being alive feels good. Maybe that's it."

Karen wanders away from Rachelle on her own, steps into the Orchid House. The soft clicking of the shutter follows her. She touches her thumb to the petal of a yellow flower. "Like, this is what I'm here for," she says, staring directly into Rachelle's lens. "This feels good."

Rachelle lowers the camera again.

"Is something wrong?" Karen asks.

"No," Rachelle says. "Incredible, actually."

Karen's cheeks warm and she looks away.

"Hey, I want to be honest with you." Rachelle lifts the camera strap from her neck, slings it over her shoulder instead. Her hand slips into her pocket and she fumbles with the recorder.

"Okay?" Karen feels that her heart has stilled entirely, as though she were suddenly suspended in time.

"I'm really into you. And not just in the friend way." Rachelle wrings her hands together. "I'm sorry about the timing, I know you're going through a lot. And I'm sorry if it rubs you the wrong way or anything, like I want you to know that I don't expect anything of you. I just wanted to let you know—"

"I like you too," Karen says, interrupting her. She steps closer. "In the more-than-friends way."

She ignores the slight tremor in her hand and slips her fingers between Rachelle's. Standing on her tiptoes, she touches her lips to Rachelle's forehead.

"Oh, we're forehead kissing now?" asks Rachelle with a giggle. Her fingers traverse the length of Karen's coat, leaving electricity in their wake. When Karen softly presses her lips against Rachelle's, all she knows is that she is doing it because she wants to be here, and because it feels good.

After some time they part. Karen asks if Rachelle has any more deep questions for her, and because Rachelle says she has enough content for the project, they walk hand in hand instead. They wander in near silence, making the same loop around the greenhouse again and again. Sometimes Karen will comment on a plant she likes. Sometimes Rachelle will say that she agrees. Sometimes they will look at each other and smile. But mostly, they are just together.

In the middle of the night, Karen's phone sounds. She has been unable to sleep, thinking of kissing Rachelle and how good it felt when they hugged goodbye and wondering at her luck and wondering why Rachelle even likes her but reasoning that it doesn't matter. She's thinking about how nice it felt to be held in public, and hoping that things will still be the same when they're back at school, and remembering how lovely Rachelle smells and how funny she is and how she has the most mellifluous of voices.

> Rachelle: I had to work on this immediately. It's a rough draft but let me know what you think.

Karen feels a slight pang of embarrassment when she sees how unsentimental Rachelle's text is. But she clicks dutifully on the private Vimeo link. It's just under four minutes long. Holding her phone above her head in the darkness, she watches a succession of still photos of herself. Lying there, she sees her vibrant coat, her audacious fedora, her exceptional skin, and that all together, they are beautiful. The video is overlaid with the sounds of the conservatory—of running water, of birdsong, of the clarity and wisdom of her own voice. It is as though the best parts of herself have finally come into view. Only love could render her as art in this way.

> Karen: So . . . we should just get married, I think?

> Rachelle: Peak pisces behavior lmao.

> Karen: I love it. Thank you so much.

THIRTY-SIX

Friday, December 21

Marisol fans herself with the instruction manual as Ola sits on the floor just below her. Assembling the arched end panels of the crib was the easiest part. The side panels and corner supports are proving difficult though. He reaches up to take the manual from her again, and she sighs in discomfort.

"Do you want me to go turn the heat down some more?" He asks, confirming the orientation of the side panel before handing the manual back to her.

"No, it's okay. It'll affect the rise in the kitchen." She leans back in the rocking chair and recommences with the fanning.

Ola nods and bites his tongue. She is doing too much and he has told her, but she claims that baking and working with her hands distracts her from the discomfort in her body. As he grabs the Allen wrench, he asks her about the thing she's baking.

"Kouign-amann," she repeats. "It's this really complicated pastry to make, they're almost like croissants but sweeter and crunchier? I want to give them to Pia."

"Pia?"

"My doula, remember?"

Ola nods, but no image comes up in his mind. That he knows what a doula is means they must have discussed it at some point.

"Cold water, then? Ice pack?"

"Water, thank you." Marisol places her hand on her lower belly and winces.

"Another Braxton-Hicks?"

She nods. He stands and the blood rushes back to his legs and feet. He comes back from the kitchen, and as he hands her the water, he watches her eyes glance over the boxes and boxes of items still to be unpacked and assembled and arranged. He sees the flash of worry in her gaze.

"I'm going to take care of all of it, I promise," he says, leaning down to peck her lips. He takes the manual from her again and settles back into his cramped spot on the floor, surrounded by screws and spindles. "How much time is left on the rise? Maybe you should go take a nap."

"But I want to stay here with you."

Ola assents. She presses his hand to her belly so he can feel the baby's foot swell against his palm, a flutter of movement at first that has become more solid and insistent.

"My mother will want to come visit after the birth. I told her maybe towards the end of the second month? And then maybe when he's around four months, we can take him down to Miami. Spend a few weeks there?"

He grunts as he pushes hard on the base of the crib so it clicks into the panels. "Okay, that sounds good. Just let me know the dates, yeah?" But internally, Ola is already dreading the trip, envisioning the myriad ways her father will subtly inform him that he is a failure of a husband and father.

"Is marriage what you thought it would be?" he asks suddenly.

She looks at the ceiling thoughtfully. "Honestly? No," she says, her eyes meeting his. "I thought we were different. I thought it would be like when we were dating. Like I would always enrapture you. But sometimes I guess it feels like I annoy you."

He wants to say that this isn't the case, but he knows she has hit on something true. Now he understands that her doting has arisen more out of anxiety than love, and what an ensnarement that must be.

"I don't want you to feel that way," he says. "I appreciate everything you do for me. But I don't want you to do any of it because you're trying to make things what they once were or something."

"I guess I just want you to love me like you used to. I thought marriage would be a lifetime of that feeling."

He shakes his head. What he felt for her before they were married, when her hair was longer and they would go out dancing and come back home and fuck for hours, was mostly a desire for possession. But what he feels now is the sense that his place is with her. Duty might not be as romantic or as thrilling, but he has come to see it as being more honest.

"I love you the way I love you now, you know?" he says. "We're in a different place from before, true. But it's probably a better place. I'm not going anywhere else because . . . I'm an equal shareholder here. Stakeholder? Whatever. I'm saying we have shared value. We're family."

She smiles brightly at this. Her timer goes off. He stands to help her up from the rocking chair and watches her waddle out of the room before he turns back to the crib-in-progress. He will stay up all night putting this nursery together if he has to.

In the middle of the night, Ola stares at his reflection and finds disappointment there. How has he not noticed, all this time, how bad the lighting is in their bathroom, so warm that it yellows the whites of his eyes and teeth? His gaze finds his hair, disheveled and, as Sola said at dinner weeks ago, uneven. A Black man without a lineup must look, he thinks, to other Black people like someone who has deserted himself.

"Baby, are you okay?" Her voice calls out to him from their bedroom, low and full from just-sleep.

"Yeah," he says, looking down at his phone. It is 2:07 a.m. He is in the bathroom at 2:07 a.m., wondering if he is ugly or not. "I'll be out soon."

He sends Dare a text asking for his barber recommendation again before turning off the bathroom light and going back to join Marisol in bed. Later that morning he wakes up to the sound of loud whistling from the kettle. Dare has replied. The place is in North Lawndale. Ola groans as he stands up from the bed.

"I'm going to the barber," he says later in the kitchen. He is buttoning up his peacoat.

Marisol is sprawled out on the living room sofa, wearing thick-rimmed glasses, sipping carefully from her cup of tea.

"Okay. Good morning to you too."

"Sorry," he says, walking over to peck her on the lips. "Good morning."

"When will you be back?"

"Two or three hours, I'd imagine."

She raises her eyebrows. "It's not supposed to take so long."

"I'm trying a new place," he says. He tries to make himself look happy, leans down to kiss her forehead.

At the door, he laces up a pair of Timberlands he hasn't worn in years.

Perhaps to prove something to himself, he decides to take public transport. The journey to the shop goes more or less as he expected; the Red Line into the Loop is mostly white; the westbound bus he connects to has some white people on it for about two stops, and then they abandon the few Black and Brown folk to their journey. Because the bus was so empty, Ola is surprised to walk into the shop half an hour later and find every chair filled, including those in the waiting area. He stands near the door for a moment, unable to find the words.

"How can I help you today?" one of the barbers asks. Ola feels all the eyes in the shop watching him, hears the hum of activity lower to a whisper.

"Uh, I just need a shape-up," he says. "Maybe take some more off the top."

"You and everybody else in here, man," the barber replies. "It'll be about an hour or so."

The "or so" makes Ola uneasy, but he sits down anyway once a seat opens, beside a young boy who is concentrating intently on the Nintendo Switch in his hands.

When Ola was growing up, his father insisted on cutting his hair at home, setting him down on a chair in the kitchen, razing his hair to an even skin cut and then applying African Pride so that the top of his head shone. It was a monthly ritual. There was no barber-shop. There was no banter. There were only the low sounds of the clippers and his father praying blessings over Ola's head, over his destiny, as he slathered the hair grease onto Ola's baldness. Ola loved him for this. But now he faults him for it as well.

The time lapses with Ola sitting there silently, taking everything in, who speaks, who remains silent, who is the philosopher among them, and who is the chorus. It feels like an eternity before the barber finally motions for Ola to come and sit down.

"Thanks for your patience, man," he says. "I appreciate it."

"No problem," says Ola. "I don't have anywhere to be."

"Who's been doing your hair? White boy?"

"Uh, no, but close," Ola says, laughing nervously. "Persian."

"Mmm," says the barber, studying Ola's hair. "How much you want off top?"

"As much as you can take off without making me look bald," Ola says. "I have a baby coming soon." He imagines he won't find time to come back within the next three months.

"Is that right? Your first?"

"Yeah. A boy." Ola buries his hands in his pockets as the barber drapes a black gown around him. "You got any kids?"

"That I do. Three. But the youngest one's mother is crazy. Fucking around with that woman was the worst thing I ever did."

Ola chuckles as the man tells his story.

One of the other barbers chimes in. "You were so excited to be messing with a Latin woman, you forgot those Dominicans will put voodoo on your ass."

"Jeeee-sus," he says. "I had to go over my grandmama house for prayer and anointing oil and everything, man."

"I'm married to a Latin woman," Ola says softly.

"Yeah? You better be careful. From where?"

"Argentina."

"Oooooh, spicy white," says someone else. "I got a white bitch too, she live in Lincoln Park."

"Nigga, if she send you money and pay for your Uber, then you the bitch," says the second barber.

The room erupts in laughter. Ola is surprised to find himself at ease. So this is the camaraderie of the barbershop, he thinks as his laughter subsides. He watches as the barber adjusts the setting of the clippers, relaxing as the familiar buzz of the trimmer against nape hair fills his ears. The men resume their earlier discussion. Sure, Chance is from the South Side, but the last concert he had, white people wearing Chance T-shirts had filled the train platforms. But wasn't it like that with all rappers, asks another, white folk pay for the music, go to see the shows, but Black folk are the ones who decide if a rapper deserves his propers. Ola listens, feeling that he has nothing to add to the discussion. He knows who Chance is, of course, but he doesn't listen to enough current rap music to have anything important to say. He again feels like an interloper. What will be his son's inheritance? Surely not the barbershop, if it has never even been Ola's.

As the barber dusts off his neck and removes his cape, Ola reaches into his pocket and retrieves his wallet, leaving behind a fifty-dollar bill.

"No change?"

"No, you can hold on to it."

"You're all right, man," says the barber.

Ola looks down at his phone. There are twenty-three missed calls, mostly from Marisol, some from his mother. Marisol has sent him a series of text messages with exclamation points and frantic-looking emojis.

"Oh shit," Ola says. "Baby's on the way."

The barbershop applauds as he leaves hurriedly, throwing his body out the door and into the wind. He almost thinks to hail a cab and then remembers that cabbies strategically avoid neighborhoods like this one. His mind goes to his father for a moment and then pushes the fact of his death away. Uber does not feel befitting for such a time as this, but he calls for one anyway, laughing nervously to himself as his fingertips go numb from the cold. He is going to be a father. Somehow, life has allowed him to bear such a title.

THIRTY-SEVEN

Friday, December 21

The Isley Brothers' "For the Love of You" plays from the speakers. Anjola is staring up at the looming bookshelves before her. She has been swaying to the music but now stops suddenly, having become aware of herself. Glancing over to her left, she studies her fellow groomsmen, chatting away happily with the bridesmaids in the far corner of the room. She had stood there with them for only a few moments before she feigned curiosity about the books and wandered away.

They are all there for the engagement dinner. The attendants mill about the room, waiting for the bride and groom to arrive. The late December days are brief and chilly, and Anjola finds it increasingly difficult to muster up anything like warmth for the people she interacts with on a daily basis. She has been short with clinical staff at work, has been avoiding calls from her mother, and was barely able to utter a kind word to anyone when she arrived at the dinner. She had half a mind to skip the event given the sleet that was falling outside after she ended her ten-hour shift earlier that evening, but she convinced herself to come anyway. She was afraid of what it might look like if she didn't show. And, she reasoned, it was probably the only chance she'd have to see the Arts Bank installation, given that she has so little time.

"It's like actually amazing that they were able to get this location," Wes says, coming to stand beside her. His hands are lodged in his pockets, and she feels a nervous energy about him.

"I know! And only for an engagement dinner."

"Right? Like, I'll forget Neil comes from money, and then he'll go and pull some shit like this," Wes says, his voice lowering to a near whisper.

Anjola can only nod, because it has always been impossible for her to forget.

"How are you doing?" Wes asks sincerely, pushing his round frames up the bridge of his nose. "Neil told me about your father. I'm sorry."

"Thanks. I'm holding up," she says, wondering what else Neil has told him. "It's all I can do."

A long table has been set up for all the guests at the center of the room, adorned with bouquets of eucalyptus and cotton and pampas grass. The table is laid with ivory china, the plates reflecting warmth from the light fixtures that look like minor constellations above them. Anjola thinks it is the loveliest thing she has ever seen. Wes's response is interrupted by a bell chime after which Neil and Giselle emerge, their fingers tightly woven together, and she sees the loveliness in this too. They are bright and gleaming, a through-line of honeyed skin and warm smiles. As she applauds with the rest of the room, she watches Neil intently, waiting to see if he will notice her. He doesn't.

Two nights ago he lay with her in her bed, intertwining his fingers with her own and then tracing them up her arm, over her neck and lips, onto the tip of her nose. They have been doing very little talking over the past few weeks. This is how Anjola has learned that the body has a language of its own. She hadn't felt guilty, not until the day before, when the third reminder email came in from Giselle's account, signed by both of them. And guilt isn't even what she feels now. Latent anger is more like it, and an anxiety that makes it terrifying to be there in her own body. Her belly grips itself tightly and will not let go. Neil hasn't so much as glanced at her. She has come for him, again and again and again, and it hasn't made a difference. She already sees that she is going to lose another thing she loves.

Wes motions to the table, his eyes watching hers with a mixture of kindness and sadness. She thinks he must know.

"Shall we?"

She takes her assigned seat between Wes and Nora, already annoyed by the conversation that will inevitably follow. As she studies the five-course menu laid in front of her, she thinks back to her father's funeral repast, the jollof rice and plantain that sat proudly above warmers in foil pans, the cans of Fanta and Sprite that guests had to plunge their hand into a cooler full of icy water to retrieve.

"How's work been, Anjola?" Wes asks as a pair of waiters begin serving the first course—watercress soup.

"Hectic," she says, "but rewarding in its own way."

The soup that Anjola barely eats is followed by a small plate of stuffed mushrooms, which she eats a forkful of before her stomach turns in protest. She looks over at Neil and Giselle, who sit to her right at a far corner of the table. His arm rests on the back of her chair, her head rests lovingly on his shoulder, and Anjola watches them and feels deeply embarrassed for herself. She thinks back to the last time she saw him, how he'd held her when thinking of her father had led her to tears, how he'd cooked her dinner, how he'd kissed her hands at the door before he left. Neil looks over at her, finally, his arresting stare stilling her breath. She hears the tinkling sound of a fork against glass.

"Everyone, I'd like to give a toast." She hears the rich timbre of Neil's eldest brother's voice, low and thick and booming like that of a proper orator. The room hushes.

"I'll keep this short," Julius says, then clears his throat. "Little brother, you are about to embark on one of the most blessed and profound journeys of this life. Marriage is a test of the spirit, the intellect, and the body. It is the constant sacrifice of your selfhood for the betterment of the collective. But you're more than ready for it, little brother. I cannot think of anyone more beautiful, more graceful, and more intelligent for you to have chosen to undertake this journey with than Miss Giselle Winters here. I also cannot think of anyone better served to take this journey than yourself. Congratulations to both of you."

Anjola feels sick. Giselle's mother is fully crying, and around Anjola rises a chorus of *how sweets* and applause. She watches Neil, who stands to hug his brother. Perhaps what hurts most is that he won't look at her again, that he denies her this brief acknowledgment of the truth they share: that Julius is wrong, that Neil has chosen the wrong person to undertake this journey with. Neil told Anjola that it had always been her, but she knows now that love is a choice, that he isn't choosing her. She excuses herself from the table.

As she walks down the hallway, she looks up at the barrel-vaulted ceiling. She studies the white coffers, how big they are, how small she is in comparison. In the single-occupancy bathroom, she leans against the wall and lets herself succumb to self-critical and pitying thoughts until she feels hot tears on her cheeks and hears herself begin to whimper.

There is a knock at the door.

"Jo?"

She wipes her tears away and lets him in. They stare at each other behind the closed door for a moment. She is conscious of how puffy her eyes are. His hands are in his pockets.

"I'm sorry," he says.

"Yeah."

"It wasn't supposed to be like this."

"Really?" She looks down at the floor tearfully. "How was it supposed to be, then?"

"I don't even know."

"You both look so happy in there," she says.

"We are."

They are silent for a moment again.

"I feel like I have no right to ask this of you," she says.

"It's okay." Neil sighs, makes a fist, and softly hits the wall behind him. "It's fair."

"You're still going through with this wedding, then."

"You know how much I love you, Anjola."

"Yeah? Clearly not nearly as much as you love her."

"Come on, Jo. What do you want me to do?"

"Isn't it obvious?"

Neil wrings his hands together. "If things weren't what they are," he says, "I would be with you. I tried to be with you for years."

"Don't put this all on me."

"I'm sorry."

"Yeah? Me too." Anjola laughs bitterly. "I'm sorry too. I'm sorry for myself."

He exhales deeply through his nose. "I have to keep my word. Because who am I without it?" he says.

It isn't that she hadn't known this was coming; it is the finality of it. Something inside her wants to bawl, wants to lay hands on him and shake violently until his mind is put right, until he sees he is making a mistake. She nods placidly instead.

"All right. Well, that's it, then," she says. She does not wait for him to ask her to be friends still, or if she will still be in his wedding party. She leaves him there in the bathroom. As she walks back down the hallway, past the entrance to the room where the wedding party eats luxurious food and fills the space with warm laughter, he doesn't try to come after her.

THIRTY-EIGHT

Friday, December 21

Karen studies the figures on the game board, soccer players in the correct uniform colors. Red, yellow, green, blue. She is always yellow. Everyone in the family knows that when Ludo is played, yellow has to be left for Karen. Ola usually plays green. Anjola is flexible, but she is normally left with blue.

They sit together at the table, playing as they did when they were children. Karen is glad she brought the game along to her sister's place. It gives them something to focus on apart from their grief.

Sola's friend Marquise emerges from the bathroom in a long leather vest, his eyes drawn with winged eyeliner. "Are you ladies sure you want to stay in?" he asks. "Because a night out dancing can work wonders."

"Please keep your wonders to yourself," Sola says with a smirk.

Marquise finishes pushing his feet into combat boots. "And here's a sign for those wonders," he says, giving Sola the finger. Karen laughs aloud, but before Sola can respond, Marquise shuts the door behind him. Sola smiles indulgently, then picks up the red game chips and places them in her house. Karen follows suit.

"So you have to roll six to get out, right?" Sola asks.

"Yep, and if you roll double six, then you get to roll again."

"The way I'm about to trounce you in this game," Sola says, squaring her shoulders as she drops the dice into the small container and shakes it vigorously. Karen gathers that it's been years since Sola has played, but it oddly pleases her to hear her sister already talking shit. No one has picked up the red pieces for a while, at least not as far as Karen can remember.

"Wow, your life is already embarrassing." Karen motions at the snake eyes that have taken the place of the pair of sixes she knows Sola was hoping for. She picks up the dice and rolls a six and a three. Karen pretends she has long hair like Sola's, flicking her imaginary tresses over both shoulders. They are giggling together.

"When are you going to tell Mom that you're switching your major? And are you going to tell her about the Fulbright application?" Sola asks, failing to roll the required number again. She hands the pieces back to Karen.

Karen shrugs. "There's a lot a young lady needs to keep to herself, I'm learning," she says in a faux posh accent.

"But you know you can tell me anything, right?" Sola asks suddenly, as though she has been studying Karen's face for signs of worry. "I'm here for you."

"I know."

"Good." She looks down at her phone. "Anjola's coming by soon."

"I'm surprised."

"Why?"

"I just never really get to see you guys. It's even wild that you're here," Karen says. "And you can tell me things too, you know."

Sola nods once and then changes subjects. "God, we need some music," she says before telling Alexa to play Afrobeats. She stands up and is opening the bottle of red wine that sits on the countertop when the buzzer sounds.

Anjola looks sick. Her eyes are puffy and the tip of her nose is red. She carries the cold with her when she enters.

"What's wrong, sister?" asks Sola.

She begins to sob, but when she notices Karen sitting there at the table, she tries to dry her tears. They are both sitting beside Anjola on the sofa now. Sola has draped a throw blanket over her legs. Karen holds her hand.

"It's been too fucking long since we've had this," Anjola says.

Karen says nothing. It's weird hearing Anjola curse, like the word is too big for her mouth, too low for the enunciated Ivy League English she speaks.

"I'm sorry," she says through her tears. "I hate that I'm such a wreck right now."

"Girl, everyone is a wreck," Sola says. "Have you seen your mother?"

They laugh, which feels cruel and deserved all at the same time.

Karen grips Anjola's hand more tightly. "What's wrong?"

"It's Neil," she says. "He's getting married."

"So?" asks Karen.

Sola shakes her head slowly from side to side, pouting. "No, she means he's *still* getting married. They started having a little affair."

Karen's eyes widen. "What happened to the guy from Thanksgiving?"

"I broke it off. It just wasn't right."

"Clearly," Sola says.

As Anjola narrates the series of events that have brought her to this state, Karen listens silently, painting the images in her mind. Sola stands to turn on the fireplace. It fills with orange heat at the flick of a switch. Karen reflects on how luxurious it feels to be resting comfortably on this grand, impeccable leather sofa with both of her sisters, how much this kind of presence has been lacking throughout their lives. They sit there for a while, trying to comfort Anjola as she weeps.

"Am I a horrible person?"

"A little bit," Sola says. "You want me to level with you?"

Anjola nods.

"The timing is kind of shady. Like even if you had done it right after he got engaged, that would be something. But then right after Dad's funeral too?"

"You think I'm disrespecting Dad?"

"No. I just think you were kind of using Neil." Sola shrugs. "And I think he deserves to be with someone who isn't just coming to him in a moment of crisis."

Karen doesn't agree with Sola, but she twists her lips, waiting to hear what Anjola will say in return.

"But I *do* love him, I *do* want to be with him. Why else do you think I even moved back here?" Anjola puts her head in her hands, and her locs fall forward like a black veil. Karen touches her back soothingly. "I would've told him sooner, the timing was never right."

"So right after we buried our father was the best timing you could think of?" Sola asks. Karen shoots her a look that she doesn't seem to notice. She doesn't think that Anjola needs a tough love approach right now.

"Sola, it was the timing I had," Anjola says. "Whatever. I mean, I guess you're right. It's over now. He doesn't want me."

They are all silent.

"He does want you," Karen says. "Life just isn't set up for you guys that way."

"Yeah?" Anjola looks up at her hopefully.

"I think it's all going to be okay." Karen is surprised by herself. "And sure, maybe you came back for Neil, but I think life wanted you here with us."

"From the mouths of babes." Sola nods. "Don't listen to me. She's the only one here with sense."

Anjola laughs for the first time that evening, drying her tears. "Jesus. I'm going to need some wine."

They all sit at the table, drinking red wine from long stemmed glasses with large bowls. Her older sisters don't seem to care that she won't turn twenty-one until the following March. They have started the game over, each taking on their correct color. Anjola is blue. The skin on the tip of her nose has returned to its normal deep mahogany color; she and Sola are laughing bitterly together.

"Little sister," says Anjola, "just don't waste your energy on men, it isn't worth it."

Sola rolls double sixes finally, brings her red piece out of its house.

"I don't," Karen says.

"Because the way Aiden did me dirty," Sola says, "sometimes I still wake up feeling like I got punched in the chest."

"What exactly did he do?" Anjola asks.

Karen pretends like this is the first time she is hearing the news, as though she hasn't read about Sola's messy breakup on influencer gossip blogs, as though she doesn't know that her sister has shut down all her accounts because of it.

"That's so heartless," Anjola says. "Is love even possible?"

"No," says Sola. "Always see to your money, ladies. It's the only thing that's loyal."

Karen thinks of her father and her mother, and of the video Rachelle made of her, and she knows that she does not agree. But because her sisters are testifying of their own pain, she holds back her dissent.

"Were you happy with him? Towards the end?" Karen asks.

"You know, my therapist asked me the same thing?" Sola leans back in her chair, sighing thoughtfully. "And honestly, I wasn't. But I had plans for us, you understand? I was committed to them."

"I think you were delivered," Karen says, bringing her piece around to eat Sola's and send it back to its house. "Interracial YouTube wasn't your dream. Now you can focus on the thing you really want."

"Not interracial YouTube!" Sola says, playfully tugging on Karen's ear. And Karen smiles because it reminds her of her father.

"That's right, the design program!" Anjola says. "Oh, I'm so proud of you for applying." Anjola looks like she is going to cry again. "You're so brave."

"Am I?"

"I don't know anyone braver." She grips Sola's hand. "I wish I had been braver when we were kids."

Karen watches as her two older sisters exchange looks that know something she does not. Sola's features tense with discomfort. But Anjola has an insistence in her gaze now, as if refusing to be dismissed.

"For you," Anjola says.

"You were a baby yourself," Sola says, attempting to shrug it off, but she glances down at the floor. Karen suddenly thinks her sister looks so young.

"What are you guys talking about?"

Sola twists her lips to one side and sighs through her nose. She gazes past them to the fire that is still going.

"A deacon at this old church we went to, he taught children's church. You were still a baby baby."

Karen's eyes widen. She's dreading what comes next.

"I was molested."

All this time she had never known, had never imagined her sister living through that kind of hell.

"Jesus," Karen says.

"I saw it happening," Anjola says, her face long, her eyes gazing down at the game board. "I should have told."

"You know? I've been really angry at you for a long time," Sola says, looking to Anjola. Her voice wavers. "I kept trying to act like I wasn't, but you were my *best friend* growing up. I felt like you betrayed me. Like why couldn't you see that I needed you to take up for me? Why couldn't you see that I couldn't do it myself?"

Karen looks to Anjola, watching her eyes well with tears again. "I wish I could go back in time," Anjola says. "Sincerely. I am so incredibly sorry."

Karen studies Sola carefully, seeing it all come together in her mind. All these things that had never really made sense to her. The deep anger that Sola seemed to carry everywhere with her, her teenage rebellion, Anjola's guilt-driven perfectionism, their mother's clueless heavy-handedness. "You must have felt so abandoned," Karen says. "For so long."

"Just let me finish," Sola says, turning back to Anjola. "I've been looking for someone else to blame for why my life is the way it is. Sometimes that person was you. Sometimes it was Mom or Ola, even Dad. But life isn't like that, you know? It's not one plus two equals three. So I'm genuinely sorry for blaming you. What that man did was all on him. And you were a kid, you know? Just like me." Sola shrugs, reaching for a napkin. "Neither of us knew what to do. We didn't have the type of home where we felt safe enough to tell."

Anjola stands up and leans over the back of Sola's chair, wrapping her arms around her. Karen rests her head against Sola's shoulder. What else does she have to offer but touch as an affirmation that Sola is loved, that she is worthy, that she is seen?

Sola stands from the table, turning away from them to dry her tears.

"Anyone want more wine?" Sola asks after a moment, her voice clear. She explains that she and Marquise are helping themselves to the small store of vintages their host keeps in the pantry. And Karen takes this to be Sola's way of saying she forgives them. If Sola is still learning to say what she feels, then Karen realizes that she, in turn, is still learning to hear what her feelings are saying: that she doesn't want to become a doctor; that she wants to date women.

Anjola accepts the glass of wine gratefully, but Karen declines. Her head is already swimming. All this knowledge feels like finally having a name for the specter that has, for so long, hung over their family. And perhaps, she thinks, this is the one gift of their father's passing: this process of unearthing answers, this exhumation of fundamental causes.

"It's your turn," Karen says to Anjola when they come back to the table. Anjola obediently rolls. The dice read two and three, the exact numbers needed for her to overtake Karen's piece and send it back to its house. Anjola looks apologetic, which somehow always makes her wins feel worse. Karen prefers Sola's loud gloating.

"Do you guys think we were happy as kids?" Karen asks.

Anjola nods. "Sometimes."

"Honestly," Sola says, "everyone's childhood was different somehow."

"Who had it best, then?" Karen asks.

"Ah. Olanipekun," Sola says, mimicking their mother's voice and causing her sisters to giggle. "Hands down."

"Oh my god, remember that party when we were teenagers," Anjola asks, "and we caught him messing around with that girl?"

"How could I forget?"

"No! I want to hear this story." Karen leans onto her forearms, setting aside the dice.

"You must have been like four or five," Anjola says.

Sola clears her throat and leans back in her seat as though she were a master storyteller. Apparently their family had driven down to Indiana for the fortieth birthday celebration of one of their mother's friends. Their mother had gone to extreme efforts to import Swiss lace for them in a brilliant pink, ferried all of them to the tailor weeks earlier, donned a violet gèlè to match their father's filà, and painstakingly tied each daughter's lace headscarf so that they would make a statement upon entry. The Longes, dressed like royalty. The party was held in a hotel ballroom, full of round tables and heaping plates of Nigerian party food.

They were there for hours—the adults were dancing, the children were playing, some of them naughtily picking up the sprayed money that had fallen onto the floor for the celebrant. Karen had started feeling ill and had gone and thrown up on the table where she sat on their mother's lap, so they were leaving much earlier than intended. Ola was nowhere to be found. Sola and Anjola were sent to find him. It didn't take long. He was in a smaller, adjacent ballroom, sitting back on a chair, a girl's head bobbing between his knees.

"Oh my god," Karen says, eyes wide with delight at the scandal. "What happened next?"

"I told Anjola not to say anything, we left quietly. He hadn't even seen us."

"And then?"

"I snitched on that nigga, please," Sola says, crossing her arms. "When me, Anjola, Mom, and Dad got back to the room, Ola was still there with his eyes closed getting sloppy toppy. Not a single clue. One hand on her head, the other on his fila, groaning."

"It was disgusting," Anjola says. "And then Mom went *in*."

Sola continues. "Mom was all like, 'You silly prostitute, you will not dissuade my son from his destiny!' Honestly I felt so bad for the girl."

"What did Dad say?" Karen asks.

"Oh, you know him," says Anjola. "He was just like, 'Pekun, I'm so disappointed in you.'"

"He barely got in trouble!" Sola says. "I was actually so pissed. It really was like he could do no wrong."

"But you know, when Dad says he's disappointed, it really weighs on you," Anjola says. Karen notices that she speaks of their father in the present tense, and she cannot bear to correct her. "I do think Ola felt bad," Anjola adds.

"To be honest, I can't imagine Ola hooking up with anyone," Karen says, covering her eyes. "I don't even know how he got Marisol pregnant."

"Oh, he used to be messy back when he was in high school," says Anjola, her eyes widening with glee. "Like he would save up money from his little summer jobs to buy himself fancy watches and take girls out on dates that didn't bring him home until five in the morning. But somehow Dad straightened him out."

"The double standard is crazy," Karen says.

"Isn't it? Anyway, now I think he's a little too straitlaced," says Sola.

"It's that white frat he pledged in college," says Anjola.

"I don't know. In my mind he's always been this way?" Karen says. She can't think of any other version of her brother than this one. Politically moderate, a little pedantic, kind and supportive, but a bit removed from the dramatic nucleus of their family.

"Well, he was definitely their favorite," Sola says.

"Maybe he was Mom's," says Karen, "but you were definitely Dad's. He argued with her for months after you left. Imagine if he'd known what actually happened between you two."

"Sola, the whole house didn't know peace until I showed him our text messages and he knew you were okay," Anjola says.

Karen shrugs. "I think they loved all of us. Imperfectly, but still."

"He was a good guy," Sola says.

There is silence for a moment, and then Sola asks, "Y'all think they'll ever find out who did it?"

"No," says Anjola. "I don't."

Sola's face remains blank. Karen turns her attention back to the game. She thinks about how life is like Ludo in that, by the sleight of some unseen hand, a soul might be pulled from its journey on earth and wrested away.

Sola rolls a six, and thus another piece is born into the world.

THIRTY-NINE

Sunday, December 30

The baby is beautiful. Anjola holds him in her arms and sits on the low stool beside Marisol's peacock chair. He has large, hypnotizing eyes like deep wells, a head full of brown hair, curly like his mother's, and a grip on Anjola's index finger that will surely steal her heart. Everyone else in her family met him during the week prior, but her work schedule has made her the last one to greet the newest addition to the Longe family.

"I've never seen anyone more lovely," she says as the baby opens his mouth and yawns peacefully.

Marisol smiles. She has a tired air, seems uncomfortable in the baby-blue ìró and bùbá that Anjola knows her mother must have insisted upon. Marisol seems like the type of new mother who belongs in linen or calico and espadrilles. Ola comes over, just as awkward in his matching agbádá. The sleeves seem like they might drown him. There is an art to throwing the sleeves over one's shoulder, and Ola does not have it. Together, the pair of them appear to be in costume.

"How's my little man doing?"

"He's everything," Anjola says. "You two made perfection in this one."

Ola and Marisol gaze at each other with loving exhaustion. According to their mother, Marisol labored for twelve hours before the baby was born in the wee hours of the morning. They are fighting about who he looks like. Sola and Karen contend that he resembles Marisol, but everyone else agrees that he takes after their father, and consequently after Ola as well.

The ceremony is to start soon. Anjola reluctantly hands the baby back to Marisol and goes to sit beside her sisters. Her mother apparently insisted on the naming ceremony. She has rented a small hall off Devon Ave. and invited as many people as seemed relevant. They know she needs this celebration of new life to punctuate her grief. No one stopped her from spending an exorbitant sum on the caterer and the drummers and the tailor-made matching outfits that she rush-ordered for them. But Sola sewed her own dress, deftly combining the light blue lace and dark blue aṣọ-òkè fabrics into a corset gown worthy of a feature on BellaNaija. If she were holding the baby, anyone might have mistaken her as the celebrant.

"Isn't he precious?" says Karen. "Mom and I have been going to theirs every day since he got home."

"He's actually gorgeous," says Sola. "And you know I would say if he was ugly."

They laugh and then quiet as their mother stands to announce the start of the ceremony. Her pastor stands behind her, unwrapping a large Bible that he lays beside the set of white bowls on the front table. The ceremony proceeds quickly enough with opening prayers and Yoruba praise songs. Marisol is directed to stand, and the pastor places the contents of the bowls on the baby's lips. Salt, he says, for a flavorful life. Honey for the sweetness of life. Pepper to symbolize fruitfulness. Kola nut to repel wickedness. Bitter kola for longevity. Palm oil for ease, a life without friction. Water because it is the essence of life itself. The baby is placid throughout all of this, barely uttering a sound. The pastor presents the new parents with the large Bible, asking them if they intend to raise this new baby in the proper Christian way. Anjola nearly chokes when Ola, the avowed atheist, affirms that they will. He takes his son from Marisol's arms, then stands before the room of attendees to speak the baby's name for the first time.

"His names are Elias, Babajide, Ramón, Longe."

Elias is a sweet name, Anjola thinks. But it is the Babajide that makes her heart leap. She knows enough to understand that this is her brother's way of honoring their late father. To confirm this, Anjola looks to her mother, whose face, though wet with tears, also beams with pride. She wishes her father were here beside her mother, smiling as he held his first grandchild. Then, with a pang, she realizes that if he were still alive, the baby would not have this name.

"That's a good name," Sola whispers. "They did good."

The ceremony ends but the guests stay for hours afterward, enjoying the food, the aunties walking up to a weary Marisol to ask if they can hold the baby. Whether out of intimidation or tiredness, she surrenders Elias to each of them until he begins to wail.

Latifat comes to sit between her and Sola, and Anjola is surprised when their mother turns to Sola and asks, "Which tailor did you take your fabric to?" Her eyes linger over the handiwork of Sola's bell sleeves.

"I did it myself," Sola says.

Their mother motions for Sola to stand and turn, and she does, slowly.

"Well done," their mother says. "I didn't know you could sew like this. All this time I've been paying these nonsense tailors and I could have asked you."

Anjola's eyes widen as she watches the two of them. She hears the regret in her mother's voice, that this is her attempt at making amends.

"Actually," their mother continues, "Funke's great-aunt is doing a ninetieth birthday party in Houston in April. Maybe you can make my skirt and blouse for me."

"I'll think about it," Sola says. "You'd have to pay, obviously, especially since you're looking at SAIC's newest Design BFA student. But I'd give you the family discount."

"What! That's incredible," Anjola says, throwing her arms around her sister before their mother has an opportunity to say anything hurtful. But when Anjola finally looks up, her mother's eyes are shining.

"Yes, Gbemisola. You've done well," she says. Sola doesn't reply, only meets her mother's words with an expression of genuine gratitude. And Anjola wants to forever crystallize this moment in her memory, knowing how rich it is, knowing it may be the closest they get.

When she gets home much later that evening, Anjola collapses onto the sofa, stripping her body of the scratchy dress she's wearing. She opens her laptop to her email and sees a message from Neil with no subject. They haven't spoken since she walked out of his engagement party, though this has not stopped her from entertaining fantasies of the potential wreckage she left behind. In her most grounded imaginings, Neil simply informed the rest of the party that she'd been called into work, Giselle looking at him suspiciously before turning back to banter with Neil's parents. In the most far-fetched, she was spotted on her way out of the bathroom, Neil emerging a few moments later looking grief-stricken and distraught. The room would have quieted to a low hush, and then Giselle would have stood up on her teetering heels and demanded that he tell her the truth. These visions had been little indulgences. This very real message floods her with waves of adrenaline. Anjola breathes deeply and then clicks to open the email.

Jo,

I don't want us to leave things the way they were left. I should call instead of resorting to this, but I find when I'm confronted by your presence I can't seem to get the words out right. I've messed up in a lot of ways and it's all I can think about. Not just over the past month. I've been thinking about our friendship over the years, the many ways I ought to have been better to you.

At the risk of confusing things further, I'd like to affirm that I do love you. I think you're the only person I've loved in this way. I love my fiancée, but I think that the love I have for you is different. It's a more knowing love. I admit that I'm confused. I admit that I had long accepted or decided that whatever I felt for you might not be realized in this lifetime. I'd convinced myself that friendship suited us better. Not because I didn't want you differently, but perhaps out of a sense of my own unworthiness, and a lingering belief that friendship is a higher love.

I still maintain that belief. I regret what happened between us these past few weeks only because I think it has cost me your friendship. Please don't take that the wrong way, Anjola. I am not trying to hurt you. Experiencing that different kind of intimacy with you was an honor, but in many ways a selfish indulgence and a pleasurable escape from the vicissitudes of my own personal life. I don't doubt the feelings you say you have for me, but I do think they might have been expressed differently under less difficult circumstances.

I guess the point of this email is to apologize. Had I been a better man we might've had the opportunity to explore the more romantic depths of our friendship in earnest. And, at the same time, had I been a better man we might never have tested those waters at all. I do care so deeply for you, Anjola, I do wish you the kind of love that allows you to be brave in the pursuit of your desires, to experience every beautiful thing this life has to offer. I do want your friendship still. Should you change your mind about things, know that you are always welcome in my home, in my life, in my wedding.

Don't be a stranger.
Neil

She is crying by the time she reaches the end. The Neil she left behind at the party was someone she resolved not to think about any longer, to blot out of the memory of her life. This Neil refuses to be forgotten. This Neil has too much nuance, and the careful consideration he demands overwhelms her. She needs a neat binary here and he denies her one. She closes the computer and turns over onto her stomach, thinking of how long, how deeply she harbored her love for him in secret, and then what that means about how little she thought of herself. That he has chosen not to be with her feels like some great cosmic wrongdoing. On the other hand, she feels that she has done it all to herself. She falls asleep with her hands as fists nestled beneath her shoulders, her narrow back curved like a tortoise's shell, protecting herself from the harsh reality of the world. But when she wakes up the next morning, her head feels clearer. She yawns loudly and stretches out her limbs and takes up space. She texts Neil and asks to meet.

He suggests a café off the Garfield Green Line stop because it's between them, as though to mean neutral territory. She walks in and finds him seated at a table near the front, his back only steps away from the exit.

He seems surprised to see her, even though they've prearranged the day and the hour. He looks well, which some small part of her is hurt by; he should have the dull pallor and the unkempt state of the despairing. His leonine hair hangs over his shoulders, and she sits down in front of him wordlessly, taking it all in. She memorizes the softness of his eyes and the hard lines of his jaw, the way his lips purse heavily, but how calm his fingers are as they come to rest gently on either side of the book he's been reading. She doesn't say anything, just turns it and glances down at the title. It is a book on liberation theology by James H. Cone.

"I didn't take you for the type to be wrestling with God," she says.

"Yeah? Well, I've been wrestling with a lot of things."

"I got your email, obviously."

"I figured."

"It was a lot."

"I know." He looks away. "You want to order some food? It's pretty good here."

"No. But if you're planning on grabbing something, I'll take a mint tea."

He nods and stands to place an order for them, coming back moments later with a table marker.

"What did you get?"

"Chicken and waffles. I'm gonna stick around and grade papers."

"Nice."

They sit there for a few seconds of awkward silence.

"My nephew was born last week," she says. "They named him Elias."

She reaches for her phone to pull up pictures from the naming ceremony and places it on top of his book.

"Oh, he's a gorgeous baby," he says in a low voice. "You guys must be so happy."

"Definitely. He's like new hope."

The silence falls over them again.

"So, are you going to tell Giselle about what happened?"

Neil clears his throat. "Uh, no. I don't think so."

"Really? Why not?" She has to admit to herself that she feels a small measure of disappointment. Some part of her wants Giselle to feel the pain Anjola has felt, for Giselle to know that Anjola has had what is hers.

"I mean, I don't think it would be as noble as it seems," he says. "I would only be hurting her in order to assuage my own guilt."

"You don't think she'd want to know?"

"Honestly? No." He cracks his knuckles. "Is this what you wanted to come here and talk about?"

A server with bright lavender Marley twists brings over his plate of food and her cup of tea, wordlessly retrieving the table marker.

"No," she says. "Your email was hard for me to read."

"It was hard to write."

"I wanted you to be a monster. You wouldn't be one."

"Jo," he says with a sigh. "I still feel like one."

"Well, your email's wrong," she says. "It isn't all on you. That's why I wanted to meet."

He fidgets with the tines of his fork.

"Neil, I've wanted to be with you since, like, the day we first met at the Lab School. I've been the coward."

He tries to stop her but she continues.

"I have. I think maybe if I was kinder to myself, I would have realized that I'm allowed to have the things I want in life and I would have told you. But I'm only learning that now. So. This is the price I have to pay. The man I want to be with loves someone else, and it's only fair," she says. "She's had the courage to do openly what I could only do in secret."

"Wow."

She takes a long sip from her tea, letting the heat singe the back of her mouth and then cool on its way down.

"We can't be friends," she says. She is surprised by how sad he looks. "We can't be friends because I haven't really been that honest with you. I've always wanted something else, and I don't know what friendship would look like for us without that."

"Huh," he says. "Yeah, I really wasn't expecting you to say all of that."

"Me neither," she says. "But I'm learning to tell the truth now."

"So that's it, then? Like over twelve years of friendship. Just gone."

"I'll always have love for you," she says.

Neil nods. "Me too."

She stands up then, ready to leave it all behind her.

"I really wish we could have had the chance to be together the way we were meant to," he says.

Anjola touches a hand to her chest. "Maybe next lifetime."

They hug, and she memorizes this too, what it feels like for his arms to bind her body to his. After a few moments, she forces herself to pull away, grateful that she can do it without tears.

Outside as she waits for her ride to come, she looks down at her phone. The House Longe group chat has left her fifty-three notifications. She clicks open the video everyone has been commenting on. Sola is on the couch at their family home, holding Elias despite his spit-up running down her arms and her hair. Ola is recording the video, his laughter echoing in the background as Sola sings a song about how Elias's parents owe her $500 for new bundles to the tune of "Yankee Doodle." Karen reaches for the baby as their mother comes to sit beside Sola, wiping her arm clean. Anjola smiles. There are a lot of things she doesn't have, but she knows now that she has them.

ACKNOWLEDGMENTS

For so solitary an endeavor, the most beautiful thing about writing a novel is looking back to see how absurdly blessed with supporters I've been. First, I'd like to thank my incredible agents, Michelle Brower and Nat Edwards. Thank you for being such wise and stalwart advocates. It has been an absolute pleasure to work with you both. I extend my gratitude to the entire team at Trellis Literary Management.

To Seema Mahanian, my exceedingly cool, brilliant, and perceptive editor, thank you. I'm forever grateful that you picked up what I was putting down. Thank you for challenging me to take these characters to places I didn't know they could go. Thank you for helping me make it make sense. Thanks also to Maya Petrillo-Fernandez for your keen eye, organizational prowess, and warm spirit. Many thanks to Pamela Dorman, Eric Wechter, Anna Dobbin, Lynn Buckley, Claire Vaccaro, Raven Ross, Chantal Canales, Julia Rickard, Emily Fishman, and everyone at the Penguin Viking team.

A thousand thanks to Curtis Sittenfeld, my mentor and friend. Thank you for loving my manuscript 2.25 drafts in and believing in its promise while it was still in an incredibly messy state (and not in the good way). Thank you for all the introductions, the many life and writing advice chats, the ice cream delivery, and for giving me so much to admire. Your support really does mean the world to me. I'm so grateful to Reese's Book Club for connecting us.

My profound gratitude to the LitUp fellowship, which changed my life. Without it, my manuscript may have been destined for a desk drawer somewhere. I'm grateful to LitUp for giving me the encouragement I needed to take this writing life more seriously. A huge thank you to Gretchen Schreiber, Melissa Seymour, Sarah Harden, Dhonielle Clayton, Zoraida Córdova, Natalie C. Parker, Tessa Gratton, and, of course, Reese Witherspoon. The most amazing thing LitUp gave me was the opportunity to connect with four exceedingly talented fellow writers. To Margot Fisher, Ashley Jordan, Bora Reed, and Allison King, thank you. I'm so fortunate to have undertaken this whirlwind journey with you all.

Thank you to MacDowell for the magic of time and space and picnic baskets.

If you, Dear Reader, happened to be on the Clubhouse app in early 2022 and were one of the five people who would write with me at 6 a.m. EST for an hour in a room called "We Write at Dawn," thank you. Thanks also to Divya Sood, who taught my Gotham Writers novel writing class in the summer of 2021 and told us to never show anyone our first drafts. I'm so glad I heeded that advice.

But thank you, Elinam Agbo, for reading my second draft. What a gift you are! Thank you for having been such a longtime supporter of my writing; you have probably read the most of it of anyone on this list actually. I consider myself exceedingly fortunate to count you among my close friends.

Thanks also to my dearest Akua Nkansah-Amankra. Thank you for lending me some of your belief when I couldn't muster any in myself. I am forever in awe of your wisdom, kindness, and directness. Thank you for inspiring me to live in spirit and in truth. The same goes for Sara Imam. In our over-a-decade-long friendship you've always spoken life into me. Thanks for your warmheartedness, your free medical advice, and for supporting me through many a career-related panic attack in my pre-author life. For various forms of support and encouragement, thanks also to Korede Osifuwa, Clarisse Baleja Saïdi, Angela Dixon, Tomi Obaro, Carolene Kurien, and Cresa Pugh.

Shefe, thank you for teaching me how to be a sister and an ally. Dad, you have been my first lesson in chosen family; thank you for calling me your daughter, even when the world didn't. Thanks for all the Barbies! While I don't know if my maternal grandmother will ever read this book, I'm so grateful for all the stories she told me, and I cherish what I remember of them. Last, but certainly most, thank you, Mom. Thank you for the àmì ohùn consultation services. Thank you for forcing me to learn to read when I wanted to play (it seems I've found a way to do both). Thank you for sharing your love of literature with me. Thank you for your many prayers over me. Thank you for your resilience, beauty, and intolerance of complacency. You have given me so much of yourself, and I thank you for all of it.